THE YEAR OF BROKEN GLASS

D1475266

NIGHTWOOD EDITIONS • GIBSONS, BC • 2011

The
Year
of Broken
Glass

Joe Denham

Nightwood Editions
P.O. Box 1779
Gibsons, BC von 1v0
Canada
www.nightwoodeditions.com

Nightwood Editions acknowledges financial support from the Government of
Canada through the Canada Book Fund and the Canada Council for the Arts, and
from the Province of British Columbia through the British Columbia Arts Council
and the Book Publisher's Tax Credit.

This book has been produced on 100% post-consumer recycled, ancient-forest-
free paper, processed chlorine-free and printed with vegetable-based dyes.

TYPOGRAPHY & COVER DESIGN: Carleton Wilson

Printed and bound in Canada

LIBRARY AND ARCHIVES CANADA CATALOGUING IN PUBLICATION

Denham, Joe, 1975–
The year of broken glass / Joe Denham.

ISBN 978-0-88971-252-2

I. Title.

PS8557.E536Y32 2011   C813'.6   C2011-900044-X

For August and Isabelle

Shine on all the fishermen
with nothing in their nets.

– Joni Mitchell

MIRIAM WAKES EARLY, before sunrise, knowing this will be the day the floats wash in. Three days ago, the *Velella velella* heaped up so thick she couldn't walk anywhere close to the tide line, thousands of blue jellies rotting black in the mid-spring sun. Then the garbage. All the way from China, from Japan, condoms and candy wrappers, Styrofoams and plastics.

Now, this morning, the full moon pulls the flood tide high up the beach and the last of the dissipating westerly pushes the floats in. The mundane and the prized, the poorly blown and the perfect, all of them precious to Miriam. All of them totems of human utility, of history, of time. Of an element fired and forged, worked and then relinquished, by chance, back to the deep wilderness of the open ocean.

She slips her warmest wool sweater on, ties her hair back and stretches a small LED headlamp over her forehead. Poseidon rubs his thick purring body against her leg, noses her hands as she pulls on her gumboots. "Coming?" she asks, stroking his silky fur. Then she steps outside, into the cool pre-dawn blue, and heads across the apple orchard toward the sea, the white cat bounding through the tall grass beside her.

Part I

I'm TIRED OF the end of the world.

Every morning excluding Sundays—that's family day, not God's day—Pamela Penner's voice works away at the hem of my dream till it's sufficiently frayed and the threads unravel. This morning I was dreaming Jin Su and I were on a big old Taiwanese ketch with all sails unfurled in the middle of the Pacific Ocean. A massive flock of albatross began to swarm the boat overhead, mewling in a great chorus over the creak of the canvas sails flexing in the wind. Everywhere around us the wide open blue, the sun bright on Jin Su, the groundswell serene. Then Pamela Penner's voice, it's 6 a.m., early morning news, something about Obama, the Middle East, as the albatross stomachs tear open and my childhood lego spills out, assembles mid-descent into flapping, screeching legotross, and I'm awake.

"Can you believe this guy actually dressed up in drag so he could use his deceased wife's membership at the Y?" Pamela reports. "Well he *is* back on the singles scene," her co-anchor pipes in. "I understand competition is fierce these days. I suppose he figured he'd better get those pecs…" That's when I press the snooze button.

Dawn's a different blue, huddled, dark, and it's sifting in through the white cotton curtains. The air I breathe is unseasonably cold for the third week in April. Must be a hard westerly blowing. Might be one of those days. Anna stirs beside me, sniffles, then rolls onto her side and pulls the duvet over her head, as she always does. I swing my legs to the floor, lift to sitting, and tuck the duvet into her back.

In the kitchen I cook up scrambled eggs and toast. I can't get the legotross and Jin Su and the drag-dressing widower out of my mind. Last fall only two million of the estimated eleven million expected sockeye returned to the Fraser River. Whole runs disappeared. Now there's a smoke-and-mirrors judicial inquiry and some talk about maybe acknowledging that parasitic or viral contamination from the open-net fish farms up and down the coast might be a factor. There's some talk of industry, and the wild fish remaining, and change. And here I am, thirty-four years of age, falling asleep to an article in *The Walrus* about the city of plastic floating in the North Pacific Gyre, dreaming of legotross and waking once more to Pamela Penner. A once-young idealist, turned workaday fisherman, cooking eggs (organic, local, free-run, of course) in my rented kitchen for myself and my eleven-year-old son, Willow, who's gotten up to share breakfast with me, as he often does, before I head out to sea with my disillusionments and deceits.

He sits at our old oak veneer table and picks at one of the de-laminated strips lifted and peeling. "Don't," I say, sliding his plate across the table as he flips his long blond bangs out of his eyes and looks up at me, saying nothing. So I say nothing back. We're both like this. Silent. Men of few words. Though I suspect that Willow is, as I am, a man of many thoughts. So we both sit here at our eggs together, thinking.

A decade ago, an article like the one I read last night about the albatross would have set me searing. Willow was an infant, Anna was beginning her master's in environmental ethics at UBC, and I, recently graduated with a degree in sociology, was riding the wave of new-millennium environmentalism from issue to issue, outrage to outrage, like everyone we hung out with at the time. But now everybody knows about the albatross, about the massive whirl-pool of plastic. And they know about the 386 ppm of carbon in the atmosphere. They recycle, eat organic and use non-disposable grocery bags. Some even supplement their grid power with solar panels, or install solar hot-water heaters on their roofs. Some drive hybrids, while others don't drive. I read recently about a group of artists who flew in carbon-dumping jet planes to Midway Atoll so they could view for themselves the carcasses of baby albatross with piles of bottle caps and flecks of plastic amongst the brittle bones. So they might be inspired.

On my thirtieth birthday, after a long night of drinking at the bar, I drove my pickup clear off the road, full speed, down a forty-foot embankment and into the base of a cedar tree, the only thing between my truck and the bedroom wall of two little girls, Claire and Christina. When I came to, blood gushing from the gash in my forehead (I still have a long horizontal scar just below my hairline), it was to the sound of their panicked screams. Shortly after, scared shitless, I walked into my first AA meeting. I've been sober ever since.

And how's that been? Sad. Uninspired. I hadn't realized how much I relied upon the euphoric binges, even the glow-over of the nightly Scotch-and-sodas, to keep my doubts at bay, to keep me searching, seeking, hoping. There's a distance around the thirty-fifth latitudes, north and south, where very little wind blows. The subtropical high. It's also known as the horse latitudes. Back in the days when trade ships crossed the high seas with only their sails to power them, it's believed the crew would throw horses and other livestock overboard to preserve drinking water if the absence of wind left them stranded for too long. That's how my sobriety has been these past five years. The horse latitudes of my life.

"You delivering tomorrow?" Willow asks, rising with his empty plate to the sink.

"Depends if there's much in the traps today."

"Wind's up," he says, leaning over the sink and looking out the window at the alders and firs swaying beyond the house.

"I think it'll ease by midday," I say, standing to join him. "That's a westerly blowing the cold air in. See in the trees which way the wind's coming from? Opposite the sun. That'll blow the rest of the clouds off, then it'll probably die down." I reach out and tousle his hair like I often did when he was young and his head was at hand height. He looks me in the eye for a moment, close, and I can't believe how far from my ship I've thrown him. My only son. But there are no words for this, only a stone of sadness in my throat, so I turn, take my thermos of coffee from the counter and leave by the kitchen door.

I wish it were a door leading not out to our driveway, to this cold wind blowing in off the strait, but to a room. A provided room perhaps in a community centre or church. In that room I wish there were a gathering of people like me, a twelve-step group for those living with no-hope. I'd walk into that room, take a Stevia-sweetened muffin from the tray of goodies, and pour myself some organic black tea, unpasteurized milk and honey. I'd sit down, listen, and when it's asked if there is anyone new who would like to share I'd rise up, clear my throat, and say, *Hi. My name is Francis, Francis Wichbaun, and I'm tired of the end of the world.*

⤳

THERE ISN'T MUCH in the traps. There hasn't been for years now. Still I come out every week and haul up whatever crab might have wandered in over the two-week soak I've given my fifteen-pot strings of gear. Over the years of fishing the Sunshine Coast I've developed a system. The commercial licence I bought with my boat, the *Gulf Prevailer*, allows me to fish 225 traps. So I keep 300 in the water at all times. Because who's ever going to check? I have 150 here in the inlet and 150 in the sandy shallows of Thormanby Island, a small island two and a half nautical miles off the Halfmoon Bay government dock, which is just up the road from our house. So, ten strings on the inside and ten on the outside. Starting Mondays I haul two to four strings a day, weather depending. Each night I hang my catch in old milk crates from the dock and the crab live in there, piled on top of each other as only hearty crustaceans can.

I hate crab. Mostly I think they've been the ruin of me, little private devils that sucked me in with their abundance and commanding market value when I first began fishing, only to all but disappear and sink to an abysmal value the very year I'd finally gathered enough money and gumption to put a down payment on this $450,000 licence and worthless tin can of a boat I've signed my life away to. Of course the reality is they're just crab. I sucked myself in. And despite all Anna's petitioning and tears, I refuse to sell and put the money toward a decent house because I don't know what else I would do with myself. I've found, among other things, that I'm a seaman, through and through.

On Fridays I deliver my catch, of whatever quantity, to Vancouver. I take the early ferry with the crab crammed into their crates, heavy sea water-soaked wool blankets draped over them to keep the heat out. It's the most primitive of systems, but it works. On Saturdays I run the boat up to the mouth of Sechelt Inlet, through Skookumchuck Narrows, down Agamemnon Channel, past Francis Point and through Welcome Pass to Halfmoon Bay, or vice versa, but not before spending the night in Vancouver with Jin Su and Emily. I leave the house Friday morning, before dawn, and don't come back until the following night. Anna knows I make my delivery, pick up supplies in Steveston, then run the boat between the inlet and the strait, but she never asks how it went, and I suppose she assumes I sleep on the boat or in the truck, or cruise at night, and I of course don't suggest otherwise.

A flock of seagulls comes from shore and swarms the boat, diving at the old bait I empty from the traps and toss overboard into the cold water. They hover above me, screeching and shitting all over the deck, and I'm reminded of the legotross as I wrestle the crab from their grips on the traps' steel mesh. I check them for their sex, throw the females back to the sea and measure the males for size. Most are juvenile, too small to be legally harvested, which I suspect hasn't stopped the other crabber working this bay from selling them to one of the cash buyers in Richmond, but I still play by some of the rules so throw them overboard, too, hurling the occasional crab at the demanding gulls.

It's a hard job, crabbing. The traps are a good one hundred pounds empty; the crabs are cantankerous at best; the rotten squid and clam I swap out of the bait cups reeks; and much of the year the weather is changeable and cold. But I work at my own pace, and I work alone. One of the things I've come to realize since meeting Jin Su is that I want and need to spend a fair bit of time alone. Often, once I've nearly finished setting a string out, I shut the engine down and leave the last trap on deck with the end of the float line tied off to the starboard rail. I sit back on deck if the weather is fair, or in my little aft cabin if it's not, and listen. To the birds ruffling and screeching in the wind, water lapping the hull. I like the space the sea affords, the instant openness of casting off from the grid of wires and roads which is the human world.

The love I share with Jin Su is like this. An open, uncharted, unsounded ocean. We've come together as two adults, with clarity and desire. Anna fell in love with a handsome, networking, ambitious young activist who promised her the world because he was too naive and self-assured to understand that the world wasn't his for the offering. Now she rattles at the bars of the cage created by being married to a man fallen from that self-constructed precipice to where I am now, sitting quietly on my boat, happy in my solitude, looking out over these inlet waters and steep, rugged mountain ranges.

The wind gusts up and I look into its cold flare. Something floating to the north on the choppy, dark-blue water catches the sunlight and shines and glimmers like a mirror. I retrieve my binoculars from the cabin and spy what looks like a light-blue, translucent ball through them. An old glass fishing float adrift, I assume. Although this is an unheard-of rarity in waters this far inland, my first thought is not to bother with it.

Jin Su gave birth to our daughter Emily on the first of January this year. Anna and I had taken Willow to her parents in Sicamous for the holidays, a tradition we established when Willow was born. The previous winter I had thought over Christmas dinner with Anna's folks to use the elevated holiday price for live crab as an excuse to bus home early on Boxing Day and be with Jin Su, at the time a new and unfamiliar lover overwhelming my thoughts and desires, my ability to be present in any place or time without her. I used the ensuing snowstorm to postpone my returning to retrieve her and Willow for two weeks while Jin Su and I huddled in the shelter of each other in the middle of the snow-hushed city. I did the same this past season, so Emily was born into my hands, wailing with her otherworldly fire, in Jin Su's little apartment in South Vancouver in the early hours of January first, dawn just breaking over the city of glass.

And ever since that day, glass is what I've broken. Unwittingly I've sent countless drinking glasses from the kitchen counter to the tile floor, shattering. I broke the tempered glass above our covered sundeck while cleaning it of cedar debris, the bathroom window while playing baseball with Willow in the yard, and Anna's stained-glass lamp, bashing into it with my head. I dropped to the tile two of the three thirty-litre glass jugs we use to retrieve pristine drinking water from the public artesian well in nearby Gibsons, and the last I tossed empty into the back seat of my SuperCab where it bounced off a tote of mending wire spools and smashed out the rear window. I've taken to wearing contacts—I'm nearsighted—which I hate, and have tucked my glasses away at the back of Anna's underwear drawer, hopefully safe from the jinx that's come upon me.

So my first thought is to consider the retrieval of the distant float to be futile, as I'll more than likely smash it to bits just trying to bring it aboard. I look again through the binoculars (it's a miracle they've thus far been spared) and of course I can't resist. So I set the last trap and buoy line out and fire up the engine. As I approach the float I drive the boat just beyond it, turn perpendicular to the northerly chop, then shut the engine down and step out on deck as the boat drifts slowly downwind. It's of the lightest blue and opalescent like oil, and as the orb of it bobs on the rippling water a rainbow of colour seems to swirl upon its inner surface. I imagine all sorts of shatterings as I drift to within arm's reach, dip my hands in, and cradle it onto the boat.

Held close, its opalescence disappears and it seems a grimy, timeworn ball of thick blue glass. Amazing—assuming that it wasn't set adrift in the inlet, but travelled in from the Georgia Strait and likely the open Pacific beyond—that it made it through those waters and the narrow, tumultuous mouth of the Skookumchuck intact. How old is this thing? And where did it come from? It's almost hypnotic, this ball of flotsam, as I turn it round and round in my warming hands, dismissing my previous fear for its integrity in my care, certain it has weathered worse. There's a large insignia stamped into the glass: a strange-looking serpentine fish with a forked, triple-finned tail, each fin splayed out and conjoined with the others at its base like a fan. It's like no fish I've ever seen or heard of, like something from another world.

~

BACK AT THE dock Svend pokes his head out of his aft-deck engine room as I pull the *Prevailer* into the berth beside his. He takes the bow line and helps me tie off as I leap to the dock. "Not much," he comments, surveying my measly two crates of Dungeness. "It's hardly worth it, eh?" Svend says this all the time. He's been fishing for decades and acquired his licence in the early days of the fishery when the government more or less gave them out for free; before restrictions, tax structure and black-market laundering drove the values far beyond real-world worth. When the crab price tanked half a decade ago and the elevated licence values didn't, Svend decided to trade his crab licence for the prawn licence he now holds. As dollar smart as that move has proven to be, it's left Svend at the dock, idly tinkering on his boat all but fifty to seventy days mid-summer, and although he will not confess to it, it's evident he yearns to be out year-round like he used to. His little *hardly seems worth it*'s are just the reiterations of a lonely, bored bachelor trying to convince himself to feel otherwise.

I climb back aboard the *Prevailer* and toss my crates of Dungeness into the small gap of water between the boat and the dock, then tie them off just inches from the bottom, all the while smirking with the pleasure of what I did bring in from the inlet today. Svend stands watching, his hands at his hips on either side of his paunch, and finally asks, "What are you grinning about?" I tie the last crate off, then return to the cabin to retrieve the float.

Svend climbs aboard to get a better look. "Huh," he says, rubbing his moustache. "What do you figure?" I ask, but he just shakes his head as I hand him the float. I do this with a little hesitation, though I know Svend to be of a steadiness of hand rivalled only by that of my Opa Hein's. Standing beside him, watching him inspect its surprising heft and dulled gleam, I see the trick of light which again rolls an oily rainbow inside the glass. He begins scouring away at the crusty film of sea scuzz that sticks to much of its surface as though it's been baked on. "This thing might be really nice

21

underneath all this," he says.

In the cabin I restart the engine, flick on the washdown hose and grab the bottle of liquid laundry soap I use when scrubbing down the deck at day's end. I give Svend a clean cloth and a cap-full of the detergent, and while I scour the boat he works away at the float. By the time I'm finished, he is, too, and what he has in his hands is something altogether more beautiful than I'd anticipated. It sparkles. The sunlight caught inside enhances its opalescent swirling, and it casts like a prism a small rainbow on the buffed aluminum deck at our feet.

"Something this nice might even be worth a few pennies," Svend says as he hands it to me. "Who knows kid, it may have been a good day's fishing after all."

∽

WITH MOTHERHOOD AND our settling in Halfmoon Bay, Anna's focus has shifted from fighting greenwashing corporations and exploitive international trade agreements to pharmaceutical companies and fish farms, but the underlying posture of resistance hasn't changed. She works part-time, for a pittance, for the Raincoast Research Society helping Alexandra Morton—a renegade cetacean biologist turned sea-louse scientist and environmental activist—with her limited PR. With the rest of her time, when she's not caring for Willow and gardening, Anna googles obsessively, digging up endless dirt on vaccines.

I always know when she's been at it most of the day. She'll be tight-lipped, smouldering through dinner, her blonde curls wound up into a bun on the top of her head, a golden halo. Once Willow is asleep she'll regale me with a litany about adjuvants, MMR, pertussis, HPV and Gardasil. She's been at it all winter about Gulf War

Syndrome and the adjuvant in the H1N1 vaccine, squalene. There are colour printouts on her study wall of hundreds of shark carcasses strewn across African beaches, their bodies drained of the oil and abandoned to rot in the sun.

I went down to the seniors hall and got shot up as soon as the vaccine was available, though I haven't told Anna. I'd have taken Willow down too if I thought I could get away with it, but her defiance is an unquestionable, impenetrable wall. *Ferris,* she'd say. *You're just like the rest of them. You've bought into their bullshit just like your mother.* Ferris is what people call me. Ferris Wishbone. Every spring, when I was a child, there was this travelling carnival that wheeled into Qualicum Beach and set up for the weekend with its gravitron, tilt-a-whirl, ring toss and bumper cars. Each year my mother took us over from Lasqueti Island, where I grew up, so we wouldn't be deprived of what was once her favourite thing as a child. When I was twelve she finally gave me ten bucks and said I could go alone, so I gorged myself on cotton candy and caramel apples, convinced the prettiest girl in class to ride the Ferris wheel with me, and on our fourth or fifth roll over the crest I puked pink bile and apple chunks all over her and the middle-aged couple in the carriage beneath us.

Wishbone is a bit more convoluted. My father Carl was born in Germany to Claus and Annette Wichbaun. They immigrated to Canada after the war and raised Carl and his sister in Windsor, Ontario. Claus worked as a machinist and was proud to be the first Wichbaun to send his son to college, which is where my father read Elie Wiesel and Primo Levi and Charlotte Delbo and built a great disgust for his German blood and heritage. Then he read Orwell and Salinger and Huxley and his disgust went universal. So he headed west and ended up at a hippie commune on Lasqueti Island, home to draft dodgers and weed growers, the disillusioned, disenfranchised and disgusted, like himself. Being comprised primarily of small-time criminals on the lam, the Lasquetians were prone to assuming and assigning themselves aliases: new-age goddess culture names like Zen and Ocean and Windchild. My father Carl became Cosmo. And, as though to rid himself finally of his last vestige of German-ness aside from his blood and every flesh-and-bone feature, Wichbaun became Wishbone. Legally.

Cosmo died when I was fourteen. To be honest I'm not one of those people who lost a parent early on and is forever traumatized as a result. The fact is I knew my father very little. By the time I was in grade school at False Bay elementary, a little one-room schoolhouse on the north end of Lasqueti, Cosmo was rarely home. He'd appear occasionally to clean out, take a break from the sea (by then he was running drugs by boat across the border to the Olympic Peninsula) and the endless Lasqueti party. He'd go upstairs to my parents' room to sleep it off and my mother would feed him soups and herbal teas. The closest I remember being to him is when I'd climb to the top of the wooden ladder which led to their loft and lift my ear to the tiny interstice between the door and the floor, listening to the deep and resonant, laboured sound of his breathing.

When he blew his heart out on a mountain of coke in the late '80s I don't think anyone was surprised. My mother, still young and very beautiful, in no time attracted the attention of an ultra-rich investment banker from New York who kept a palatial property on the southwest of the island, a perfectly secluded bay of pebbles and sand he flew into once a summer by float plane via Vancouver International. They courted for years, on Lasqueti and in New York, and when I was finally off to university, they married.

So when Anna hurls a comment at me like, *You've bought into their bullshit just like your mother*, which she does almost nightly these days, it takes aim at the fact that my mother, a born and raised back-to-the-lander, is now the divorcee of a small-time Bernie Madoff with scruples, living in a Manhattan apartment on his alimony payments and what's left of her inheritance now that Oma and Opa have died and their quarter-section on the south end of

Lasqueti has been sold off. But there's a whole subtext beneath such a comment that takes aim at me too.

We were at the University of British Columbia together when we met, in the time of Ani DiFranco and the organics explosion— a time and place where a couple of years of liberal arts education could sweep a beautiful, athletic, small-town girl in her time of easy influence into the seedy, new-age Y2K dustbin where genuine hippie heritage like mine was like street cred and a young man like me was a prince. God knows I played the part, because let's face it, pretty much all of a healthy young man's socializing in his early twenties is about getting laid, and I'd found the ace up my sleeve. So Anna fell in love with me before I knew who I was. And before I'd figured that out, or anything about anything out, she was pregnant.

I took a job on a small commercial crab boat at the mouth of the Fraser River, which Anna liked, as it fit the wild-man-of-the-land-and-sea image I'd sold her. After she finished her master's we moved from the city to Roberts Creek. It was 2001, housing was cheap, the price of crab was upwards of six dollars a pound, and Willow was weaned. I'd say we were happy. I was commuting to the Sand Heads crabbing grounds three days on, three days off, and had taken a lease as a skipper on a little twenty-five-foot aluminum day skiff by then. So we had money and friends, and we would still share a bottle of wine once Willow was down for the night, making love to cap off the evening more often than not. When gentrification and the housing bubble made Roberts Creek unaffordable and undesirable, we set our sights up the coast on Halfmoon Bay and found the rental we still live in now. With my mother's financial assistance, by way of a co-signature on a high interest commercial bank loan, I bought the *Gulf Prevailer*.

For the who-the-fuck-am-I-and-how-shall-I-carry-forth anxiety that comes on with early parenthood, I did nothing, till I told my long-time crab buyer to go fuck himself, and walked into a competing buyer's office across town. Which is where I found Jin

Su, working behind the receptionist's desk, small and lovely, and every bit the answer to a question I'd forgotten even to ask.

↬

ANNA'S IN THE bath reading and Willow's in bed. It's actually been good between us lately. I've learned to let her snide comments slide off my back, more or less, so excluding her little freak-outs whenever I break glass, it's been calm. Tonight I nearly broke her crystal two-in-one salt and pepper shaker. Anna has all these "heirloom" things all over the house that she was given when her grandma died, mostly semi-antique junk, though ever since I've become the proverbial bull in the china shop they're suddenly priceless gems to her.

Willow and I were jousting with the broom and the mop in the kitchen when I accidentally swatted the shaker from the shelf above the stove. It bounced off the stovetop and Willow caught it mid-flight while I just stood there, wincing as it flew, already anticipating Anna's tirade about my carelessness and juvenility. Sword fighting in the fucking kitchen! Of course I would counter that, given the heaviness beset upon him by our marriage—we've never actually had a wedding, though we've always considered ourselves man and wife, and if ours is not a marriage, what is?—times of lightness and play need to be indulged in and encouraged with our son as much and as often as possible, good riddance to heirloom trinkets.

I'm out on the front porch smoking some of Anna's homegrown tobacco, the westerly subsided now and the night warm beneath the late-April stars, the scent of new growth and old rot rising from the alder-bottom beyond our house. I can't stop thinking about the float I found earlier today. Before I left the boat I packed it in an old tote with rags and crab floats for padding. When I arrived home I stowed it high in the rafters of the garage where Anna wouldn't find it. Svend had been adamant about the fact that it might be worth a bit of cash, and if so it will be money I'll give to Jin Su.

"Thirty thousand," Svend says, as I answer the vibing cellphone in my hand. I think about this for a second before understanding that he's referring to the float's value. "You're shitting me," I reply, trying not to raise my voice with the exhilaration that sum brings. "I'm not. I've been on the computer for hours now. There's this guy, Stu Farnsworth, he's the big fishing float guru. Anyway, he's got an 'Antique Floats Wanted' page on his website, and on it he's got pictures and drawings and descriptions of all these rare floats he's always on the lookout for. Most fetch from five hundred bucks to five grand. But there's this one grouping of seven or eight different emblems, and that fish on your float is one of them. Those ones he's offering up to thirty grand for!"

Svend is so excited his voice is leaping through the phone into my ear. An old fisherman, forever in love with the thrill of the big haul. "You know, I'm thinking," he continues. "Who do you sell your crab to?" I know it's a rhetorical question, and I'm not sure where he's going with it, but I answer: "Nelson Chow." To which Svend replies with another obvious question. "And what's he?"

"He's a fucking fish buyer Svend. Why, you think he's looking to get into the glass fishing float market or what?" I'm a bit exasperated, a bit excited, and I want to know his point.

"He's a middle man, kid. Now I've been surfing around for hours looking into this thing, and it turns out Stu Farnsworth isn't the only person buying floats online. In fact, there are as many people buying them as there are people selling. Or more. There's pages of these things up for bid on eBay."

I'm starting to get where he's going with this. It's sort of a knee-jerk reflex for most fishermen to want to cut out the middle man. We spend countless hours on the docks and at coffee shops scheming ways to get our catch directly to market. The prawns Svend catches and sells to the buyers in Vancouver for five bucks a pound sell for fifteen dollars or more once they make it to Toronto and LA. They sell for upwards of fifty dollars a pound in Japan. The middle men are making more money from their cushy offices moving our product than we are risking our lives out on the water fishing for it. It's an old story. And it's an age-old desire for fishermen to want to find a way to bypass them and keep for ourselves the inequitable slice they take from the pie. "Somebody, somewhere, is paying a pretty penny for these things Ferris." We're both hanging on the line, digesting the implications and the possibilities. Through the open window beside me I hear Anna rising from the bath. "I've got to go Svend," I say.

"Do you know of anyone?" he asks. "Anyone who might know about these things?" I picture hundreds of glass fishing floats still held in their twine encasements, strung together like beads on a string, swirling and clonking in the breeze like a great wind chime beneath Fairwin' Verge's treehouse.

"Yes," I say. "I think I might."

FAIRWIN'S TREEHOUSE, OR "Fairwin's Fort," as it's known on the island, sits high in the mid-section of a massive thousand-year-old Douglas fir near the top of Mount Tremeton, the highest point on Lasqueti. A steep staircase winds up the trunk leading to an octagonal structure enwrapping the tree, its timber floor-system set on massive forty-five-degree braces spanning from the building's outer perimeter back to the trunk. Long strings of fishing floats hang in threes from each outer point of the octagon, bejewelling the dark tree and Fairwin's Fort to scale. Svend's never seen anything like it. He stands beneath, hands jammed in his jean pockets, looking up in awe and perplexity, shaking his head as though to say, *Why would anyone bother?* And most wouldn't. But Fairwin's another sort.

Farevin Verge spent his working years as a lighthouse keeper up and down the west coast of BC, from the fortress on Triple Island to the estate-like grounds of Cape Scott, to his final posting as the last keeper of the Sisters Island light, a humble light tower and living quarters built on a tiny upsurge of igneous two miles northwest of Lasqueti's northern tip.

The feds switched the Sisters station over to unmanned automation in the early '90s, so after thirty years of isolation on the lights, his only companionship that of the CBC and his books, Farevin took early retirement and settled on this: a life built high in a majestic tree, with materials of scrap and salvage, driftwood and blowdown, fed by the sea, the forest, and a trickling spring of pristine groundwater.

It wasn't long before the Lasquetians (all 350 of them) made the reclusive, elusive Farevin one of their many subjects of community gossip, coining him Fairwin', as in "Fairwind"—tongue-in-cheek for his gruff demeanour and weather-worn, windblown appearance.

I place my treasured blue float (still packed safely in its tote) at my feet, then reach up on my tiptoes to grab and swing a dangling strand of floats so they knock and clang, announcing our arrival. "Fairwin'," I call out, my bellow dampened yet carrying through the old trees. There is little understory in the Lasqueti forest, the island overrun by the flock of sheep set feral when the Lasqueti Wool and Dye Company died with my Oma and Opa. With no animals of prey to speak of the sheep population has increased to the point of infestation, so the forest floor is one of sheep-shit-speckled moss and loam, and sapling shoots gnawed of leafage. A massive culling is in order, but the year-round community, ninety percent of whom make at least a portion of their living off the annual marijuana crop, oppose it. The sheep's understory thinning makes for easy bushwhacking and planting, and although the Lasqueti forest of the future will consequently be devoid of its beautiful fir and cedar, for now it's the best of both worlds.

"Ferris Wishbone, you've your father's timbre," calls Fairwin' in response, not down from the tree, but up from the last leg of the goat path Svend and I have just climbed. I turn to watch him—looking much older than when I last saw him—climb toward us, a basket of nettles in one hand and an old urn filled with water in the other. He ascends, puts his load to the ground and, as he has never done before, embraces me. "How long has it been?" Fairwin' asks, letting me free, and I almost sense a quaver of sadness, an audible tear in his voice. Nine years, I think. Nine years since I was last on Lasqueti. He introduces himself to Svend, who shakes his hand heartily and introduces himself in return. "You've brought me something?" Fairwin' asks, looking down at my tote, the lid duct taped shut. "Let's take it up," I nod. And we do, 101 steps up the winding staircase into Fairwin's fort.

⤳

SIX HOURS LATER we're driving west through Cathedral Grove, a token highway-side stand of vestigial old-growth fir preserved as park and viewing for the four million tourists who pass through this way to Pacific Rim National Park, Ucluelet and Tofino each year. Dusk is sifting down through the tiers of their splayed branches, the dash light of the mid-seventies Dodge Dart I'm driving starting to cast its dim green hue on my hands as I steer through the trees.

One look at the insignia stamped on my float and Fairwin' was alight with an idea. "I know a woman," he'd said. "Miriam Maynard. She owns a lodge out in Tofino, the Glass Globe beach house. She's a major beachcombing buff. I met her at a workshop there years ago." Fairwin's far less excitable than Svend, so though he was enthusiastic, his voice was calm. "A workshop?" I asked, amused by the idea of Fairwin' in attendance at any gathering of people, much less a workshop. "Yes. A beachcombing workshop. She gave a bit of a talk that weekend on some of the more rare and sought-after floats to be found."

We caught the last ferry off the island and agreed with some Lasquetian unfamiliar to both Fairwin' and I to pay two hundred dollars for the two-day rental of this gas-guzzling though groovy piece of shit I'm now driving. We were happy to pay it, none of us looking forward to the otherwise near-hopeless enterprise of a scruffy-looking young man, an overweight middle-aged man, and a freaked-out-looking old man trying to hitch a ride to Tofino in the dark.

Anna thinks I'm delivering in town or running the boat around from the inlet, and I called Jin Su to tell her I'd be coming early next week instead of tonight as I normally would be. I've yet to figure out what lie to tell next to rectify the discrepancy. I'm tired and hungry, but also excited by the possibilities at play here. What kind of money, if any, will this Miriam lady be able to lead me into, and what liberty will that then afford me? If I could, I would buy Anna out of what little equity we own in the *Prevailer* and begin our separation. I'm not sure beyond that; how I'd then approach my life with Jin Su and Emily, or how I'd explain them both to Anna, Willow and my mother.

I've often wondered if Anna's seeming indifference to my whereabouts the Friday nights I spend each week with Jin Su and Emily is indicative of her own infidelities. Perhaps she's more than happy to be rid of me, making it easy to rendezvous with whomever her lover might be. And that could be anybody. Anna is one of those women who is every man's type. I've come close many times to asking her, in the midst of one fight or another, but I fear such an unfounded accusation would only indicate my own betrayals, so I resist.

Svend is quiet now in the back seat. I peer at him in the rearview and he appears to be dozing off, his thick head wobbling above his shoulders. "So what happened to you?" Fairwin' asks, his voice rough yet frail over the old car's many whirs and rattles. "Last I saw you, you had that beautiful woman at your side—Anna right?—and that plump son of yours on your shoulders. Then, no more of your mother, no more of you." I think for a moment about what to tell Fairwin', and what not to. "I'm a crab fisherman," I say. "And I have a daughter now. Emily."

"Emily. A daughter of yours and Anna's must be very beautiful."

"She is," I reply, then consider for a moment whether to, and how to, elaborate or clarify further. "Though some may not think so." Fairwin' takes his eyes from the road and looks toward me as I say this. "She was born with a port-wine stain on the left side of her face," I continue. "On its entirety, from the base of her neck to the top of her forehead." Fairwin's look is one of puzzlement and concern. "Do you know what that is?" I ask.

"I've never heard of it."

"Neither had I. It's one of the symptoms of Sturge-Weber Syndrome. It's a vascular malformation in which the blood vessels, the capillaries at the surface of the skin, don't contract, so the blood is always pooling to the surface, like a newly forming bruise. You know Gorbachev, that purple birthmark on his forehead? That's port-wine."

Fairwin' considers this for a moment, ever-thoughtful as he is, then asks. "And so like Gorbachev's it will not go away then? Is there any treatment these days?"

"There's a thing called pulsed-dye laser. It's painful, and to give it to her now we'd have to put her under general anaesthetic."

"How old is she?"

"She'll be five months May 1st. Ten days."

"And this laser treatment, does it work?"

"I guess it varies. It's hard to say whether it's worth it."

"And what is this Sturge-Weber Syndrome? You said this was the outward presentation. Is there more?"

Jin Su and Svend are the only people I've spoken with, other than our GP and the doctors and nurses at Children's Hospital in Vancouver, about Emily's condition. I realize now, telling it anew to Fairwin', the magnitude of the stress I feel, the worry, for my daughter's well-being, for her future. "There can be," I reply. Svend lets out a great sigh, then begins to snore in the back seat. I look again to him in the rearview. He's flopped over against the windshield and the sound of his snoring rising from his silhouette is enough humour to lighten the mood I've begun darkening into. "There's the threat her left eye will develop glaucoma because of the pressure built up by blood pooling in the sclera. Also, it's unlikely, but sometimes the damage travels up the trigeminal nerve to the brain, then calcifies the brain tissues and causes all sorts of problems, from seizures to severe retardation."

"So you're worried, of course. And Anna—how is she taking it?"

That's a good question. I think of the polarities of darkness and light I've brought home with me from Vancouver since Emily's birth. How Jin Su and I have rode the highs and lows together of sadness and elation at our daughter's existence, of fear and hope and anticipation as we wait to see what she will become, whether her birthmark is indicative of further damage, or the brunt of what she will be asked by chance of her particular genetic complexity to bear. It will be months, if not years, before we know. Anna and Willow have both unwittingly rode those highs and lows, and have lived in the shadow of anxiety the precariousness of Emily's future casts around me. "Hard," I say, in answer to Fairwin's question. "I think it's been really hard on Anna."

⌒

WE ARRIVED AT the Glass Globe beach house well after midnight last night. We pulled down the long driveway as quietly as we could, then Svend and I waited in the car while Fairwin' hobbled his old bones up to a little cedar-shingled, wisteria-shrouded house. We watched him enter, and waited another fifteen minutes till he re-emerged and led us down a dimly lit path, over a long cedar foot-bridge, to the Globe House. Fairwin' gave us each a key to our own room and I fell asleep quickly, exhausted, and slept soundly to the rhythm of the Pacific swell rising up and breaking against the shore.

I woke up in the late morning to Svend at my door. "What's up with these hippies and their houses," was the first thing he said as he stepped into my room. "Really, what's so wrong with a good old-fashioned rectilinear rancher?"

I chided him then for being a redneck, but standing outside on the deck of the Glass Globe now, I see his point. It's one of the more ridiculous buildings I've ever seen. It's hexagonal, perched on high timber girders thirty or forty feet over a sandy beach. The long cedar bridge we walked out on last night connects it to the high bank property Miriam's house sits upon some hundred-odd feet inland. But what really puts it over the top is not its location or elevation, but the building itself. It's comprised of six separate, triangular rooms, touching only at each tip. The whole thing is connected by a single roof which, at its apex, houses a common, interior room from which a swirling staircase descends to the beach below. The six rooms have on their two exterior walls a large, bulbous, round window, each a different colour of the rainbow, with violet being the colour of the massive bubble skylight above the building's central room. Svend and I are walking the perimeter deck of this thing, dumbfounded by the scale of its gaudiness, when Fairwin' comes toward us over the bridge with a middle-aged woman in tow.

Miriam Maynard is, judging by the aesthetics of her establishment, not what I had expected. She's dressed in pleated slacks and suit coat, her grey-white hair pinned up behind her ears, a hint of mascara and lipstick tastefully applied—a businesswoman! Not the nightie-wearing, slippered, tea-sipping old hippie crone I'd have pegged as the owner of such a place.

Fairwin' manages introductions, then Miriam leads us up to her home, which is equally well kept and, well, as conservative in its decor as her dress and demeanour are. She doesn't entirely diverge from the neo-hippie I'd imagined though. The living room walls are adorned with the work of Roy Henry Vickers and other contemporary Native artists, there are wood and soapstone carvings on the shelves, and her home has the smell of cloves, garlic and lemon. She brings us chai tea and raisin scones as we sit down in her living room to discuss my glass float. As I lift it from its tote her eyes light up and she quickly reaches out for me to hand it to her. Again I hesitate, then notice them all notice, feel foolish, and set it into her slender, manicured hands. She turns it round and round, its opalescent sheen swirling in the room's lamplight. "Beautiful," she says, and it truly is. She inspects the insignia, drawing her eyes very close to its surface, then hands it back to me. "Follow me," she says. "You need to see something."

Miriam's house sits on a property that juts out and eventually drops—a scraggy, northwest-facing point of basalt—to the sea. At each side of the point are two fields. One of long grass bisected by a slender footpath which leads to the bridge and the Globe House; the other a large apple orchard which gives way to forest and a steep trail of root-strewn, sinuous earth. The three of us follow Miriam slowly down till we come to sea level. We traverse swampish terrain, little ochre-tinted pools and fans of devil's club, then a narrow trail through thick salal, tall, dry grasses, and finally out to a ball-field-sized dune of soft white sand rising up to the west and again falling away toward the sea hundreds of feet beyond. There is a wide horseshoe of stones piled waist-high to the seaward side of the dune. Set down in the sand, arranged in patterns and lines, are hundreds and hundreds of glass fishing floats of every size and colour.

"The wall keeps them from being buried by windblown sand, and even with protection it's a daily duty to tend to them," Miriam explains. "They spell ʔukʷiiyaʔum ciłciłii," she says lightly. "That's Nuu-chah-nulth, the indigenous people's language, for *Safe journey, grey whale.*" Miriam leads us toward the glimmering floats, the morning sunlight reflecting in their array of colours. "Some have nothing embossed on the seal," she explains, pointing to the row of floats now at our feet. "Like these ones. They're generic floats made in Taiwan and China, probably within the past thirty years."

Listening to Miriam tell of her beach full of glass floats I realize something I'd been trying to place while following her down through the forest. In the soft yet self-assured, authoritative tone of her voice is the echo of Anna's. It's a dead ringer. And I see in this woman, this stately, upright, elegant woman, her eyes kind and body relaxed, the woman I once imagined Anna growing into in her older years. What happens? You spend a decade living—eating and sleeping and working and dreaming—side by side with someone, and through that time and sharing that person is altered, till suddenly you watch her in the light of your shared kitchen cutting carrots, or from a distance at a street corner talking with someone she knows well and you don't. Or you look at her beside you in your bed, the bed you have loved each other in, conceived and birthed your child in, and she is asleep, her brow furrowed, her jaw clenched down and grinding in the night, and you don't recognize her, don't know her, have never known her, though it's clear by virtue of the years that she's now closer to you than ever.

"There are floats of all sizes and of many shapes," Miriam explains as we follow her further through the rows. "Now this one," she nearly whispers as she stoops to lift a cylindrical, transparent float from the sand, brushing it off with the care one might show dusting a dish of fine, centuries-old china. "This one was blown in Japan, probably post-World War II. See the kanji symbols?" Miriam hands me the float, its insignia set not on either end's seal but instead along its side. I run my fingers over the raised kanji, then pass it carefully to Svend before the jinx I've been under catches up with me. Miriam waits quietly till we've all inspected the float, then takes it from Fairwin', sets it back down in its pocket of sand, and steps over it, reaching for a round float of green glass a few rows beyond. She brushes the sand from it as attentively as she did the last, and a little smile plays across her face.

"This float was brought here by a guest visiting from France. People come from all over the world to stay at the Globe House and place a piece of their own collection on this beach." She holds the seal-end toward the three of us so we can all see it. The markings on the seal are of the capital letters C and M. "The C is for Christiania, the M for Magasin. This float was blown in Norway around the turn of the century. At that time, what is now the city of Oslo was known as Christiania. Magasin means Market. In 1898 the store contracted four Norwegian glassworks, Dramman, Hundal, Hadeland and Biri, to manufacture floats and emboss them with its own CM trademark to be sold on its shelves." She hands this float to me too and the three of us again pass it around.

There's an offshore wind arriving high in the trees where ravens clonk and skip from branch to branch. The surf can be seen and heard rising on the other side of the small cobble wall. I think of Anna at home, Saturday morning, maybe out in the garden by now, putting seeds in with Willow at her side. And of Jin Su and Emily in the confines of their little apartment high above Main Street. Perhaps Emily has finally learned to sit up unassisted and she's doing so now, teetering, smiling her fiery smile with her mother seated beside her on the polished bamboo floor. They'd be looking out over the city together through the thick-milled floor-to-ceiling glass. Out to the downtown high-rises and the still snow-capped mountains above, which go on and on north beyond the city, peak to valley, peak to valley, giving way finally to tundra, then to the Bering and the Beaufort Seas. It's a calamity inside me. There are so many worlds. And here I am, on this crazy beach in Tofino, searching and hoping for a stroke of luck, some quick cash, a patchwork fix for the mess I've made, am making, of mine.

WE HIKE BACK up to Miriam's house in silence, each of us contemplating where we've just been. There are places on this earth which, by virtue of human creation or some localized perfection of the planet's biorhythm, seem home to some energy, sacred, elevated beyond that which is normally sensed. Jin Su says it's why the monks always live high in the mountains, where the energy is clear, unmuddled by human cacophony. She says she's never felt it, always in the city as she is, inside the electricity. I think I have, alone on the water, though only to a degree, and wonder what it might feel like on a wind-powered boat in the middle of the open ocean. At any rate Miriam's beach of glass has that sense, that marriage of human homage and nature's magnitude, and it sets us all outside of time a bit as we climb back up the steep embankment together, offering and taking each other's hands when needed, and walk through the brightening orchard and into Miriam's home.

"There's one more thing I'd like to show you," she says, and leads us down a hallway to a door at the back of the house. Taking a key from her pant pocket she unlocks it, ushering us into a room lined with hundreds of shelved books, most of an aged appearance. There are pencil sketches of fishing boats, wharves, trees and children's faces pinned to the walls. At the far end of the room there is a rustic hutch upon which a small collection of glass fishing floats sits. She leads us to them and lifts one of clear glass into her hands.

"This float was blown in 1949 by the Northwest Glass Company in Seattle. It's thought there were only twelve made. Of those twelve, only five have been found." The float is in the shape of a doughnut, with a walled hole clear through the centre. "The hole is for hanging the float line through. It was a good idea, but proved too time-consuming for mass production. I was given this one by an old patron from Alaska when she passed away. She found it on the shore of Bristol Bay while collecting seaweed for her garden." Miriam smiles and sets the float down, not offering this time for us to hold it, then lifts another from the hutch-top. "This one is a binary

double ball, not as rare a shape, but see the violet hue at each base."
She holds the float up into the daylight coming through the room's
only window. "That's the fire's colouring, also rare." She shows us a
large, unblemished float of deep cranberry and explains how the
Japanese used gold to create the hue; and a float of light green with
a thin spindle of glass falling through its centre like a stream of
water in stasis; and another clear one with a small amount of water
trapped inside it—water, she tells us, which was absorbed through
porous imperfections in the glass while suspended in Arctic sea
ice, where it was found by some of the first Canadians to attempt
the North Pole on foot.

"And this is my most prized," she says, lifting from the hutch a
rather ordinary-looking dark green float, still encased in its beige
twine mesh, with *BV* embossed on the seal. "The trademark is that
of Biri Glassworks, one of the four I mentioned earlier who made
floats for Christiania Magasin. This float was one of the first blown
there in 1841, and was given to me by my mother's father, Kjell Biri,
the last of the Biri glassblowers. It was never sent to sea." This float
she sets in my hand, holding onto it still by the bind of its meshing,
and looks me closely in the eyes.

"These are all very rare and valuable treasures, Mr. Wishbone,"
she says, a little grin rising in her lips as she says my name. "But
their rarity and value are nothing compared to what you have
brought here with you." She lifts the float from my hands and places
it back on the hutch, then turns and waves for us to follow, which
we do, back down the hallway to her living room.

"There is considerable mystique around the float which you have
found," Miriam continues, seating herself on the chaise lounge
beside my float. She lifts it again from its tote. "To my knowledge
there have been less than a dozen discovered. No one knows where
or when they were blown, though all those found have been in the
North Pacific. Most agree they were likely among the first Japanese
floats, blown just prior to the First World War. Every one of them

is now owned by a single collector, a Mr. Sunimoto in Hawaii. I've never seen one of these floats before, but this one is remarkably unworn for its probable age, and its exceeding thickness and opalescence is of particular uniqueness as well. I couldn't put a price on it, but through the right people this float may fetch you a very substantial sum."

"We've noticed Stu Farnsworth is offering upwards of thirty thousand dollars," Svend pipes in, almost leaping from his chair with excitement.

"And that's a considerable sum, Svend," Miriam responds. "Though it would be unwise to sell this to Stu." She looks to me now dead-on. "If I were a shrewder woman I'd cut you a check right here and now for that same sum, and I'd be sure to double my money, maybe triple it, by sundown. One phone call." Svend is sitting back smug as she says this, finally triumphant in his scheming to sidestep a middleman. "Instead, I'm going to make that call for you, Mr. Wishbone, free of charge, and in return you're going to stay with me another night and we're going to feast of the sea, be happy, and give thanks for all that the ocean provides."

MIRIAM DROVE US in her fully loaded Prius out to a beach on the east side of the Esowista Peninsula. We harvested oysters and clams, then drove further on to town where we bought fresh crab from one of the local fisherman and a bag of expensive food from the local market. By the time we started back toward her house I'd simmered in myself a broth of dislike for Miriam, for her pat expropriations of the Native customs, art and language (at least those convenient to her lifestyle and aesthetic); for her ease and self-assuredness and easy environmentalism, her fifty-thousand-dollar hybrid car and her organic wool sweater. Then I thought, watching the forest whiz by her back-seat window, how my knee-jerk contempt was just like Anna's, almost instinct, and I resolved then and there to put it aside.

When we arrived back at Miriam's house I went out onto the front deck to call Anna. On the car ride I'd resolved to tell her the truth of where I was and why, thinking again that if the float was as valuable as Miriam suggested I would use the money to finally break with Anna; if it wasn't, it was of no consequence other than to give her more fodder to fling my way.

She wasn't angry at first, not expecting me home still for a few more hours. But as I told her about the float and what it had led to, she grew more and more irritable, launching into a tirade about my desperate financial schemes, my head always off in the clouds dreaming up some fucked up way to get us out of the mess I'd gotten us into buying the stupid fucking boat in the first place. Of course I fought back, our voices growing louder and more hostile, till I realized the others were most likely hearing my every heated word inside the house.

So I told Anna she'd see and she'd be sorry, and I hung up and went back inside, my anger re-bloomed inside me like an algae in the harsh light of Anna's reprimand. But now it had its familiar object of attention, my wife, back in focus, which left me free to celebrate with Miriam when she emerged from her study with the news that a buyer representing Mr. Sunimoto would indeed be in Vancouver on Monday to exchange $150,000 cash for the fishing float I nearly broke when—later in the evening and drunk on the first bottle of wine I'd drank in nearly five years—it dropped from my hands and rolled the length of Miriam's kitchen island before falling to the forgivingly soft fir floor.

Svend, Fairwin' and I journeyed back this morning at first light, Svend and I nursing our collective hangovers. Fairwin' drove the Dart—the whole time with this little schoolboy's smirk upon his face, unlicensed, and having not driven a car for nearly fifteen years—through the mountains to French Creek, where we took Svend's boat across to Squitty Bay. Fairwin' stood in a grove of huge old arbutus and watched us motor back out into the strait. From the stern, as I puked my guts out into the southeasterly waves heaping up on Point Upwood, I could see his lone figure climbing out onto Poor Man's Rock, a barren buttress of scoured igneous protruding from Lasqueti's southern tip like a prow into the sea.

Back on the Coast I drove to Sechelt with Svend and bought some new Levi's, a couple of t-shirts, underwear and socks. I picked up some toiletries at the pharmacy and went with Svend back to his house to shower, shave and call Jin Su. All to avoid going home to Anna. I considered hauling Willow from school for a walk or lunch, to spend some time with him and get some grounding in the midst of all this.

Ever since Miriam pronounced the figure $150,000 I've been hovering six feet off the ground, oscillating between elation, nervousness and fear. Will the approaching exchange, with such a large sum of cash involved, go off without a hitch? Is that even possible? It seems that my every turn of fortune these past few years has been, though not catastrophic, certainly not without its foibles. I thought better than to have Willow see me in such an anxious state, to expect that he might be able to calm me down when quite likely he would be disturbed by my preoccupation.

Then I considered driving down to the dock and loading up what little crab I had hanging, maybe three hundred pounds, into my pickup before heading to town. But I was clean and dressed in my new clothes and quite frankly still exhausted, though wired, from the journey and the excitement and the booze still flushing from my body. So instead I headed straight to the late-afternoon ferry, where I fell asleep in my truck, still aware of the wind howling through the upper car deck.

I dreamt I was with Miriam making love in her big bed of driftwood and white linen. When I woke up, I stumbled from the truck to the side of the boat and threw up again into the wind and the tumultuous seas below. Back in the truck I thought of my drinking and of Miriam. I cursed my slip back to the bottle, but consoled myself with the fact that she was indeed a beautiful woman, attractive still for her age, and had clearly made advances toward me once Svend was snoring on the couch and Fairwin' had gone off to bed. Advances that, despite my drunkenness, I'd denied.

I felt better as I pulled the truck off the ferry in the dusk, my body having ejected the last of the poison and my mind calmed by the thought of soon being with Emily and Jin Su, of the love that awaited me there, still untarnished and strong.

⌐)

JIN SU ANSWERS the door in boxer shorts and a kimono when I arrive. She leaps up into my arms and wraps her legs around my waist before I've even made it in the door. The pent-up lust of my dream on the ferry rises up to meet hers and we make love frantic and heated on the couch, little Emily already down for the night in the bedroom. It's a world of difference in comparison to the love Anna and I seldom, if ever, make anymore: the occasional attempt at romance between us always leading to a lovemaking that proves only to reaffirm and widen the chasm between us, so we lie naked and darkened afterward, turning away from each other, each to our own arms.

Jin Su and I lie entwined now on her grey leather couch, her light body on top of mine, her head on my chest and her hand up behind my neck twirling my hair with her small fingers. She stares toward the door and finally asks, "What's in the box?"

I'd set it to the floor as she'd leapt at me, then slid it into the room with my foot as I closed the door and carried her to the couch. "It's a surprise," I reply, just as Emily starts to stir, then sputters a cry from the bedroom.

Jin Su lifts herself off me, slips into her kimono, and wrinkles her nose. "She's fussy," she says. "Cutting her first teeth I think." Then a scream like a battle cry issues from the bedroom and Jin Su springs away to tend to our daughter.

Emily was born ablaze, a roaring inferno from the first breath. She's all fire, from the birthmark spreading perfectly from the midline across the left side of her face to her tuft of light red hair standing up static on top of her head, despite her mother's dominant Chinese gene and my own head of dark brown curls. She has a wiry body, a rambunctious disposition, and a ferocious, though often playful, howl. She is, frankly, foreign to me, as is Jin Su, having come swiftly like a fresh wind into my life. Though it's a wind that feels hospitable, carrying an undercurrent of settling and the unexpected scent of home.

I gaze around Jin Su's apartment. There are some baby toys by the window, a small collection of rattles and stuffed animals and little musical instruments, a tambourine and a bean shaker, a drum and sticks. There are painted wooden blocks and a couple of old Chinese dolls, a baby boy and girl, from Jin Su's childhood, all ordered neatly on the polished floor. She's arranged a collection of photographs of her large family back home on top of the piano and another on the wall space between the dining room table and the floor-to-ceiling window. There's a tiny alcove kitchen beyond the table, and though I can't see it from here, above the stove is a picture of me in rain gear on the deck of the *Prevailer* sorting a trap loaded with crab. Jin Su took it soon after we first met, the one and only time she's been out on the water with me.

Taped to the stainless steel fridge is another picture taken at our request by a stranger on Granville Island one sunny Saturday in early February. We're all three bundled up in winter clothes and smiling from beneath our toques and hoods, happy together in the mid-winter sunlight. I can hear Emily suckling in the other room, contented, and I'm amazed that I am here, that this is my life, in stark contrast to the one I share with Anna and Willow. Somehow it seems there's more of me here in this relatively tidy, relatively empty apartment than there is or ever has been in that other rental home with its half-acre yard littered with my spare traps, motors, haulers and crab crates, my heaps of clutter and scrap.

Having failed at her attempts to nurse her back down, Jin Su brings Emily from the bedroom and plops her down on my stomach. Then she retrieves the tote from the entryway, sets it on the floor beside me, and sits down at my feet on the couch. Emily pounds my chest like a drum, a wily grin splayed across her face. "Take it out," I say, sliding the tote toward Jin Su, and I can tell she thinks it's some kind of present I've brought for her, which in a way it is, though it's evident she's both disappointed and intrigued by what she finds as she unpacks the glass float. "Careful," I can't help but caution her as she lifts it to her lap.

"Oh, it's quite beautiful isn't it?" she says, after turning it around in her hands. Emily reaches back and gives it a swat. "Careful sweetie," Jin Su says, holding Emily's hand for a moment as she does. "Where did you find it?" she asks.

"In the inlet. On Thursday afternoon."

Jin Su carries the float across the room and places it on top of the piano. She turns the little piano-top lamp on beside it and sets three of Emily's blocks around its base to keep it from rolling off. Its opalescent sheen swirls up now under the light as Emily lets out a yowl, pointing firmly toward the float and her blocks.

"It's okay sweetie," Jin Su assures her, taking two more blocks from the floor and handing them to our daughter. Then she says something to her in Chinese followed by, "Daddy brought us a pretty pretty ball," in her quiet, calm voice. I feel almost reluctant in telling her, though I know the money is more of a gift than any glass ornament could be for Jin Su, so I do: "I'm meeting a man at a sushi restaurant on South Granville tomorrow and he's going to give me $150,000 for that thing."

"What?"

"Cash. It's all arranged. Through this woman, Miriam Maynard, Svend and I,"—she doesn't know anything about Fairwin' Verge and I don't feel like explaining right now, so leave him out of it—"we met with her a couple days ago in Tofino. She's some kind of aficionado when it comes to these things. She says this one's among the most treasured in the world. So she made a phone call, and wham, $150,000!" I stand up as I say this. I'm still naked, I've got Emily in one hand hanging off my hip, and I feel ridiculous, but what the hell, it's just finally setting in what this means, here now with my daughter and Jin Su, as I tell her the news. I set Emily down and slide my jeans on, then reach out and take Jin Su by the waist while Emily beats her blocks against the floor. "What are you in to?" she asks me, with some suspicion, and blooming joy, in her eyes. "One hundred and fifty thousand dollars?" And I repeat it. "One hundred and fifty thousand. Enough to buy Anna out of her half of the boat. To break clean."

There's a sadness that enters the room as I say this. It settles like a fog in the valley formed between our two bodies. Perhaps it's the wrong time to point out that opportunity, those intentions, as it suggests a future, a near future, of both renewal and loss, pain and healing; of change and upheaval, redefining and reconfiguring. I sense in Jin Su an immediate resistance, which strikes me suddenly as something I might have anticipated in her, as organized and tidy and conservative as she is. I kiss her on the top of her head—something I often do as it's right at mouth level—and reassure her. "It'll be good Jin Su," I say. "You'll see." Though I wonder if it's not myself I'm reassuring, because I've been here before, at this place where choice and commitment suddenly weigh in like the Achilles heel of the horse you've put all your money on; like the little rattle in the engine room, the sound that's not quite right—you search and search for its origin without luck, and so assume the best, and grow to accept it as just another sound.

⌒

"It's up to you Jin Su," I say to her through the dark. Emily is asleep between us, restful, the pain in her mouth finally subsided as her little teeth relax their heaving at the surface of her gums.

"What's that?" she asks sleepily. I flick the bedside lamp on and walk out to the living room to retrieve the float. Back in bed I lie down and hold it on my chest.

"However this works out tomorrow, whatever this brings, if we do get that money like Miriam has said, it's up to you what we do with it." Jin Su turns over, props her head up and looks at me, then rests it back down on the pillow, flipping her long black hair from her face as she does. She slides her hand over and places it on my hand where it steadies the glass.

"It's up to both of us Francis," she says, and closes her eyes again. "I love you. And I'm ready for whatever life you're ready for." The room is warm and silent, the three of us close in this little bed together, her gentle hand on mine and our daughter's small breathing between us. Her hand eventually goes limp and slides down to my chest as I stare for a time at the orb of glass till it takes me as if by trance, in the dim light and the sweet scent of my daughter's new life, into sleep.

⤻

WE WAKE TO a loud bang, as if something far off has exploded or collapsed. Then the walls and window start to undulate and the bed begins to shake with the floor which is heaving and bucking. I bolt upright and the glass float rolls from my chest to the bedside table, as the floor-to-ceiling window explodes, sending a spray of tempered glass out into the early morning air. I grab hold of Jin Su, all I can think to do, and we ride out the racket of shearing wood and cracking concrete with Emily in our arms between us, stunned, then screaming, as the earth far beneath rumbles and shakes.

The sound is of a million wine glasses being stomped underfoot by a million people stampeding. It suspends time, so it's as though we lie on the bed like this for a moment and an eternity concurrently. Then it's over, and the city around us falls to a tenuous silence that hangs in the air like a single strand of spider's silk. Then the grind and shatter of glass again, buildings creaking on one last precarious point-load, and a splintered, agonizing moan issues from the throat of a woman far below us.

As more cries of the injured begin to rise into the day, I come back to myself, turning toward the window just as the float rolls the last few inches of Jin Su's bedside table and drops into the void left in the window glass's absence. I look back to Jin Su holding Emily tight to her breast, our daughter wailing now in fright, then leap to the buckled floor and scurry on all fours to the edge. All I see with my nearsighted eyes is a white blur of broken glass on the street twelve storeys below. I squint and squint and think I see a spot of blue on the other side of the street, so I wave Jin Su over.

"Are you kidding," she cries at me from the bed, one tear streaking down her face.

"You're okay right?" I ask, looking back at her, Emily hysterical in her arms. I get to my feet for the first time since waking, go to the bed, and hold them both, just hold them tight for a long time till Emily's wailing turns to sobs, then sniffles, then finally stops.

"Okay," I say. "We're okay." I wipe the last of the tears from Jin Su's eyes and Emily decides to smile, which lightens her mother as I lead them both to the ledge. "Is that it on the other side of the street?" I ask. "I see blue there, is that it?"

Jin Su looks at me incredulously, then finally begins to scan the street below. "It might be," she says. "I'm not sure. And anyway, even if that is a portion of it, it's bound to be cracked or blown apart. We're twelve storeys up." I think about this for a second, then I think of how it flew from my hands at Miriam Maynard's and landed unscathed on the other side of the room, and I wonder. What are the chances?

"I have to go down and check," I say to Jin Su as I start looking for my clothes.

"Are you kidding Ferris?" she says. She only calls me Ferris when she's displeased with me, but I don't care because she's all right, and the baby's all right, and I'm all right. If that float is all right too I want to be the first one to it. Short of being one of the first looters downtown at Birks, it's my only shot at setting my life somewhat straight, a little gift from the gods, and I'm not going to give it up till I've seen it ruined or in shards with my own eyes, up close.

"You just have to trust me, Jin Su. We have to get out of this building anyhow, right now, so let's go. Grab whatever you can and let's get to the fire escape before the rest of the building does." Jin Su thinks only for a moment on this, she's sensible, before she grabs a bag from the closet and starts filling it with clothes and diapers for Emily, whom I hold as Jin Su changes herself. Thankfully she has no mirrors in her room, no glass other than the window that ejected out onto the street, so we walk unhindered to the entryway. "Boots, Jin Su," I say to her. "You'll need the thickest soles you've got." I pull on my steel-toes, then Jin Su laces up her hikers and ties Emily in her mei tai close to her chest while I grab some bananas, apples and bottled water from the kitchen.

We try the door, but it won't open. The framing is buckled so I slam my body into it. Still it won't budge, wedged tight in its jamb. Instead I go to the bedroom with one of the dining room chairs and smash a hole in the drywall. Then I smash a few more and tear the sheathing away, then the insulation, then kick between the studs and break through the drywall on the other side. I keep kicking till I've made a large enough hole for us to slip through, and we do, out into the darkened hallway. Jin Su flicks a little flashlight on and we walk swiftly to the fire escape door, which opens, then we descend the concrete stairs, turning down and down, twelve flights to the ground floor.

In the lobby there's an old woman with tempered glass in her hair and clothes. Her face and arms are bleeding and she's just sitting stunned and huddled in a corner. Jin Su starts toward her. "We've got to get out, away from the building Jin Su," I say, thinking that if the aftershocks come, if the building isn't sound…

"Just give me a minute with her," she says, and turns to the old lady. "Mrs. Maven, it's Jin Su." She takes her by the glass-gouged arm and lifts her from sitting. "Where is your husband Mrs. Maven?" Mrs. Maven is gasping and choking on her own attempts to breathe, in shock, unable to answer Jin Su's question.

Beyond the lobby, out on the street, a massive shower of glass falls to the sidewalk. I'm not sure whether it's safer inside the building or out now, so I tell Jin Su to wait in the lobby and step out and up onto the heaps of glass, the most recent shower of which was kicked out by a cluster of elderly people and a young woman who seem to be trapped in an apartment on the fourth floor, calling out for help to the few people standing below them. I start walking down and across the street, to its opposite side, to where I think I saw the gleam of my float's iridescent blue from high above. There are branches and wires down and it's nearly impossible to walk, the glass is everywhere and it shifts and cracks underfoot. There's a building fire raging up the block and black smoke is starting to billow toward me, obscuring the sky.

Then I see it. It shines at me. Shrouded beneath a tree branch I catch its opaline swirl in my peripheral vision, just a tinge of it. I'm nearly on top of it, and reach down and lift it from amongst the oak leaves. With my shirt sleeve I brush some flecks of dirt and glass from its surface.

A water main has burst and everything is wet. There's a river running beneath the wire, glass and steel in the street. I don't know enough about the grid to be sure, but it occurs to me that this quantity of fallen high voltage wire and water seems questionable. Some of the glass is starting to slide on the flood and it feels altogether unstable and frightening beneath my feet.

I tuck the float under my arm and make my way back toward the lobby. People are scrambling from the building now, and I'm struggling against them, against their panic, within my own, trying to get back to Emily and Jin Su. Then they emerge from the crowd, Jin

Su takes my hand and we start down the street, away from the fire and the flooding waterline. Saying nothing, we just walk, toward another building in flames further down, and another, through a city strewn with glass and rubble, wire fallen everywhere, and people, some wailing, some starting on the looting, as the choppers begin to circle overhead, their blades thumping the smoke filled air—we walk toward the only place I can think to. We walk together down to the sea.

Forty blocks through the smoke and clamour, glass everywhere underfoot, and Emily, poor thing, falls asleep against her mother's chest. Every so often another explosion splits through the din of screams and sirens, another cracked gas line flaming. We get to the bottom of Main then head west on Second Avenue to Fir Street. There's a ragtag of fishboats and scuzzy live-aboards tied to the floats at Fisherman's Pier. I'm going to, if I can, commandeer one of these things and get us out of here.

Jin Su waits on the dock while I jump aboard a little shrimp trawler. It's unlocked and I go in, but there's nothing to it, gutted of everything but its engine. I scramble off the bow to the stern of the next boat along, an old fifty-foot wooden troller. The cabin door is padlocked so I smash the captain's window out and squeeze through. Inside, the boat reeks of rats and rot, a damp winter untended. There's no key in the ignition. I try the start button anyway, but nothing turns over or clicks. So I throw my body at the cabin door, bust the latch clean from its screws, and tumble to the deck. I lie on my back for a few seconds looking up at the sun, a hazy ball of dark orange above the burning city, ash drifting like snow through the air.

Jin Su peeks over the bulwarks from the dock. "Are you okay?" she asks, and climbs aboard as I start laughing. I can't help it: she's standing above me on this shitty boat in the middle of a whole city of pandemonium, holding my stupid fishing float below the lump of our sleeping daughter tied to her chest, somehow calm. Sensible.

Anna would be through the fucking roof. Emily starts to stir, then screams. "I've got to feed her," Jin Su says, handing me the float. She unties the mei tai and sits down on the hatch coaming to nurse.

"Give me your flashlight," I say, and Jin Su digs it out from her jeans pocket. I turn it on and climb into the cabin, down into the fo'c'sle, then crouch into the engine room in the bowel of the boat. There's a single battery hooked to a Constavolt charger with a single wire coming off it, to drive a bilge pump no doubt, but the rest of the battery bank is gone. I swing the beam of light over to the engine and look it over. It's an old pre-war Perkins. I remember Svend telling me about these motors, how they can be started by hand, one cylinder at a time, but I've never done it or seen it done.

First I open the fuel lines from the two huge steel tanks port and starboard, then I open the drain on the inline fuel filter to make sure there's fuel flowing through. I turn my light back to the Perkins and think. It's been my saving grace countless times at sea that I'm able to work out mechanical solutions on the fly. I've got a natural aptitude, most likely come down through my mother from my Opa Hein. He was always fixing or inventing something on the farm and I've gotten through most of my fishing career thus far in the same fashion, creating makeshift gaskets of underwear elastic and sections of gumboot, helm wheels of vice grips and screwdrivers.

There's a valve on the head of the first cylinder, which I figure must be a compression release, so I open it wide and hand-crank the cylinder till it sputters to life. I release the compression on the other three till each is fired, then climb back up and out of the dark, the Perkins chug-chugging away with its good-old-reliable diesel sound. It gives me confidence when Jin Su asks if it's going to be okay. I have to wonder exactly how much fuel might be left in the tanks, but it's a short haul to Halfmoon Bay, maybe six or eight hours up the shoreline.

"We'll be fine," I tell her. Although I know I'm hedging my bets (as any seaman knows he is whenever he sets out on the water, even in the best of conditions and with the most proven, well-maintained equipment) I look at this woman I love, and at my daughter drunk on good milk grinning her big smile, and I believe it will be, the glass float set on the hatch coaming beside them like some good luck talisman keeping us safe from all the surrounding chaos and destruction.

I reach down and kiss Jin Su, then take the float and carry it off the boat to the dock. On my knees I dip it into the cold green water and wash the last of the glass flecks away. Lifting it dripping and smooth before my eyes I can't keep from laughing again, it's so ridiculous, this fishing float of great mystique.

I'm holding it in the midst of a city buried in broken glass, the bright sound of its shattering still ringing out from every direction, and this float, lighter than my daughter, hasn't a scratch upon it. Turning it over and over in my hands it's perfectly intact, unscuffed and gleaming, as though it is still in the cradle Jin Su built for it with toy blocks on her piano last night. As though I'd never taken it, like any old piece of happened-upon flotsam, from its endless drifting on the sea.

WE'RE HOVERING OVER my home on the Esowista Peninsula watching a wall of water wash over it. When the earth finished rumbling I lay stunned in my bed as an image I'd seen years before played through my mind: a shaky hand-held shot of a great wave surging onto the Thai shore and slamming into the hotel the cameraman was filming from; water rising in swift, swirling torrents toward the third floor perspective. Then I leapt from bed and jammed myself into the first clothes I came upon. I thought for a moment of Poseidon, my cloud-white Persian, but knew trying to find him was futile.

So I ran from the house, across the orchard and up the sandy embankment, my panic-driven feet slipping out beneath me. I could hear the ocean pounding the beach far below; I could almost feel it surging, and thought, as I entered Jim's forest, of the Good Friday Tsunami that destroyed Port Alberni in 1964. The epicentre of the 9.1-magnitude quake that caused that tsunami was far north of here in Prince William Sound, some seventy miles east of Anchorage, Alaska. I had no way of knowing, as I ran through the trails Jim cut between my house and his, what the severity of the quake that awoke me was or where its epicentre may have been located. All I knew was the fear Jim imbued within me on our many walks through those trails together. A fear of the worst. Of the wall of water now washing over both our homes.

In the forest I became disoriented, panic confounding my thoughts and my sight, until I was no longer on the trails but stumbling over and through the forest's thick ferns and blowdown without bearing. I can't say how long I struggled like that, lost, until I saw the wide relief in the treetops that could only indicate a clearing. Keeping my sights trained upon it and my ears on the helicopter's percussive roar, I came out finally into the acres of green surrounding Jim's house.

He was already seated in the cockpit, the prop blades whirring above, when I raced over the grass toward the helicopter, ducking down low as I climbed up and in beside him. He'd waited for me to the last moment, just as he'd promised he would if, in the event of an earthquake or some other emergency, we were forced to evacuate.

He lifted the helicopter off the ground perhaps a minute before the tsunami broke shore and we've hovered over our homes ever since watching the water stampede toward them. Now the sea is washing over the land like it normally does the intertidal zone, runnelling through the age-old forest as though it were just a rock-clinging bed of kelp.

Jim turns us to the east, and we fly. Up the Tofino Creek Valley, over Great Central Lake and across the shoulder of Mount Arrowsmith. As we crest the mountain, massive clouds of dark grey ash suspended over the Cascades come into view, and I know that one of the many long-dormant volcanoes north of the city has erupted in the earth's convulsions. The helicopter shudders in the wind funnelling down through the valley off Qualicum Lake, Jim steering it adeptly over the ruins of the town, the magnitude of the quake made apparent by the heaps of brick and wood that were once Qualicum Beach's older buildings. We travel down the island's eastern coastline to Schooner Cove and Jim spins us low over the rows of yachts tied snug in their slips.

One of my late husband Horace's great ambitions was to sail the world. It was never going to happen, him lacking the necessary bravado for such an undertaking, but there was nothing stopping him from buying an open water-ready sixty-five-foot ketch and keeping it spit-polished at this exclusive marina. We made a few weekend forays on the *Princess Belle* to the sandy beach of Tribune Bay on Hornby Island and the blue shallows of Home Bay on Jedediah. We even stopped in False Bay and hiked up Mount Tremeton to visit Fairwin' Verge at his tree fort.

Then Horace, gaining confidence, decided we should venture further afield, so we took the *Belle* up to Princess Louisa Inlet to view its glacial till, aquamarine waters and the majestic Chatterbox Falls. On the way back we nearly lost the boat (or so Horace's story went—to my mind it wasn't as close a call as he imagined) when he misjudged the residual whirlpools passing through Malibu Rapids at high water slack and the hull sucked over, leaning so far to port the jack-line saw green. After that Horace—the wind gone out of his proverbial sails—gave up his seafaring dreams.

There she is, *Princess Belle*, long and dark and regal in her slip. Jim sees her, too, and pulls the helicopter up high over the trees, then spins down into the ballpark just a few blocks from the marina. I unbuckle myself and so does Jim and we hug each other in the roaring cockpit, the blades still slicing the air above us. "I'll be there," Jim calls to me over the deafening noise of his machine.

"You take care," I holler back, and jump to the soggy grass, my legs a little weak beneath me. Running from under the blades I turn and stand in the helicopter's heavy thrashing of the air as Jim lifts off and circles northward over the trees and out of sight. I have this foreboding feeling that it will be the last time I see him, but it's to be expected, I suppose, under the circumstances. So I swallow it and start walking.

So far, things have gone as we'd planned. Jim is en route to his home away from home, a modest, self-sufficient house on the south end of Reid Island where he can wait out the storm with his radio and his books and his six-month stores of non-perishables; I'm on the way to my boat, fully fuelled, stocked with food, and with seaworthiness and sails to hoist and power me wherever I need or desire to go. This may be straight up to Jim's to wait out the aftermath with him; to marry the *Belle's* resources to his so we can both live with more, and in good company, while we wait for the world to recalibrate.

Walking out along the finger the *Belle* is moored to, I hear the unmistakable cry of an infant rising from one of the houses perched above the cove, and it strikes me just how little of the human damage I've seen thus far. From the air Qualicum Beach and Parksville looked like ruined ghost towns, the odd emergency vehicle making its way through the streets, but nothing more. No mobs of people in panic. Perhaps the quake occurring early in the morning as it did has been a blessing, most people still in the safety of their homes when it hit. As the baby's cry rings out again it occurs to me suddenly and with urgency that I have to call my girls. They'll be worried sick for me.

I dial Esther in Halifax and leave a message reassuring her I'm fine and asking her to contact Mirabelle, who's been living in India these past few years. For a moment after I hang up I feel that same sense of foreboding I felt when Jim lifted out of the ballpark, and I want nothing more than to be with my girls. But it's not to be, not now, and I know it, so I climb aboard the *Belle* and walk the length of her teak deck inspecting the rigging and masts as I do.

I climb down into the cabin, walk to the nav station, and turn on the sounder, inverter, computer and GPS. Then I turn the engine over and the little diesel purrs to life, quick as Poseidon would from a nap when he was a kitten... Poseidon, who's gone now to his namesake's domain. Gone. My bedroom with the white silk curtains drawn and tied so I can wake with the morning sun spilling across the field of tall grass falling to the sea. Gone. My photos of the girls when they were growing, and their father Yule in his eternal young-manhood. Gone. My morning walk to retrieve the mail at the top of the drive. Gone. My tea on the back porch in the evening watching the sun ignite the western sky magenta, pink and gold, Poseidon brushing against my bare legs as I lean back in my old rocker to take another sip of this good, good life.

⤙

I'VE BEEN MARRIED three times. Once for love, once for company, and once for money.

My first husband was a fisherman from Victoria. The son of a son of a Norwegian fisherman. We met at an anti-oil rig rally in front of the provincial legislature. The Social Credit government of the time wanted to open up the BC offshore to oil and gas exploration, much as the current government intends to do now, almost thirty years later. I was young, the daughter of a conscientious objector and socialist, my father; and a wealthy girl married below her class, my mother, who raised me on nostalgic tales of her enchanted summers at the family estate in southern France, idling the days away on the sandy beaches as whales sang endlessly off the shore. I was studying literature and women's studies at the time and so was naturally there to oppose the proposed industrial despoiling of our pristine coastline. Yule, my first husband, was there to oppose any possible disruption of the fish and his freedom to hunt and catch them.

He trolled the west coast of Vancouver Island each summer and fall for chinook, coho and sockeye, and shortly after that rally I finished my second-year examinations and headed out with him on his white and blue Wahl-built troller, *Misty Girl*. Yule schooled me in the ways of hauling and gaffing, gutting and glazing, fellatio and cunnilingus. It was my youth, the times, and his ruggedness that made me love him so fervently, and we were married that fall and set off for the Sea of Cortez where we wintered on his little ferro-cement sloop, eating liberally of the sea and each other. That was love.

Five years later, while I was still pregnant with our second daughter, Yule went down with the *Misty Girl* somewhere on the early chinook run northwest of Cape Scott. A nearby lighthouse keeper heard his last call on the VHF as the water rushed in the wheelhouse door. And that was that.

Shortly after, I married Yule's best friend, Ray Harving, and ex-cept to say that he got me through the raising of my two girls in more comfort than I'd have been without him, there wasn't much there. Losing Yule had put the fire out in me, and I passed through that time in what I realize now to have been a suspended state of grief. My poor girls, I was gone into the sorrow that swelled up when Yule and the *Misty* went down.

When Ray sank with his tuna boat just off the mouth of the Col-umbia River I awoke to my life as though out of ten long years in a coma. With my girls approaching their university years, and myself almost forty and penniless, I decided on one course of action: find a rich husband, a landlubber, or at the very least not a fisherman. Someone I could love and wouldn't lose to the sea. Three times lucky. So I began sailing lessons at the Royal Victoria Yacht Club in Cadboro Bay, possibly not the best place to find a non-seafaring man, but certainly a place to find a wealthy one, which I did.

Horace Maynard, the son of a land baron in England, was old, old money. I recall him actually saying to me around the time we first met that he'd come to Victoria to get a taste of the colonies, as if Canada's ties to England were anything more than those of history and formality; as though the Empire of the world was still British and not American. Horace was an idiot, but a rich one and a loveable one in his well-bred, benevolent arrogance. He considered himself a philanthropist, and so I easily convinced him in the mid-90s to buy a very expensive waterfront acreage south of Tofino where we built the Glass Globe beach house, a small and outrageous-looking accommodation (thanks to Horace's flair for innovative design). The idea was to offer it as a free residence for scientists and journalists, academics and artists, and whoever else was working for the betterment of the world's oceans, which we did; and to rent it as a short-term bed-and-breakfast accommodation to the tourists through the summer months, the proceeds of which were to be donated to Greenpeace and Sea Shepherd and the like.

Not long after the Glass Globe was built, Horace and I bought my mother's old family estate in southern France from the family who'd owned it since my grandfather passed on. It was there we wintered most of our eleven years together; there we had a grand swimming pool built and housed in glass on the Mediterranean shore. And it was in that pool, filled with the fresh sea water we had pumped in to avoid the fish-killing chemicals used in conventional pools, that Horace had an aneurysm and drowned.

So I've lived alone in what was once our modest summer residence at the Glass Globe for almost five years now. In that time I've had some exceptional company—I've shared a table with Sylvia Earle and Tim Flannery, David Suzuki and Robert Kennedy Jr.— but as I idle past the breakwater at Schooner Cove, all the while cursing Horace for insisting on the purchase of such a large, impractical boat, it's one particular conversation with one particular guest that I can't keep from flooding my thoughts.

It's been over a decade now since the Children of Mu, a little motley group of characters obsessed with the life and ideas of a man by the name of James Churchward, first descended upon the Glass Globe for a week-long convention. I have only a very peripheral knowledge of Churchward and his ideas, gleaned from the many lectures I received over dinners with Horace. He and the leader of this group, Monsieur Arnault Vericombe, were kindred spirits, and the friendship they immediately fell into inspired my husband to become enamoured with Churchward's life and his theories of Mu. As a young soldier in the British Army, Churchward was sent to India during the famine of the 1880s. There he fell in with a rishi at a local temple and, in the off-hours of his army duty, he studied an ancient language which the rishi claimed was the original language of mankind and originated in a place he called Mu, a continental landmass the size of South America which supposedly sank beneath the Pacific Ocean twenty thousand years ago in a storm of fire and water; the Atlantis of the Pacific, essentially.

At some point during this affiliation, Churchward's story goes, the rishi produced from the vaults of the temple a number of clay tablets brought to India between twenty and fifty thousand years ago by explorers and colonials of the Naacal, the civilized people of Mu, more advanced in their arts, sciences, technologies and religion than those of Churchward's time. Purportedly, Churchward and the rishi worked tirelessly at the deciphering and translating of these tablets, and it's upon these that all Churchward's subsequent theories and writings were based. Of course, he never produced these tablets or his rishi mentor as supporting evidence, but he insisted that the many discoveries he made circumnavigating the globe in search of further signs and artifacts of Mu substantiated his claims.

Following his travels, Churchward settled in New York and became a very rich and successful inventor and entrepreneur. Horace mentioned once that Churchward held over thirty patents in the United States, several of which were the first alloys of titanium, chromium, manganese, nickel and steel: stainless steel. I often thought that, aside from his friendship with Arnault, it was Churchward's adventurous and innovative mind and spirit that so engaged my husband, not the elaborate and outrageous claims Churchward put forth in the five volumes he wrote on Mu and the

Naacal in the later years of his life.

Successful entrepreneur or not, Churchward was a quack. Aside from insisting upon the overnight sinking of a continental land-mass, he also made various outlandish claims of the Naacal's pervasive influence on subsequent human civilizations and religions the world over. He asserted, for instance, that Jesus's lost years were spent studying with the elusive Naacal Brotherhood, the keepers of the ancient religion, in the mountains of Tibet. Of course, all his claims are soundly debunked by the most basic archaeological, geological and genetic sciences of today. But that hasn't stopped Churchward's books from being in print nearly a century after he penned them, and it hasn't dampened the beliefs of Arnault Vericombe and the like.

Shortly after Horace's passing, Arnault again brought his band of "Muologists" to the Glass Globe for another convention. At first I thought he'd done so as an excuse to check up on me, and I wondered if Horace had asked him to do as much in the event of his passing. Arnault and I had never been close, but he lingered in my home each evening well past dinner, well after all the other guests had retired to the beach house. We reminisced about Horace the first few evenings over wine. Once that wore thin, Arnault began finding or creating seemingly random topics of conversation to carry our evenings along, which led me to wonder whether his interest in me was in fact of the romantic nature. If it was, he never made his feelings or intentions the least bit explicit.

Regardless, his last night with me Arnault told the most outlandish story, one that I thought at the time he had most certainly dreamt up while lying alone in his bed down at the beach house, pining, listening to the Pacific break against the shore in the near-distance below. Now I'm not so certain in my skepticism. As I motor by Parksville, hugging the shore on a track line north to Lambert Channel and through to Reid Island, surveying from the sea the damage I've just recently viewed from the sky, there's a crack opening in the wall of reason and doubt I built between myself and Arnault's fantastical tale of glass floats, magical fish and mountains of fire. A crack just wide enough for me to slip through as I turn the boat ninety degrees eastward and set course instead for Lasqueti Island.

I'M LYING IN a bed of lambskins listening to the wind's light breath in the high branches above me. Fairwin' has fallen asleep at the far end of his fort and he makes no noise.

Earlier in the day I motored around the bottom end of Lasqueti, up Bull Pass, and dropped anchor in Boho Bay, a bit southeast of Mount Tremeton, the safest place I could think to leave the *Belle*, stern-tied and locked up tight. I imagine False Bay, with its band of dockside boozers and petty crooks, to be a less than wise place to leave a boat such as the *Belle* at the best of times: under the current anarchic circumstances, I may as well hang a *Take Me* sign from the taffrail.

It took much longer than I thought it would to hike up here from the boat, the dirt roads empty, not even the occasional truck passing by. Fairwin' tells me this is to be expected, Lasqueti being so sparsely populated and Lasquetians, in general, especially those living south of False Bay, being of the homebody type who rarely venture off their acreages. So I arrived in the dimness of last light, the trail up a tricky negotiation in the dense darkness of the forest at dusk. Fairwin' behaved as though he'd been expecting me as I finished climbing the irregularly spaced treads of his winding staircase and entered his home. He served me a bowl of bland, though hearty, kale and lamb soup and we talked of the earthquake for a short time as we ate. After our meal, Fairwin' shuttered his glassless windows and blew all the candles out, so the night's dark is absolute. Coupled with a silence punctuated only by the wind's occasional and very light gusting, it makes remembering my conversation with Arnault Vericombe as effortless as dreaming.

He and I were sitting in my living room when he told me the myth of the Sohqui. It was late in the summer, cricket song ringing through the open windows from the tall grasses beyond my house. We had been sharing the last of a bottle of sherry and discussing the recent re-election of Bush and Cheney when Arnault got up and crossed the room to the front entranceway. He took from his coat pocket a piece of paper that he unrolled as he walked back and sat down on the couch beside me. On the paper were dozens of symbols, I assumed drawn by Arnault himself, which he explained were taken from Churchward's third volume, *The Sacred Symbols of Mu.*

"This one," Arnault explained, pointing to a pencil drawing of a seven-headed serpent, "is the Naacal symbol for creation and the creator. This one," he continued, pointing to an image which looked to me like the birds-eye view of a four-bladed helicopter prop, "symbolizes the creator's four sacred commands. These other symbols comprise the Naacal's hieratic alphabet. And this one we've only recently discovered the meaning of," he said as he turned the piece of paper over. On its backside was a drawing of a fish with a three-finned tail, almost identical to that which is embossed on Ferris's float.

"Have you ever seen a float with this image on it, Miriam?" he asked. At the time of course I had not, though I told him the recent rumour of certain floats being bought for considerable sums of money, all of them with unusual, unknown markings. I couldn't tell if his reaction to this was one of relief or disappointment, but regardless, his mood thickened. When he asked if it could be trusted that what he was about to tell me would always and only stay between us, I almost answered no. It was late, I was already tired from our week of long evenings together, and was thinking I might prefer to have a hot bath, curl up in bed with Poseidon, and listen to the crickets. But instead I said yes, and Arnault began.

"This image was first discovered many years ago by Augustus Le Plongeon, a contemporary and friend of James Churchward's who worked tirelessly on the deciphering of tablets he found in the Yucatan," Arnault explained, pointing again to the drawing of the fish with the three-finned tail. "More recently, some Naacal tablets were found on the Marquesas, once some of the high mountain peaks of Mu, which have finally shed light upon what this image represents."

He went on to tell me the myth of a wondrous sea creature called the Sohqui (as in, sew-key), a fish the size of a right whale with the whiskered head of a tuna, a long, scaly body, and a three-finned tail. According to the legend, the Sohqui was a deep-sea creature living in the dark saline waters at the bottom of what was then the ocean floor off the east coast of Mu and is now the Mariana Trench. They were translucent, as the only time light touched their bodies was on full moon nights when, drawn by the pull and shine of the moon, the Sohqui would surface. On such nights a fleet of fishermen would await them. It was believed the Sohqui's oil brought virility, strength and longevity to anyone who ingested it, so it was the most precious of commodities, the gold of the Naacal. Anyone supplying the emperor enjoyed the full favour of his court and vast lands and riches as a reward.

To catch the fish, the Naacal fishermen set long lines of glass floats upon the surface of the water to attract the Sohqui with the moonlight reflected within. The fish would open their great gullets and attempt to swallow the floats, at which time the fishermen would unleash their spears upon them. Apparently, the tablets tell of a golden time in Mu when the Sohqui were plentiful and the

Naacal and their emperor lived long and healthy lives, prospering on the flesh and oil of the abundant fish. Then the Sohqui began to decline, and the civilization began its decline concurrently, until the last Sohqui was killed.

Arnault went on to explain how the last Sohqui, a massive old fish said to be the original mother of all those taken by the Naacal before her, swallowed the float of glass which had attracted her to the surface and swam back down to the depths with it and several spears plunged into her side. This is when the earth shook and erupted a volcanic storm of fire, and the waters rose and buried Mu beneath fifty million square miles of sea. The Sohqui died there at the bottom of the Mariana Trench, and over many years the glass float lay trapped in its carcass of bones, both glass and bone preserved by a coating of the coveted oil. Eventually the float drifted free and floated up to the ocean surface, where it has drifted the world over for some twenty thousand years.

Since that time, Arnault insisted the tablets said, the very fisherman who set the float of glass upon the moonlit water and drove his spears into the last Sohqui's side has lived immortally upon the earth, cursed to seek out the float, smash it to pieces, and cast them into the conduit of the Mauna Kea, the highest volcanic mountain of Mu and that of the greatest vertical elevation, if measured from the ocean floor—which was, according to the legend, once the sea-level land of Mu—on earth. It is said upon the tablets (here Arnault appealed to my knowledge of industrial overfishing, of coral bleaching and acidification, of the great auk and the whales) that until that float is found, broken and cast into the mountain, the oceans will be caught in the throes of an exponential extinction crisis that will eventually threaten the very ability of humans to survive on earth.

I didn't know then whether to laugh at the absurdity of Arnault's tale or applaud his gifted imagination. I assumed he'd seen a picture of one of the rare fishing floats of the like Ferris Wishbone has now found, and had subsequently woven it into the stuff of his life's obsession, the Lost Land of Mu, to create his fantastical tale. I've half-expected to receive notice of Arnault's book these past few years, *Sohqui and the Oil of Immortality: Why the Continent of Mu Was Lost*, and I've kept him off my spam list just to keep tabs on his activities.

That night, as I considered what my response might be to all this in the awkward silence that followed Arnault's outpouring of the myth, I remember noticing suddenly that the crickets had stopped their singing. The silence wasn't only awkward, it was complete. This seemed, at the time, to lend a particular weight to the evening and to Arnault's telling, and it inspired in me a fleeting but undeniable feeling that Arnault's tale might, in fact, be less of a fiction than I'd been thinking while listening to him tell it.

"If you ever find or hear of a float that bears any of these symbols upon it, Miriam," Arnault said, "contact me without delay." He put the piece of paper with the many drawings in my hand. "There are those who, knowing too of the myth, would rather the float remain unfound. Or if found, unbroken, so as to keep the curse intact."

It was with this claim that I could no longer contain myself, and I burst through Arnault's gravely serious tone with a near-hysterical fit of laughter. Poor Arnault. After all that, to feel the compulsion to cap it off with the suggestion of some conspiracy theory. Though as he rose and left me on the couch, doubled over Poseidon on my lap, it seemed it was him who pitied me.

Shortly after I used the piece of paper he'd given me as fire starter, and I've thought nothing of it since. For a moment it crossed my mind when Ferris first revealed his find, and I thought fleetingly that I might call Arnault as he'd requested. But really I've always considered him a kook, much like my dear third husband, a man born of great wealth who was never forced to grow beyond his childhood daydreams and flights of fancy. I imagined Arnault insisting that he come to see the float before anyone else is contacted, and then further dragging the whole thing into some fantastical and ludicrous scenario. I knew that even if I, out of some respect for the friendship he once shared with Horace, had the patience for such things, a young and eager man like Ferris most probably would not.

Now I'm lying here remembering the thick black clouds of ash hovering over the Cascades today, ash that is probably by now falling on the forest around me, and I can't help but consider the coincidence. Fish float found, fire in the sky. One of the particulars Arnault had told me about his magic fishing float of Mu was that it could not, in any way, be broken by anything or anyone other than he who had created and set it out upon the water, the killer of the last Sohqui. The myth said that he was to find it, and take it from the sea, and that when he did he was to break it and throw it to the depths of the Mauna Kea immediately. Arnault claimed further that if this were to not happen, if it were to be lost or waylaid, or to fall somehow into the wrong hands, that a fury of fire and water of the magnitude that took Mu and the Naacal to the ocean's depths would again be set upon the earth.

There's something about this fort, about this creepy island, full as it undoubtedly is of individuals living beyond what is generally considered sanity (I've heard Lasqueti referred to a number of times as the "open-aired asylum"), that makes fertile ground for such far-fetched thoughts. But Ferris's rendezvous was set for noon, and there's no way he could have made the exchange beforehand... unless he sold it elsewhere or had it stolen from him. Both unlikely, which leaves two options. Either Arnault's tale is true and the float possesses some conscious power to pre-emptively conjure a catastrophic earthquake in order to avoid being given over into the wrong hands, or Arnault's story is, as I'm inclined to think, hogwash. But still there is that sense in me that there may be some truth to the myth Arnault told me so many years ago. Which is why I'm here in Fairwin's fort, waiting for sleep to take me and carry me into tomorrow, resolved as I am now to break my vow of secrecy to Arnault and tell Fairwin' the story of the Sohqui and the float, so he will leave with me on the *Princess Belle* at first light to go search for Ferris Wishbone.

⌒

WHEN I WAKE, dawn light pixelating through the shutters, it's with a sense of renewal and foreboding both, and I know this upheaval of my life brought on by the earth's is altering my sense of things, making me take and consider actions that are perhaps against my better judgment. I lie in my warm bed of lamb pelts as Fairwin' lights a candle and his little cookstove, then pours water from a large brass urn into a glass pot, setting it on the stovetop. He starts in on some strange form of stand-in-place qigong, all he would have room for amidst the clutter, patting and slapping himself up and down his body, rapping on the back of his head, his fingers tapping on his closed eyelids, all the while breathing ferociously. Then he settles back into an open-armed stance, like he's holding a large ball to his chest. His breathing eases to inaudible and I close my eyes again, not prepared yet to abandon the luxury of my nest for the bareness of the coming day, and think instead of Ferris.

The night Ferris dined at my home he and I were in the kitchen with his big oaf of a friend Svend snoring soundly on the couch, and strange old Fairwin' Verge gone off to bed. I'd arranged earlier in the evening, with more ease than I'd anticipated, to have a buyer pay Ferris $150,000 for his float. So naturally his spirits were high, celebratory, and I'd played on that all evening, fixing a succulent feast of oysters and crab, thyme-roasted potatoes and a spinach, pear and chevre salad, with a dessert of chocolate ganache cake and a gooseberry reduction. I'd brought from my cellar fine wines: a

'73 Chateau Margaux and a '84 Chateau Latour, among others. So there we were, pleasantly full and mildly intoxicated, comfortable in conversation, sharing the task of washing the evening's dishes, a task that, despite its mundane domesticity, has always seemed to me to possess a hint of the romantic in such a circumstance— two complete strangers sharing a very commonplace household ritual.

"So, a fortunate weekend for you," I said to him, wiping the last of the cheese and crab-shell bits into the sink. I rinsed my hands under the tap, then turned to him seated behind me on my wide maple island. I ran my hands up and down his thighs to dry them, looking up into his eyes with unveiled intent. My side of the air between us was electric; bolts of it rushed up my fingers to my breasts as I touched his legs, something I hadn't felt in so long I'd forgotten or given up on its possibility. "What are you going to do with all that money?" I asked, which I understood immediately to be the wrong direction in which to steer the conversation. I lifted my hands from his legs as his eyes winced.

He looked away. "It's complicated," he replied, and slid drunkenly, more drunkenly than I'd expected, from the counter. Then he slipped away from me into the living room, where he lifted the float from its tote on the floor. Holding it at eye level, he stared into it like it was a crystal ball, as though he were viewing within it his future, swaying on his feet ever so slightly as he did so.

I poured our wineglasses full and carried them as quietly and elegantly as I could into the living room. I'm not an unrealistic woman. It was clear to me that Ferris is of the calibre of man who can pick and choose his women, so I knew if I was going to have any chance with him it was going to be then and there in my own home. I seated myself on the chaise lounge, trying to give him space to come back to me from wherever it was my question had sent him off to. Svend coughed and buried his head under a pillow on the couch opposite us.

"Why is this thing worth so much money?" Ferris finally asked, a perplexed and incredulous, almost angry look on his face. "That's a good question," I offered in reply, holding his wineglass up to him. "I can't say I entirely know."

He looked down at my answer and the proffered glass of wine in seeming disgust, then carried the float into the kitchen. He placed it on the counter and pulled a drinking glass from the drying rack, which I'd stacked, I'll admit, in a rather haphazard, drunkenly fashion. The other glasses tumbled one after the other to the counter and floor, shattering around Ferris's feet.

"Fuck!" he yelled, grabbing the float which had been set in rolling motion by one of the toppling glasses. He wheeled quickly around and moved toward me, which is when his feet slid out from under him on the scattering of glass. As he fell the float ejected from his arms onto the island. It rolled toward me across the wood, and it was all I could do to stand in time to see it drop from countertop height to the floor.

I rushed first to Ferris to see that he was all right, helping him up. "Jesus Christ," he exclaimed, brushing the glass from his jeans and shirt. "The float!" We both stepped over the glass to the far side of the island, where I reached down and lifted it off the floor. I turned the overhead halogens on and we inspected it in the bright light. Not a scratch. Ferris sighed in deep relief, glass shards still glinting on his shirt and in his hair. I swept him off, looked his hands and feet over for cuts and embedded glass, then suggested he take a shower down the hall in my ensuite bathroom.

While he did so I swept the glass from the kitchen floor and wiped a few small drops of his blood off the fir. I recall being aroused again by the rawness of this, dipping my pinky finger into a spot of it and taking it to my lips. I could hear the sound of the water falling across his body, and had half a mind then to disrobe and slip into the shower with him uninvited. Instead I waited, and finished wiping the glass from the floor with a wet cloth, listening as the water stopped, and shortly after as he stepped from the bathroom and the springs of my bed flexed as he lay his body across it.

I washed my hands again in the sink and loosened my hair from the bun I'd kept it wound in all evening. It fell beyond my shoulders, still long and shiny, though whitening and thinning, as I ran my hands over my breasts and belly, wondering for a moment if I was up for this, if I truly had it in me still. Then I took a last sip of wine from my glass and left the kitchen, dimming the lights as I walked down the hallway to my bedroom, where I found Ferris splayed across my bed, naked but for a towel around his waist, asleep.

I approached the bed and tried to rouse him, placing my hand lightly on his arm and quietly calling his name, but he was done. The sight of his still-wet and muscled body was a bit too much for me. I leaned over and kissed him on the forehead, my breasts alighting as they brushed across his naked chest, and the next thing I knew I was practically running down to the beach house. There I knocked on the door until Fairwin' answered, then proceeded to have my way with him. It was a rough, unfulfilling fuck, he and I having never had any spark, and both of us too old for our libidos to make up for its lack. Though it did serve to attenuate my desire enough that I could, in its easing, drift off to sleep beside Fairwin' in a bed that has since been washed away by the sea.

Now I'm lying on Fairwin's floor thankful both that I was not swallowed by the sea along with the Globe House yesterday morning, and that Fairwin' made no mention before bed of that evening and what, in my inexcusable lust, I'd instigated between us. Recasting it all in my mind as I have this morning I feel a touch shameful and every bit the fool, and it has put in question for me the very premise of my being here. What is it that I'm after, the float or Ferris? It's disorienting, everything that's occurred in the past twenty-four hours, and I feel as though I can't trust my own sense of direction, like I'm a ship unanchored, unpowered and drifting.

So I resolve to slow down, to get in touch with Arnault Vericombe, and to keep his myth to myself until I'm able to do so.

ARNAULT WON'T ANSWER. I try his numbers several times without success as Fairwin' and I hike down to Boat Cove to harvest oysters. Fairwin' barters with the other islanders for what he can't find or catch in the forest or sea. The rice we ate for breakfast, for instance, he trades for each fall with salmon he cures in a small smoker below his fort. It's his one transgression, he says, the rice that forms the main carbohydrate staple of his diet, grown and shipped up from California. Otherwise, his is the five-mile diet, and those five travelled by foot or by oar.

We each carry with us two plastic five-gallon buckets procured from the Blue Roof Bar and Grill in False Bay. After an hour and a half's walking we reach the bay, a beach of jagged and barnacled rock giving off to a long littoral sand-flat. There are old Salmon Enhancement Project signs along the roadside fence bordering the ravine and the little creek trickling down to Boat Cove. Once the object of some of the locals' best intentions and efforts, the creek is now clogged with blowdown along its length, the mouth jammed with stormed-in driftwood. I remember when spawning-ground enhancement work was the new idea, it was going to save the salmon, and for a time every environmentally concerned citizen was out there cleaning creek beds of debris, building fish ladders,

JOE DENHAM

digging, planting, fencing. Then it was on to the next thing. Water quality, clearcuts, organic gardening, emissions... Now, some twenty years after these signs were set in the ground so hopefully and proudly signifying our efforts at atonement, the salmon are nearing extinction.

If only Arnault's prophecy were true. If only everything, if only anything, were that simple. Though I have always believed that in-deed there are more things in heaven and earth, dear Horatio... and so I haven't ever gone to the extremes of Fairwin' Verge, my über-hippie hermit friend picking his way adeptly over the beach, filling his bucket with some of the hundreds of oysters clinging to and strewn amongst the rocks. He says this will be one of the last harvesting days before the algae blooms turn the bivalves toxic, so he's stocking up.

For my part, I walk more tentatively over the inhospitable rocks. I suppose the past fifteen years living with Horace's money, on beaches of fine sand, in luxury, have left me soft. I fill each bucket half-full, not wanting my arms stretched down to my ankles by the time we've ascended back to the fort. Which I suppose is emblem-atic of our varied approaches, Fairwin's and mine, of the different lengths (pardon the pun) we are willing to go to.

Fairwin' has chosen a life beyond reproach. He told me last night, as we were discussing the failure at Copenhagen this past winter, that his years alone on the lights gave him the clarity to see that we were beyond hope. There was something, some frenzy we stirred in one another that kept and would always keep us from coming anywhere close to the collective acuity necessary to come to terms with ourselves, and to live on the earth with dignity. His chosen path, he said, is the result of that understanding. Because, he said, given the slightest entry point the comforts of modern-ity are insidious, and the resulting ease breeds a laziness which the mind clings to covetously. Somehow, in his matter-of-factness and his accepting countenance, he related this without any tinge of condescension, regardless of the fact that I am, from his perspective, obviously one of the lazy who have chosen to buy into the collective mind's cheap delusions.

Which is fair enough, I suppose, though I'm not so certain all our innovations and efforts are to be so easily dismissed. Tidal power, solar and wind, geo-engineering and bio-mimicry, though they won't bring us back to the Garden of Eden—to Arnault's Lost Land of Mu—are certainly not to be scoffed at. I suggested to Fairwin' last night that he might be throwing the baby out with the bathwater, which he conceded, though he countered that my argument would be made irrelevant once there were no babies born but those of humans, and the earth and oceans were rendered toxic, scorched and entirely ugly, as we'd now become, with our desperate creations built of metal alloys and concrete and plastics.

"Don't flail outward any longer Miriam," he'd said. "We're too old for that now. Turn the lights out and live in the darkness, as your precious whales do, and you will hear how saddened their singing has become." Then he blew the candle on the floor between us out, said goodnight, and slipped silently away to his bed on the other side of the fort, leaving me to fumble my way to the heap of lambskins he'd set out for me, blinded, my eyes straining but unable to adjust to such an absolute, unfamiliar darkness.

Now Fairwin' leads the way back up his scraggy trail, which climbs like a stream in reverse, meandering upward. He hikes adeptly, the iconic mountain hermit, his feet unshod, over the mountain's loam and stone. I struggle on the steep sections, my feet sliding out beneath me. "The shoe is the root of our human ills," he says. "That, and dehydration." He leads me down a fork in the path, traversing the side of the mountain for a time, until we come to a spring, a small hole in the ground with a silty bottom and a foot or so of water held within it. There's a dented tin jug on a moss- and fungus-laden log beside the spring, and Fairwin' dips it into the spring and offers it to me. "This water filters down through fissures in the coastal range," he says, waving his hand out toward the distant mountains we can see through breaks in the fir and hemlock branches. There is still a great plume of ash above the mountains to the north, though the westerly which brought with it the sunshine we've spent the day walking in seems to have broken it up, carrying it eastward over the hills, up the Fraser Valley, to the higher hills beyond. "It travels under the strait, then trickles back up here. It's as pure as it gets. Try it." I take the water to my lips and it washes cool and complete through me, a great essence, an elixir.

The only rebuttal I can offer to Fairwin's very positional manifesto is one beyond reason, beyond words. It's what keeps me hoping, despite the dire daily evidence of decline and the very convincing arguments of futility, of *ignis fatuus*, set forth by Fairwin' Verge and the like. It's something I learned in pregnancy and in caring for my daughters. It's a very small and vital, a very elemental truth I would not expect Fairwin', whom as far as I can gather never fathered children, to be able to wholly grasp; and I wonder if any man actually, ultimately could. It has something to do with a deep interconnection—and by that I don't mean to invoke the scientific connotations so common in modern environmentalist dogma; I don't mean to slip into pat ideas about the air we breathe being composed of the same molecules Jesus once exhaled; don't mean to infer we're all walking on water—it's that underlying thing that interweaves us, like the mycelium to the mushroom, or rather the under earth which holds the mycelium. The rhythmic surge of the tides and currents upon which the salts and waters of the wide ocean fall and rise. Something like that, though perhaps without the poetic flare.

"There was this time, about a year into my first taking up qigong, a long time ago now, when I thought for a while that we as people might possess the necessary strength to evolve, with it all part-and-parcel, our technologies and luxuries intact." Fairwin' takes the jug from my hand and bends down to scoop from the pool as he says this. I watch him, wondering if he's been reading my mind, or if there's simply something about drinking water high on a mountain from a deep-source spring that stirs such thoughts. We've spoken very little today, for two people walking together alone, and what conversation we've had has been about the earthquake and its aftermath, and Ferris. And the unfortunate timing of it all, him being possibly in downtown Vancouver when it struck—the last place one would want to be in the event of such a thing.

"I felt an energy upsurging in me," he says. "Something I hadn't sensed before and didn't know the source of, something boundless and universal, and it felt so great it seemed conceivable that a shift could occur, something beyond ready explanation, some real spiritual awakening in humanity, and things could still be set right." Fairwin' places the tin jug back on its log and begins the trek back up the path as he says this, and I follow. "But then I became accustomed to the feeling, it was simply that of my body's energy flowing properly, and the intoxication subsided and I realized that it was an individual discovery I'd made." He stops there, as though that were the end of it, and quickens his step a bit, his arms hanging tautly at his sides, the two buckets of oysters riding against his thighs.

"Sure," I reply. "But that implies it's a discovery that can just as easily be made by others." Fairwin' scales the side of a steep abutment of rock, then sets his buckets at the top and scurries back down to retrieve mine. He leans in close to me as he takes them from my hands, his forehead and bushy eyebrows glinting with sweat.

"Yes. And no. A different mind might experience the same energy and make of it a conquering power, not one of healing. A corporate executive in New York might take up the practice of Kundalini and use the energy and newfound clarity to win a mega strip mining contract in Ecuador. It's an individual discovery, and each individual will make of it what their life's ground provides for. I was a hermit long before I chose to live in this way Miriam." There's an intense resignation in Fairwin's eyes, not a sadness exactly, but an acceptance. "It was the most sensible and natural evolution of my being, but for another it might be to engineer rocket trips to Mars, or better ways to extract oil from bituminous sands. Which seems good for them, for their individual lives. But it's not so good for those whales you love. And it most probably won't be so good for their grandchildren either, though it's not going to be any spiritual awakening that's going to make them see that, not in the profound way necessary to realign things as needed." Fairwin' takes the oysters and shoulders them up onto the rock, then reaches down and offers me a hand as I climb behind him.

"What is it then?" I ask. "What is it that's going to make them see?" I'm feeling frustrated with this now, this hopelessness Fairwin' has espoused.

"It," he replies. "The actual damage. They'll see it when it's right before them. When the oceans turn and the earth's oxygen goes thin. When the heat comes and the famine. When those grandchildren can't properly breathe, haven't enough to eat—when the world's emptied of everything but us. But by then it will be too late."

"But there are options Fairwin'. Radical ideas and possibilities for rejuvenation," I contest.

"Yes, ideas and possibilities," he counters. "And then there are probabilities. Which aren't easy, at this point, to live with, because they're awful and unthinkable and might mean you'd have to give up that fancy car of yours, hybrid or not, because regardless it's still made of metals mined and intensely machined, and plastics that poison those seas you so love. Our technologies are mind-boggling Miriam, I'll concede that. They're of the greatest complexity and accomplishment, but they're mostly damaging, and we've lost sight of what it means to live without them. We've lost the wherewithal to live in the world, with the weather, and the desire's not there now to learn."

A quizzical look comes over his face and it appears as though he's going to burst into laughter. "Can I use your phone for a second?" he asks. I'm taken aback, it being an odd request at the end of such a diatribe. I reach into my pant pocket, turn on my cell and hand it to Fairwin'. He promptly hurls it from our perch to the forest below. As it lands with a crack somewhere beyond sight, he hoists my oysters onto the rock and resumes his brisk pace up the trail.

"What the hell?" I call at his back, but he doesn't turn as he hollers his reply.

"I just saved a bee colony. You'll thank me next time you drink your tea with honey."

I scurry up the rock, grab my two buckets, and hurry behind him, not quite incensed, but agitated by his arrogance, his impenetrable certainty. I catch up with him just as we come to what I suppose you'd think of as his yard, the space around the base of his fort, a circumference delineated by the fishing float strands hanging down from the fort's underside. Fairwin' drops his buckets by a fire pit to the outside of the perimeter, a heaping pile of shucked shells already forming a midden beside it.

"What the hell was the point in that?" I ask him, indignant. "I might've needed that in the near future. We did just have a major fucking earthquake Fairwin'. My home was buried under ten fathoms of water yesterday, and that phone is one of the only things I've got right now."

"And you won't make do without it?" he asks, and I can see by the cheek in his eyes that he's enjoying this now, my dander being up as it is.

"That's not the fucking point, you asshole," I say, raising my voice considerably, and I realize that I'm enjoying this too. A good row. I also realize that this is what it was like the other night, us having sex, two lonely hermits taking it all out on each other. So I decide to dig in deeper. "You wouldn't have done that if we hadn't screwed the other night."

"Perhaps not. But we did, didn't we?"

"Much to my displeasure, believe me." I'm stomping up the winding staircase behind him now, raising my voice in congruence with the climb.

"That wasn't my idea was it, Mrs. Maynard?" He looks back at me from the top of the stairs, grinning.

"Well don't worry, it's not a mistake I'll make twice," I bellow at him. "I'd rather service myself, thank you very much, than have your hairy heap of grunting sweat on top of me again." I climb through the door as I say this and before me is Svend, presently bursting into hysterics, and behind him Ferris, laughing in a less gregarious manner, the Sohqui float cradled and glimmering in his arms.

Part II

The Eve of, or Deliberations

SHE SAID, "WE should go." This was like the parable of the forbidden fruit, but in reverse: she was proposing abandoning knowledge for bliss. He didn't fully know this, couldn't read her intentions, couldn't feel what she had felt all along, the insatiable pull of her to him, him to her, because his mind was like that of a long-caged animal's, desperate and withdrawn. She knew he needed the clarity of the offshore, with its seeming endlessness, to see her. So although she found her own words dubious, she spoke them nonetheless, and convincingly, because for her it was the understory beneath the words she was telling. She said, "And so Mu sank in a storm of fire and water," and she was saying, *My body is an ocean. Dive.* She said, "Cursed to search the world over, for tens of thousands of years," and she was saying, *I am your orb of perfect glass found, young fisherman. Break me open.*

"This time of year, south around the high and into the trades, it should take us twenty days, give or take." She only knows this by virtue of conversations overheard, but she speaks it with certainty, tries to make it sound easy, like an everyday journey.

"Have you ever done it?" he asks, seeing through her facade.

"There are lots of things I haven't done. That's no reason not to now."

"We've both never been out there."

"You're a seaman, aren't you? The boat is as seaworthy as they get, a sixty-five-foot hull of hand-laid fir and yellow cedar. She's on the hook in Boho Bay, waiting. It's the fastest way."

"Maybe the airports will reopen."

"The whole ring of fire is erupting!"

"We don't know that."

"Svend?" she appeals to his friend.

"That's what the CBC is reporting."

"I know what the CBC is saying, Svend, I heard it, too. But that's just the news. It's probably sensationalist reporting. There's no way I'm taking a sailboat to Hawaii because of some crazy myth a cult fanatic cooked up."

"You just dropped that thing from a twelfth-storey window," Miriam counters his disbelief, swallowing her own spittle of self-doubt as she does.

"I didn't drop it, it fell."

"Yet there it is, round and perfect as ever. How else can you explain that?"

"Physics."

"What?"

"Chance."

"Chances are, that thing should be busted to smithereens. Look Ferris, I know it's a lot at once, we're all going through this, but think of it this way. If the prophecy is real, we save the seas, possibly even the planet. If it's fiction, we find Sunimoto and we get your money. In fact, we get more money than he's already agreed to. Sunimoto must believe the myth is true, which is why he's paying such a high price for these floats. Now that these earthquakes and eruptions have occurred, he's likely to be convinced that your float is the one he's been looking for. And he'll be desperate to have it. So we set the price. A half-million? A million? Then we're back within six weeks, eight tops."

"And how do you propose we find Sunimoto? We're just going to show up in Hawaii and ask someone at the nearest gas station if he's around?"

"I'll make some calls. We'll arrange it."

"Okay. So let's just say this whole hocus-pocus thing is actually real. Doesn't the earthquake mean that Sunimoto's not the man, that it's not him who is supposed to find the float after all?"

"But it wasn't actually him you were going to meet. How do we know Sunimoto's man had Sunimoto's best interests in mind? Maybe it works this way: you find the float, you deliver it to the hands of Sunimoto. Any deviation sets the earth to shaking. How are we to know? Sunimoto has bought every one of these things known to have been found for an exorbitant price all within the past six years. Aside from those few purchases, he's not known as a collector. We know he lives in the town of Hilo, at the base of Mauna Kea. What better do we have to go on?"

"I have a wife and a son, Miriam, and there was a major earthquake yesterday." Francis looks at Svend as he says this, affirming his confidence. Jin Su and Emily, their secret. "There's no way I'm sailing off with you to Hawaii based on some stupid fairy tale and some hare-brained speculations."

"Then what are you doing here? Why come to Fairwin's in the first place?"

"What was I supposed to do? This thing just fell from the top floor of a twelve-storey building and didn't break!"

"Exactly."

Miriam takes the float from the knee-high table. She does it swiftly, and swiftly she makes for the door of the fort. She thinks better of what she's about to do as she's doing so, a skeptic of the Mu myth herself, but follows this line of reasoning: if it doesn't break, he's hooked, we all are. And if it does, I'll give him the 150 grand myself, and besides, there's more than one way to skin a cat.

She leans out over the fort's deck railing and hurls the float into the trees. It tinkles through the branches, then lands with a thud far below. They all watch it bounce, and roll, and bounce, and roll down Fairwin's path, out of view. "Don't think it broke," she says. "We'll leave tomorrow then, first light."

"Are you fucking nuts?"

"Better go find it before dark. Keep your eye out for my cell while you're down there," she says, and shoots a playful look at Fairwin', at peace with him now that their fight and approaching evening alone has been interrupted by Svend and Francis's timely arrival. "Though its curse is of a different sort." This time she winks at Fairwin'. "And I doubt it fared as well as the float."

༄

HE DOESN'T TRUST her. She's a dragon, obviously. He finds it pathetic how she wants him, the way she leaned across his nakedness that night on her bed and kissed him. The way she pushed her breasts to his chest as he pretended to sleep. He can see that she was once very beautiful, perhaps more so even than Anna. But what of it? Even Anna's beauty, not yet lost to age as Miriam's is, fails to stir anything inside of him. She's a bored, rich woman well past her prime, unable to face up to her age. So ungraceful, despite appearances, despite her natural way of movement and demeanour. And un-genuine. He can tell for sure she doesn't buy her own bullshit. The float is heavy, obviously blown thick, which would explain its being of a larger than normal size for such a thing, and might too explain its resilience. Further, earthquake or not, Francis remembers enough from Geology 101 to know that land masses and the ocean floor are of very different composition. No major continental lands have ever sunk, nor could they have. He knows this, and he knows that she does too.

But he can't go back to Anna's—he already thinks of their home as "Anna's," not "his" or "theirs" so long has he been removing himself from it emotionally now—he's just come from there, and it was ugly. And he needs the money to leave her. If this old Sunimoto guy actually believes he's some immortally cursed fisherman, however that works for him, maybe he will pay more than 150 grand given the recent circumstances. Maybe it's time to strike while the iron is hot. So he's going along with it, because Miriam's certainly right about one thing: what else has he got to go on? It'll be futile to harvest crab for market any time in the next few weeks, and he's not going back to Anna, not ever. He's done. So he will sail with Miriam for Hawaii, her sights clearly set on him, his set on the horizon.

First Light

HE FEELS THE strength quiver out of him as he sets the dog on
the windlass and Miriam starts motoring the boat out of Boho Bay.
What kind of an idiot am I? he's wondering of himself. But now
they're heading out into Bull Pass, a light westerly astern, and it's
past the time for second-guessing. He's asked Svend to provide a
home for Jin Su and Emily, knowing they couldn't be in safer, more
trustworthy and capable hands. And though he's not sure if Anna
will even let him through the door, he's asked Fairwin' to go and
stay with her and Willow, at least until the earthquake's aftermath
subsides. He also took him aside and told him about Jin Su and
Emily, and he's asked both his friends to ensure Anna and Willow
don't discover who Emily is to him. To them. Willow's sister.

There is a hint of nausea in Miriam, something she's felt off and
on since this past winter, a feeling she can't put her finger on, except to say it seems to start in her core and radiate to her spleen
and up into her larynx. She suspects its cause to be of an emotional
nature, and feeling it now tells her only that she's experiencing the
anticipatory anxiety which one would expect at the outset of such
a journey.

They're motoring at six knots, the wind too light for sailing, southward in the middle of the Georgia Strait, the gravel-pit scar above Sechelt to port and the big-box suburban sprawl of Nanaimo to starboard. The sun is cresting over Mount Elphinstone to the east. Francis takes the wheel so Miriam can go below and make coffee. Off the stern-quarter now he can see into Halfmoon Bay, between South Thormanby and Merry Island, its little lighthouse rising like a steeple from the rock, and he thinks of his son and wife, still asleep for certain, in their small cabin just beyond the bay.

The morning after the earthquake, before he left with Svend for Lasqueti, he stretched and fastened poly over the blown-out windows and looked over the emergency food stores and supplies to ensure they would be adequate. Anna lives with a perpetual distrust of the grid-dependent life, so she's well prepared. Still, he hopes she will let old Fairwin' stand in for him while he does this thing. The anger he felt when last he saw her gives way to an instinct for protection, and that feeling gives way to a sort of sentimental compassion. So in the light wind, in the brightening blue of sunrise, he feels deeply ashamed of all that he's done, what he's become, a desperate man with a child born of an adulterous affair with a woman he has to confess, if he's being honest, he barely knows. And he is being honest with himself in this moment, perhaps for the first time in far too long, perhaps because he's cast off now on this journey and it is swiftly setting a distance between himself and his life. He can feel it now being just beyond focus, his life, like something receding in a rearview mirror, and he wants to slow down, to stop, to go back and take a closer look, but he knows he can't because it will just ambush him then, will consume him and offer no clarity, and so he knows all he can do is continue, that the only way forward is to keep this boat on course for Boundary Pass, Juan de Fuca Strait and the unknown, open Pacific.

⌒

PASSING BY FRANCIS's old crabbing grounds, Sand Heads, the Fraser's fingered mouth, memories like ghosts rise off the cold water. *I wouldn't go back there*, he thinks of that time, the eighteen-hour days, his back like a wall of bricks, crumbling. It's unthinkable, only a decade beyond, the intensity of the work a young man can bear. Hour after hour with his head down, beating crab pincers free of steel mesh, wrestling hundred-pound pots about the deck. How much of a seaman is he? Never been outside the tide-churned waters of the strait, never on the open swell, never beneath a billowing sail. "How much have you sailed?" he asks Miriam, wondering suddenly, with full gravity, what he's gotten himself into.

"My entire childhood, every summer, on the Mediterranean." She's lying, usurping a bit of her mother's life story to fill out her own. "My first husband and I wintered on a small sloop in the Sea of Cortez for many years. And then my last husband, Horace, he bought the *Belle* a few years before he passed away." She looks him up and down for a moment, his hands on the big stainless steel wheel, then looks back to the sea. "It's not difficult, Ferris. It's like anything, a little knowledge, some good equipment, a little luck, and you're off. Complete morons set sail for Hawaii every summer. You see them kicking off, dogs and grandchildren yapping away from the yacht club floats as the boat pulls from its slip, their son-in-law filming the whole scene with a fancy little digi-cam, their daughter at his side flapping her arm in farewell, trying not to sob. RVers with boats. They make it to Hawaii, get drunk for a week in an all-inclusive, feeling all the while smug and triumphant, then fly home and wait for the hired skipper and crew to complete the somewhat more difficult return leg of the journey and deliver their baby back to its berth."

It kind of ransacks the mystique, her response, but it eases

Francis a bit, and warms him to her as well, the wryness of her tone, her little *c'est la vie* smile at the end of her answer, something he can understand, something of the resignation of his class. And he sees there is more to her than he'd accounted for, that really he knows nothing about this wealthy woman with the tongue of a dilettante, with the eyes of one who's stood fast in the strongest of winds, with hands smooth and fingers long and slender as coral, into which he has chosen, against his better judgment, to place his life's safety and care.

⌐⌐

"OKAY, I MADE some calls on the shortwave and I've finally got it figured out," she says to Francis, emerging from the cabin to the cockpit. Francis used the last of the charge on Svend's cellphone battery to call Anna and Willow last night, his own phone long forgotten on Jin Su's bedside table, so Miriam has been below deck most of the morning using the shortwave. She hands him his third cup of coffee of the day. He hesitates before taking it. "You don't get seasick do you?" she asks him, wondering at his hesitation. "No, heartburn. And I get a little... unsettled I suppose would be the word." He grins at her as he sips from the hot brew. "I think that's the idea, isn't it?" she quips back. They're passing through Haro Strait, motoring with the afternoon ebb, and the quake damage on shore becomes evident again as they pass by Sidney Island and the houses of Cordova Bay come into view, a whole swath of them and their manicured yards stripped away some ten feet above high water, the last casualties of the tsunami before it broke up and receded on the scattering of islands Miriam and Francis have just passed through.

"Sunimoto's on a large, fenced property above the town, and I've

been given a password to get us through the gate when we arrive."
He looks at her with the question. "Pineapple," she answers, before
he can even ask. "It's Pineapple."

"That's ridiculous."

"I didn't make the game."

"Is that what it is, a game? I mean, let's cut into it here. You don't
actually buy all this sunken continent curse shit, I can tell, so what's
in it for you?"

Miriam lets the question linger for a few moments before answering. She can tell Francis is irritable, probably tired and hungry,
a bit overwhelmed—though she has yet to discover just how overwhelmed he is, or why—and getting a bit jacked on the fine, very
potent Ethiopian Harrar.

"Look at the shore, Ferris." And she pauses again for him to do
so, for it to sink in: the torn shoreline, its newly exposed striations
of soil like some secret script exposed, the long-closed vault of geological time flung open in a human instant. Houses buckled and
sheared from their foundations, teetering above the beach. "Imagine what my home looks like right now, if there is even anything
left of it. Most likely there's not, and the beach house is most certainly gone, and my cat, and the orchard, too. What's there for me
other than ruin? This boat is my home for now, and what better to
do with it than sail the westerly trades to Hawaii? In everything an
opportunity, Ferris, it's what gets me up each morning." And she
isn't entirely being untruthful in this answer, though it's incomplete, it's what she knows is appropriate, knowing very well that
everything is timing—luck, love, life—and so keeping the rest, her
heart's stowaway cargo, for what she knows comes next. The lightness and relinquishment when land's gone from eyeshot behind the
unperceived arc of the earth.

Drinking, Alone

THEY HANG OFF the hook in Neah Bay at the mouth of Juan de Fuca Strait to sleep for a night before the sailing begins, before the revolving watch schedule they've agreed upon alters their biorhythms, before leaving land behind. Under normal conditions, most sailors on this route would top up their fuel and water tanks, but the marina has been decimated, and they'd thought twice of even using the bay as anchorage for the night given its shallow waters and the boats inevitably sunken beneath. Just past midnight, the strait uncommonly calm as the winds slackened before backing, they threw caution to the wind, so to speak, Francis squinting into the black water off the bow with a bright hand-held spotlight while Miriam, eyes trained to the digital sounder, steered them slowly in. It was a first test of their compatibility as crew hands, co-sailors, and they passed.

In the morning, first light, they pull up anchor and round Cape Flattery, past Tatoosh Island and Hole in the Wall. The southeasterly is still flowing through so they motor into it, despite their every inclination to conserve the precious, finite diesel. The pull to move with every moment closer to Hilo Bay is just that much stronger, their sense of urgency trumping any common sense of frugality.

They have decided they'll share mornings at watch. From six until noon they'll work the helm and the galley together, sharing breakfast and coffee, sunrise, and each other's company. After lunch they'll each work a three-hour wheel watch while the other sleeps, then a couple hours together again for dinner, then two more five-hour shifts traded off between sailing and sleeping. All weather and other variables depending, but it's a blueprint to build the days by. It's no small task for two to sail a vessel the size of *Princess Belle* on such a crossing, but the time of year couldn't be better, and they are both, in their particular ways, proficient at sea.

Just past noon the wind finally veers to the northwest, so they raise the main and jib and cruise with the gathering wind abeam on a gentle angle from the coast, heading two hundred degrees south-southwest, each hour taking them only slightly farther from shore. Miriam fixes a meal of miso soup, rice, canned salmon and canned peas after her late afternoon nap, and brings it out to the cockpit with a bottle of red wine to share with Francis. The wind is a light ten to fifteen knots, but with the spinnaker now hoisted the hull cuts quick and smooth through the water. The evening air is chilly as they sweep through it, but they dress warmly, Francis in one of Horace's many merino wool sweaters still folded and stowed neatly in the locker of the aft stateroom. "We've got food for a good sixty days on board, but I can't say it's the most appetizing fare," she explains as she hands him his plate.

"I'm not fussy," he says, which is true. Francis would eat almost anything, gobbling it down with such haste it's a wonder he tastes it at all. Anna has always insisted he's host to some voracious parasite, but Francis has always refused to be tested. In consequence, she's insisted he submit to various fasting and purging regimes over the years, masticating bowls of raw brown rice and wincing back vile concoctions of wormwood and black walnut, resulting always in his dropping in weight and gaining in irritability, but never in any decrease in his appetite or change in his desperate-dog style of eating. It is this same tendency to gorge and guzzle which has led to his tumultuous relationship with the bottle, which gives rise to Miriam's confusion and disappointment now as she offers him a glass of red.

"I don't drink," he says. "The other night, that was a mistake. Other than that I've been sober for almost five years." Over their meal he tells her of the drunken accident, the cries of those two little girls calling through his concussive unconsciousness, and the narrowly avoided catastrophe they signify, those cries, how they haunt him still, and keep him on the straight and narrow.

"Don't you think that's enough, drunk or not, to keep you from making that kind of mistake again?" she asks, spooning the last of the fish from her plate.

"It's not that simple," he says, and pauses, wanting, and not wanting, to say more. This is the nature of what it is to be out on the water, alone with just one other person on a boat. The need for communication, for companionship, and the sense that the world is dissolving down to the single point of the self and the other on-board, awakens in one a desire to spill forth all the secrets and stories of one's life. Sea yarns. So all that is needed is the quizzical look she gives back to spur his explanation on. "I can't trust myself," he continues. "When the liquor gets in me it's like a little flame, and I'm a tinder box. I can't keep it contained and the next thing I know, anything goes."

"Are you sure the liquor's the flame?" she asks. "Maybe it's just the bellows."

"That's irrelevant."

"Maybe. Or maybe your thinking belies a deeper notion. What if the flame's already inside you, Ferris? What if you are, for whatever reason, keeping it so suppressed that it flares with the smallest fuel, only one of which is alcohol? What if your focus on the booze as the source, your attending AA and whatnot, what if that is missing the point, keeping you from the truth, from real happiness?" Miriam says this knowing it's pushing the boundaries of what is comfortable between them, but she has a strong sense that she is right, and knows that no matter what she says they are stuck together on this boat now, which shifts the point of leverage.

Francis answers her question with a long silence, looking back to land for a time. She waits him out. "It doesn't matter, that stuff," he finally says. "Because the day-to-day reality for me, in my life right now, is that I've got work to do, bills to pay, mouths to feed. I can't say how much you know of what that's like, though it seems that if you ever did there's a good chance it was long enough ago that you've probably forgotten." He waits for a moment, expecting from her some sort of rebuttal that doesn't come, then continues. "Anyway, what it comes down to is this. However it works, whatever explanation you or I or anyone can come up with, the fact is I can't drink, because I can't trust myself when I do. The easiest way to deal with that is to just not do it."

"But that still leaves you as a man who can't trust himself, entirely, and if you can't trust yourself, who can you trust?"

Which is a good question, Francis thinks, because if you can't even trust yourself, if you're that suspicious of and estranged from even your own heart and intentions, what does that say about how alone you really are? But he doesn't feel completely alone in his life, not now, and therein he finds her answer. "Jin Su," he says. "I can trust her." Though even as the words pass through his lips the day is darkening swiftly to night—it does this on the open water—bringing with it many of the doubts and questions not considered in the light of day, and he is beginning to wonder.

Calm as Glass

THROUGH EACH DAY they tow two things off the stern of the boat. On the starboard side, attached to the taffrail, is a small generator with thirty feet of line spooled off it, a small propeller at its far end. The prop spins in the wake, the line spins with the prop, and the generator spins with the line, sending a small trickle charge to the battery bank below so they can light the cabin and deck, run the in-line water pump and the autopilot, and use the single sideband to radio into the Pacific Seafarer's Network, report their position, receive the weather forecast, and hear any other news of relevance.

In this way they've learned over the past two days the extent of the damage which has occurred throughout the Northern Pacific Rim. Mount St. Helens, Mount Pinatubo, Mount Fuji and the Mauna Loa have all erupted almost concurrently with a plethora of minor volcanoes. The Aleutian Trench is in spasm. Tsunamis have decimated the Asian coastline as well. There has occurred an unthinkable seismic chain reaction. All air traffic at the few airports still functioning throughout the region has been restricted to relief efforts. People are desperate, world leaders are overwhelmed, and seismologists are baffled. All this while Miriam and Francis sail the coastline in light winds and the luxurious comfort of the *Princess Belle*.

On the port side they tow a nylon fishing line with a hoochie and a double-barbed hook. They're cruising thirty miles offshore, skimming the line where the cold northern water flowing downward along the coast, the western edge of the North Pacific Gyre known as the California Current, collides with the warm waters of the greater Pacific. This is where the feed fish thrive, anchovies and sardines, where the tuna run. Just past noon one strikes, a ten-pound albacore, and Miriam reels it in with little effort. The tuna trolling is her thing, sport fishing being something Francis has never had the time or inclination for, it being the last thing he wants to do when not out on the crabbing grounds. But Miriam has a long-standing love for trolling, reaching back to her days on the *Misty* with Yule, and today she decides to forgo her nap in order to watch the line and nurture the flow of their conversation, which picked up first thing in the morning where it had left off last night.

Francis speaks of his newfound love with Jin Su, their daughter's birth, and his plans to leave Anna. He recounts the disintegration of his and Anna's life together, their love's failing, and of the shame he feels in that failure, in his infidelity and deceit. How he's come to often avoid his young son, a mirror he can't bear to look into.

Now they're above deck in the cockpit again, it's past 9 p.m., and the schedule they'd decided upon just two days previous has already devolved into nothing but a loose itinerary, a basic intention. The wind has fallen slack, the boat making no more than two knots an hour under sail by the time they decide to fire up the diesel and cruise under power through the night. The diesel's steady drone and the streaming stern-wash sets a background to their conversation, like the light din of chatter at a dinner party, so their talk is candid and fluid. Miriam has had another bottle of wine over dinner, rice with the tuna she caught earlier in the day, and she's feeling again like it might be time to push Francis further into her confidence.

"Why do it then, really? Why go to another woman after all that time, after everything you'd been through and built with Anna?" Miriam wants to know, honestly, because as much as she had thought to leave Ray all those years, and considering how easy, how un-messy it could have been just to pack some things, take her girls and leave, she didn't.

"Springsteen has this song," Francis starts. "Are you a Springsteen fan?"

She answers with a smile. "I'm more of a Nina Simone kind of gal."

"Anyway, the song's on his *Ghost of Tom Joad* album. Around the time I met Jin Su it was the only CD in my truck, so I'd listen to it on the long drive to and from Vancouver every week when I was delivering my crab. This one song, 'Dry Lightning,' has this verse: *You get so sick of the fighting, you lose your fear of the end. But I can't lose your memory, and the sweet smell of your skin.* I listened to that song over and over until it sunk in just how sick I was of our fighting—and I mean fighting, not just bickering—and I started longing to be the guy in that song, alone with my melancholy and my memories, you know, without anyone in my face. Then I met Jin Su, she pursued me, and I felt I had no reason not to be with her because I'd already decided on finding a way to leave Anna. Though I certainly didn't think it would lead to what it has. It was just sex at first, before she got pregnant. Which believe me was the last thing I saw coming."

"And you don't think the exact same thing will happen in your relationship with Jin Su?"

"No, I don't. I think we understand each other better, we're more compatible. Anna and I were young when we met and had Willow. We didn't really choose each other, it all just sort of happened. Jin Su and I have though. When she got pregnant we decided to have Emily because we're two adults who know themselves, and so know what they want, and what we both want is each other."

"But how can you be so sure if the only life you've ever lived together is this one in the shadows, hiding from Anna and your son? How do you know it won't turn out the same in the end?"

"I just know. For instance, the way Anna and I fight. Jin Su and I don't do that, we never have. Anna's an angry, confrontational person, she always has been, and so we've always fought, about everything. I mean, we've fought ourselves out to the point that Anna's had to resort to the most ridiculous and petty things, anything she can find, to fight with me about."

"Like what?"

Francis has to think about this for a few moments, not because there aren't examples, but because there are so many it's like a fog in his mind, a million little particles of memory clustered together to form the one monolithic storm cloud of Anna's anger.

"Okay. I like to take a bath in the evenings. So does Anna. It's so important to us that the first thing we did when we rented the house we live in, before we'd even unpacked all our stuff, was to replace the old standard tub with a really nice sixty-six-inch clawfoot. Anna's always working in the evenings once Willow's gone to bed, and she likes to go to bed later than me. But she refuses to have a bath after me. She wants the fresh water before I soak in it. It's something that started when she was pregnant, and it seemed reasonable then, you know, hygiene, but she's upheld it as a rule since, even though there's no real reason for it now other than that she doesn't like the bath once I've dirtied it up. Anyway, most nights I get tired of waiting for her to come out of her study and have her bath, so I draw one for her to move the whole thing along. Sometimes it works, sometimes it doesn't. Often whatever she's doing on the computer is just too important for her to put on hold. So the bathwater goes cold—unless I nag her, which is asking for a fight—and she refuses to add more hot because it's an energy waste. Of course this is my fault. So I started some time ago filling the tub with only scalding hot water, adding no cold, so it would take a long time for it to cool. It seemed the best solution, seeing as there's no way to get through to Anna about the fact she might be in some way to blame for those cold baths, that she might consider my side of things. But it didn't work. She started complaining about the bath being so fucking hot on those nights she'd actually go to get in right away. How she'd have to let some of the hot water out in order to make room for the cold she'd add to cool it down. That this was a shameful waste too. I couldn't win for losing. So then I'd tell her she should consider herself lucky she has a husband that goes to the trouble of drawing her a bath at all, let alone one who waits for her while she has it first. Which would always lead to an argument, to her railing about how I don't appreciate what she does around the house, and to me railing about how she's inconsiderate and wholly incapable of sharing a home with others. At least not in any harmonious way, everything always having to occur on her time, how she likes it."

"That doesn't sound too out of the ordinary to me Ferris. You know, I've been married three times, and each of those marriages has had its share of my-side-of-the-bed-your-side-of-the-bed kind of conflicts."

"Sure, but get this. A couple of weeks ago Anna has a headache, so she draws the bath for herself early, as soon as Willow's gone to sleep. She's at the sink flossing her teeth, still wrapped in her towel, when I get into the tub. It's the perfect temperature, and I say so as I sink in, in an isn't-this-luxurious kind of a way. She turns to me and says something like, *That's 'cause I fill the thing properly*, in this nasty tone. She just digs in, and I'm so tired of her spewing her anger onto everything, even a pleasant moment such as that one, that an anger rises in me to equal hers, and by the time it's all over we've been yelling at each other for half an hour, we're in the kitchen with towels wrapped around our waists, the floor is littered with broken glass from the Mason jars Anna has thrown across the room at me, and Willow is in his pyjamas, crying in his mother's arms, his bare feet bleeding from the glass he stepped on when he came running from his room, crying at us to stop."

Of Different Worlds

To the sound of the little diesel resonating through the hull, Miriam sleeps through the early hours and dreams of dreaming beside Yule in the fo'c'sle of the *Misty*. She wakes with the scent of him, salt water, fish blood and tobacco, the slightest base of grease and diesel, as though caught and lingering in a dream-cloud around her. There is that pain to the left of her abdomen again, both dull and sharp at once, radiating upward through her body, and she wonders if it has something to do with the onset of menopause, with the fallowing of her ovaries. The boat is bucking a bit with the waves, so she knows the wind is up, the rigging chiming above deck.

She fixes two bowls of instant oatmeal, the default breakfast each morning, neither of them too keen on the dehydrated egg powder. Out in the cockpit, Francis is dressed in a full flotation suit. Through the night the rising northerly wind cleared the sky of the high overcast cloud cover that settled in when the wind died yesterday, and the temperature has dropped dramatically.

"Cold night?" Miriam inquires, handing him his bowl. The sun has risen now over what they can still see of Oregon's coastal mountains and the volcanic ash hovering above them, the upper ridges and peaks forming a thin, obscured, blue-green band on the horizon. The day is just beginning to warm beneath the cold northerly bite. "You might want to put a couple sweaters on if you're going to stay up here. Did you get some sleep?"

He's noticed Miriam is one of those people who look a wreck in the morning, like all her energy has crawled deep down into the cave of her body and hasn't yet risen to the surface though she has risen from sleep. By noon she's one of the most radiant, pleasantly energetic women he's ever seen, of any age, which makes her morning appearance all the more surprising, almost disturbing, and intriguing, as it signifies for Francis—he doesn't consciously articulate this thought, it's more a visceral recognition—a complexity and a depth to Miriam, a ground-source to her character he hadn't first perceived and hadn't expected. It also signifies her need for coffee. "Take the wheel," he says to her, just as she's about to answer his question, to start telling him about the dream still hovering at the fore of her mind, and he jumps down the five steps of the companionway and into the cabin.

He emerges ten minutes later—Miriam's morning fog already lifted, blown off too by the steely, crisp wind, shivers just setting in—with extra sweaters for her, and hot, black coffee. Now she's thinking of her life with Yule from beyond the trance of her dream. "My first husband and I used to fish these kinds of mornings, offshore of Winter Harbour, trolling for coho and springs this time of year. It's so clear, isn't it?"

Francis knows little of her life previous to the one he's seen her living at the Glass Globe, and hearing her say this he feels a mixture of shame for using her as a sounding board so much these past couple of days, for not reciprocating her curiosity; and understanding, because something in her seems too much like home to him, and the fact that she was once married to a fisherman, that she once fished herself, is a puzzle piece clicking into place.

"A northerly always feels like a fresh start, doesn't it, like the whole world's slate has been wiped clean," he offers, trying not to let his emotions surface, wanting to hear more.

"If only that were true," she says, taking a good sip of her coffee and smiling at him, the blue in her eyes seeming to darken and deepen against the backdrop of the day's light equally darkening and deepening the wind-waves as they begin to churn around them. "Yule always said there were two worlds, the one out here, and the one back there." She tips her gaze toward the diminishing sight of land. "He maintained that if everyone was made to spend some time out at sea then the world would be changed for the better. That people would come to appreciate the magnitude of the natural world and so would learn to live with reverence, not narcissism and arrogance."

"I think it's a lot more complicated than that."

"Me too, but Yule was still in his twenties when he died."

"Before the romantic death rattle sounds."

"That, and he was—we were—profoundly in love." As she says this that love is still almost present, not something lost to the sea nearly thirty years ago, but just carried off with her dream-cloud on the northerly wind. She has just lain, less than an hour ago, in the warm cave of his arms, his thick beard rough down her neck. "I don't think many people find that kind of love. That's why they can't believe things could be, are, as simple as Yule believed."

"Don't you think that's a bit presumptuous Miriam, a bit condescending?" he asks her, irked by her Anna-esque certainty, her moral authority.

On any other day she would have agreed with him. With the disillusionment of two marriages of convenience behind her, and the love she and Yule shared hardened with time to a statuesque fact—something for her mind to dust off, polish and occasionally ponder from the perspective of observer, not creator—she would have asserted that no love is transcendent; that romantic love is, ultimately, delusion. But this morning, still held within her dream's gravity, she thinks differently. She thinks, yes, if only each person could spend a month at sea, or better yet a lifetime in love, real love, the kind she and Yule shared those days they fished alone together on the *Misty*; those nights they spent sleeping on the deck of the *Florence Five*, their little sloop, anchored somewhere in the Sea of Cortez in a secluded bay on one of its volcanic islands under a net of stars too numerous to contain.

"Let's hoist the sails," she says, by way of avoiding his question, not wanting to get further into a conversation which will lead inevitably to disagreement; to waste such a splendid morning doing the old tête-à-tête clackity-clack down that dead-end track. So they do, working for an hour to establish the right sail pattern, Miriam's limited knowledge the only thing to guide them as they try various configurations before setting a double spinnaker, two genoas poled out, and the *Belle* assumes a natural downwind course and cuts across the swells at hull speed.

They lunch early on the remainder of yesterday's tuna, then Miriam takes the helm and lets Francis sleep away the afternoon, well through his three-hour allotment. She can see he's tired, and would be too, she concedes, if she were carrying the burden he's set upon himself. The wind courses across the water at a steady twenty knots, the waves stirred to a not-uncomfortable four feet, the *Belle*'s high stern solid with the following seas, so the steady, easy sailing affords Miriam time to reflect, and consider.

A week ago, this time, she was preparing dinner for herself in the warmth and comfort of her well-arranged and well-appointed kitchen. Poseidon would have been most likely having his late-afternoon nap on the couch, or just waking to demand his dinner. She was probably considering what pretenses she might invent to seek out Francis, as in her at the time was a thirst for him that seemed unslakable. Now she's headed for the fortieth parallel, without a home, lost in her old love for her first husband, with Francis sleeping his torment off below deck, seeming less like a man to be desired than like a confused, frightened child. Which he is, it's becoming clear to her. A boy not much older than her eldest daughter, albeit inhabiting a man's body, a strong and perfectly balanced, beautiful body that could fire desire in the most frigid of women. And now she's on this boat and there's nothing to be done but make it through to Hawaii, to find this man Sunimoto, whom she's been assured by several old and good acquaintances does indeed live there, as they have been assured by their old and good acquaintances, whom have been assured... It's a mug's game, possibly, the entire thing.

Francis finally wakes just past 5 p.m., climbing to the cockpit with sleep still in his eyes. He rubs them heavily, then squints out off the port side, toward the eastern horizon. "It's gone," he says, and she looks out too. She'd been so engrossed in her own thoughts all afternoon she had not noticed the last of the distant mountain peaks disappear from view. "I've got to say I never thought I'd see it. No land. Wow," he says. "I'm not sure about his ideas on love Miriam, but I'll go with your husband on this. It's definitely a different world out here."

Nightwatch

THE NORTHERLY PERSISTS, pushing them past the fortieth parallel. Through the night Francis holds to a downwind track, south-southwest, keeping the wind and waves astern so Miriam can sleep comfortably below. They'll keep to this course until they've crossed the thirty-fifth parallel, the horse latitudes, then they'll catch the northeast trade winds and set a direct course southwest to Hawaii.

Francis likes the night watch. It's eerie, the sound of the hull creaking and splashing through black water, the stars scattered from horizon to horizon against a sky lit by the light of no moon. It gives him shivers, the immensity of space surrounding and the cold north wind, so he lights the propane lantern in the cockpit to keep them both at bay. He wishes he had a pack of smokes, a bottle of rum... and thinks about opening one, perhaps a bottle of Scotch to warm the blood; thinks about what Miriam said of the flame being inside his head, his heart, not the whiskey, and concedes to himself her point. Perhaps with Jin Su things will be different. Perhaps they'll share a bottle of wine over dinner and it won't lead to a scathing fight, to him tearing out to the bar for more, to escape her suffocating reprisals, pushing the fire at his feet hard and fast down the dark winding highway, his anger like an anvil on the accelerator.

That's a world away to him now, those dark nights, and Francis thinks instead about what lies ahead of him, all things going with grace, the new lease on life the fishing float will provide at this journey's completion. He sets the autopilot and goes below to take the float from its tote stowed beneath the main salon bunk. Carrying it out to the cockpit, he studies it by the pale lantern light. Not a scratch. It's something he and Miriam don't talk about because it's ultimately beyond explanation or comprehension. Like crop circles. Or the tiny ball of light he and Anna saw once while lying in bed a few days after Willow was born. It flitted about above them, streaking across the room, then hovering, then again streaking on another angle until it suddenly disappeared. What to say of such a thing? Tinkerbell? Extra-dimensional crossover? Extraterrestrial visitor?

Holding the float fills Francis with a feeling of presence, of reverence, of being in possession of something sacred, even perhaps of being in its possession. It's a feeling he's felt since he first lifted it from the waters of Porpoise Bay, but holding it now he can't be sure how much of it is inspired by the object and how much by the events of the past week, by the stories Miriam has told of its mythological powers. If pure belief were possible it would be made so on a night such as this. But Francis has always had a hard time with Step 2: *Came to believe that a Power greater than ourselves could restore us to sanity.* It's why he stopped attending AA meetings years ago. Faith's not an answer for him, it's delusion. Though in the suspension of time and space that blooms in perception when the sailor crosses the barrier of the continental shelf, the living ocean deepening beneath, in the dark of the new moon beyond the limits of the cities' light-surge, a fold of *anything's possible* opens that even the staunchest atheist would be liable to fall into.

Francis shuts the lantern's fuel off and it hisses and flickers out, leaving him again with the boat's creaking and clinking and the unfathomable stars. The glass feels warm in his hands, in contrast to the cold wind curling around them. What if the stories of the Naacal and the Sohqui are true? Sunken continent or not, it doesn't rule out the possibility of an unacknowledged, anciently ancient civilization. It doesn't nullify the possibility of some super-spiritual curse. There's no question the ocean, the whole earth, is in the throes of an extinction crisis. And what of the Mayan 2012 thing, or is it 2018? It must signify *something*. Pop-fluff. Self-fulfilling prophecy. Francis knows better.

He takes the float back inside and stows it away in its tote, safe and unaffecting. Above the bunk, in the upper salon cabinet, are the stores of alcohol. A row of shiny bottles holding liquids of clear and amber and gold. He considers, then takes a bottle of single malt, a single glass, and returns to the cockpit. He's feeling good, substantial, surprisingly grounded given the lack of ground beneath him. So good riddance.

He pours himself a drink. Sweet Scotch. The stars are like little bells ringing above his temples. Sweet music. He drinks to Willow and the Wichbaun blood humming behind his ears. He drinks to Anna and her variable ugliness and beauty. His mother asleep in her filtered air above Fourth Avenue, and Miriam in her wide forward berth below, dreaming to the rhythm of the hull sliding through the sea. Jin Su curled around Emily, warm in Svend's spare bed, enwrapped in the cocoon their two hearts keep spinning, synchronized, in the little microcosm he'll soon call home.

⤳

ONE HAND ON the taffrail, one hand guiding his stream, he recites to the nightscape while pissing into the wash:

Man's sole gesture of defiance
at a hostile or indifferent universe
is standing outside at night
after the requisite number of beers
and with a graceful and enormous parabola
trying to piss on the stars
failing magnificently

It's all he remembers of the only literature course he ever took, Introduction to Canadian Poetry, an easy second-year credit. It's a poem by Al Purdy entitled "Attempt," though he remembers neither the author nor the title, and couldn't say now if he was asked what precisely the word "parabola" means. But he does recall that the single most common cause of fatality at sea amongst fishermen worldwide is falling overboard while pissing off the deck. The thought sends a second shiver down his spine as he zips himself back up.

⇋

HE CONSIDERS HIS choices, the mickey of Scotch soundly downed, and decides on a bottle of Jägermeister, for old time's sake.

⇋

HER SMELL IS of lavender and ice. Of red wine and coal smoke. Of sweet grass. Of thyme. All these things at once. It lures him to her door. He stands, swaying slowly, wanting to enter. *The dragon's lair,* he thinks, and sucks in the ensuing chuckle. He puts his hand on the doorknob and twists, then comes to his senses, realizes he's being creepy, and goes back out on deck.

⤺

HIS VOMIT PROJECTILES out into the wind, into the dark. *How many sailors follow that overboard?* he wonders. *Yo-ho-ho and a bottle of rum.*

⤺

IT'S ANOTHER SONG by The Boss, "Local Hero," that's been playing through Francis's mind since they set sail from Neah Bay. *These days I'm feelin' all right, 'cept I can't tell my courage from my desperation. From the tainted chalice, well I drank some heady wine.* He belts it out at the top of his deep, booming voice. He bellows Bruce up at the stars. Then he sobs, big drunken breached-levee sobs, because Anna and Willow and Cosmo and Mom; because if Miriam's right then Jin Su and Emily too; because the ocean is so wide and the stars are so many; because his moments of joy are so few.

⤺

MIRIAM RISES BEFORE daybreak, dresses warmly, and comes to the cockpit shining a little hand-held flashlight. They're using house lights only when necessary now as it's been days since they last ran the main and they've discovered the tow-generator provides only a nominal amount of amperage. The beam catches first the gleam of the near-empty bottle of Jägermeister and the drinking glass, then the image of Francis curled up on the stern bench, cradling both, fast asleep. She smiles to herself at the sight, then descends below, returning with some woollen survival blankets. She takes the bottle and glass from his hands, and tucks the blankets over and around him. She's in the afterglow of her second consecutive dream of Yule, still a-swim in tenderness and affection, so she places a long, soft kiss on Francis's forehead. Then she pours herself a drink and sits back to savour the residual dream-flow; the contrast of the warm liquor and the cold, cold wind.

The Looming

FRANCIS SPENDS THE rest of the day sleeping it off and puking it out. He won't eat. Miriam drinks a pot of coffee after dinner and stays up well into the night keeping watch. They haven't seen another boat in almost three days, but she's heard horror stories of massive cargo ships barrelling over boats the size of the *Belle*, crumpling them like pop cans. The wind goes slack in the sails some time before dawn, and the softening swells lull her fears to rest. Exhausted, she clips to the jack-line and lowers the sails. Then she sets the radar alarm with a twenty-mile radius and curls up in the cockpit on the same bench seat Francis slept atop the night before, wrapped warm in the survival blankets and some of Horace's thick sweaters. His was that British man's smell of aged cheddar and mothballs, and the faintest trace still lingers in the wool. She thinks of how proud he would have been to be out on the high seas, on the *Princess Belle*, drifting across the thirty-fifth parallel, the fabled northern horse latitudes, with plenty of water and provisions, and a good steady British motor to power them through. Horace trusted technology, provided it was engineered properly and built flaw-lessly, which it was sure to be if done by British minds and hands.

She says a little prayer to his ghost, and has a laugh at the irony, having presently put her life, and Francis's, solely in the hands of a Japanese radar. Then she drifts as the boat does, off into sleep.

∽

WHEN SHE WAKES it's to the sound of a lone humpback exhaling, a great burst of air startling her from sleep. All she sees upon bolting upright, her worst fears of cargo ship collision sending a shot of adrenalin to her blood, is the plume of sea water drifting away from her and the tail flukes descending as the whale sounds. Then nothing. She scans the water around the boat, but the whale must have surfaced once, then dove.

She's oriented now, though, having walked the length of the deck to the bowsprit, then back to the cockpit. She's wide awake, which makes the mountain peak she sees suddenly hovering over the eastern horizon, a snow-capped precipice floating, solitary, north of the rising sun, all the more unbelievable. They haven't seen land for almost two days now. They couldn't have drifted back that far while she slept? She does a double, a triple take, but there it is. Jumping down into the nav station, she checks coordinates on the GPS, and sure enough they've drifted southeast of their position, but barely, it's only been four hours since she set the radar alarm. She pops her head back out of the cabin and it's still there, clear as day, so she slides Francis's stateroom door open, leans in and shakes him awake. "You've got to get up, Ferris," she says. "You've got to come see this."

Francis wakes easily, having more than slept off his stupor, dresses and hurries to the cockpit. "You're sailing us back?" he asks, squinting up at the mirage on the horizon. He's instantly annoyed. "Look Miriam, I know I fucked up, but it's no reason to give up..."

"I'm not," she interrupts him. "I didn't. I don't care about that. We've been sailing on course. We're almost two hundred miles off the coast of central California." Miriam's excitement is settling into a reverent awe now—now that she knows Francis sees it too and she hasn't gone mad.

"That's impossible. There's no way we could see that if we were."

"Go check our position. You'll see," she says, not taking her eyes from the horizon, the pale-orange morning sunlight flashing in them, widened and entranced. Francis descends to the nav station and does as she has just done, then hurries back up on deck with the binoculars in hand. "Jesus Christ," he says, peering through the binoculars at the mirage.

"Something like that," she agrees. A perfectly clear image suspended in a cloudless sky. She takes his hand in hers, she can't contain herself, she needs the connection to keep steady on her feet. There's the sense of an immense, godly energy coursing through her, through him. They have to hold each other as they stand, watching for minutes that seem like hours, each of them surrendering to this inexplicable appearance, this otherworldly vision, until eventually it dissolves into the distant blue.

❧

THE WIND STAYS down all day, so they cruise under power on a course to magnetic southwest. By sundown the fuel tanks measure half-full, but they're sure to catch the trade winds soon, as reliable a source of propulsion as any diesel engine. The weather is warm suddenly, balmy, and they strip down to shorts and t-shirts and soak up the sun. They scrub the deck and clean the cabin. They each shower, and Francis replaces a burst seal on the galley water pump, the only breakdown thus far. They knock on wood, both feeling so optimistic, so smiled upon, they almost don't think to do so, each assigning as they have a disproportionate spiritual weight to the sighting. They have been shined down upon. Their quest, their association, blessed.

At sunset, they watch the sky together again, both with their eyes fixed on the blazing ball of deep, darkened orange as it falls. The instant the last of its circumference sinks below the horizon-line an instantaneous flash of bright emerald green ignites across it, a burst of light and colour radiating laterally and upward from where the sun has fallen.

Flotsam and Jetsam

THE SLACK HEAT persists. They deliberate in the morning, questioning their fuel consumption, but both are beginning to wonder, on account of yesterday's sightings, if indeed there is something to Arnault's tale. They both think and say so, unashamed now at admitting to themselves, to each other, that each has always given some credence to the possibility. They've both felt since the outset that this voyage may be about much more than retrieving some money. Perhaps time is more of the essence than they can even possibly imagine. So they motor onward, holding their course straight southwest.

So far, by virtue of the changeable weather and their only-just-getting-to-know-each-other banter, they've more or less avoided the onset of boredom which is to be expected on such a trip, and is indeed the norm on any open-ocean crossing. The mind needs something to munch on, so once the exhilaration of being beyond sight of land subsides, the great, irreducible magnitude, the vast unending blue, becomes, well, reducible. The reverent mind becomes irreverent. A piece of garbage, a white Styrofoam cooler, say, or a plastic dinner plate, floating by on the flat sea becomes an occurrence.

They are both starting to sink into this state of mind, despite the remnant exhilaration spilling over from yesterday's sightings, and so, with nothing more of chores or cleanup to keep them busy, they decide on a mid-afternoon bottle of wine. Miriam brings from her special stash spot below—the storage locker beneath her bed, though Francis doesn't know this, having found the liquor cabinet, obviously, but not her wine, which he's noted she seems to have a fair quantity of—a Chardonnay of fine vintage from the Burgundy hills of France. It is, as far as she's concerned, the finest bottle aboard, and she brings it out now to toast the majesty and magic of yesterday.

The miraculous mountain in the sky was in actual fact a type of optical phenomenon known in the lexicon of meteorology as a looming. Currently, there is a deep temperature inversion on the coast of California caused by the particles of volcanic debris still floating in the lower atmosphere from the multiple eruptions which took place last week, the remnants of which have blown down with the north wind over the past few days, holding the sun's heat trapped above the cool northerly air below. The light rays carrying the image of the mountain peak to Francis and Miriam's eyes were refracting, bending as they bounced off the lid of warm air downward toward the dense, cool air rising off the ocean. They began beyond the geometric horizon, arcing over the distance in a manner somewhat parallel to the circumference of the earth, but Miriam and Francis's minds assumed the light rays to be straight, as they normally would be, and so saw a mountain peak hovering where clouds would. In this way sailors throughout the centuries have seen visions of "ghost ships" sailing in the sky; real ships that were positioned well outside the sailors' standard line of sight, just as the looming peak Francis and Miriam saw was far beyond theirs. Loomings are the most common of the superior mirages, and every time a person stops to watch the sun rise or set over the horizon one is seen, if just for a few moments, as the sun's image rises to or descends from view before or after the sun actually does.

The flaring streak of green they witnessed together at sundown can be similarly explained. Because light moves more slowly in the denser air of the lower atmosphere, the sunlight rays, again, refract. And because higher frequency light—green and blue hues—curves more than lower frequency light, these rays remain, for but a second or two, visible to the eye after the others are gone. This phenomenon is known as a green flash in meteorological vernacular, and is not an uncommon sight over the open ocean. Which is why Miriam, in the sobering light of the day after, has not entirely given herself over to the belief that yesterday's mirages were of supernatural origin. She has seen green flashes before, from the boat with Yule and from the Glass Globe with Horace, and though these were far less dramatic than the one she witnessed with Francis last night, it's enough to make her suspect, though she isn't certain, that there could very well be some plausible, scientific explanation for both of yesterday's sightings.

This still wouldn't, in her mind, completely eliminate the possibility of spiritual attribution. Just because science can explain something, does that then negate all mystical significance or the possibility of otherwordly origin? Regardless, she can tell that Francis is sold, hook, line and sinker, and what she does know is that somehow, as a result of yesterday's happenings, her lust for him has returned to its former fury. Playing into what, as far as she can tell, is his unquestioned conviction that they have been visited upon, seems to be working in her single-minded favour, and she'll drink to that.

And so they do. And for most of the afternoon it seems to spur just the sort of light-hearted palaver and whimsical flirtations Miriam hoped for when she popped the cork.

⤸

HE TAKES HIS shirt off and shows her the scar. "See, that's where the knife went in." He's been telling her a tall tale about being attacked on board his crab boat by a rival fisherman. As it went, Jerry Phillips, a crabber out of French Creek who occasionally gets the idea to blast across the strait in his overpowered aluminum skiff with a couple strings on board, rammed the *Prevailer* in a fit of rage, then hopped aboard, looking for blood, only to find Francis waiting with a very long, very sharp pike pole at the ready. Francis gave him one good smack upside the head, and that was enough to send Jerry clambering back onto his own boat, very nearly ending up in the drink as he did so. But as Francis tells it to Miriam, it's a gruesome affair, a bloody deck brawl with both men bruised and bleeding as its outcome, a rusty line-knife plunged into Francis's side.

"That's an appendicitis scar," she says, calling him on his fib. Then she lifts her shirt and shows him hers. Identical. Then she lifts her shirt above her head and off.

⤸

HER BREASTS ARE surprisingly shapely and pert. He's never seen a middle-aged woman's breasts before, not even in the movies, but he's always imagined them to be something akin to deflated balloons pinned to a corkboard. Hers are two cousins of the mirage he saw yesterday, laid on edge. He'd like to hold one. Just one. He's had too much wine.

⤻

SHE THROTTLES DOWN and shuts the main engine off. The boat slows, then comes to a standstill. She slips her pants off and strips down to her underwear of fine white silk. She dives in and under as far as she can swim, then re-emerges just beyond the bow, treading water, her whitening hair a waterfall in stasis across her shoulders. Francis dives in, too, coming up beside her. There's over two thousand fathoms of water beneath them. Cold water, dark, saline and thick. But the blue they swim in is warm and clear like the inshore waters of the Georgia Strait never are, never could be, there being too much sediment washed down off the mountain slopes.

"It's a bit creepy, isn't it?" he says. She doesn't respond, floating back with her face to the sky instead, a gesture of absolute trust and surrender. Her answer.

⤻

"THIS IS THE first time we've stopped since we left land," she says, cradling her dripping legs to her chest. She licks some of the salt water from her knee and looks over at him sitting beside her. "Not exactly," he corrects her.

"Right, there was your little episode." She springs to her feet and strides to the cockpit to retrieve the bottle of wine as she says this. "I suppose we should drink to that then, should we not?" She takes a good swig, standing above him with her fine legs and figure, still naked but for her underwear. He takes the bottle when it's offered. *Sweet sin*, he thinks to himself, though there's no god's stricture he's submitted to live under. Just his own law, now three times broken. Three times lucky. Three times gone.

ᶒ

ONE THING THAT can be said of fishermen, as a rule—and to be clear there are not many things can be said of fishermen inclusively, them being a motley and unruly bunch the world over—is that they almost invariably have a somewhat manic-depressive, red-hot to icy-cold temperament. Either it comes with them to the job, or the job, by nature of its ups and downs, bonanzas and busts, infuses it. Whichever the case, it's there, and it is why Francis rushes to the stern and heaves Chardonnay-laced bile over the rail almost immediately after their first kiss.

ᶒ

"I ACTUALLY THOUGHT it was quite nice," she says, making light while handing him a wet towel. "I can't do this Miriam," he says, not interested in making their drunken kiss smaller than it is. "It's not right."

"There's just you and me on this boat, Ferris."

"Francis," he says. "My name is Francis."

"What?"

"My name is Francis. Francis Wichbaun. Do you think you could just be one of the few people in this life who actually call me by my real fucking name."

"Gladly. It's much more suiting of you, Francis." She walks toward him and puts her slender fingers on his flushed cheek. "Are you okay?"

"I've already got one woman too many in my life," he says to her, realizing as he does that he's not entirely sure what that means, which woman he's referring to.

"Perhaps, Francis. Or maybe you've got one too few of the kind of woman you need."

"And which is that Miriam, your kind?" He's angry now, at her brashness, her lack of obvious boundaries, of decency. "Jin Su and Anna are the mothers of my children, for Christ's sake. What are you? Some rich woman with a thing for antique fishing floats and men half her age?"

"That's unfair," she shoots back, her voice quavering slightly.

"Is it?" he counters, unrelenting. It's his downfall in arguments. At the first sign of weakness he eschews the opportunity to diffuse things with compassion. He goes in for the kill instead, against his better judgment and his heart's intent. She wants none of it. And knows enough to see a man whose deepest vulnerabilities have surfaced, the aggravation that inspires, and how alcohol elevates such emotions to unreasonable proportions.

So she says nothing in response. Instead she scissors her legs over the starboard rail and dives back into the sea.

Albatross, Albatross

THE ALBATROSS ARRIVES with the wind. High noon, and the smooth sea starts to ripple, then curl. Francis and Miriam made their peace over a breakfast of oatmeal, orange juice and canned peaches. Only eight days out. What choice but to do so? "I'm sorry," she'd said to him, ending the silence. "I shouldn't have pushed you."

Through the night he'd lain awake thinking through it all, Anna and Jin Su and the alcohol, and now Miriam too caught up in it, his little shitstorm of confusion, until his anger had melted back to self-derision. "You didn't push me. I should have been more clear from the get-go. I need to keep off the booze out here." This is spoken not as an emphatic statement but as a request, for support, and Miriam understands it won't be an intoxicated entry party into his heart. His is of the heavier sort, and if he's to be opened to her it will have to be by virtue of a gentler lever. A quiet affection. She's beginning to know him for the old-fashioned romantic that he is. Which is fine. There's still weeks and weeks to go on this expedition, together, alone.

So, in answer to his declarative question, she takes his empty bowl from him and climbs down into the galley. Minutes later she emerges with Francis's blue tote emptied of the float and filled instead with bottles of liquor and wine. She hauls it with great effort through the companionway and drops it at his feet. Saying nothing still, she tosses one of the bottles over the stern. "Miriam don't," he says, reaching up and holding her wrist firmly. She looks him square in the eye.

"It's fine," she says. "I want to. I do." She nods at him lightly until he releases her arm, then she proceeds to throw the rest of the bottles overboard. The full ones sink fast where they fall. The others, the half-full or near-empty, float in a line behind them so they look like a string of glass floats, from a time now past, glinting in a new day's sun.

⤳

THEY HOIST THE main sail, then the jib, and as the latter takes the first of the trade winds to billow it full Francis feels the dark bird's shadow cast a stream of cool across his skin. Above him its wide, grey wings, six feet tip to tip, glide. He viewed a flock of Laysan albatross through the binoculars while off the coast of Oregon, but this is his first up-close visitation. Those Laysan, the albatross he's seen in photos and movie footage, even his dream albatross, have all been of a predominately white plumage, so Francis doesn't recognize this black-footed albatross for what it is. But Miriam does, and she quickly begins reeling in the hook they're trolling behind the boat. "Albatross," she says to Francis, winding the reel. "Lucky it didn't dive on the hook before we noticed it." The bird turns its black beak down at them, assessing, and issues a loud shriek. "Let's feed him," Francis says, and leaps down into the galley to open a can of tuna.

"And a good south wind sprung up behind. The Albatross did

follow, and every day, for food or play, came to the mariner's hol-
lo!" Miriam recites to Francis when he emerges back on deck. "It's
from 'The Rime of the Ancient Mariner.'" Francis responds with a
blank look. "Samuel Taylor Coleridge?" she tries.

"I was never really into that old poetry stuff," Francis finally offers her, tossing the tuna into the sea. The albatross dives, nabs it in
its bill succinctly, and chokes it down, twisting back up into the air.

"Me neither," she says. "But Yule was always reciting verses from
that poem. He knew the whole thing, word for word. Every time
we'd see an albatross while trolling, without fail, he'd pipe in." She
puffs her chest out, pulls her shoulders up and back, reciting in a
deep-voiced caricature of her late husband. "At length did cross an
Albatross, through the fog it came. As if it had been a Christian
soul, we hailed it in God's name." Then she relaxes back into herself. "It's always stuck. It's funny what we retain, isn't it? I've got
this song in my head, from when the girls were little, when we
lived with my second husband." She leans back this time, relaxed,
a crooning posture. "One two three, four five six, seven eight nine,
ten eleven twelve, ladybugs came to the ladybug picnic," she sings.
"There's more to it, but that's all I remember. The thing is, I swear
to God, that song runs through my head a good ten times a day. It's
totally random."

"I know the thing," he pipes in, laughing at her display. "Here
comes the rain again, falling on my head like a memory, falling on
my head like a new emotion…" he belts out.

"Annie Lennox," she says, "I love Annie Lennox."

"You can have her. I hate the shit. But I swear, every time it starts
to rain, doesn't matter where or when, I hear that stupid song." The
albatross squawks at them for more scraps, to which Miriam puffs
out her chest once more. "'God save thee, ancient Mariner! From
the fiends that plague thee thus!—Why look'st thou so?'—'With my
crossbow I shot the Albatross,'" she bellows up at the bird, which
watches her display curiously, then again squawks its request.

"Yule used to shoot them?" Francis asks.

"No," she replies, her tone rising back to her own, turning serious. "But we killed our share. It was the seventies. Back then we didn't think much of them as by-catch. It was just the way things were, always had been."

"And always would be," he interrupts, an unveiled accusatorial tone to his voice.

"That's right. I wouldn't expect you to understand. It was a bit before your time."

"Not before Rachel Carson's though, was it?"

"No. But chemicals and fishing by-catch are two different things."

"Are they?" He's starting to grow agitated again. *Short fuse Ferris*, she thinks to herself, pondering what to say next to redirect the conversation.

"It certainly seemed so at the time. You do use toilet paper, don't you?" she asks, throwing his own critique back at him. He wants to refute the point, but he knows he'd be wrong in doing so. Which is the crux of the entire thing. Where's the line, and who draws it? For a time, when he and Anna were first living together, they lived with no toilet paper in the house, using instead an old yogourt container in the bathtub to wash with after shitting. Then Anna got pregnant and it started to seem unsanitary to her. The neighbourhood health food store sold 100 percent post-consumer recycled toilet paper, nowadays a regular grocery store item, but back then a rarity. It seemed a reasonable compromise. And of course they never went back to the yogourt container and tub routine. So instead of a bit of tap water there's energy-consumptive manufacturing, bleach, plastic packaging and shipping. DDT and by-catch. Oceanic acidification and ass-wipe. There's nothing to be said, and he knows it. Touché.

"Do you think if we keep feeding him he'll keep following us?" he asks, an olive branch.

"That's what old Coleridge says," Miriam answers, "though I wouldn't get too carried away, Ferris." His old moniker seems appropriate to her here, an appeal to the more playful aspect of his nature. "We've still got a ways to go before we get to sing 'Bob Dylan's 115th Dream,'" she says, trying for common ground.

He smiles, and launches right in. "I was riding on the *Mayflower* when I thought I spied some land..." And she joins in too, right after he imitates verbatim Dylan's false start on the original track, recorded in 1965, three years after Rachel Carson first wrote of a future denuded, defiled, without birds left in the sky for us to sing to or hear sing.

THIS EARTHQUAKE WON'T be any good for the salmon. Threefold. First of all, twenty to thirty million Atlantic salmon will have been released into the wild as a result of the tsunami damage to the fifty fish farms on the west coast of Vancouver Island. Of course, this is nothing new. As it is, there's anywhere from fifty thousand to a half-million escapees a year due to storms and negligent pen-tending. But every Atlantic means a graver threat; means an invasive, non-indigenous species spreading disease and competing for what spawning grounds remain, which are always dwindling. There used to be over one hundred spawning streams in the Vancouver area, not including the Fraser and its tributaries. Now there are two: one in Stanley Park, and one in Port Coquitlam. They're both stocked. Between forestry, mining, and hydro-electric damming and diversion, good grounds up and down the coast have been decimated.

Currently there's some 750 creeks and rivers in development or application under the provincial government's new run-of-the-river independent power project initiative. Plutonic Power, a General Electric subsidiary, is about to start building a 1,000-plus megawatt project just a few hundred kilometres north of my house. Green power, as they spin it. Two hundred and fifty kilometres of road, 450 kilometres of transmission wire, 140 bridges. They'll drive their excavators into the stream beds at low water and build a few token groomed spawning pools. They'll call it good stewardship. Then they'll open the pipes and siphon up to 95 percent of the annual flow off seventeen different Bute Inlet tributaries. But the turbines will spin and the power will flow and everyone will go on using their energy-star approved hot-air dryers in the middle of the summer, comfortable knowing that their power doesn't come from horrendous coal like those nasty Americans and backwards Indians and Chinese.

Then there's the inevitable diversion of money and resources away from what little efforts are being made on the salmon's behalf. The damage to our all-important human infrastructure will take precedence, and both government funding and community initiatives for salmon will be some of the first to be siphoned off. People will rebuild houses, not spawning grounds, and the government will be all too eager to accommodate the shift in priorities and energies back to one reflected in the markets and the tax purse.

A shift that will be indicative of the greatest problem, as I see it. Public sentiment. We've been fighting an uphill battle for a decade now to get even a fraction of the public to notice the salmon. It took the disappearance of an estimated nine million fish from the Fraser runs to land just enough front-page coverage and galvanize just enough public concern to force the Conservatives to order a judicial inquiry into DFO's mismanagement of the salmon.

And now we've got it, and the earth picks this fine time to rattle. Mid-swing, in the midst of the public consultation process. And you can bet the government will keep the timeline clock ticking. Whole communities of people who were just gathering enough information and gumption to step up and speak for the salmon will be derailed, defused. It's a near-miracle when any one issue takes hold with people these days, oscillating as we all are with a sort of low-swell panic. Our endemic fear. We flit from one issue, one cause, one solution to the next.

My husband—a bit of a misnomer as we're not married, though it's what he'd have me call him; I think of him more as Willow's father, the man I co-parent and cohabitate with—Ferris, he took off the day after the earthquake on an insane wild goose chase to find some guy in Hawaii who he says is going to pay him a wad of cash for the glass fish float he found. That's what I mean by low-swell panic. Everyone's going from one desperate scheme to the next.

We didn't even get off the ground with alternative energy, I mean real alternative energy, and emissions reduction, before carbon sequestering and geo-engineering became the order of the day. And in the midst of it all, who could really care about a few genus of salmon? Especially now that the earthquake's made basic amenities an issue. Now that everybody, once again, has got bigger fish to fry.

ᠸᢇ

WHEN FERRIS SHOWED up the day after the quake and told me he was leaving right away for Lasqueti I just about packed his bags for him. All his bags. To be honest I've been waiting for him to pack up and leave for a while now. It's not an easy place to come to, realizing that you no longer love someone, and for me it has been that much more difficult because of Willow. But eventually such a thing becomes undeniable, and I'll always remember the night, the moment, it happened for me.

We'd been fighting fiercely all summer. To be fair I should say that fighting is nothing new for Ferris and I, but I can say for myself, and I think for him too, that there's a critical point where it just becomes tiresome, a song you've heard a thousand times too many, and we'd reached it. Which is when it either stops, which it didn't for us, or it becomes detached from all passions other than hatred. That's where we'd gotten to. Then Ferris came home early off the water one day in late August last summer and told me to get dressed in my finest. Which is to say, my black spaghetti-strap dress and thin black sandals and the gold-filigreed silver leaf earrings my mother gave me when I left for university, all remnants of my school girl days when fashion and adornment still mattered. I protested, wanting to know what he was getting at, but he held steady to his secrecy, saying only that I was going to love it, and, thinking back on it now, I wonder if it was that word, love, which convinced me to go along with it. I'm one of those women who's got the same figure at thirty-five as I did at twenty, lucky I suppose, so I slipped on my dress, brushed my hair out long down my back, and climbed into the Volvo.

As it turned out, Joni Mitchell was giving an advanced screening of her new film, *The Fiddle and the Drum*, at the Ruby Lake Resort's outdoor amphitheatre that night. Ferris had gotten what he had understood were exclusive tickets, for one hundred bucks apiece, to dine at the resort restaurant with the owners, their close friends and Joni Mitchell herself. I should say in Ferris's defence that I flat-out loved Joni Mitchell in my early twenties. I might even go so far as to say that if it weren't for the fact that Ferris was the first guy I'd had in my bed who would lie awake with me listening to *Blue* and *For the Roses*, we might never have fallen in love to begin with.

The irony of it was, there we were almost fifteen years later, dressed to the nines, trying to salvage some shred of what we had shared back then, and Joni didn't show. Not for dinner. And not till we'd stood around afterwards in a chilly wind and rain waiting for her to arrive at the amphitheatre for nearly two hours. When she finally did, she offered the hundred-odd people who'd showed for the screening some flippant excuse about running late in an interview with PBS and *having* to stop at home for a salad because she had been absolutely famished. Then they screened the video, one of the more sorry excuses for art I've ever seen. Joni's been hit-and-miss through the years, but this was taking lack of discernment to a level beyond forgivable, an hour-long debacle of sappy song and ballet with that triumph of human spirit, courage and love over ecological disaster message the baby boomers all default to in the absence of their willingness to own up to the world of shit they're leaving us.

But what made the evening fall flat on its face, and with it Ferris's efforts to rekindle something that just won't be, was not all that. Even if Joni had been at the dinner and the screening had been amazing, it still would have failed. It was doomed from the start. Because the premise only worked to illustrate how much we'd diverged, and how little Ferris saw of who I actually had by then become.

I have no time for Joni Mitchell now. I put *Blue* or *For the Roses* on every once in a while when I'm home alone and feeling sentimental. I'd say they're albums more suited in theme and tone to my life and to our relationship now than they were when I listened to them incessantly so many years ago, but it always irks me. How could a woman so capable of such beauty, and so apparently concerned with the state of the earth, how could she be building that ten-thousand-square foot mansion of concrete and glass she's now having constructed just up the highway from here? It's irredeemable. Paving paradise with her architecturally engineered palace. I'd like to be a fly on the wall of her mind when she's talking herself into feeling good about that decision. I'd buzz my wings as loud as I could just to try and drown out the bullshit. I think I've said that very thing to Ferris. I've ranted on ad nauseum about the incongruence of Joni's lifestyle and her message, but he doesn't really hear me. I mean, he hears me, he hears me all the time. I've made very few friends in this town since we moved here. It's full of old-school rednecks, retirees and forty-something urbanite yuppies who've moved from the city to raise their kids in "the country," bringing the city with them.

So in the absence of any other sounding board, Ferris has heard my every diatribe under the sun concerning everything I can't figure of how others are living their lives these days. But he thinks I'm just being angry, stubborn, unrelenting, and so his listening is like that of a patient parent's—I've seen him do it with Willow, he stands a certain way, his arms crossed against his chest, his eyes wide as though attentive, but ultimately hollow, his thoughts elsewhere. He dismisses my ideas before I've spoken them because he's prejudged them as adolescent. If he hadn't, he'd have understood that the way back to my heart was not with some overpriced, decadent dinner and a glimpse of Joni Mitchell. But he didn't understand that, and by the time we got home, I was furious for it.

Ferris had sent Willow to Svend's for the night—"Uncle Svend," the closest thing to family Willow has got in this town—obviously expecting romance. But I just railed at him, about the supreme indignity of expropriating the agony of other species' dying for the sake of making art. About Joni's arrogance and self-aggrandizement. And he eventually railed back, accusing me of being unduly harsh and equally arrogant.

I often wonder why he doesn't just agree with me, like he used to, but he's become incapable over the past few years of assigning blame where blame is due. Since he quit drinking he seems to have this need to forgive everyone, as though, on top of all the luxuries everyone takes for themselves, forgiveness is deserved, too. It's not. All in all, we're vile creatures, and our only shot at redemption is to admit it, to ourselves and to each other, and to get on with the hard work of setting our wrongs to right. He looks at me with disgust whenever I say so, and I know it's why he hasn't wanted to have another child with me. He calls me recalcitrant. I used to think it was cute when he'd use words like that, words beyond the normal range of his vocabulary. I used to find his intellectual limitations and his little attempts at obscuring or overcoming them endearing. But now I just find it pathetic.

I've heard it said that successful—which is to say lasting, possibly even happy—marriages are almost invariably comprised of two people whose IQs are within five points of each other. That's definitely not the case with Ferris and I, though he'd never acknowledge it, and if I were to say so it would be just another example to him of my arrogance. Which is the reason why I haven't wanted to have another child with him. Not to mention that it's probably the last thing the world needs me to do, give it another human mouth to feed, another appetite of desire to satiate. What the world needs me to do is fight for it because it can't fight for itself. As his mother, that's what Willow needs me to do. To fight the corporate fascist state for a future not poisoned and oppressed by its toxic oligarchy. To try to pioneer a way around what we've become. It's what he needs his father to do, too. But somewhere down the line Ferris capitulated, and our love was handed over in the terms of his unconditional surrender.

⌒

IT'S BEEN OVER three weeks since Ferris left and we haven't heard a word. He should have landed in Hawaii days ago, though this morning we awoke to news reports of a massive earthquake there now, too, so what to hope for? That he didn't make it in a safe and timely manner? That has its own potentially frightening implications.

The CBC reports that the lid has been blown right off the tallest mountain there, one of the volcanoes scientists had deemed dormant because it hasn't erupted in over 4,500 years. All I can hope for is that Ferris arrived safely, tended to his insane business, and was already on his way home by the time the eruption began last night. Poor Willow. I'll never forgive Ferris for not calling.

They've been talking all day on the radio about James Lovelock and Gaia's revenge and ridiculous stuff like that. It's just like people to cope with harsh realities with confabulations and self-delusion. By three in the afternoon I've had enough, I can't listen to another inane minute, so I decide to head down to the beach to find Willow. He spends most of his summer days there. It's heaven for him, out of school, out of doors, away from his parents' watchful eyes. He's a good kid, Willow, and I trust him to himself. One thing I can say for Ferris is that he's capable. Street smart and sea smart. It comes down to him from his grandfather, or so Ferris has told me, and it has come down to our son, too. I'm glad for it. He'll need it in the coming days. When things really do collapse. When things constrict. Which is to say, when it gets so incredibly difficult to be anything other than poor that the only dignified life for people of our class will be the one wholly outside of and completely non-dependent upon the urban system. This will occur in my son's lifetime, and so I leave him to roam as much as I can, to teach him independence, emotional self-reliance.

I find him down in the estuary of Halfmoon Creek building a dam in the intertidal zone out of old driftwood and rocks. There's a family of ducks drifting out in the bay, and there's a young mother, an Asian woman, and her baby, nursing on a drift log set into the sand above high water mark. "Hey Bub," I say to get his attention. He works so diligently and intently at his projects, a bomb could go off and he wouldn't notice. (Hopefully a bomb never does go off...)

"Hi Anna," he answers back. He gets this from Ferris, calling me by my first name. Ferris rarely refers to his parents as anything other than Cosmo—or Carl, if he's expressing anger or resentment at who his father was, something he did often before he quit drinking, and seldom does since—and Alexi-Lynne. Willow has followed suit. "What are you building?" I ask him, trying to pry his mind from his imagination. Selfishly, because the truth is without

Ferris around I'm lonely. Arguing or not, his companionship in the evenings takes me away from myself, and without him here I've spent too much time alone.

"A dam, like the ones you're always talking about with Ferris. When I'm done I'm going to smash it."

"Why would you do that?" I ask, already certain what his answer will be.

"Because that's what you always say we should do to them. That's the only hope."

The only hope. Jesus. Ferris always says I'm going to turn Willow into some sort of eco-terrorist extremist talking the way I do, and I suppose here before me is his supporting evidence. Of course, eco-terrorism may be the only truly appropriate and courageous response to his world by the time Willow's an adult, but that's not a direction I want to lead him in. Truth is, I suspect it may be the only appropriate one now, though I'll confess also to being full of piss and vinegar when talking of such things, but a chickenshit when it comes down to brass tacks. I'm far too timid to actually act on any of it. I fight my fight with words and civil actions, without physical violence, because I ultimately agree with Ferris on this one point: you can't fight fire with fire, not when what you're fighting for is to put the fire out.

"I don't really mean that when I say it Bub, I'm just venting," I respond to my son, but I can tell he's unconvinced. I suppose my rally-cries are a tad more persuasive than my recanting. Anger is a powerful passion. "Do you want to come up to the bakery with me for a cookie and a cool drink?" I propose, wanting to change the subject. Sometimes once a hole's been dug with children the best thing is to let time's detritus fill it in. At least that's what I tell myself when I'm stumped with Willow.

I take his hand as we start up the beach, but he quickly shakes it loose, running ahead toward the marram grass and flowering blackberry brambles above the rocks and sand. When we first moved here, when Willow was still an infant, I used to come down to the beach to sketch the old houses and the shoreline and sometimes Merry Island in the distance. That's when I still believed art had some transformative power, a position I've grown suspicious of over the past decade. There's no shortage of artists addressing the woes of the world now, nor has there ever been, but if that's contributed to its betterment it has obviously been in so small a way as to be negligible.

I come back to Joni Mitchell painting her post-apocalyptic paintings and singing her requiems for the earth, and for what? So some fans can convince themselves of the self-delusion that they're different because they choose her over Celine Dion or Madonna? Because her CDs come in cardboard packaging, because she cares. Obviously, I'm bitter. This world isn't the world I wanted or want, this world of cellphones and all-inclusives and rich artists building mansions on the beach. I suppose I hold the artists more accountable than most because art *should* be transformative, and if it's not it's because the artists haven't pushed themselves to the point of necessary transformation themselves. Ferris accuses me of self-exemption. He points to my computer and my internet connection and my car as evidence that, to scale, I'm no different. But that's naive. This *is* a war. The Poles on horseback stood no chance against the blitzkrieg. There is necessary weaponry, and there is luxury. There is a clear and easy distinction there, and Ferris's refusal of it comes from his own desire to legitimize his acquiescence, his cowardice, which in his heart of hearts I know he can't, and I know it's turning him slowly into one of those broken men, hiding from the world inside himself behind a patchwork of flimsy ideas that hold no water. Ferris's are like the clepsydra that hangs on the wall above his dresser, the one passed down from his father, given to Ferris by his mother on the tenth anniversary of Cosmo's death. One of those ancient clocks the Saxons used to keep time, a wooden bowl with lines carved into it and a tiny hole in the centre. They would set it floating in a basin, and as water entered the bowl the time was indicated by whatever line it had risen to. Eventually, of course, the bowl would sink, just as Ferris will, I mean figuratively, of course, and knock on the closest piece of wood I can find as I think it, a washed-up, sea-worn timber, as any fisherman's wife would.

⌐

ONE THING THAT'S been good as a result of the quake has been the lack of tourists in town. Usually they're swarming this time of year. City-slickers in convertible beemers and on fancy motorbikes cruising around checking out the scenery and the real estate prospects. Usually the bay is busy with speedboats and water skiers. But it's been quiet these past few weeks, eerily like it was when we first moved here, as if the quake set the clock back a decade. Aside from some blown-out windows and a few fallen power poles there was little damage done to the area, so by physical appearance alone you'd almost think the quake hadn't occured. But the city's become a bottleneck that virtually nothing can pass through, so things have been altered insofar as supplies, primarily food, have been scarce. The bakery just reopened a few days back, and the general store's shelves are still relatively empty.

Willow and I each get a muffin—it's either that or strudel or a croissant—and the only drink available, a glass of water. The Asian woman and her baby are seated out at one of the two tables in front of the store, so we sit at the other. I say hello, and she responds with only a timid smile. Her baby's another matter, practically leaping at me from her lap, bursting at the seams, a wide grin across her face. She's got the dark Asian eyes and fair skin of her mother, aside from where it's been blemished dark red over the entire left side of her face. "What's wrong with her face?" Willow blurts out, indiscreetly. It's not like him to speak so insensitively, though he's picked up more and more of those types of behaviours over the past five years at public school.

It's another one of the repercussions we suffer as a result of Ferris buying his stupid crab boat. Who of our class spends $450,000 in their twenties on any business, let alone one as precarious as fishing? If things were different I'd home-school Willow, or send him to Waldorf down in Roberts Creek, but as things are I can't afford not to work and we can't afford the Waldorf tuition, so he's at Halfmoon Bay Elementary, and he has morphed into one of those kids who say inappropriate, even cruel things without thinking as a result. Like now, asking a perfect stranger what's wrong with her child. Some of the contractors' wives around here would lay right into Willow for it, but this woman very politely answers his very rude question.

"She has a birthmark," she says. "She was born with it."

Willow takes a bite of his muffin and then responds, his mouth half-full still. "Oh, I thought she was burned or something."

"I'm sorry," I interrupt, embarrassed by my son's lack of manners. "I'm Anna," I continue, trying to change the subject. "And this little ruffian is Willow." I tousle Willow's hair, hoping to illustrate that he is, after all, just a rascally kid.

"I'm Jin Su and this is Emily," she replies, smiling a reassuring smile my way.

"She's very beautiful," I say, and mean it. Her birthmark isn't ugly as you might expect, it's just different, and I for one find it stunning. It looks like the underside of a bird's wing outstretched in the wind. It's the type of diversity in humans and in the world I've grown to love. Not the kind built of artifice, of intention, but the organic kind. That which is as it is, beyond any conscious meddling or manipulation. This baby's birthmark is such a thing, and it's captivating. It seems to lift more of her to the surface, and she's obviously a boisterous and beautiful spirit. "I've only just noticed you around these past few weeks, since the quake. Are you staying with relatives or something?"

"With Svend," she says, and I'm surprised.

"Svend is a good friend of ours. He's like an uncle to Willow." Willow has taken his muffin and wandered across the road where he is climbing the retaining rocks of the steep embankment. "How do you know him?" I ask.

She takes a moment to answer my question, fussing around with her baby girl, repositioning her on her lap. "He *is* my uncle," she says, again to my surprise.

"I didn't know Svend had any family in this part of the world?" I say, the question caught in my inflection.

"He doesn't," she answers, and pauses as though to think again before speaking. "He didn't, until I found him. His eldest brother is my real father, but I didn't even know until a few months ago. I grew up in a Chinese family in Vancouver, but I was adopted. When I got pregnant with Emily I started looking into my real family, and I found my father. He lives in Norway. When he came to meet me last summer, he told me about Svend. We've been e-mailing ever since."

"I met Svend's brother last summer. But he didn't say anything about you. We thought he was just here to visit Svend." Emily starts clawing around at her mother's chest, so she puts her back on the milk. I flash a look across the street, but Willow is gone. Probably run up the trail across the road to the little waterfall he likes to climb in and under this time of year.

This Jin Su is quite stunning too, and I'm realizing talking to her that she's not as young as I'd assumed from a distance. She has fine, unlined skin, and eyes that don't show their age, but I can tell by the way she conducts herself, by her composure, that she's a woman of my age or older.

"Do you live in Vancouver now then?" I ask, though the answer is obvious. She explains to me in her soft voice how her apartment was ruined in the quake, and how she'd been trying to cross the city to get to her adopted parents' home, but by way of circumstances ended up coming on a boat here instead, landing at Svend's door. The baby drifts off to sleep on her mother's breast, to the lilt of her voice as she tells me her story.

"The boat you came up on," I ask. "Who was driving it?" Again she takes her time answering, and this time it seems almost as if she doesn't know how to respond, so I ask her flat out. "Was it a guy with dark, curly hair named Ferris?"

"Yes," she says. "I was trying to remember his name, and that was it, Ferris. I met him in the street below my building." Ferris had said when he got home the night of the quake that he'd slept in his truck in a parking lot up by Queen Elizabeth Park. He'd said it was probably the only thing that saved him because there were no buildings around. He told me he stole a boat from one of the docks near Science World, but he had said nothing of any passengers, let alone a niece of Svend's. "I was crying in the street, holding Emily, and he came up to me and asked if I had anywhere to go. So I told him about my parents on the North Shore, and about Svend, and he told me he knew Svend and could take me to his house."

I explain to her that Ferris is my husband, and Willow's father. "How is he?" she asks. "Have you heard from him?"

I respond to her only with a questioning look, not immediately understanding why or how she knows Ferris is gone.

"Svend told me," she offers without my asking. "I wanted to find Ferris to thank him for helping me, and Svend said he had gone away. On a sailboat to Hawaii for some reason."

"We haven't heard from him. Did you hear about the eruption last night?"

"No!" she almost leaps from her chair, the baby fidgeting at her mother's raised voice.

I explain to her the reported magnitude of the quake and eruption, and I could swear she's fighting back tears by the time I'm through. She gets up from her seat, her baby tucked in against her chest. "I'm sorry," she says. "I hope he's okay. It was very nice to meet you." Then she turns from me and heads up the road.

⌇

JIN SU TOOK the news of the earthquake in Hawaii harder than I would have expected, and all afternoon I've wondered why. If I didn't know better I'd almost suspect her to be Ferris's lover or something. I've always wondered where he stays on his delivery nights, but I don't ask because really, I don't care to know. If Ferris has a lover, it's all the more to keep him from me—from any more pathetic romantic overtures like the Joni Mitchell night. I decided a long time ago just to get through this thing with him till Willow is on his own two feet, and if his taking a lover makes the whole thing easier on him, then it's easier on me, and so on Willow, too.

But there are two reasons that make this woman being Ferris's mistress a complete improbability. First of all, she's Asian, and given the disdain for that ethnicity which Ferris has developed through his many years of difficult dealings with the Chinese buyers in Vancouver, it's safe to say she's not his type. And secondly, she's got an infant, which would almost certainly make Ferris the father, which is impossible. Ferris is congenitally incapable of keeping a secret, especially for any sustained period of time. If he had fathered this woman's child I'd have found out long before it was even born. So it's not that she's Ferris's lover, but something stirred her when she heard the news of the eruption. What? And where *is* the father of her child? Eventually my curiosity got the better of me and I marched up the road to invite her and Svend for dinner.

"He came. I let him stay for a few nights, then I asked him to leave." I'm explaining to Svend why Fairwin' Verge isn't still here with us. I assumed Svend had taken him back to Lasqueti, and Svend assumed him to be here all along. I've been angry with Svend for the role he played in the whole fish float shenanigan, so we haven't seen each other over the past few weeks. Now we're both finding out that wherever Fairwin' is, and however he got there, it's otherwise than what we expected.

"Whatever," Svend says. "That old bugger could survive in the desert without water. I'm sure he's fine."

It's a good segue into the question, so I ask Jin Su, "Where's Emily's father?" Svend shifts around, a bit uncomfortable, obviously, and I suddenly dread what I hadn't considered given Jin Su's predominantly calm disposition. What if he died in the earthquake? Perhaps that's why the news of the eruptions in Hawaii seemed to strike such a raw nerve in her earlier today. I'm about to apologize, to tell her she doesn't have to answer the question, when she clears the air.

"He's in Toronto. He works for Nike. He's in sales. He was at a training seminar for the week when the earthquake happened. He's still there, waiting for YVR to open to commercial flights. We're fine here with Svend, and there's nothing but a ruined city to go back to right now, so he's better off there anyway. We're thinking it might make the most sense for me and Emily to fly back east, actually, once we can. His parents have a nice place in the suburbs, and it helps that it's still standing."

Listening to her answer I realize that I haven't yet asked her if she's heard from her parents, her adopted parents, the ones whose house on the North Shore she was trying to get to when she met Ferris. I decide not to ask, thinking it best to let sleeping dogs lie. "I'm just going to check on the salmon," I say, and leave them sitting on the couch with their mugs of peppermint tea.

Willow is out in the yard building a fort with his driftwood. He carries a stick or small log home with him every day from the beach, and he's built up a good pile through the spring. Now he's stacking them up in an interlocking pattern like a log house. It's just a few days since solstice and the evening air is warm and clear, well past 6 p.m., with hours of daylight to go. Every day it seems he grows more and more to resemble his father. Maybe it's because of Ferris's absence that I see it as such, or maybe it's that time in his life, just pre-puberty, when his more masculine features are starting to emerge.

Either way, watching him now from the kitchen window is like watching a miniature Ferris at work, and it sets in unexpectedly how much I miss him. It's the last thing I would have seen coming, but I'm flooded with dread as I turn to pull the salmon from the oven. Where is he? Somewhere out in the middle of the Pacific, hopefully, on his way home. I place the salmon on the stovetop and sit back against the counter for a second to gather myself before calling Willow in for supper. I can't help but wonder if I pushed Ferris to go out on that sailboat. If all my bitching at him about buying the boat has pushed him to do something as stupid and desperate as that for money. It must be. Why else would he be in such a hurry for the money other than that he sees no other way to bring our life back to the relative harmony it had before he got the loan with his mom and bought the boat?

I feel ill. How many times have I accused him of not being the man that I agreed to have Willow with? As if I've not had a hand in moulding him into what it is he's become. I always thought I'd be happy if he'd just leave me, if he'd just be the one to end it so I wouldn't have to choose between enduring more years in this house, this life, or being the one to leave. Being the one in the story of our son's life who left. But I never fully understood what it would feel like with him gone. How could I? And I'm petrified, suddenly, standing in our kitchen where we've fought and fucked and fed together. Where we've provided our son with a sense of family, however tumultuous it has been.

It's not these strangers I want at my dinner table with me. That's why I sent Fairwin' Verge away. I don't need company, I need my family, together. I need Ferris home, whomever he's become and however he wants to be, and it's setting in just how far away from me I've pushed him with my resentment and my inability to let him live his life in the way he needs to. So far away from me that he's somewhere adrift in the middle of the Pacific, best-case scenario. I don't want to think of the worst-case scenario, but I'm unable not to, to wipe it from my mind. Jesus. What if in my uncompromising, unrelenting expectations, I've pushed the father of my child, my best and only true friend—I'm feeling right now even still my lover—to embark upon a journey from which he may not return?

I'm on my knees in the bathroom, dizzy and nauseous, and I hardly remember rushing in here. I'm hyperventilating and sobbing uncontrollably, and I can hear Svend calling from the living room, asking if I'm okay. I wipe the saliva from my mouth. "I'll just be a minute," I manage to call out. I run the water, strip down, and climb into the shower. The water's near-scalding, my skin lighting up bright red, but I can't feel it. I step back out of the water's stream. All I can feel standing in the steam, watching the water swirl down the drain, is the emptiness at the centre of myself, the one Ferris is supposed to fill, for better or for worse, though till this moment I've not allowed myself to see it clearly as such.

〜

Ferris,

The moon is near full and through the small spaces between the houses across the street I can see its light skipping across the water. Time is much kinder at night. John Berger wrote that in his latest novel, a book of letters written in the voice of a middle-aged Palestinian

*woman to her lover in prison. I've just read it cover to cover this even-
ing. Svend was here with his lovely niece Jin Su and her daughter. We
ate a chinook he caught off Point Upwood, an early catch, with rice,
and salad from the garden. The quake didn't seem to upset the let-
tuce! When they left I read Willow to sleep, then thought I'd do the
same for myself. Now it's late, or early, I suppose I should say—it's the
middle of the night, and I'm out on the front porch wishing you were
here, wanting to say so many things. So I'm writing to you instead, as
Berger's A'ida would do each night to her incarcerated soulmate.*

*Earlier in the evening I made myself sick thinking of you lost at
sea. I can say it's a fear I'd learned to live with long ago so I could care
for Willow when he was an infant and you were out off Tsawwassen,
hauling in the gales. Now I'm wondering what part that has played in
all that has become of us. How much has the fear of losing you in that
way I can't control forced me to push you from me in the ways I can?*

*I've just smoked the last of my tobacco. We'll have none till the late
fall now, till the Perseids, but I knew we would run out long ago. I
planted twice as many seeds this year, and they're all thriving in the
heat, so we shouldn't run out again. It takes a lifetime to learn a life, I
think. Just when you think you know what you need, you need more.
Or less. Or different. I'll confess I had convinced myself I didn't need
you anymore Ferris. That we didn't need each other. I would be surprised if you said you hadn't done the same. But now I wonder. No, I
don't wonder, I know that is wrong.*

*Absence is the aphrodisiac of the soul. I don't remember who said
that. It's from some book or movie we both loved once I think. If you
were here you would tell me exactly which one. You've always been
the one to sift the chaff from the grain for me Ferris. Here's one I can
recall. Distance is the soul of beauty. Simone Weil. Come back to me
Ferris. Come back to me, and come back to me. Time is much kinder
at night, Berger writes, there's nothing to wait for. But he's wrong. Because this night here is unkind without you, and I am waiting.*

Your love,
A.

I fold the letter four times, carry it to the bedroom, and slip it under Ferris's pillow, for him to find when he returns. I know he will. With everything around me silent and asleep now I can feel him. I know he's still in the world, that he's left Hawaii safely and is on his way home to me. I say a little prayer for him to whatever god or gods might still be here, then I lay my head down on his pillow and curl up on his side of the bed. There's a little songbird—I haven't the faintest clue what kind—nesting with its young in the attic above our bed. I've never seen it, but every so often it sings in the night. Short, pretty trills. Tonight they fall through the dark like a song of blessing answering back from wherever my prayers might be heard.

⤴

THE WORLD IS elevated in the light of love found or love renewed. I'm not naive to this. It brings the soul to the surface, the way some deep sea fishes rise to the light of the moon on clear nights. I don't resist it. Willow heads off to the beach in the morning and I go out into the garden. It's a hot June day, no wind, and I spend it watching the bees trip from stamen to stamen, then fall asleep in the shade of the broadleaf maple behind our house and dream of a day a lot like this one, back when we'd first moved from the city. Willow was teething, fussy, so we loaded him into the crummy and drove up the east side of the inlet to Tuwanek, then up the logging roads into the Tetrahedron Range. Willow fell asleep before we even left the pavement.

Somewhere in the mountains we pulled the truck over beside a small creek and made love on the front bench seat of the cab. It was muggy and hot and we finished with a slick film of sweat and dust coating our bodies. We got out to wash in the creek, the world around us silent but for our splashing and the ticking of the still-cooling engine close by, in the distance a float plane lifting into the air from the inlet waters far below. I dreamt this all clearly, exactly as it had been. Ferris came up behind me while I was bent over the stream washing my legs in its cold glacial water. He leaned over me, so I thought he was going to take me again from behind, right there on the side of the road. Instead he put his mouth to my ear and whispered, "I'd pick you one, but it doesn't seem right. Come see what I've found."

On the far side of the creek the blasting scree rose steep and barren back to the trees. In amongst the granite cobbles and shards were these little bunches of flowers. Tiny, with yellow petals and purple sunburst centres. They were the only growth on that inhospitable slope. Perfect clusters of flowers, growing as though out of nothing. So small in relation to the magnitude of their surroundings—the aggressive man-made road cut through a slope of towering firs and hemlocks, the wide view of the sky to the downslope side, the long inlet below—those flowers would have been impossible to notice if it weren't for the afterglow of our lovemaking.

I woke up with this in my mind, and have been lying here a long while savouring the feeling of that day as it still lingers inside me, watching the late-afternoon sun illuminate the chlorophyll in the maple leaves above as they rustle in the lightest of winds now blowing in off the bay. I've also been thinking of something else I read in Berger's novel last night. I want to recollect it properly, as he wrote it, so I rise and go to the house to retrieve the book. It's on the front porch where I left it and I quickly find the quote I'm looking for.

What lasts is women recognising the men they come to love as victors whatever happens, and men honouring

each other because of their shared experience of defeat.
This is what lasts!

Which is why, I'm realizing, the kind of love we had on that mountainside hasn't lasted us. I've not seen Ferris as a victor, regardless of his ill-fated decisions and his failures. I've not honoured him despite his defeats. But even as I think this I feel the counterweight of other thoughts, dissentious thoughts, leaning in. Should a man then be honoured regardless of the ill stride he takes his defeats in?

A few pages on, perhaps the passage that struck me the most last night:

> *And what we today can show ... is that victory is an illusion, that the struggle will be endless, and that to continue it, aware of this, is the only way to acknowledge the immense gift of life!*

Somewhere along the way Ferris decided he didn't want to struggle any longer. He started acquiescing to dimwit ideas like, for instance, the one of plastic, as a product of human ingenuity and synthetic manipulation of terrestrial material, being natural. And therefore acceptable in whatever quantity we deem necessary, or so I've always assumed the rest of the argument must go. All our destructive designs being somehow inevitable, unavoidable, foreordained, and so permissible. He started questioning the solidity of the ground we'd staked out and stood firmly upon, regurgitating pat aphorisms like, *We can't just throw the baby out with the bathwater,* or *Let he who has not sinned cast the first stone.* Questioning whether it was right, for instance, to call people like Joni Mitchell to task for signing a record contract with Starbucks; or David Suzuki for making a deal with the devil when he broke ranks with Alexandra and Salmon Coast and founded allegiances instead with Ocean Harvest, the largest aquaculture corporation in the world.

We don't need to work with the industry, we need to eliminate it! It takes five pounds of feed-fish to grow every pound of farmed salmon. This will not change without radically changing the salmon's DNA or increasing their already heavy hormone regime. In what way then can this industry be made to be sustainable, closed containment pens or not? But Ferris would stand steadfast by Suzuki's collaboration-with-industry approach, saying I'm foolish to question a man of such experience and broad-based knowledge. Coward's talk. How can I see it otherwise? How can I call the author of such feeble-minded thoughts my victor?

Our parents might have said the future was what we were struggling for. Not us. We were fighting to remain ourselves.

That's Berger's A'ida again. It's the articulation of the unspoken mantra Ferris and I lived by, together, before he gave in to the fear of what's lost—financially and socially—when you're anything but a fence-sitter in these hyper-conservative times. Forgetting to keep his sights trained instead on the personal dignity retained, Ferris lost his allegiance to those tenacious, impossible flowers, and since then he's been lost to me.

⌒

"YOU'LL END UP old and bitter and alone," Ferris said to me the last night he was here. He was on his hands and knees picking window glass from the carpet in the dining room. I'd come at him hard when he told me he was leaving the next day for Lasqueti to try to arrange another meeting with the fish float buyer. I'd told him he'd bought into the system so far when he bought the boat that he couldn't see anything clearly anymore, that he was just another panicking worker on the rat-wheel, lost in the racket of his own whirring. And I meant it. "It's not that fucking simple Anna," he'd fought back. "Everything for you is so fucking black and white."

"That's right, it is. You're either scrambling for money with the rest of them, poisoning and killing whatever you have to along the way, or you're not. Which is it, Ferris? Which are you doing with your life?"

"The best I can with what I've got to work with is what I'm doing. Put it into whichever box you want Anna."

"I have, and I will."

"That's right. There's me and everyone else, destroying the precious world in one box. And you in the other. Immaculate Anna, sitting at home all day with your fucking Apple computer and your iPhone, saving the world."

"Don't start at me with the hair shirt shit Ferris, it's pathetic."

"Alone Anna. You're all alone. There's a whole world of people out there struggling together to make things work and you sit in this house passing judgment. I won't do it. I can't."

"Cause you're a fucking coward like the rest of them. You've gone soft. Which is all fine and dandy for you, isn't it, but the whales don't have that choice Ferris. And the salmon and the albatross and the fucking sea turtles. Why don't you ask the great auk whether they figure all those people out there are trying hard enough? Oh, wait a second, I forgot, they're already extinct. Fucking gone, Ferris. And the salmon will be the next to go while you and all the rest of the doing-our-besters are easing into the idea that we might need to seriously rethink some shit here. I won't join in, Ferris. And if it means I live and die alone at least I'll do it with dignity. Something you used to have before you went and made fishing the end instead of the means."

"As if that's what I wanted. As if what's happened in the fishery is all my doing."

"It's a sinking ship, Ferris, and you refuse to jump."

In my disgust I turned my back on him and stormed into the kitchen. He got up off the floor and followed.

"What would you have me do then, sell the boat for a hundred-thousand-dollar loss? And then what, get a fucking job on the ferries?"

The knife I'd used to dice the vegetables for supper earlier in the evening was sitting there on the counter beside me, so I grabbed it, and waved it in Ferris's face. "I'd have you lie down right here on this kitchen floor so I can cut your heart out and find out once and for all what's happened to it," I said.

"You're fucking nuts. Put the fucking knife down," he yelled at me. And I did, tossing it with a loud clang into the cast iron sink.

"What the fuck is this about anyway?" he asked. "What? Why are we having this same old stupid fight again. I'm so sick of this. I can't even remember what started it now." He had that look old people get in the early stages of dementia when they suddenly realize they've lost their bearing and have no idea where they are, what they were doing, or why. For a moment I felt an upwelling of tenderness toward him, and I realize, revisiting this now, that this feeling, one I often feel in the more heightened moments of our fights, must arise from the fact that yelling is the closest we come to sharing ourselves with each other. In the absence of lovemaking, of dreaming and envisioning our future, of laughing together, fighting has become our only intimacy.

"Maybe that's the problem," I said, and meant it, hoping maybe the fight might turn to the crux of the matter for once, to the thing neither of us wants to out-and-out say.

"That's not what I meant," he said, sidestepping.

"It's about the fact that there's just been a massive earthquake, and you've just arrived home, and you're already planning to leave tomorrow morning to go chasing after money, as if that's the least bit important right now."

"Right. Exactly. And that's exactly what I'm doing."

"Whatever Ferris. You do whatever you want," I'd said. "Just don't expect there to be a place in this home for you when you return." It was the last thing I said to him. I left the kitchen then and went off to bed. I listened as he had a shower, then lay down to sleep on the couch. When I woke up in the morning, he'd already left.

I came home from the beach that evening to a message on the machine explaining that he was sailing to Hawaii, that he was on a good safe boat, and so he'd be fine. He said that Fairwin' would be coming to stay with us. Then he told Willow he loved him, and to take good care of me while he was gone.

The Shifting Poles

DAY NINE ON the water, and they finally enter the trade wind's perpetual flow. The sails stretch taut, full of the strong and steady northeasterly, and the hull rides smooth on the following seas. The journey is a rhythm in and of itself now, and the only thing is to submit to it. A day in and they begin to keep, finally, to the watch schedule they'd agreed upon when first leaving Neah Bay.

Their relationship too falls to a different rhythm. The charades of the first week behind them, they turn from that romantic potential to a more congenial, cordial exchange. They share with each other the stories of their lives, both avoiding anything that might be suggestive, that might reawaken the tumult of days previous. Because it's there still, their desire, and they are both constantly aware of its powerful, single-minded force.

THEY ARE LIKE two magnets, each backed on one side by steel. If one turns away from the other, the other attracts. If they both turn, each feels only the slightest pull to spin and face the other. If they do, and at the same time, the force is one that pushes, repels. Until one turns away again, and they come together.

The magnetic poles of the earth are in constant flux. What is known as true north and south are static points, zero degrees lat and long, north and south, from which all official maps and charts of the world are based. They are an agreed-upon human convention and, as such, are fixed. But the magnetic poles that the compass needle swings to are forever in motion, moving in swirling loops up to fifty miles in a day. And for reasons greatly speculated upon but not fully understood, the poles occasionally flip. This hasn't happened in almost eight hundred thousand years, and no one can predict when next it will occur, or what on earth may alter as a result.

In this way neither Francis nor Miriam can completely predict the movements of the magnetism between them. This is the essence of emerging love lived. It won't be contained, corrected or controlled. It won't be fixed as a constant by which one can navigate. But as a force it can be harnessed nonetheless, and it is through this they each develop an awareness of the other that is kinesthetic: she knows precisely his location on the boat whether he can be seen by her or not, just as he knows hers. They speak less and less because so little need be said. When she brings him coffee, it's with plenty of cream and sugar. When he brings her coffee, it's black. When he tires, she gives him room to be alone. When she's tired, he tells her a story, or coaxes one from her. They each take an interest in the deeper workings of the other. When one speaks of their waking dream, the other keeps quiet, and listens.

St. Elmo's Fire

A WEEK IN the trade winds goes by in an instant and an eternity. Such is the nature of monotony. When inside it, it seems the gears of the world's clock have worn all their teeth away so the passage of time has ceased. But when one looks back over a week of such days they seem to have passed as a single, uneventful instant. Often there are no points of reference inside the trades, no significant shifts in wind or wave pattern to mark the passage of time in one's memory. The sun rises and sets through the unbroken blue, the stars cast their net over the night, augmented only by the odd airplane's passing, and higher up the sight of satellites orbiting by—little glints of light being pulled as by an invisible string across the sky.

But on the morning of their sixteenth day at sea the sun rises behind a blanket of thick grey cloud gathered on the eastern horizon. By midday the clouds approach from every direction, at first diffuse, then thickening. Thunder rumbles across the ocean, and by early evening they're inside a squall of rain, intermittently dumping sheets of water down upon them. There is a taut intensity to the air in the intervals. Sounds of hissing and crackling begin emanating from the mast and bowsprit. Then the lightning starts in the far distance, bolts and sheets, approaching through the deepening grey.

⌒

ST. ERASMUS OF Formiae. St. Elmo. Beaten around the head and spat upon by his Roman captors. Flogged with leaden mauls until his body burst with blood, then thrown to a pit of worms and snakes and doused with a mixture of boiling oil and sulphur. Still he sang his Christian God's praises. A great storm of thunder and lightning descended, and electrocuted all surrounding the pit, sparing the saint. Later, according to the legend, his teeth were plucked from his mouth with iron pincers, his skin torn with iron combs, and he was roasted upon a gridiron. Then, with his eyes plucked from his head, his Diocletian persecutors laid him out naked, tied withes around his neck, arms and legs, and stretched him until his body broke. Still, he sang. But it is commonly thought that the account of his first round of torture, of his being spared and protected, even avenged, by the great lightning storm, made him the patron saint of sailors.

It is also thought to be the etymological origin of "St. Elmo's fire", the name given to a particular phenomenon witnessed often in the midst of thunderstorms. A searing, flame-like blue or violet can be seen at night emanating from the tips of tall, sharp objects, accompanied by a hissing or buzzing or crackling, as of fire. It is this sound that Francis and Miriam have heard projecting from the mast and bowsprit throughout the early evening, and as night falls the darkness makes visible its luminous glow. Miriam has seen this once before while crossing from La Paz to Puerto Vallarta with Yule, so she knows it for what it is: a coronal discharge; the result of what's known as an electron avalanche, an exponential ionization of the air. They are both in the cockpit when the blue becomes visible, each unable to rest in the heaving tumult. The sea has turned sinisterly unpredictable, sending waves at them from every direction, and though the rain has ceased, there is a constant churning of ocean spray in the air.

"St. Elmo's fire!" she hollers to Francis over the racket of the thrashing waves and wind.

"I see it," he calls back, holding the wheel hard to their downwind course. "What the fuck's happening on this boat?"

She laughs at this, leaning into his side. "It's natural. It's an electrical charge thing, like the lightning."

"It's fucking spooky," he says to her now, and she can tell that he's kidding, but also means it. "They didn't say anything about this storm on the network last night," he says, and she sees now what's spooking him. His first offshore storm. A storm in sight of land, within the vicinity of safe harbour, is one thing. But out on the open ocean, at the full mercy of the elements, it's something entirely different. It can make a coward of the most courageous, a whimpering miscreant of a moral man.

Miriam can see that Francis is fighting to hold to the sane side of fright. "The *Belle* is built for it. She can take whatever the sea throws at her," she says, not wholly believing her own words as she speaks them.

"Natural or not, those things are freaky."

"They're supposed to be a good omen," she says. Francis doesn't buy it. His empiricist underpinnings may have been shaken by last week's sightings, especially the looming, but it's still a long way from where he stands to the realm of petty superstitions and religious faiths. She tries a different tack. "If they didn't even mention it last night it can't be more than a little system blowing through." It seems a reasonable enough line of logic, and she decides to follow it. "I mean, how bad can it get?" she hollers at him as a massive wall of water broadsides them and she's forced to brace herself against the awning struts to keep from falling to the deck. It's a question she regrets asking just as soon as it has passed through her lips, and she realizes that her attempts at reassurance are as much made for her own sake as for his. So she trains her eyes on the little blue flare atop the mast and says a little prayer to their patron saint.

The Beaufort Scale

In 1805, Admiral Sir Francis Beaufort developed what is known as the Beaufort Scale, a twelve-point scale meant to help sailors estimate wind speed by way of visual observation. Beaufort's answer to Miriam's question, "How bad can it get?" is Force 12, *Hurricane: The air is filled with foam and spray. Sea completely white with driving spray; visibility very seriously affected.* Doesn't sound so bad until one considers what kind of weather would constitute a *sea completely white with driving spray*: mammoth waves perpetually cresting and breaking, colossal walls of water curling over troughs as deep and wide as canyons. Pure, uncompromising chaos.

One of Francis's closest childhood friends took a job on a black cod and halibut boat when they were just out of high school. The *Bull Performance*, a ninety-foot steel-hulled trawler converted to a longliner, was a boat built to beat the weather. At the tail-end of the halibut season, late November, after a month of fishing the furious gale-driven seas south of Cape St. James, the southernmost tip of Haida Gwaii, the winds flared from Force 9 to Force 11, *Violent Storm*. The skipper bucked the Bull Performance into the fifty-foot waves and roaring wind for two sleepless days and nights before their luck expired and a massive wave broke over the boat, slamming with its full weight and force against the two-storey steel cabin, blowing out every storm window and shearing the walls from their welds. The crew abandoned ship, and three of the seven, Francis's friend being one of them, never made it out of the black and icy water into the inflatable life raft. The next night the surviving crew was found hypothermic but alive, drifting in the aftermath fifty miles southwest of where they'd signalled for help, just thirty miles downwind from where the *Bull Performance* was found, still afloat, its cabin twisted and set back six feet onto the back deck.

It makes Francis weak to his very core thinking of it now as the wind and waves rise around him. He's always sworn he would never fish the open waters; that he'd never put himself at the mercy of the merciless wind. And yet here he is, at the wheel of a boat he doesn't know the capacity of, one he's never seen more than a six-foot chop in, in the middle of the North Pacific. The sails are near-bursting with wind and the rigging is a clangorous cacophony of straining steel. He leans to port and pukes his guts out. He hasn't the slightest clue how to sail through this storm as it ratchets up moment to moment.

The lightning has ceased, St. Elmo's fire has extinguished, and they're in one dark, howling cavern now, sailing downwind with the main reefed halfway down, which might seem the preferable direction, not having to scale the front face of cresting waves growing steeper and taller with every successive ascent. But Francis knows better. He knows every time the boat catches the crest of a wave and careens down into its trough, gaining speed until it slams into the base of the wave-back before it, is the height of seafaring danger. The boat's centres of gravity and buoyancy go ass over snout every time it surfs down a wave, and it's only a matter of time before the centres slide past each other and the boat does the same, flipping aft over bow. It is the cause of the majority of all capsizing occurrences, and Francis knows they're sailing on the brink.

But there is something that happens inside a person at sea when caught inside a storm. There is a point where fear surges into further territory. Into grandiose fright. The eye of the sailor peers inward and finds a reservoir of defiance not normally called upon and not often known of until that moment. A moment of fierce self-awareness. Francis shifts into this state, with a steeled resolve. To survive. To meet the storm head-on, with strength and will, and not surrender his clarity and dignity to the raging sea. A very sad, very human posturing in the face of a power so much greater than we are the mind balks at the magnitude, then reduces it through such devices. *So that's how it's going to be is it? Alrighty then. Bring it on, baby!* A product of adrenalin, ignorance, fear and delusion. But it works for Francis, gets his equilibrium re-established, gets him in the game when Miriam emerges from the cabin with a harness and a plan. "Put this on and clip into the jack-line," she yells over the wind. "We've got to reef the rest of the main down and batten down the hatches."

The wind has reached Force 10, *Storm: Very high waves with long overhanging crests. The resulting foam, in great patches, is blown in dense white streaks along the direction of the wind. On the whole the surface of the sea takes on a white appearance. The "tumbling" of the sea becomes heavy and shock-like. Visibility affected.* Stability affected. The ability to steer the boat affected. To work the rigging and sails, to reef them in, affected.

"Wait until I tell you, then spin the wheel to starboard," Miriam instructs him, calling through the driving rain. "We've got to get the nose to the wind to get the sail slack." She hands him the boom line. "Haul this in as the boat turns to the wind. Keep the boom steady." She snaps into the jack-line and jumps out of the cockpit.

Francis doesn't have his contact lenses in, so he squints hard into the pelting rain and the foam-furrowed dark. The boat is keeled so far over, walking the deck is like traversing a mountain slope of rushing water, the hull shuddering underfoot as it slams to the bottom of another steepening trough. Miriam struggles along, half-hanging off her connection to the jack-line on the upside of the slope. When she reaches the mast she raises her arm in the air. And when she spins it above her head in the starboard direction, Francis spins the wheel.

Erasmus of Formiae

THE EXACT REASON for St. Erasmus's designation as the patron saint of sailors is in fact a matter of contention and speculation. The story of his initial torture and persecution is but one supposed origin. As another tale goes, he was giving a sermon on a ship at sea when the sky suddenly darkened and a tempest descended. Undeterred by the storm, Erasmus is said to have continued preaching as the sky filled with wind and rain and lightning, one of the bolts striking him clear in his praising, uplifted hand and surging in a crackling flash through his entire body, igniting the floorboards at his feet. And still he spoke the word of God.

Here's another speculation. The origin of his other saintly designation, that of intestinal ailments, of colic in children and the cramps and pains of women in labour, is undisputed. Legend has it that after having his limbs and neck stretched on the rack, Erasmus somehow escaped his Roman captors. He fled to Mount Lebanon, and for a time survived in the wilderness on the scavenged scraps the local ravens fed him. Eventually recaptured, he was brought before Diocletian's co-emperor, Maximian, who once again had him flogged with whips and beaten, then stuffed into a barrel full of protruding spikes and rolled down a long hill. Following his barrel-roll, he was coated with pitch, set aflame and thrown into a dark, solitary dungeon to starve. Again he escaped and roamed the Roman provinces emboldened, preaching the story and message of Christ, converting pagans to Christianity, until he was again recaptured in Salona, the capital of the province of Illyricum, in what is now Croatia. This time he was sent directly to Rome, back to Emperor Diocletian, who ensured this would be the last time Erasmus would be dealt with. He had his men spike him to a table and carve his stomach open. Then he had them cut his intestines away from his abdomen and wind them around a windlass. A windlass, the same device used to haul a ship's anchor from the ocean bottom.

Intestinal pain? Stomach ailments? Francis's retching attests to the seafaring relevance as he again heaves his guts out onto the deck at his feet. He can't stop, and is near useless, despite his recent resolve not to cower in the midst of the storm's anger, its obstinate aggression. He drops the line Miriam gave him and the boom swings free on its hinged clamp, port to starboard, with each pitch and roll of the hull. He lunges forward, groping on the cabin roof for the boom line, but is blinded by the pelting rain and the tears welling in his eyes from his stomach's spasmodic convulsions, so he doesn't see the line or the boom as it swings toward him and slams him in the head, knocking him down, instantly unconscious, folding like a torn sail untethered to the deck.

St. Vitus's Dance

HE WAKES INTO a bright beam of light. Hears Anna calling from somewhere far beyond its source. *Wake up*, she is saying. *My God, I can't do this without you. Wake up.* He feels her hands on his skin not because of their coldness (his flesh is as frigid), nor their rhythmic kneading on his naked chest (he's gone numb), but because they are hers, and he would know them anywhere.

～

A POOL OF darkness. It sways and rumbles and pounds. Like inside a hollowed heart. The thrum of omphalos blood. Anna, six months pregnant. He comes inside her, then dissolves between her legs, his head on her belly, ear to her womb. *Hey little one*, he whispers. And the little one responds, a gentle nudge to his skull from beneath her skin. Afloat in that warm saline dark.

෨

HE'S CONVULSING AND she's holding him, trying to steady him, trying to soothe. It moves through one limb, then another, St. Vitus's Dance, an inaudible measure moving in his mind.

෨

WILLOW HAS THE blunt edge of a maul rap-rap-rapping on my skull. Anna's watching from the window with a smile. Open your eyes, *she's saying.* Open your eyes.

෨

WEEPING. WRAPPED IN a warm body weeping warm breath in his ear. *Anna? Miriam: the boat: the storm.* Fear, a convulsion cascading from the coccyx to the crown chakra, a pulsating stream. The fontanelle gushing out and sucking in the dream. The way an infant comes to this world with the other still clutched in its eyes, dark portals, diminishing in this world's wanting light.

෨

WHEN HE RESURFACES from beneath the waves of shock and concussion, it's to the wind-chime ringing of the stays and halyards lightly clanging. The hull gently rocking on the settling seas. The smell of metal and sweat and salt, and Miriam, her smell of grass-lands and apple cider, enwrapped in her legs and arms and chest. He puts his hand to her face, the air passing lightly from between her lips. He puts his lips to hers and pulls her warm air in, little ventilator, resuscitator, spirit bellows.

⌇

IT IS SAID trauma and orgasm are two of the temporal paths to timelessness, to God. To be concussed is to be set adrift on an ocean of ethereal unknowing. To fuck is to dive in, shallow or deep, as many depths as swimmers and crystals of salt. To orgasm is to dive down to the stars—a wormhole loop—and for an instant and an eternity at once, brightly burn.

⌇

THEY ARE LYING in the aftermaths, of the storm and of *their* storm. Drifting like the boat, without course or bearing. Just waking. "Are you okay?" she asks, passing a finger over the point of swelling at the top of his skull. "It didn't even break the skin," she continues. "It's been two days. You've been sleeping. I've been mending the mainsail." He focuses his eyes on the teak and mahogany inlay pattern on the ceiling above Miriam's bunk where they lie. He groans a long, long exhale. "Where are we?" he finally asks.

"A few days from Hawaii still. Three, maybe four," she answers. "We're not under sail," she continues in a whisper, her mouth close to his ear. "The storm passed overnight. We've been drifting for al-most two days. I've been down here watching over you, afraid you might break into fever. You've been in and out of sleep."

"I know, I remember," he says. And the image of her arched back in orgasm above him flashes through his mind. The feeling of being in her thighs like being swaddled, and the sickness passing from him, and the coolness after, falling again into sleep. He remembers shaking, and shivering, and then receiving her around him, and the ensuing calm. "I feel fine," he says, finally answering her question. "I'm fucking starving, but I don't know, it feels like nothing happened." He says this in a way to address his injury and their lovemaking both, and she comprehends it as such. She runs her hand down his arm as he sits up, the blood pounding between his eyes. He's lying, of course, on both accounts, and he knows she can tell. But Francis isn't one for dwelling or complaint, for drawing out in conversation the obvious, and he feels the world coming back to him, and with it his sense of urgency.

"I'm fine," he reiterates, easing his naked body down from the bunk. "Come on. Let's hoist the sails."

The Tears of the World, I

THE PEAKS OF Mauna Loa and Mauna Kea are the first sights of Hawaii to come into view on the western horizon. Neither of them thinks to break into Dylan. The night before, eavesdropping on the chatter of various ham radio operators, Francis had overheard word of Mauna Loa's and Mauna Kea's simultaneous eruptions. Another strong quake shaking the mountains at their base. And now they're sailing straight toward the spewing mountains, just as some of the island's inhabitants, and all its tourists, are attempting to flee. "This is fucking ridiculous," Francis says. "What the fuck are we supposed to do now?" He's noticeably irritated, and has been, more or less, since waking from his concussive sleep three days previous.

Miriam steps lightly around his moodiness, and so hesitates before addressing his concern. "We'll just have to land and see what's going on," she finally says.

"What's going on is that people are evacuating the island. Look at all the boats," Francis retorts, handing her the binoculars. There is a motley armada of sailboats and cabin cruisers offshore of Hawaii, headed northward to the island of Maui. Likewise, the air around the island is filled with a swarm of small aircraft, float planes and helicopters. "It's uncanny," she says.

"It must be the float," Francis says, and jumps down into the cabin. When he returns it's with the float in one hand and a cast iron frying pan in the other.

"What are you going to do with that?" she asks, knowing the answer already.

"What do you think?" he says, and puts the float on the cockpit deck. He lifts the pan over his head and brings it down fast and hard, as though he's clubbing an ancient sturgeon over the head. It ricochets off the float and bashes him in the shin. "Fuck!" he wails, dropping the frying pan to the deck, grasping his shin, hopping up and down on his unharmed leg. The float rolls with the lean of the boat and settles in the sternward portside corner of the cockpit. "You've got to be kidding me," Francis yells at the float and Miriam both. "What the fuck is going on here?"

Miriam isn't sure whether to laugh, as she's inclined to do at his childish temper tantrum, or to talk him down. Given his recent trauma to the head, she decides to take the cautious approach.

"What the hell are we supposed to do with that thing?"

"We're supposed to deliver it to Sunimoto, like we've arranged."

"Wouldn't you say the molten lava running down those mountainsides might be a bit of a sign to the contrary? I mean, first the earthquake in Vancouver, now this!"

"What else have we got to go on Francis? Obviously you or I can't break the thing. Maybe this Sunimoto is the man who can. Or he knows the man who can, or will be found by him. Or maybe it's all just another of the countless everyday coincidences and there's no meaning at all to be ascribed to those mountains erupting." She feels this last point may be overextending the argument, but she makes it anyway, an attempt at some sober-minded rationale in the midst of a situation which is swiftly sliding far from the comfortable bounds of reason and predictability.

"Come on Miriam," he grimaces back at this. "Drop it. You know as well as I do there's way more going on here. Shit. I just hit that thing so hard it should be in a million pieces at our feet. But it's not. It won't fucking break. What are we supposed to make of that?"

"I don't know Francis. But the fact is, you need to calm down. We've sailed all the way here and the only thing to do is deliver it to Sunimoto and get your money." She pauses for a moment, an epiphany of remembrance washing over her so strongly that she can't believe it hadn't occurred to her sooner. "I'll tell you something. After Arnault first told me his story, I was skeptical, but still curious. So I did some research on what I could, on Churchward and plate tectonics, on the possibility of any sunken continents, and on Mauna Kea. One of the things I found out was that Mauna Kea is a dormant volcano. It hasn't been active for almost five thousand years. It's a post-shield volcano, which means its caldera has been filled in by various layers of cinder cones. If there's no caldera, then how are the shards supposed to be thrown into it? It seemed like such a simple and major flaw in Arnault's story that I called him to ask if he'd maybe gotten it wrong, if maybe Mauna Loa was the mountain. I told him that as I understood, Mauna Kea is less than fifty metres higher than Mauna Loa, and that height is a result of magma accumulation which has occurred much more recently than the supposed sinking of Mu. But he said no, it was Mauna Kea, the tablets from which they had deciphered the myth were quite clear, it was to be the tallest volcano of what remained of Mu into which the shards were to be thrown."

Miriam bends down to pick up the light-blue float at her feet, then continues. "When I asked him how he thought this would be possible given that there was no longer any caldera atop Mauna Kea, he replied quite simply that the mountain would erupt, contrary to all geological precedence and predictions, and the conduit would be reopened to receive the glass. And there it is, Francis." She points to the high mountain now in plain view on the horizon.

"Just like Arnault said. And it might be we're here to do as we are. To deliver this thing to the one man who can do with it what needs to be done."

⌐

GERMAN ASTRONOMER JOHANNES Kepler, widely considered one of the fathers of the Scientific Revolution, the contributor of a link in the chain of ideas which led to his contemporary Sir Isaac Newton's law of gravity, believed that volcanoes were ducts for the earth's tears. Tears of smoke and fire and scalding hot molten lava. Francis doesn't know that the thought he is having is one that once occupied, resolutely, one of European history's great minds. Nor is he a proponent of James Lovelock and his Gaia theories. He's unwilling to anthropomorphize the entire planet, or anything for that matter, an insulative stance not uncommon among modern fishermen. To anthropomorphize is to risk empathizing with another species or object. Sympathy is one thing. But to empathize with the object of one's own mass slaughter is a slippery slope—not one Francis has been willing to even approach the edge of.

But as Miriam steers the boat into the north end of Hilo Bay, inside the mile-and-a-half-long man-made spit of rip-rap breakwater extending across the bay, he thinks it: *the tears of the world.* It's in keeping though, with the aspect of silent sadness Francis has assumed in recent years in response to the world's dwindling and decline, antithetical to Miriam's excitement and anticipation as she cruises the boat parallel to the rock wall's inner perimeter, to its far southern end, into Radio Bay. The closer she gets to the impossible flowing and billowing of the Mauna Kea, the more an acceptance of what once seemed preposterous settles in. *Horace,* she thinks. *You kooky old sod. If only you could see us now.* And she can't help but wonder, in the light of all that's transpired, if it might be possible that in fact he can.

If Francis knew her thoughts at the moment he'd be liable to smack her. He's morose about the prospect of Sunimoto being locatable in the current state of crisis sure to greet them on land, if indeed he hasn't already evacuated the island. A cacophony of sirens can already be heard ringing out from the streets of Hilo. Francis imagines pandemonium: a state of desperate emergency, people everywhere crying out and rushing in panic to escape the flood of molten lava slowly sliding down the mountainside. Which makes his surprise twofold when they reach the dock and a very small, very calm Hawaiian man takes the spring line from his hand and helps to tie off the *Princess Belle*.

"Francis Wichbaun and Miriam Maynard," he says. "Welcome to Hawaii. My name is Tito." They both look at him with incredulousness and incomprehension, to which he laughs a warm, friendly laugh. "We have a car waiting to take you to Mr. Sunimoto. I will explain while we drive. Please, come. As you can well see, time is of the essence."

～

IT'S INSANE, THE feeling of moving so quickly within such narrow, confined margins only moments after stepping from a three-week cruise on the open ocean. They're in a white SUV with tinted windows from which they watch the countryside of green fields, macadamia and palms careen by as the driver barrels the vehicle up the winding asphalt. Tito explains how and why it was he was there awaiting their arrival prior to their landing at Radio Bay. "Mr. Sunimoto is an exceedingly wealthy man, and he is a man with only one desire. To find what it seems you might possess there," he says, indicating the blue tote set behind them in the back of the vehicle. "When the mountains exploded, as we'd expected they would, we knew it to be a sign that you were close, and so Mr. Sunimoto has had me stationed at Radio Bay waiting for you since last night. It is the only easy moorage in Hilo, so it was a safe assumption you would arrive there, which you have. And welcome to you! Although it is not the most ideal of circumstances, we are more happy to have you than you can imagine."

Francis's head is spinning and pounding and he is having trouble getting his bearing, his grounding, as the vehicle moves at a fast clip winding further and further out of town and into the hills. He grabs hold of Miriam's hand and grips it tightly in his. "Pull over," he says. "Now! Pull over." Tito has his driver pull over and Francis falls from the vehicle and ejects the contents of his stomach onto the roadside. Outside the air-conditioned suv, the day is oppressively muggy, and Francis breaks into an instantaneous sweat. He retches again, then scans his sightlines. *Where the hell am I?*

"Are you all right Mr. Wichbaun?" Tito asks from his unrolled front passenger window. Francis wants to say no and run. Nothing feels all right to him. Not this place, not Tito, not driving farther and farther away from the boat toward the slow river of lava flowing down the Mauna Kea. But he knows he can't be sure of his instincts. That they've been altered by his time at sea, his injury, and his being enveloped in Miriam's presence these past three weeks. He's an animal out of his natural element—all the green is too green, too bright, the air too humid, the earth beneath his feet too dusty, yet dark—and so he's without power, which may be all that is giving him pause. He climbs back into the vehicle and takes the bottle of water offered by Tito. "It's going to be okay," Miriam whispers in his ear. "We'll deliver this thing, get your money and we'll be gone."

The driver idles the car by the roadside while Francis drinks. "You're all right then?" Tito asks. Francis nods. "Good. I'm sorry to have to ask you to do this," he holds two black sheets of cloth out as he says this. "But could you please tie these over your eyes." It's not a question, quite obviously.

"You're kidding, right?" Francis says, looking to Miriam for backup.

"I'm sorry Mr. Wichbaun. Mr. Sunimoto must maintain absolute secrecy as to the whereabouts of his home. I'm sure you can understand."

"No fucking way," Francis says, feeling instantly claustrophobic at the thought of wrapping his face in Tito's black cloth. Miriam takes his hand. She's feeling uneasy too at the prospect of being taken blindfolded up into the hills of a foreign island by these two strangers, but she trusts enough in those who originally put her in touch with these people to not let it get the better of her.

"Again, I'm sorry Mr. Wichbaun. But there is no way we can proceed from here without you putting on the cloth. It's for your own protection, too." Tito drops a cloth in each of their laps. "Not proceeding is not an option. So you must please put these on."

"I don't like how this is going," Francis says, and he tries to open his door, which is locked. "Open it," he says to Tito. "Open it!"

"Please put the blindfold on," Tito says, no longer with the soft and patient tone he's thus far maintained.

"Open the fucking door!" Francis shouts, lunging at Tito, who lifts a small handgun from his side and presses it to Francis's oncoming forehead. Francis freezes, then eases back into his seat as Tito guides him with the end of the gun still pressed firmly between Francis's eyes. Tito looks at Miriam, who settles back, too.

"Look," he says. "I'm sorry we have to do it like this. But it's just the protocol we have to follow. We're not here to hurt you. Quite to the contrary. If we were going to cause you harm we would have done so a long time ago. Now, Mr. Sunimoto is waiting. It is supposed to rain later this afternoon, and if it does, it won't be safe around here any longer. Please Mr. Wichbaun. For everyone's sake, just put the blindfold on and we'll proceed."

Miriam leans over and takes Francis by the hand, then looks to Tito to indicate he should back off. Tito takes the gun from Francis's head and recoils to his seat. "We have to trust them," she says to Francis. "There's no other way to do it. We're in this now for better or for worse." She takes the cloth from his lap and folds it over several times, then lifts it before him, leaning in. "We'll make it through this," she says to him. "We've made it this far, haven't we?" She places the cloth over his eyes and his sight goes black, then she reaches behind his head and ties it off tight.

Francis listens as she ties her own over her eyes, Tito and the driver sitting silently up front, waiting. He'd like to ram that gun up Tito's ass. He doesn't take well to intimidation, but he knows there's no winning in this scenario. Miriam places her hand on his leg. It's warm and loving, the way she holds his thigh, and he allows himself to drift back into the concussive dark of her bunk and their slow, feverish fucking. She's taking him inside of her, all of him, as the suv pulls back out onto the road.

The Tears of the World, II

UNEASY OR NOT, they're both thinking more or less the same thing as they step from the vehicle to the cobblestone driveway: what *does* a twenty-thousand-year-old man look like? Of course, there's been no clarification as to whether this Sunimoto man is indeed the guy, or is even standing in for the guy, but much has been insinuated by Tito, and so much might be assumed. And it still stands that neither Miriam nor Francis is wholly sold on the whole Mu thing, though it is undeniable to both that the evidence is mounting. "I am so sorry about the blindfolds," Tito says to them, handing Francis his tote. "Please follow me. There is very little time to spare."

Sunimoto's house sits backed against a high cliff of rock in a small clearing surrounded otherwise by trees. There is a black helicopter parked on the lawn behind a house much more modest in its size than in its detailing. It's octagonal in shape, like Fairwin' Verge's treehouse, but the similarities end there. There are posts of ornately carved teak and wide windows, some inlaid with stained glass patterns of vine and leaf. A two-tiered glass pagoda rises up from the centre of a copper-shingled roof. There are three doorways to pass through, two separate vestibules, before entering the living area of the house. At each vestibule Tito punches in a code on a security pad and the next door slides open. Francis is wondering if PINE-APPLE is what he's keying in, and thinking so sparks enough of his sense of humour to relax his shoulders a bit and unlock his jaw.

Tito leads them into the centre of the house, the living room, above which the pagoda rises, infusing the house with daylight. No men with guns. No shadowy corners. Not what Miriam and Francis were expecting following their blindfolding. "Please, sit down and be comfortable," Tito says. "I will bring you cold drinks and inform Mr. Sunimoto you have arrived." He leaves them both to seat themselves on the triangle of couches at the centre of the room. Miriam sits down and looks to Francis to do the same. "I'll stand," he says, stiff-lipped.

"Relax, Francis," she implores him.

"We're not safe here. Something's not right Miriam. I don't like this place."

"You're overreacting. Come sit down."

A middle-aged Japanese man strolls toward them. He has silvery hair and smooth skin. A bright face. "Welcome," he says to them. "Miriam and Francis, I'm Minoru Sunimoto." Again, not what either of them was expecting. No arthritic, hobbled wrinkle-face, this Sunimoto. He shakes their hands and seats himself opposite them on a blue leather loveseat. "You've had a long journey. I can only imagine. It's been a long time since I've been to sea."

Tito brings them drinks and seats himself beside his boss. He looks up to the pagoda above. "We need to move this along. The rain is starting." They all look up and watch the thick drops begin to pelt and stream down the glass. A sound like distant thunder can be heard approaching. The sucking thump of helicopter blades. Tito stands, as they all cast their gaze skyward, wondering.

Before they can react further, the pagoda explodes in a shower of tempered glass. They tuck into themselves as it rains down upon them. When it stops, Tito is the first to spring from his curl. The helicopter hovers above as thick lines of rope unspool into the house. Two figures fall from the helicopter, rappelling toward the hole in the roof. Francis and Miriam are uncurled now too, stunned. When Tito pulls his gun from his jacket and starts to fire, they bolt for the doors.

One body, then the other, drops from the sky to Tito's feet. One lands on top of the tote holding Francis's float still within it. Francis wants to retrieve it, but Miriam holds him back and Tito waves him off.

"Go!" he hollers. "Go to the truck." He fires more rounds through the hole in the roof, then tucks Sunimoto under his arm and runs toward the back of the house as bullets start bursting through the hole onto the floor.

An entourage of armed men approaches the front entranceway and the doors slide wide open. All but one of the men race into the house past Francis and Miriam. The one who stops yells at them to run for the SUV over the racket of gunfire and helicopters. There are now three hovering above the property, disgorging machine-gun fire and rappelling lines. The army of men who have emerged from the forest perimeter return the fire, thwarting any attempts by the attackers to rappel to the ground.

"It's fucking raining bullets out there," Francis screams back at him. "No fucking way." The armed man hurls Francis into the driveway, sending a spray of bullets toward the two helicopters within firing sight. Then he does the same with Miriam.

They're both out in the open, exposed in the torrential downpour now dumping from the thick clouds overhead. "Run," the man screams, sending more bullets skyward. Francis and Miriam both make it to the white SUV and dive in, Francis at the wheel, Miriam in the back seat. The key dangles in the ignition. Francis turns it over and slams the vehicle into drive, spinning around on the wet cobblestone and flooring it down the driveway. Miriam watches out the rear window as the man who hurled them toward the SUV falls to his knees, then his face.

One helicopter spins out of control into the cliff-face behind the house and explodes as Sunimoto's lifts into the sky. One of the two remaining ambushing helicopters pursues it. The other hovers while three men rappel successfully to the ground, then it spins and propels itself through the air in pursuit of Francis and Miriam as they catapult down the long, slick driveway. A cluster of bullets slams into the SUV, shattering the window glass Miriam looks through just as they pass into a tunnel of overhanging trees.

Francis is a single thought in every aspect of his mind and body: *Drive.* "We've got to stop. Stop the truck Francis," Miriam yells at him. He doesn't respond, pushing his foot further to the floor. "They can't see us right now through the trees. Once we're out from under them, we're fucked. Stop the truck Francis." But he hardly hears her inside his focused fear. She leans over and puts her hand on the wheel. "You have to stop the truck Francis. When we come out from under these trees, we're fucking dead." *Fucking dead*, and her face thrust beside his gets through.

He looks at her, then up to the trees. "Okay what?" he asks, pulling the truck over. "What do we do?" He's panicking, she can see that. She files through their options in her head, all of them the shits, then she decides. "We've got to get into the forest," she says. "We can't stay in this truck."

Miriam leaps from the SUV without another word or thought, running, then nearly free-falling down an embankment reminiscent of the one that leads to her beach of homage to the ocean, or did, before the tsunami washed her vast collection of glass floats, and the rest of her life, out to sea. She's a woman untethered—her two girls launched into their own lives and so more or less estranged—sliding down a rain-washed bank with nothing but her survival to run for. Nothing but her survival and her love for the man now falling into the forest behind her.

The Lahars

Lava flows at differing speeds, depending on its composition and viscosity, and of course upon the degree of slope down which it slides. The lava spewing from the Mauna Loa and the Mauna Kea is basaltic, and has been, until now, creeping slowly down the two neighbouring mountainsides. The Mauna Loa is a continuously active volcano, having a major eruption on average every twenty-five years. As a result there are fixed channels, the hardened flows of the past runnelling down its various faces, which the fresh lava moves over or between, unhindered. The Mauna Kea hasn't erupted in 4,500 years, and so it is more consistently forested below its barren alpine slope. But this upper slope is nearly twice as steep as the Mauna Loa's, so the flows, though obstructed by the forest, have enough momentum to keep pace with those of the Mauna Loa. Now, with the rain dumping over both these flows, the water is thinning their viscosities and slickening the earth over which they descend, mixing the lava with mud to form lahars, lava-heated slides building in breadth and velocity. Hilo is the wettest city in the United States, and one of the wettest in the world, measuring over two hundred inches of rainfall per year. When it rains in Hilo, it pours.

Francis and Miriam are trudging down the northern bank of the Wailuku River, through thick groves of unfamiliar trees. For three hours they have alternately bushwhacked thick brush and traversed open riverside fields, neither of them knowing where they are, only that the river will lead them to the shore, and on that shore will be, hopefully, the *Princess Belle* still tied to the dock in Radio Bay awaiting them. They are both soaked, fearful, hungry and exhausted, the river flowing full in a torrent of white beneath them. It grows louder and louder until they find themselves at the top of Rainbow Falls.

If either knew the geography of Hawaii they would know they were less than two miles from the boat. But instead they're both feeling lost, dusk is falling, and Francis is the first to assign blame. "I told you it didn't feel right Miriam. For Christ's sake. Now what? Even if we get to shore and figure out where the boat is, who is to say they won't be waiting for us there?" They're standing on a large outcropping of black pyroclastic rock above the falls, the rain relentlessly pelting down. At the edge of the rock, an eighty-foot drop into an emerald pool of water, the falls roiling the water to white at its high side. They yell to be heard above the swollen, raging waterfall.

"It's not like we had any choice, Francis. You think if we refused to get in the truck with Tito he would have just left us with the float? Not a chance. Evidently someone wants it bad enough they're willing to kill to get it."

"I'd say they have it by now, wouldn't you, Miriam? Don't you think maybe it would have been smarter to stay home and wait for them to come to us?"

"Wait for who? Sunimoto's boys with their machine guns, or the guys in the helicopters? What makes you think we'd be any safer at home than here?" When she says this the thought of Anna and Willow flashes through his mind. Jin Su and Emily, too, and he realizes how stupid he was to come here, to this foreign island, where he's at the mercy of things he has no resources to control. Where he can do nothing to protect his family, both his families, and he again feels sick to his stomach. He turns from Miriam toward the forest, readying to retch, when he sees the grey-black liquid running out from beneath the underbrush. It streams in thin rivulets down into the river.

"What the fuck's that Miriam?" he asks, turning to her. The rivulets widen, and widen, until there is a continuous flow spilling from the forest, steaming and hissing as it enters the river.

"It's lava," she answers. "That's a lava flow, Francis," she says again, comprehending what's suddenly upon them. She swings her head around, scanning their surroundings while Francis watches the dark liquid gush just beneath their slightly elevated perch. "We have to jump, Francis. We've got to get under the falls." Francis looks down into the pool below, still green though the white froth of the falls is starting to blacken with the infusion of the thickening lahar now risen to within inches of their feet. "We have to jump!" Miriam yells as she grabs his arm and, running, pulls him over the edge into the air.

In the Cave of the Goddess of the Moon

"I'm cold, Francis," she says, shivering. It's his turn to hold her body still now. On any other night the fall's white water would be illuminated by the moonlight, but tonight the Wailuku River runs black, a cascading curtain across the cave mouth, so Francis and Miriam huddle in a darkness thick as that in Fairwin's fort. They've both stripped off their drenched clothes and are sitting side by side on a low rock shelf at the back of the cave. Exhausted and disturbed beyond the prospect of sleep, they both stare silently into the roaring dark, reliving the day, bewildered.

Miriam can't comprehend how Tito knew they'd be arriving at Radio Bay when they did. She'd lied to Francis when she said she'd arranged the meeting with Sunimoto over the shortwave that first day on the boat. Without her cellphone, she was unable to recall any of the contact numbers she would have needed to do so, so she passed some time at the nav station putting in another call to her eldest daughter Esther instead, then lied to Francis to keep the boat moving westward, knowing she could always sort things out once they got to Hawaii.

She doesn't know that Fairwin' found her phone, or that he had its memory recovered. And even if she were to guess at that, and at his contacting of Arnault Vericombe, she wouldn't ever suspect or imagine that Sunimoto was in fact an employee of Arnault's. So she's perplexed, just as Francis is at the more obvious intrigue of the day's events. Who is Sunimoto, really? And what about the men who attacked his compound by helicopter? Francis accepts that Sunimoto knew he and Miriam were coming because he doesn't know of her deceit. But what about the ambushers? How did they know of their arrival? And why, really, is the float of such value? If it truly was to be broken by Sunimoto and thrown into the Mauna Kea's reopened conduit, who would want to stop him? And why?

Miriam has asked herself the same questions, and she's thought to voice them, but has remained silent instead knowing any speculations would be only that, and so without purpose or consequence. When she finally speaks, it's because the air in the cave has become a creeping chill up and down the naked skin of her back and she can no longer bear it. "Please hold me," she says to Francis.

"Where are you?" he asks—meaning *in what way do you want your body against mine?*—but she is already leaning against him, easing him down onto the rock. She curls her back into his chest, pulling his arm across her stomach. His hand cupped in hers, she presses it over one of her breasts.

The lava cave beneath Rainbow Falls is said to be, in some accounts of the Hawaiian myth, the former home of Hina, Goddess of the Moon. It's said that Hina lived there with her mortal husband and her two sons until the day she grew weary of her worldly work and family and decided to climb the rainbow that forms in the mist at the base of the falls. It is said she first attempted to climb to the sun, but its intense heat overwhelmed her once she was above the protection of the clouds. So she returned to the earth to regain her strength. Then one night she climbed up on the moonbow which forms also at the base of the falls. Her jealous husband fought to keep her this time, wounding her leg onto which he clung, before she kicked free of his grasp and ascended to the moon, where she has resided since, and always will, at peace in her home in the heavens.

The first time Miriam and Francis made love was marked by a desperate intensity. It was devoid of temperance and tenderness, awash as they both were in Francis's sickness and the sea's still-waning temper. But being inside the cool, dark, resonating ground is pure yin. Miriam takes him into her, plunging like he did into the pool as she pulled him from the edge of the ravine at dusk. His body falls deeper and deeper into hers, unseen in the unriven dark. When orgasm finally flushes through him he exhales, only then realizing that for a long, long time he's been holding his breath, a diver caught in an undercurrent of water; and lying intertwined with her afterward, he thinks of the bliss supposedly felt when one dies of drowning.

〜

SHE DREAMS OF hovering over her house in Jim's helicopter, watching the tsunami wash over her orchard. Then she's standing amongst its apple and plum trees, the crickets singing in the tall grass beneath a full and radiant summer moon. She smells the first windfalls turning on the earth, the salt breeze up from the beach. The helicopter is ascending swiftly, vertically toward the sun. A single plum in her palm, broken, so summer soars out. Its sweet scent and kaleidoscopic light. The whirring blades lifting, lifting over the earth. A dragonfly's-eye view. An endless humming of insects from inside the grass. Yule. Francis. Yule-Francis. Her womanhood beating like insect wings inside her. The blurring propeller overhead. She unbuckles, unlatches the door and dives from Jim's side into the air, ascending through the blue sky as though rising up through water, through water to moonlight cast above a surface of rippling waves.

He dreams, too, the archetypal dream of breathing underwater. He dreams her—Miriam, Anna and Jin Su—amalgamated in a single, ever-fluxing body of water. His soul's ocean, or so he dreams it. He's carrying Willow and Emily, both as infants, in a sac of flesh on his back like a seahorse does his young. Emily and Willow grow larger as he swims, now stretching from his lumbar to his shoulders, now from the back of his knees to the crown of his head. Then they swim off, and in the blindness of the depths Anna's voice comes through the pressure roaring in his ears. He feels cold, through and through.

For a long time he hears the voice only as a distant, drifting melody, like listening to her hum in the shower down the hall while cooking dinner in the kitchen of their home. He's set the table for two, a single candle burning at its centre. He hears her open the bathroom door and start toward him down the hall, her gentle footfalls, the shower still running, as he takes two plates of food to the table. He sets them down, steps to the window and looks out over their front yard to the quiet country road beyond. Anna comes up behind him, naked, wraps her wet arms around his chest, and looks over his shoulder at the moon he's been staring at, too bright and too close in the sky. Everything appears pale and frigid, as though coated in frost.

When they wake in the first light of morning they're in the opposite position to that which they fell asleep in, Miriam cradling him now, warm despite her naked back being open to the air, Francis huddled and shivering in her arms.

I'm OUT ON the front deck smoking the last of a pack of tailor-mades I bought after the homegrown ran out. I wouldn't have thought I'd have so much trouble going without the nicotine, but since hearing news of the eruptions in Hawaii last week I'm at my wits' end, so I'm taking my smoking of shit-tobacco in stride. Willow's at the beach again. The weather has been our saving grace, hot and humid every day and night. It helps to keep the mind in the immediate. Helps keep a relatively positive outlook on things, which is all I can do, given the lack of any word from Ferris. I've got to keep it together for our son; keep him convinced that everything's all right. I lied to him a few days back and told him his father had called, and ever since then the anxiety that was starting to wrinkle his forehead has relaxed and he's been down at the beach long days again instead of hanging around the house worried and clingy as he was starting to do.

I haven't seen Svend or his niece since they were here for dinner, but I can't stop thinking about Jin Su. It was like déjà vu having her in the house. Almost like I'd seen, even known her before somewhere, somehow. I thought maybe she'd been at UBC in the years I was there, but she said she hadn't been. Then I thought maybe we'd been neighbours, but when I told her where I'd lived in the city she said she'd never lived anywhere near those places. She seemed uncomfortable after that, so I stopped asking. But it's been bugging me ever since. She just seemed so naturally *here* to me. Like she already had some place in my home, in my life. It must be what kindred spirithood feels like, an instant familiarity. It's like I've already known the particular smell of her. And her way of quietly pausing before she speaks.

So I've tried to see her several times since, but there is never anyone at Svend's when I go by. Which is probably for the better. I know I'm just looking for distraction, someone to talk me out of my own head, of the worry whirring around, keeping me up all night smoking. And all day too, sitting out here on this front porch with my little pack of corporate sinsticks and my dog-eared copy of *The Plague*, possibly not the best medicine for my affliction, except it has in it for me, in some of its passages, a nostalgic familiarity that's comforting.

> *But the narrator is inclined to think that by attributing over-importance to praiseworthy actions one may, by implication, be paying indirect but potent homage to the worst side of human nature. For this attitude implies that such actions shine out as rare exceptions, while callousness and apathy are the general rule. The narrator does not share that view. The evil that is in the world always comes of ignorance, and good intentions may do as much harm as malevolence, if they lack understanding. On the whole men are more good than bad; that, however, isn't the real point. But they are more or less ignorant, and it is this that we call vice or virtue; the most incorrigible vice being that of an ignorance which fancies it knows everything and therefore claims for itself the right to kill.*

What's interesting to me is how people today call upon our

ignorance, our collective unknowing, to justify their killing. People won't stand against the fish farms because the science is incomplete, inconclusive. So too with global warming. And of course it always will be, as the scientific method is not designed to address problems of such magnitude. It encourages exclusiveness, not synthesis. Specification, not generalization. And so people have turned to our inability to shrink the intricacies of the natural world down to lab-sized proportions as their excuse for carrying on with business as usual. The diesel's burning cleaner, but it's still diesel. Everyone still does the once-a-decade reno, but now it's LEED-certified. There was a time in the movement when people were hopeful. They thought that if the public just knew what was going on, if the information was made available, or even better, if it was made saleable, marketable, packaged up and sold in theatres and on television, that things would surely change. They agreed with Camus insofar as they thought too that people on the whole were more good than bad; that callousness and apathy were not the general rule. Which they may not have been, in Camus's time. Ours has shown otherwise.

Of the two, our modern apathy is the vice that seems to get all the attention; it's a kinder, gentler killer. It assigns responsibility elsewhere, whereas callousness assumes it. Given the knowledge that the acidification of the world's oceans is killing off marine life—from krill to coral to blue whales and cod—and that this carbonic acidification is caused by shipping food from across the globe to our refrigerators, or flying ourselves around the world to gorge at all-inclusive smorgasbords, most people continue to fill their cupboards and fridges with box-store groceries. Even of those who make the leap to locally grown, organic food, most still see the virtue in a quick flight down to Mexico mid-winter for a week-long stay at some swank gluttony palace. What, other than an all-pervasive callousness, can such obvious disregard be attributed to? Near-sightedness? Weakness? Stupidity?

> *In this respect our townsfolk were like everybody else,*
> *wrapped up in themselves; in other words they were*
> *humanists; they disbelieved in pestilences. A pestilence*
> *isn't a thing made to man's measure; therefore we tell our-*
> *selves that pestilence is a mere bogey of the mind, a bad*
> *dream that will pass away.*

People can't see beyond their own noses. Or if they can, they don't seem phased by the fact that the view is of a world diminishing in our poison and ill care. It's their own ambitions and dissatisfactions, their own anxieties and fears that occupy their minds, when you get right down to it, not the dwindling of species, not the desert we're making of the future. I've been thinking for days of how to save the salmon from the farms under such conditions. The judicial inquiry Alexandra has put so much hope in is shaping up to be a whitewash. So what's left if not the courts, the government or the people? Eco-terrorism? But how do you sabotage fish farms without doing collateral harm to the wild species you're acting to protect? And what does one person rotting in jail for such a crime accomplish?

There are over 130 fish farms in BC, or there were before the tsunami. So there's still probably 100. Who cares? Sometimes I feel like the fight has been pared down to a few delusional contenders shadowboxing in their little corner of a ring no one's watching. Sometimes I think Ferris is right, I keep it up out of sheer habit. Last fall he wagged the latest issue of *The Walrus* in my face, insisting I read the cover article. *The Fix for Planet Earth: How human ingenuity will save the day*, the title set over a front cover painting of futuristic airplanes and some kind of massive particle emitters towering into the sky. "Get that trash out of my face," I'd said to him at the time, and if it weren't made of glossy magazine paper I'd have used it for fire starter. I found that issue under his bedside table last night and sat up reading the article he'd so wanted me to nearly a year ago now. It's full of pathetic statements of dark resignation dressed up in glittering facades of courage and hope: *Our future will be very, very different both from today and from some idealized pastoral past, likely much more artificial, and yet luminous in the constellations of possibility it offers.* What a load of urban-centric horseshit! But I had to pause at the author's critique of the movement when he quoted the aphorism, *Insanity is doing the same thing over and over again, but expecting different results,* because that's what we, what I've been doing all these years.

Despite all our efforts, things get exponentially worse. For the salmon, the whales, the bats and honeybees, our children. So where does that leave me? With a choice between resigned complacency or anarchy? Between inaction or terrorism? The future decline is a *fait accompli.* But there's still the question of what kind of world we'll build within it. It's a redundancy, my sitting here thinking this all out on my front porch. But it helps, my time-worn copy of Camus and this ongoing argument with Ferris occupying my afternoons. Helps me forget that I'm only passing time here, a simple small-town girl with a head full of half-baked ideas, trying not to think of him as he is now. Out there. It helps take my ear from its anxious anticipation of the silent telephone in its cradle.

⤸

FAIRWIN' VERGE COMES through the garden gate and up the front path with a tall, skinny man in tow. He's got a pencil-thin moustache, this man, and he's wearing glasses thick as engineered glass. They're both marching in a very hurried and deliberate manner. I hardly get out of my chair and they're already up the stairs and beside me on the stoop. "Where'd you get off to?" I ask Fairwin', but he doesn't address me with an answer.

"Where's Willow?" he asks.

"He's not here. Why? Who's your friend?" I don't trust a single person I've ever met from Lasqueti Island, especially not crazy old Fairwin', and I don't trust this spindly bespectacled man he's brought along with him either. Then it strikes me as possible that they've come with news of Ferris. News of the worst kind, and my knees almost give out beneath me. "Have you heard from Ferris?" I ask, my voice cracking under the strain of my fear.

"No," Fairwin' says. "I'm sorry," he almost stammers, and he actually seems for a moment to be embarrassed by his lack of empathy and manners—which is, from what I can tell, a cornerstone of his character. "We haven't heard anything from Ferris. We were hoping you had. This is Arnault Vericombe. He's a friend of Miriam Maynard's, the woman Ferris is sailing with." I shake this Arnault man's hand. He's got a limp, slippery handshake that makes me want to shriek him right off my porch and out onto the street. I can't see his eyes, not really, through the thick haze of lens he wears over them, and it makes me uncomfortable.

"I'm Anna," I say, not offering him my last name, something I often do to people who creep me out when I first encounter them.

"Monsieur Arnault Vericombe," he says in a tense, nerdy voice. "A pleasure to meet you." There's nothing worse than a nerdy voice with a French accent. He's wearing a casual suit, white slacks and shirt and a grey blazer. Obviously he's very wealthy, or at least wanting others to think of him as such. If he is wealthy, it's new money, and there is definitely nothing worse than a man with new money and old-world blood. It gets my hackles up.

"What can I do for you?" I ask, trying (unsuccessfully, I think) not to descend to Fairwin's level of gruffness and lack of decorum. "What do you want with Willow?" I address my questions to Fairwin', who looks immediately to Vericombe.

"It's a bit complicated," Vericombe answers. "Perhaps we could discuss it over tea or something of the sort?"

I was looking for the short answer, hoping my pointedness might get them on their way and me back to my Camus. "Of course," I say. "I'll put some on. Or maybe you want something colder? I haven't got much, just water and…"

"Tea will be fine," Vericombe interrupts me. "We'll wait out here on the porch," he says, seeming swiftly and suddenly exasperated— perhaps, I'm thinking, by my less-than-easy answer to their inquiry as to my son's whereabouts.

When I return to the porch with a pot of tea and two more mugs Vericombe is seated on the couch beside my rocker, alone. "Where'd he go?" I ask, not really interested in the answer. The only thing I want to know from these two is anything they might be able to tell me about Ferris. I set the mugs and tea down at Vericombe's feet. He's wearing classic leather deck shoes, dark blue. Asinine-looking, everything about him.

"He said there's a store a little further down the road. He's gone for supplies."

"Unless supplies means magazines, pop or Twinkies, I don't think he'll find much. They're still running pretty low on stuff."

"I'm not sure what he's after," Vericombe offers. "He is an odd man, isn't he? I don't pretend to understand what he's up to. He tells me he's a good friend of your husband Ferris though." He says this as if it were a question, and I realize that this Vericombe man knows Fairwin' perhaps even less than I do, so I ask.

"You don't know Fairwin' very well, do you?"

"We've only just met yesterday. He called me on my cellular three days ago. I was home in Seattle at the time. I arrived on Lasqueti last night and we came directly here this morning." I offer him no response or encouragement, so he continues. "It is of the most urgent nature, the matter we've come to discuss with you. I'm not sure where to begin." He looks at me closely in the eyes. Or so I think. His go so screwy it's impossible to be certain of their direction. He's like that idiot on that *Trailer Park Boys* show, only worse. I find it disconcerting, dizzying. To my relief he looks down at his mug and takes a sip, then continues. "Did Ferris tell you why, miss...?" He's asking for my last name. He's just the kind to do so.

"Anna. Please call me Anna," I say, spinning it politely back at him.

"Anna, then. Did your husband tell you why the float he'd found was worth so much money?"

"No. I mean, he said it was very rare. But something tells me there's more to it than that."

"Indeed there is. I see you are a reader Anna," he says, dropping his screwy gaze to my ratty Camus. "Albert, one of our greatest treasures. Ultimately a bit of an ass, but brilliant nonetheless in his time. Are you familiar with the work of James Churchward? No? I'll give you the much-abridged version, Anna. The float your husband found is intricately connected to the sinking of the continent of Mu some twenty thousand years ago, and to the deterioration of the oceans today. This is not something widely known, obviously, nor is it something well understood by those who do know of it, but it is clear that your husband is now a part of it, of its unfolding, and we think he might be in the gravest of danger as a result." I start laughing. I can't help it. He lost me at the sinking continent bit, his little pencilly moustache wriggling away above his upper lip.

"Listen. I know it sounds ridiculous to you. I won't try to convince you to think otherwise. But consider this. Your husband sailed to Hawaii to deliver his float to a man for the sum of $150,000. The man he delivered it to was an employee of mine. This man, who has worked for me in a loose affiliation for over seven years, has since gone missing. His helicopter departed from my compound outside of Hilo and never landed in Maui. We don't know what has become of him, but we suspect the worst. So we are charged with three things now. To find him, to find the float, and to find Miriam and your husband."

I've reined in my laughter and I'm listening now. "Who's we?" I ask, realizing that, as goofy as this man and his story are, this involves Ferris, so I'd better get a grasp on it.

"We're a loose network of followers of Churchward and his ideas. We call ourselves the Children of Mu. I assume you've never heard of us before, either?"

"I can't say I have," I reply matter-of-factly. "But that's irrelevant. Where's my husband, Mr. Vericombe?"

"We're not certain. That's what I wish to find out. There are others in our organization who are seeing to the whereabouts of my employee and the float, but it is up to me to try and locate your husband. We suspect, we hope, he left Hilo Bay heading north on Mrs. Maynard's boat a couple days ago. Other than that, it's a big ocean, if in fact they're even upon it."

"Well I haven't heard anything from him since he left. So what do you propose to do now?"

"I have a boat. It's fast, safe and equipped specifically for this expedition, with all the tools and equipment needed to find your husband. We would like you and your son to come with us to Hawaii to do just that. Today. There's not a moment to spare."

I can't help but to laugh again at this. As if in a million years I would do such a thing. "Not a chance," I tell him, letting my irritation show through in my tone. "There's no way I'm getting on a boat with you and fucking Fairwinner, and there's definitely no way my son is."

"I understand your concern Anna. But be assured you are safer with us than you are here alone. Please hear me out for a moment. The people we suspect have taken both my employee and the float are likely operating under the same assumptions as we are. Those assumptions are as follows. First of all, the glass float your husband found must be shattered and thrown into the conduit of the Mauna Kea in order to halt the snowballing extinction of marine species worldwide. Secondly, your husband, being the one who found it, may be the distant but direct descendent of the Naacal fisherman who made it. And thirdly..." he pauses here for a moment. "Tell me," he diverges. "Is your husband's grandfather or great-grandfather still alive?"

"No," I answer.

"Good. Fairwin' has already informed me that Ferris's father passed away when he was young and that he has no brothers," he says, before I get a chance to ask what relevance his question has. "Thirdly, being the living direct descendents, it will be only by your husband's and your son's simultaneous efforts that the float will be broken. These are things we have learned through our deciphering of many ancient tablets found in both the Marquesas and the Yucatan. Our understanding that breaking the float falls to all those living in the patriarchal line of the man who finds it is one that we have done our best to keep secret for as many years as we have known of it. My employee in Hilo was set up under the alias of Mr. Sunimoto and we've worked to create a mystique around him, disseminating a false myth that suggests our Mr. Sunimoto is the ancient fisherman himself, cursed to live until his task of finding the float and destroying it is completed. In this way, the Children of Mu have bought and destroyed every float known to be found of the type your husband possessed, looking always for that one that will not be broken so we might teach the one who finds it what must be done with its shards. It was me your husband was to meet in Vancouver. When the earthquake hit I tried desperately to reach Miriam, who had set up the meeting between us—though she did not know it was me whom she had arranged for your husband to meet. But her home was destroyed in the ensuing tsunami. I had no way of finding her, or your husband, or even knowing if either had survived, until Fairwin' called."

He licks and sucks at his lips, then smooths his fingers over his moustache, uncrosses his legs and leans in closer to me. "The float won't break, Anna. According to Fairwin' he watched it fall from his treehouse forty feet up, bounce off a rock, and continue on for some distance down a steep, rocky slope. When they found it, there wasn't a scratch on it."

"Not a single scratch, Anna," Fairwin' adds. He's standing in the doorway, having obviously come in through the back of the house from the lane. He's holding a large tin of tomato juice and a pack of playing cards. "You've got to understand, I was skeptical, too, but if you had held that thing, felt how fragile it is, and then seen it hit that rock and bounce off it like a soccer ball... I was still skeptical, even after that..."

"But when the Mauna Loa and the Mauna Kea erupted, he called me right away," Vericombe interrupts. "See Anna, the tablets predict such disasters if the float does not reach its proper destiny in a timely manner once removed from the sea. It is the myth's own self-corrective power. If the float is in danger of falling into the wrong hands, it triggers a natural disaster akin to that which sunk Mu. Earthquakes and volcanic eruptions. Tsunamis."

"Miriam told us all this the night before she and Ferris left. I thought the whole thing to be a bit of a stretch at the time. But it all adds up Anna. There are too many coincidences to have no meaning, and what other meaning could there be?"

I light myself a smoke while they both banter at me, their voices rising in volume and excitement as they feed off each other's enthusiasm. Fairwin' is almost frothing at the mouth, little spit bubbles forming at each corner. They're both sweating. I take a hard drag. It's too hot on top of the heat of the day and it triggers a coughing fit in me. When I finally recover myself, Fairwin' has opened his new deck of cards and spread them out on the worn deckboards at my feet. "Pick three cards," he says. "Any three."

"Oh for Christ's sake," I say to him, and cough again.

"Please Anna. Choose three." I look at him sideways, then I slide three from the floor as Vericombe looks on. "Now pick up the rest of the deck and shuffle them back in." Why not? I play along, reshuffling the cards several times. "Now spread them out as they were before." I do this, too. Fairwin' reaches down and selects three cards, then turns them over. Ace of diamonds, jack of spades, two of hearts. The three cards I selected. "How did I do it Anna? Was it magic or sleight of hand?"

There's a presence in Fairwin's eyes I've not seen before, a focus of thought, and it strikes me that I've perhaps written him off unduly because of his association with Lasqueti. Perhaps there's more to this man than I've assumed. I lean back and take a lighter drag. "Of course it's not magic," I say, exhaling, with only the slightest of doubts as I speak. "Are you certain Anna? So certain you'd be willing to bet Ferris's life on it? Ferris is somewhere out there Anna. And even if you don't believe all this, there are people who do. Dangerous people."

"We've tried as much as possible to disguise the true identity of the one, or ones, as the case is, who must break the float. But your husband's meeting with Sunimoto was ambushed, and though we've been given a detailed report of this, and we know, or think we know, that your husband and Miriam both escaped unharmed, we don't know how the very secretive whereabouts of our location in Hilo was known to those who carried out the ambush. If they believe the false myth we've propagated, then our Sunimoto is already dead, and your husband and son are in no danger. But if they know the truth of who it is who must break the float, as I suspect they do, they are hunting your husband as we speak, if they have not already found him. And they will be coming here for your son, too."

⁓

I'M RUNNING DOWN the beach screaming for Willow. Where is he? Across the sand, over the rocky point, out onto the intertidal estuary. Barnacles, mussels and muck sucking and crunching underfoot. I scream out his name again, wheeling around on my heels. He's not here. The waterfall! I run toward the mouth of the creek and start thrashing my way through the ferns and salmonberry bushes, over blowdown alder and erratic boulders. I find him tucked in behind the trickling little falls, caving. That's what he calls it. Caving. He's built a bed of twigs and moss up beneath the overhang and placed a little log above it which he's using as a bench to sit upon while he picks pebbly stones from the cliff-face as though he were an archaeologist. He studied the Coast Salish peoples in his social studies component this past school year, and he's spent these few weeks since the quake scanning the beach for smooth little stones with a hole bored through the centre, sinkers the Sechelt and Sliammon made to hold down their fishnets, or digging for arrowheads and other rare artifacts up here at the falls.

"Willow," I call out, but he's so engrossed in what he's doing that he doesn't hear me. When I get closer I can hear he's singing a little song to himself, not one I recognize. Most likely one he's made up while sitting here picking at the earth. I duck under the dank overhang and put my hand on his shoulder. He turns to me. "Mom. What's the matter?" I'm out of breath, and I've got leaves and twigs clinging to my clothes and tangled in my hair.

"I couldn't find you at the beach. I was worried." He's perplexed. I'm usually pretty lax about his whereabouts. As I said before, I trust him. He's a careful child.

"But you know I'm always here if I'm not at the beach," he says, picking an alder leaf from my hair. "I know Bub. I know." I'm still trying to catch my breath as I talk. "I want you to come to the house, okay?"

He lifts a stone from his bench and holds it up. "Look what I found," he says excitedly, beaming up at me. I take the stone from his hand and inspect it. It's flat, palm-sized, roughly triangular. It could easily be mistaken, in a child's wishful eyes, for an arrowhead.

I haven't the heart or the time to burst his bubble. "You found an arrowhead!" I exclaim. "Finally."

"Yeah. And I bet there's more here too. I knew I'd find artifacts here Anna. This is a midden."

"That's great Bub." I hand him back his arrowhead. "Why don't you come home for lunch now, sweetie. There are some friends of Ferris's here I want you to meet." Distress washes over his face when I say this.

"Is he okay? Is Dad okay?" Willow only refers to Ferris as Dad or to me as Mom when he's frightened.

I give him a big hug, holding him tightly to me. "He's fine," I say, still holding him tight so I don't have to look him in the eyes as I lie. Then I release him, holding him in front of me at the shoulders. "But he's broken down out on the water and these friends of his have a nice big boat for going to get him. And they want us to come with them. So you've got to come. They need us to leave with them right now."

⤺

I'VE HAD SECOND thoughts ever since we kicked off the dock. Both of these Frenchmen are nutty and now I've put my life and my son's life in their hands. But what else could I do? All the asinine myth stuff aside, if any of what they've told me is true, about people hunting Ferris and Willow, then I need to help find Ferris and I need to keep Willow safe—though I'm not sure being on this boat with captain coke-bottles qualifies. The boat's huge, though, and seems sound enough. She's probably over one hundred feet long. Some kind of small freighter. *Naacal Warrior*. For the love of God! There's a little blue helicopter strapped down tight to the front deck with *Churchward's Angel* painted on its tail, and beside it a big, high-powered inflatable skiff with *Sohqui* emblazoned across its bow. Whatever that means. I imagine there's a good quantity of rust beneath the fresh blue, green and white paint Vericombe's had the ship's hull and cabin coated in, but the engines seem to be purring along nicely, and the engineer, a stout and stocky man introduced to us as Figgs, seems serious and capable. Willow's taken a shining to him since he took us down into the engine room to show us around. Still I'm uneasy.

I put Willow to sleep in the second-storey stateroom we were assigned aft of the cabin—the boat's three storeys high: galley, head, first-aid and storage on the main, bunks above, and the wheelhouse deck above that—but I couldn't sleep, so now I'm up playing rummy with Fairwin', who also can't sleep, though not on account of any uneasiness or anxiety, but because of the engine noise. "There was a time I wouldn't have batted an eye. When I worked the lighthouses that diesel sound was always there, day and night. But I've been living in the forest so long now," he explained to me when I first wandered into the galley. He was playing some kind of solitaire when I came in. Now he's got me roped in with a cup of herbal tea and his insistence I sit down for a game of cards. I want to know what Fairwin' really thinks of all this; of Vericombe, and this glass float mythology that's claimed my husband and child as its unwitting heroes. So I've taken his tea and he's presently walloping me at rummy. "Vericombe tells me you haven't known him long," I say, laying down a low run of spades.

"He arrived on Lasqueti yesterday. It's the first time we've met."

"So what? He's a friend of this Miriam lady, right? Did she leave you his number before she left in case something went wrong or something?"

Fairwin's wrinkled face brightens when I ask this and he seems to be lost in his memory for a moment. "I suppose you could say that," he says, grinning. "Miriam dropped her phone from the cliff below my house the day before she left. I found it last week in the alder bottom while looking for oyster mushrooms. It was all smashed up, but I brought it up to the house anyhow. I thought I'd throw it in the garbage next time I went to False Bay. When I heard about the eruptions in Hawaii, like I said earlier today, I thought maybe it was too much coincidence to be just that, so I had this guy I know on Lasqueti recover the phone's memory. I recognized Arnault's name as the man Miriam said had told her the myth, so I called him."

"And here we are."

"And here we are. Rummy," he says, and lays down the remainder of his hand in one go, a straight flush of diamonds, seven to king, three aces and three fives. I fold my cards on the table without acknowledging his latest in a string of wins.

"You don't actually believe any of this shit do you?" I ask. "I mean, I'm here because there's obviously a bunch of quacks who believe in this stuff and I'm convinced it's possible that some, if not all of them, are dangerous. And I want my husband back. But it's a little much, don't you think?"

"There was a time, Anna, when people thought the world was flat."

"That's right, and they also thought it was the centre of the entire universe. But it's not. We know that. And we've known the story of Atlantis is just a story for a long time too, Fairwin'. So what gives? All of a sudden Hawaii's the tip of a sunken continent and my husband's found a fish float that sets off major earthquakes whenever it doesn't like the way things are going?"

"Possible. It's possible."

"I suppose. In the same way it's possible that hell can be reached by passing through seven gates at the end of Toad Road in York, Pennsylvania. Come on. This is fanatical cult stuff, Fairwin'. I wouldn't think an old misanthrope like yourself would go for it."

"I'm not a misanthrope, Anna. I'm a recluse."

"What's the difference?"

"The difference is I'm not absolutely suspicious of every other person's motives. And I don't assume superiority because I know better or more than others."

"That's not my point, Fairwin'. My point is these people have got my family all wrapped up in something that shouldn't have anything to do with us."

"As far as they're concerned, it has got everything to do with you. Or at least with Ferris and Willow."

"And what if we're getting caught in the crossfire of some battle between two factions of this cult, this Children of Mu thing?" I lift my pack of sinillators from my pocket and take one out.

"You can't smoke that in here, Anna," Fairwin' reminds me.

"Honestly," I say, as I light the smoke. "Do you think I give a shit? Vericombe gets my son. I get to have the odd smoke. Seems fair enough to me."

"No one forced you onto this boat, Anna. You and Willow could be home alone right now if that's the way you wanted it."

I consider this for a moment. Have I made the wrong choice, getting on this boat? What if Ferris shows up at home while we're off in Hawaii looking for him? The magnitude of it, the ludicrous idea that we could just go find Miriam and Ferris. But what if he is in trouble or danger and we don't go searching for him? And once again, what if there really are dangerous people coming after him, and Willow, too?

"There's a big difference between what I want and the choices I've got," I say. "I may be here Fairwin', but it doesn't mean I don't think this whole thing is fucking insane. These people want to believe in some stupid myth about ocean life dying off because of some curse put on a fisherman and his glass ball tens of thousands of years ago? It sounds to me like a particularly hare-brained attempt to not acknowledge responsibility where responsibility lies. I'd have an easier time being on a boat with the global warming detractors. At least they're dealing in real world matters. Sort of."

My second-hand smoke is hanging as a thick cloud between us, obscuring my view of Fairwin' as he leans back beyond the glare of the one shaded bulb burning above us. "There are matters in this world beyond politics Anna," he says, the condescending fucker. I'd like to stab his weathered eyes out with my burning cherry, but instead I stand up.

"You know what I think? I think you're as unsure about this whole thing as I am. I think you're scared," I say.

"I saw that glass float fall Anna. It didn't have a scratch on it. I'm convinced there's something going on here. It may not be all that Arnault believes, or exactly as he believes it, but it's not to be brushed aside because we can't comprehend it. If there's one thing I've learned in my life Anna, it's that things are often much more, or much less, than they seem. Either way we're just along for the ride and all we can do is hope things don't get too bumpy along the way."

Cliché statements like that don't deserve a response, not in my eyes. So I scoff instead, get up from the table, cross the galley and exit out the cabin's side door.

It's cold out on deck. There's no moon visible through the light cloud cover that blew in as the sun was setting. I lean my head over the railing and watch the steel hull skim through the water. We must be travelling at twenty knots or more. The breeze built by the momentum, refreshing earlier in the day, lifts and ducks under my clothes at the neck and waistline and sends shivers down my arms. It gives me goosebumps. I walk to the stern to take shelter and light another smoke. I know Willow's sleeping soundly. I've done a good job, at least, of convincing him that this is okay. That this is what we should be doing and that everything is going to be fine. I'm not so sure though, and I wish more than ever that Ferris had never found that float. Or at least that he'd not been so desperate to get the money from selling it, or to get away from me, that he chose to embark on this whole thing.

It's times like these more than any others that I need him. He used to have this ability to keep me centred when the whole centre of the world seemed to be spinning out of control. And I imagine he still does. That he could still do so if he were here, if I would let him. If I would trust him enough. But I know I haven't trusted him since he bought the boat. I knew it was a bad idea; too risky for our position in the world. The irony of course is that Ferris's ability to take risks is one of the things that first drew me to him. He was so ballsy and bold, he'd stick his neck out and try anything, undeterred by the perceivable obstacles, when he felt that things were right or worthy. He has good intuitive instincts, something I suppose he gained from growing up on Lasqueti, out in the world with the wind and the sea.

It does something, the wind and the sea, as it is for me now. It blows away all the crap so one can find clarity. I can see myself from a distance in my mind, tucked away in my office, avoiding Ferris. I can hear him pleading with me to stop hiding. Stop blaming him. To come out and help him sell his fish privately for good money, to make the fishing business work. And I can see myself instead slouching further and further over my own work, digging my heels in deeper and deeper, drawing a perimeter line around myself I refused to let him cross.

Life hasn't felt as precarious as it does now since before I met Ferris, when I was young and alone in the world, and it strikes me just how easy it's been to take for granted what his presence in my life provides. The stability of knowing he's always there. For better or for worse. He's asked me a dozen times or more through the years to exchange that vow with him. But I always assumed it already spoken, somewhere beyond words. I always assumed so many things. Simple to see, now that nothing can be assumed any longer, not even that Ferris is alive. Simple to see how easy it is, in the midst of it all, to take the one you love for granted, as if they'll always be there. And even more, to feel smothered by them *because* of this sense of permanence. And for a prevailing resentment to build up, a sort of sustained claustrophobic panic that obscures the reality of what and who that person is. Your family. Your home. Your one and only place in the world.

Now I'm wishing I'd said yes to Ferris. To his need to buy that fishing boat and all that it's brought us. To his need to stop fighting the world and instead build something he believes in within it. Because I can see now that's what he's wanted to do. To build a life that will be lasting for us, us and our son, something solid and stable, something with the prospect of longevity regardless of how the world changes or crumbles around us.

We've just rounded the southern tip of Vancouver Island and we're heading up Juan de Fuca Strait. I can see the odd bright light on the shore where Victoria once burnt its electric fire deep into the night. They're starting to rebuild already, crews working through the night under the light of glaring generator-powered halogens.

When he bought the boat, Ferris thought it would be our ticket out. A source of making a living somewhere further north, away from the city. Cortes Island, Malcolm Island or Echo Bay. Possibly even Haida Gwaii. Maybe Ferris was right. Is right. There's no stopping it. Them. Which is the same thing, I think, though some people like to speak as though it were otherwise. As if we're all just being driven by the momentous thrust of technology. The technology we design and build and implement. The machines we drive into and across and over the earth.

When I find you Francis Wichbaun I'm going to start saying yes. To leaving together. To building together. To being together. I'm going to leave the fight to those who have nowhere better to go to. Because I do. With you. For better or for worse. The next line's unthinkable, so I leave it unsaid, for now, with the million other things still unspoken. I flick my butt into the wake and watch it blink out when it hits the water. Then I head back in, calmed, to offer Fairwin' an apology. Ready to accept my decision to be here on this boat with these men on this journey. Ready to take on whatever comes next with as much courage as I can muster. With the kind of courage Ferris would have if he were here. The kind I know he has now, wherever he is out on this crazy sea.

The Variables

WITHOUT THE GLASS float or money, they motored out of Hilo Bay, both uplifted, despite all that had transpired, by the *Princess Belle* being still tied to the dock awaiting them. Uncertain what approach to take, they cruised northwest up the island shorelines, past Maui, for three hundred miles. They felt there was safety amongst the number of boats out on the water—many still shuttling people away from the calamity caused by the eruptions and the lahars—and both feared returning to land for the possibility of being found. Still, for two days they watched the skies instinctually, their ears keen to the possible *wump wump wump* of approaching helicopter blades, until their trepidation eased and they joined in line with the armada of boats waiting in Nawiliwili Harbour on the island of Kauai to refuel. With tanks topped up they set a course to magnetic north, hoisting the sails to take the trade winds abeam, and settled in again to the rhythm of the sea.

It's counterintuitive, under normal circumstances, to feel a sense of relief when watching from a boat's deck as the last sight of land slips from view, but Miriam and Francis shared a loosening sigh when they lost sight of the Hawaiian Islands over the southern horizon, putting the fear and failure of that place behind, leaving them to themselves—the now-familiar world of living and sailing together on the *Belle*—and the long journey home.

↩

THEIR NIGHT IN the cave below Rainbow Falls works like a harrow in both their minds. Miriam had known she desired him, but that night she'd experienced what she hadn't expected: love. The kind she'd had with Yule when she was young. A love so entirely clear it was like the cadence of the moon's tides moving through their bodies in the dark of the nowhere and everywhere they were together, a place their union took them outside, beside, space and time, a portal to something perfect and pristine both beyond and within this world otherwise altered. It's upon this otherworldy ground that any and every true marriage—consecrated or not before any god or church or state or otherwise—is founded. And it is upon it also that these marriages flourish or founder.

It's what has kept Francis and Anna together, ultimately, and it is also what has torn them apart—because it is ground too sacred to keep to for us despoilers, us little rogue beings. We want it like a drunk wants a drink, or a junkie a fix, always after the bliss of that first kiss, indescribably sweet, the taste we carry hauntingly on our tongues. Some addicts will spend their life's last cent, will submit the last of their body's ability to survive, to re-attain what they experienced when the heroin first shot like the cool breath of god across their brain, a cheap synthetic facsimile of the flood-waters true lovers swim together. Similarly, some lovers will fuck each other to the other side of love to swim or drown again, for even the slightest taste of that elixir, then try to wring it from each other in fits of rage and violence until one or the other or both lie breathless by the other's hand. It's completely beyond the realm of the rational.

For Francis, the waiting has required more faith than he has had the capacity for. His first few years with Anna were woven together by the occasional ascension back to that ground, and so it was easy to keep the rope that bound them together taut. Of course they fought, and fought more and more as their love slipped into routine, unsuccessfully scaling the heights of the walls their day-to-day lives built between them. But then there would occur a re-infusion, a reconnection, a re-journeying to that place Miriam and Francis have now shared. And so they would start afresh, falling back with time into a mundane, profane familiarity closing in on them, claustrophobic, until they would begin to turn acrimonious toward each other, fucking almost aggressively to fight the feared, inevitable spiritual and sexual ennui, until they would somehow push past it, back to that place of rejuvenation and replenishment.

But since Willow's birth, they have not been back there. Anna has understood this, due much to her mother's counsel through the years, as a not-uncommon state for those in early to mid-parenthood, and so she has held to her memory of what she and Francis once shared, and to her love for the child they do share, and though their love's estrangement has lasted much longer than she'd expected—on account of Francis's straying into his other life with Jin Su—Anna has not thought more than fleetingly of stepping from their marriage.

Without any sibling or close parent as confidant, for many years it was Anna who acted as both best friend and counsel in times of trouble for Francis. But when the afterglow of Willow's birth and infant year diminished, and he bought the boat despite her cautioning and reservations, she became more and more his adversary, until he lost sight of what she'd once been to him, of what they'd once shared, of the love they'd achieved. He began to doubt in his mind that it was ever anything other than the desire-induced hallucinations of the young, naive and mutually solipsistic.

But what occurred with Miriam in the cave has reawakened him just as it has reawakened her. To love's potential, to its true essence. And to the love each still has for the one with whom they first attained it. Which has cast them both into a state of divergent clarity and confusion, him longing for Anna and her for Yule as they both simultaneously desire each other. They sailed north of Hawaii for eight days without either of them properly noticing time's passage. Countless occasions they set the autopilot and radar alarm and ducked below deck to Miriam's bunk, or made love in the hot sun on the smooth teak capping the cabin roof. They fucked each other raw trying to get back there, to that precipice, and it wasn't until the wind died five days ago that they sobered up and it set in for each that what they'd found in the cave had somehow been given by some force beyond their control—just as the wind was, and now was not, filling the *Belle's* sails—and it was not again to be found together, no matter the desires they submitted to or efforts they made together to make it so.

〜

THE HORSE LATITUDES. The calms of Cancer. The variables. On the ninth day from Hawaii they passed into that zone again, multifariously named, where the cold recirculating winds of the Hadley and Ferrel cells converge in the tropopause and sink, creating two hundred miles or so of variably light to calm winds; a place of pause amidst the massive machine of the world's ever-churning winds. For anyone sailing on the conveyor-belt coursing of the trades it comes as a sudden jolt to the system, as though some god has flicked a massive reset switch or cut the wire that sends the winds their ever-present power. Everything changed for Francis and Miriam the day they crossed over, though it wasn't the wind's recession exclusively that put a tether on their mutual obsession, but rather two things that happened concurrently.

The night the wind subsided Francis was at the wheel while Miriam slept in her stateroom below. Exhausted as he was from the upheaval and turmoil of the past month coupled with their insatiable lovemaking as of late, Francis had fallen asleep in the cockpit again inside a cloud-covered night so black keeping watch was staring into an immediate, oppressive abyss. He woke up to the sound of the sails flapping in the diminishing wind, the boat bobbing on the waves, making no headway. So he lowered the sails and started the diesel, which woke up Miriam for a moment as it sputtered and rumbled, warming to its duty, then sung her with its vibration back into sleep.

For a few hours Francis motored northward, kept awake by the thrumming diesel, until it sputtered and choked and abruptly died. This time Miriam was deep into her dreams, and she did not wake. Francis went below and pulled up the floorboards to access the engine room. He found water in the primary fuel filter when he drained it off, and it was black with dirt and grime when he removed it from its housing. He replaced it, then unscrewed the secondary filter from the block. It too was full of water, so he replaced it and crossed his fingers.

By the time he began trying to restart the main engine Miriam was coming out of her dream, and the undesirable sound of the starter labouring to no avail brought her back to the boat from the one she'd been on with Yule in the Sea of Cortez, drifting on that bright turquoise blue. She felt a great pain in the left side of her abdomen again, the one she'd been feeling many mornings over the past month, and she became overwhelmed by mild, retching convulsions. Just as she heaved up a pool of bilious blood onto her pillow, the main engine surged to life. Francis revved it up full throttle to try to blow any air, water or gunk out of the head, and for a time it roared in the middle of the cabin, belts whirring. Miriam wiped her mouth clean, removed the soiled pillowcase from its pillow, and climbed from bed, holding her searing and tender ache with both hands. Then she collapsed to the floor, again spitting up blood into the pillowcase, as the main engine's revs dove, went quiet, then heaved, heaved again, and quit.

The Calms of Cancer

ON ACCOUNT OF their mutual, twofold ignorance, the tragic irony of *the calms of Cancer* is lost on Miriam and Francis both. Firstly, though they have each often heard the more common *horse latitudes*, and have their own vague ideas of why it is or may have been termed as such, neither has heard the thin windless region of the northern hemisphere they've entered referred to as *the calms of Cancer*—as opposed to *the calms of Capricorn*, south of the equator. Their other ignorance is of far greater consequence and is why the nature of the irony is tragic.

The first time Miriam fell into one of her depressions, half her lifetime ago, when Yule was still alive and Esther was still a breast-feeding infant, it had been symptomatic of her contracting the Epstein-Barr virus. Because both her daughter and husband didn't get sick themselves, and because her physician mistook her lethargy, depression and general ill-health as symptomatic of Seasonal Affective Disorder—sending her home with a bottle of little blue pills and a suggestion to return to Mexico as soon as possible—it went undiagnosed.

In oncology and haematology it's becoming widely understood

that viruses can trigger or lead to various forms of cancer. With Epstein-Barr, that is several of the eighty some-odd types of indolent, non-Hodgkin's lymphoma, one of which has been in Miriam's blood for nearly twenty years, at times flaring inside her so that she's gone back into the lethargic, depressive state she experienced when first contracting Epstein-Barr.

The pains she's been feeling in her abdomen with waxing and waning intensity for the past year have been caused by the swollen, hardened lymph nodes in her para-aortic and spleen regions, and more recently by the deterioration and disintegration of her spleen organ. If they were anywhere near a hospital she would be rushed to ultrasound and doctors would detect an extreme amount of fluid inside her abdomen. Her cascading blood pressure would indicate the fluid to be blood and an emergency laparoscopy would be performed. In the operating room, the surgeon would lift a mushy ball of flesh, her disintegrated spleen, from her abdomen. They would vacuum out the excess fluid, suture her and keep her in the hospital for a week or so on IV-drip antibiotics while they monitored her recovery and ran a battery of tests on her blood and body. They would find she was suffering from indolent lymphoma, stage two, possibly three, and they would send her home with a watch-and-wait protocol, as little else can yet be done by allopathic medicine for her illness. She would take it upon herself, because she is a fighter, not a flighter, to use her money to seek out alternative treatments throughout the world, and she would live many more years, in relative health, with an ever-renewing sense of happiness and spiritual contentment, knowing she was living on stolen time having come so close to death, all the more grateful for each blessed day she'd been given.

But on the *Belle*, the fuel tanks full of water and crud from the contaminated dregs of the holding tanks they filled from in Nawiliwili, she is drifting on the northward current further into the windless zone. The shortwave is overwhelmed with news and calls for help as a result of the massive simultaneous earthquakes in India and southwest of Indonesia occurring just days before, and of the ensuing tsunami damage to shoreline countries throughout the South Pacific and Indian Ocean, and Francis's calls for help go unanswered while Miriam, green-faced and weakening by the hour, drifts in and out of agonized delirium.

Without surgery there is nothing to be done for her. Francis finds an old prescription of T3s in Horace's head closet and tries to get her to drink them down, but they come back up in a pool of blood. She writhes through the days, drying and parched, the sun beating hot and unrelenting down upon them. Nights he lies beside her, in her rancid bed, and tries to sleep though she twists and wrenches, whimpering in the otherwise eerily silent darkness.

In the daylight he busies himself trying to get the main up and running. He drains the fuel lines and then refires the engine, rigging a clamp-and-cast-iron-frying-pan contraption to the ignition button so the starter will turn over while he bleeds the air from each injector. A couple of times he gets the engine to start, only to die within minutes as it again fills with water-contaminated fuel. The fourth afternoon, grease-smeared and defeated, he stands beside the engine, sweat dripping from his forehead, listening to the silence following the engine's once-again failing. He knows he won't be given another chance, the batteries too weak now to power another round of cranking the flywheel over.

Miriam groans from her bed below the bow. Beyond her closed door he hears her coming to, in unfathomable pain, and he's stripped to conceding that his attempts at restarting the engine have been admittedly futile; that they've been nothing more than his way of doing something, anything, in the absence of knowing anything else to be done, not wanting to give over to the inevitable death being brought on beyond her door. He lifts himself out of the engine room and replaces the floorboard. Climbing to the cockpit he scans the horizons. Identically unbroken, unaltered blue in all directions.

The first two nights of her sickness he'd fired flares up into the night sky, hoping to be seen from any boat over the horizon. But nothing. They're alone out here with whatever evil or ill energy has descended upon them. He thinks perhaps a jinx fixed by the float they failed to deliver soundly, by whatever consciousness it has which sets the ground to shaking—as it most likely has now in India—and sets the seas to swallowing the land.

He strips off his clothes, climbs onto the taffrail and dives, swimming as far out underwater as his lungs will allow. Then he resurfaces and continues swimming away from the boat, the water cool and enlivening around him, until he finally stops and spins onto his back, filling his lungs so he can float and stare up at the sun. He considers which will take more courage, to exhale and sink, or swim back to the boat, imagining the long, cold descent into the depths juxtaposed with Miriam's dying in her foul bed. As he turns his back to the sun and starts swimming for the boat, having made his choice, he feels like nothing but a coward for having done so.

⃊

FRANCIS REALIZES THAT, though he can't fix her, can't save her, he can come out of his shock, his panic and lack of presence, and in so doing there are things to be done to alleviate for her the worst of her suffering. He makes a bed of the salon and cockpit cushions above deck, at the bow of the boat, and carries her carefully—her bones turned brittle beneath her skin—from her stateroom to the open air. He lays her down, her body aflame with fever, and places sea-soaked towels over her naked skin, her gaunt, flaccid limbs so swiftly deteriorated from those toned and smooth that he'd groped and held less than a week before. In the sun he can see her body greying before him, her eyes darkening and receding in their sockets, and he knows it won't be long until she's gone.

For the past few days nothing but faint, indecipherable whimperings and whistlings, like light wind through cracks in a thin wall, have passed from her lips. He lies down beside her finally to listen. Inside the pain she is cutting the threads that connect her consciousness to her body. She imagines herself like a seamstress working to reset an elaborate garment, *snip snip*, go her little scissors. With each strand cut she recedes from the pain, further into a plane of light that flares with each beat of her struggling heart. From that place she felt him carry her from the dimness and into open sunlight, so she is surrounded both inwardly and outwardly by it, the heat unbearable but for the cool cloaks of water he sets across her. *Snip snip*, she cuts herself away as he lies down beside her. *Snip snip*, inside the red, sun-stained dark behind her eyelids.

He washes her, limb by limb, and holds wet cloths to her lips. He places his hand on her distended abdomen, but she winces, so he instead holds another wet cloth to her forehead, stroking the feverish sweat from her hair. When dusk comes he brings the sheet from his bed and lies beneath it beside her, speaking of their past month together, of his childhood, his own children, anything to keep the sound of his voice calmly flowing into her ear. He imagines it helps her, his being there, though for her his lilting voice is like a faint and distant seabird's calling carrying from the shore out to the boat she is on, the *Misty Girl*, with her two girls on the back deck and Yule at the helm, steaming away from the rising sun, out to the fishing grounds for another day of hauling and setting.

⌒

DOWN DROPT THE breeze, the sails dropt down, 'twas sad as sad could be; and we did speak only to break the silence of the sea. These verses—Coleridge's, though she thinks of them always as Yule's, the words he'd whisper in the morning to break the days of silence that would always follow whenever they'd have a roaring fight—these verses sing for days at the tip of her tongue, until on deck there in the early morning light she lets them pass by her lips, the iron taste of blood in her mouth, into the waking, windless air. Francis rouses from his sleep to the sound of her recital, comprehending *to break the silence of the sea*, as he comes to, a rush of hope lifting him to sitting as he does. He looks down at her eyes still sunken and dark, her skin lined and sallow, aged thirty years through these days of agony. Her searching eyes find him, as does her hand. He cradles it in both of his, cold and empty as it already seems, as the life lifts or falls from her eyes, he's not sure which, only that it's gone, she's gone, instantaneously so. There's no sense of her still in the body beside him, no lingering warmth of spirit to attend. Just this inexplicably wrecked body, the gas passing from it, vulgar and sickly. Death, in the guise and withered form of the woman he'd given himself over to, in fever and fear, and found in return a clarity of mind and heart he'd long thought lost; a clarity coming now into infinitesimal focus, coming terrifyingly clear in the absolute aloneness he's caught within.

The Horse Latitudes

HE ROLLS THE limp body into the sea. It flops like a rag doll over the deck-edge, arms dragging and slapping against the rail stanchions and the hull before landing with a splash supine upon the water. Upon, because the body floats, buoyant beside the boat, its wide eyes staring up at Francis as though with recrimination. As though to say, *How could you abandon me?* Though Francis knows he's only anthropomorphizing what is now no longer human. Death, in the guise and withered form.

Lowering the dinghy off the *Belle*'s stern into the water, Francis climbs in and paddles to the bow where the body nudges the hull. He ties a line from the stern to the body's arms, then he paddles out, away, all the while cursing the name of Horace for being so old-fashioned as to have a rowboat, not a powered skiff, for a dinghy. Had it been otherwise he may have devised a way to attach the small outboard to the *Belle* to use as a makeshift kicker, and in so doing he may have been able to drive them southward back into the wind. Then Miriam's fortunes may have been different; maybe a ship with medicines and medical personnel would have noticed his flares or responded to his calls for help. Maybe she'd be recovering and he wouldn't be towing this bloating, ruined vestige of her upon this desert of ocean.

A few hundred yards from the boat he stops and unties the line from the stern. The water is flat as glass, no swell, so the body lies still, unmoving. Francis waits beside it for a few moments. Forgetting himself, he sends a small prayer out for her in his mind, to wherever, whatever might be listening, though it's more from some sense of protocol that he does so. There's nothing out there. Francis can feel it, the vast emptiness of the air around him. If there are gods, or a God, they're not with him now. He has half a mind to keep rowing, and rowing. He thinks of that wife and husband from Vancouver Island who crossed the Atlantic by rowboat and lived to tell and write of it, to speak on the radio and tour their story across the country. To gain fame, and some fortune, by the fruits of their endurance. As he rows back to the boat he thinks of the story he'll have to tell of these weeks at sea, and with this thought the implication of Miriam's death seeps into his mind like a fear-borne contagion and he begins to consider the possibility he too may not survive. And then he thinks further, for the first time in weeks, beyond his immediate predicament, and wonders if he does survive who in his life—his children, his women—might still be alive to hear it?

⤺

FRANCIS HAS LEFT the dinghy tied off to the taffrail, floating in the relentlessly slack water, and occasionally he rows away from the sailboat, filled sometimes with a flush of false hope, sometimes with fear, sometimes with the emotion, less extreme, of out-and-out boredom. He's moving slowly northward on the current through the world of no-wind he's stranded within, but without any points of dead reckoning to reference he has no way of knowing this.

So the day after her passing, after an afternoon and evening spent in utter inertia, sleeping and staring into the emptiness of the air around him, he starts taking stock. He empties the galley cupboards of all their contents and determines he has food for another fifty days, sixty if well rationed. Beneath Miriam's bunk he finds two bottles of champagne, a corkscrew stashed between them. A night's worth, a celebration. He wants to drink them down fast, consecutively, but he places them instead back beneath the bunk, good keeping for when and if needed, and turns instead to the realization of his first major oversight: water.

There's no agreement amongst mariners or historians as to the etymology of the term, *horse latitudes*. The most accepted and agreed-upon theory of its origin comes from the time when there was a great amount of trade between continental Europe and the West Indies via the seas. It's said that quite often, stranded in the crossing of the subtropical high, Spanish sailors would be forced to corral their trade-horses overboard so as to conserve the water they required. Another, less popular theory contends that the horses were driven mad by the hot, stagnant skies, and were thrown to the sea so the sailors could be rid of their beastly insanity. Less popular still, some accounts insist the horses were in fact kept on board and slaughtered so the sailors could eat of them and drink of their blood.

With the batteries drained low from his many attempts to fire the main, the little one-hundred-watt solar panel won't provide the high amperage required for deep recharge. So although he's getting enough juice from the sun to keep the radio and lights on and the inline water pump delivering water to the galley tap, the desalinator won't make it past start-up surge, which leaves him only what's left in the storage tanks to drink from, plus any unlikely rain that might fall. Without tearing the boat apart so that he can get a good look at the size of the tank, he has no way of guessing how much water remains. He needs help. It's all he can think as he contemplates himself parched, dehydrating to death in the inescapable heat. In hindsight he sees that all the while he was trying to restart the main he should have been conserving battery power and focusing on somehow attracting rescue. Which leads him to his second oversight, which he will never see clearly, but will lead him to his third, which he immediately will.

In the first few days of Miriam's dying, consumed as he was in the panic and shock of the inexplicable thing that was happening suddenly inside her and the Murphy's Law scenario of simultaneously losing propulsion power, he'd obsessed over starting the main engine, stopping his wrenching only to tend to her and occasionally send out a distress call on the shortwave. Several nights he had spent hours radioing out into the ether without result. Why hadn't anyone answered? Sporadic chatter came through as always, but when he called out, no one called back.

He looks over the shortwave but all he sees is a simple radio with a volume, channel and squelch dial. He checks the handpiece connection at the back as he has many times before and as always it's secure. If he were to unscrew the radio from its mount and turn it upside down, he would find on its underside a little recessed toggle switch labelled CALL STOP. It's one of the many silly customized retrofits Horace decided upon, a means to prevent any future grandchildren from sending out a false SOS call while inevitably playing, against his "captain's rules," at the nav station.

What Francis hasn't known, and what Miriam in her agony had unsuccessfully tried to tell him several times, moaning almost incomprehensibly the two words, "stop calling," whenever she would regain cognition within the pain long enough to try—what he eventually misunderstood as her request for him to stop calling for help and instead tend to her, to be with her while she faced her final hours—was that she switched it on when they first left Hilo Bay, afraid that outgoing communication might alert any possible pursuer to their position. A superfluous precaution taken in the midst of the fright-induced, unreasonable paranoia they shared and re-inforced for each other those first few days following the ambushed meeting with Sunimoto. So Miriam had lay dying while he hollered frantic pleadings for help that were never transmitted. It wasn't, as he had thought in the absence of any other explicable reason, that there was no one listening within his transmission range, or that all emergency monitoring had been narrowed only to the areas af-fected by the Indian quakes.

The oceans, as the world, are no longer that large. It's rare that any boat is ever more than one hundred miles off from another, and shortwave single side band transmissions from even the weak-est of radios can normally be picked up across ocean distances of three hundred miles or more. If he were more of a seaman he would know this and so he would perhaps turn the radio upside down and inside out searching for its flaw, but there is one thing Francis doesn't get the guts of and that's electronics. So it doesn't cross his mind to consider inspecting the radio further, but in thinking again about what he assumes to be its limited range, he begins to search the nav station storage drawers for the radio's manual, which is when he finds the EPIRB.

Because there had never been one on any of the little Georgia Strait crabbing skiffs he'd worked on, and because the *Belle*'s had been stashed away, out of sight, in the drawer he's now found it in, the EPIRB was not something he'd had at the forefront of his desperate, overwhelmed mind over the past week. He certainly knew what an Emergency Position Indicating Radio Beacon was, and had learned all about them and the global search-and-rescue network they connected their carriers to in his Marine Emergency Duties courses. He'd held and used several in practice sessions, but had failed to think of doing so when the time had come in the throes of this very real, exceedingly stressful situation.

Francis climbs to the cockpit, EPIRB in hand, and scans the emp-ty horizon. Then he lifts it from its cradle, pops its cap, and flicks the switch. Intermittently the light at its top begins to flash, indicating that it is, provided all is working as it should, sending its coordinates and SOS signal up to one of the many satellites swarming the earth, which should in turn be relaying that signal back down to the US Coast Guard Rescue Coordination Center in Honolulu, triggering an effort to have some sort of rescue crew, by boat or plane or helicopter, sent his way. He leaves it on deck and descends back to the nav station. He'll put his call out again, and between that and the EPIRB it will only be a matter of time, he's certain, before someone arrives to take him from this cursed boat.

↩

INSANITY: DOING THE *same thing over and over again and expecting different results.* Six days into his stranded seclusion he recalls this quote from the *Walrus* article he had wanted Anna to read in the months leading up to Emily's birth. He's been pacing up and down the decks of the *Belle*—memories of Miriam and Anna and Jin Su and his children, and of the float, the pristine, unbreakable float, whirling and clanking about in his mind—calling out his distress on the shortwave at closer and closer intervals, each time to no response but silence, the unnerving silence, also unbreakable now that his own voice and footfalls seem to bleed into and not disturb it, a sunburst of sound, the ceaseless ceasing of the wind. The random radio chatter also so familiar as to seem unheard, word upon word, he screams into the handpiece and up to any god, up to the full and bright-as-daylight moon in the nights that pass without sleeping, with a dread sense of haunting, of being helplessly alone, a fear of somehow having slipped into some sort of twilight zone from which he won't return. Six nights and days of this, each one worsening by degrees, and he's sitting at the shortwave, naked, calling out to the anywhere that won't answer back, when he thinks of the aphorism and decides to break out the bubbly. What the hell? He has to shirk the spell the past week has put him under, and a good piss-up should induce the much needed capillary break. It so often does, doesn't it?

As he pops the cork and pours a glass, he thinks how old this pattern in his life is—the freight train speed and intensity of the tracks of trajectory he gets moving on and the derailed wreckage that ensues. How the fuck did he end up here exactly, on this boat somewhere in the North Pacific—his seamate, his lover, dead; his wife and first child at home; his mistress and their daughter dumped off at Svend's, while he's spent the past month driving himself headlong into a world of trouble he should have nothing to do with? His is an extreme tendency to get lost in the moment, swept up into whatever storm has blown over his life. No wonder Anna has shut him out. How much could she be expected to go along with? He'd bought the boat, on a market high, in a gust of ambition and inspiration without really running the numbers, without listening to her reasoning when she had diligently done so, and the ripple effect has trapped her and their son in a little shit-box rental in a town she ultimately would love to leave and never return to. All the while he's blamed her for not standing by him?

He pours another glass. And now he's gone and thrown Jin Su and Emily into the mix, barrelling forth without pausing to take bearing, to get a real sense of his heart and feelings as he's told Jin Su time and time again that his leaving Anna is only a question of timing. Which is a fallacy, isn't it? If he truly were ready to leave her he'd have done so years ago, before ever taking up with Jin Su, or at least before the birth of their daughter. And now he's compounded his infidelity these past few weeks with Miriam, acquiring both clarity and confusion in so doing, and where now does that leave him? On his third glass of champagne, eyeing already the second bottle he'd sworn to himself he wouldn't open, losing hope of anyone coming to rescue him, praying to the oppressively bright sky for storm.

⤿

No REGITATIONS OF poetry this time as he drunkenly relieves himself over the side of the boat. Instead, a memory of watching Megan Follows play Anne of Green Gables on TV with his Oma and Opa when he was a child. He's staring down at the dinghy as his stream trickles into the water beside it, envisioning the scene where Anne acts the part of the deceased Lady of Shalott being set adrift in a leaky old dory. He climbs down into the dinghy and unties it from the *Belle*. Then he lies down, naked, in the bottom of the boat, his arms crossed over his chest as he recalls hers were. He closes his eyes, reciting his own rendition of the funeral rites he seems to remember she spoke, though he can't be sure that's what she did, but it doesn't matter, he's drunk and drifting away from that boat turned sour with the stench of his sweat and that of Miriam's bodily emptyings he's yet to clean from her forward stateroom. He can't face it, her aftermath. He's been running as far from what's happened to her as he can, though there's nowhere to run, is there? And he's been nothing but a childish coward all this time, for years now, Miriam's death and this stranding being only his latest mess. Lifting himself up, he hurls his guts out yet again into the sea, and the sobs start, his eyes stinging with the tears, until the convulsions subside and he lies down foetal in the bottom of the little boat, falling fast asleep for the first time in days under the blistering hot sun.

⤿

HE UNPEELS HIS eyelids and focuses through his alcoholic haze on a small knot in the wood of the dinghy's hull. It's a knot that was crosscut in the milling, so it tails off across the one-by-four board like a comet streaking the sky. Around the time Willow was born he and Anna dreamed of buying some land out on one of the islands, maybe Salt Spring or Cortes, somewhere they could live more with the creatures of the world, with the unobscured stars and the sea. They'd stay up late nights together sketching floor plans and elevation profiles on graph paper, imagining the perfect home for the life they would have, the big kitchen for canning and preserving and drying, the root cellar off the northeast corner, a large attached greenhouse to the south, all heated by a central masonry stove. Anna read books by Michael Reynolds and learned about greywater systems, rain catchments, R and K values and site design, the azimuth angle and the differing qualities of clay, gravel, sand and soil. There had been a point though where her enthusiasm outpaced his own, and that's where things started going sideways. She'd wanted to cobble whatever money they could save, beg, borrow or steal and get whatever piece of land they could afford as soon as possible. She wanted to get started. She talked as though that were the only answer, the only real response to what was happening in the world and the only decent way to raise their son and the children they would have in the future.

Francis, having grown up on Lasqueti, knew better. He'd seen countless young adults come with their idealized dreams from all over—small towns, suburbs and cities—to end up living in plastic shacks and half-finished huts on land that offered nothing more than space and solitude. No good wood to work, soil to sow or water to drink and harness for power. They lived in the cold and the dark through the winters, their water lines frozen or clogged with crud, their roofs leaking, host to families of rodents that shat and pissed in the insulation until their homes stank of musty dens and their children grew sickly from the mould that proliferated in the walls and roof cavities. Most lasted less than five years, and the ones who stayed aged quickly, living as they did with cold floors and the endless struggling with inadequate supplies and equipment and know-how to build and furnish a life off-grid, in isolation. So he and Anna locked horns, neither listening to the wisdom of the other, and their life together has remained stuck like that since. Her wanting more than anything to leave the small-town suburbs behind, and him wanting that, too, but even more so to not end up like so many he's seen before: a wrecked rural sawyer with a beat-up old Wood-Mizer mill and a back just this side of broken.

He peels his body off the ribs and hullboards and feels the ache of his sunburn as he stretches out his limbs and spits out the taste of vomit and the parched, sticky saliva from his mouth. He needs water. He rows back to the boat and ties the dinghy off to the taffrail once again, then climbs slowly aboard and down into the galley. When he twists open the tap it sputters, spitting out intermittent bursts of water and air. Thirsty as he is, he gulps back what he gets, two and a half glasses, until the pump pushes out nothing. He closes the tap and starts to laugh. What fun God, whatever that is, must be having with him.

The glass he's drinking from shatters as it lands at his feet. Then he empties the cupboards in front of him of their contents, the glasses and plates and bowls crashing to the floor, those that are breakable scattering in pieces across the cabin. He rips the cupboard doors from their hinges, winging them across the cabin like Frisbees. When he finally feels the blood trickling from his punctured and sliced feet, he climbs up to the cockpit and grabs the EPIRB he'd left out on deck days before. He waits for it to flash, indicating that its signal is being sent, but it doesn't. What? How long has the EPIRB not been transmitting? He hadn't even thought to check, hadn't noticed it not blinking, blinded by boredom and fear as he's been, cloistered below deck, hiding from the oppressive magnitude of the endless emptiness of his surroundings.

When Horace bought his new Category 1, 406/121.5 MHZ EPIRB, he was in Madrid on business, a loosely-termed practice of his that constituted old friends, wine, polo and talk of investment opportunities over fine Scotch and cigars. After the long flight back to Vancouver he got a room at the Hotel Georgia and over the course of three days met individually with his money men: his accountant, his stock broker and his financial planner. When he finally arrived home at the Glass Globe he found that the EPIRB had been accidentally activated in his luggage. He switched it off, resolved to replace the battery, and shortly after stowed it in the nav station drawer where Francis found it. Of course he never gave it another thought, the EPIRB not being a priority piece of equipment for the short inshore trips he and Miriam took on the *Belle*.

Francis bashes it against the side of the cabin door several times, each time staring it down and cursing its inactivity. Each time nothing happens. So he flings it in a rage spinning out into the ocean. Then he hobbles down into the nav station and again starts hollering into the shortwave. "Where the fuck are you, you stupid fuckers?" he screams. "Where?" He tugs at the handpiece until its cord stretches and snaps from the unit, the little sheathed wires shearing apart. He throws it too across the cabin and tears the radio from its mount. His thumb slides over the little CALL STOP switch at the bottom and clicks it off as he hurls the shortwave to the floor, picks up one of the cupboard doors he'd Frisbeed across the galley, and beats the radio to bits at his feet.

Water, Water, Everywhere

IF MIRIAM'S HUSBAND Yule were with Francis he would recite these, some of the most famous lines from Coleridge's epic: *Water, water, every where, and all the boards did shrink; water, water, every where, nor any drop to drink.* At this point in the poem the mariner has just slain with his crossbow the blessed albatross (for reasons not wholly conveyed) which has travelled many miles in dense mist and fog with his ship and crew around Antarctica. The mariner's crew, two hundred strong, had embraced the bird as one of good omen, as upon its arrival the ice that gripped the hull cracked free and a sailable breeze began to blow. Upon the mariner's slaying of the bird, conditions improve even more, the fog lifting finally and the breeze strengthening, and the crew applaud his killing. Then they come to the subtropical high and the winds die, as does the crew, all two hundred men, of starvation and dehydration. All but the mariner, who is eventually returned by a supernatural wind to land, where he is cursed to roam in perpetual penance, forever telling his tale to the strangers he meets.

But Francis didn't slay the one albatross that visited them so many days ago, and he holds little hope for the help of any divine intervention. The sails haven't more than fluttered over the past week, and though there truly is water everywhere—not just the endless volumes of the sea, but also that which is in the bilge, the cooling system of the main engine, and in each cell of the lead-acid batteries—none of it is drinkable. There may be some still sloshing about in the bottom of the tank, and they'll be a few drops in the lines, but this he knows won't amount to more than a day's worth at best and he's already thirsty, mildly dehydrated as he is from his drinking earlier in the day.

Some doctors say that, on account of the natural anaesthetics the brain produces within a few days of it being denied nourishment, the process of dying by dehydration is not as painful for the sufferer as it might seem. Some even suggest the experience includes hardly any discomfort at all, since the coma-like state that is soon reached negates any perception of pain. Others refute this, saying the pain is excruciating, as can be seen in any sufferer's agony. Regardless of what the sufferer actually experiences, death by dehydration isn't pretty. The skin hangs loose from the flesh and becomes dry and cracked and scaly. Nosebleeds, on account of the skin cracking, occur frequently. Highly concentrated urine burns from the bladder while the eyes sink into their orbits and the sufferer dry-heaves as the stomach lining dries out. Those are the early symptoms.

Convulsions begin as the brain cells burn and coughing brings up thick secretions from the dried-out respiratory tract causing the sufferer to fight for breath. Within five days the parasympathetic nervous system is impaired as a result of toxic buildup, the regulatory mineral balance of calcium, potassium and sodium thrown out of whack, and the muscles stop working, including, eventually, the heart. There are claims that people have survived as long as three full weeks without fluids, but of course the irreparable damage to their bodies and brains was done long before they actually died. Francis knows he doesn't have long to live without water, and so he starts tearing into the walls of the boat.

With the claw-side of a hammer he strips away the mahogany panelling, exposing the lengths of wiring and hosing beneath. He follows the water line to its source, sucking what little drops of water he can from it as he goes, until he comes to the tank buried behind his bunk in the stern. He rips the panelling away and exposes the bulk of the tank's stainless steel sidewall. Cutting into it is another matter, and as he thrusts the claw repetitively at the shiny steel, he wonders if there will be enough water in the tank to replenish that which he's perspiring as a result of his exertion. By this method he manages to tear away enough of the sidewall to get his arm in with a cup in his hand and scoop up that which the pump couldn't draw. A few litres. He mops the rest up with paper towel, wringing it out into the plastic and steel bowls and cups that survived his temper tantrum. He plugs the sink and sets these down into it, and when he's done he stands for a long time and contemplates these precious vessels, a few days' worth of water at best.

And then what? Is he supposed to just sit here waiting for the rescue that should have already arrived? For the miracle of wind that won't blow despite his prayers and self-effacing promises to be a better man, to come clean to Anna and Jin Su both and be a steadier father to his children? It's the deep-seated though vague vestige of his grandparents' Catholicism coming to the fore in him, in his time now of utter desperation, staring into these cups and bowls of what little time he has left, an image of himself he hardly recognizes—bearded, sunburnt, scared and broken—staring back.

Life Is But a Dream

IT'S AGAINST OUR basic nature to do *nothing* in the face of imminent disaster. Which is why those long-ago sailors threw their valuable horses to the sea, perhaps a bit rash given that a boat will usually drift free of the subtropical high within a couple of weeks (though who's to know if that was widely known and trusted knowledge in those days). Regardless, it seems equally true that it defies our nature to do the most sensible, prudent thing in such circumstances; it's a rare person who thinks well and clearly under real stress, the kind brought on in life-threatening conditions. Francis, far as he is from being one such person, decides.

First he transfers what water he has left into the two empty champagne bottles—careful as he's ever been not to spill a drop—corks them, and wraps them in Horace's wool sweaters. He collects the survival blankets from the emergency closet, the first-aid kit and a survival suit. He takes pillows and blankets and clothes from his stateroom, rolls of toilet paper and sunscreen from the head. Cans of fish and veggies (the water they're preserved in more precious than the food itself), a good knife, spoons, a can opener, a flashlight, candles and a box of matches. Sheets, shower curtains and rods for shade-making. All this he places with the fishing rod, gaff and tackle into the dinghy. Then he writes a small note. *Paddling due south in a white dinghy. Find me.* He duplicates this twice and tapes one to the galley table, one to the nav table and one to the cabin door. Then two last things, binoculars and a compass, and he climbs down into the little boat, unhitches the line from its bow cleat, sets the oars in their locks, and heads out with renewed vigour and hope, rowing for Hawaii.

⤳

BOTH THE VIGOUR and the hope fade fast. He'd begun to think the *Belle* was genuinely cursed, and thought maybe if he rowed free of her he might eventually cross paths with some other mariner. Could it be though that it's he who is cursed? It's not hard to get sucked down into the whirlpool of such thoughts when thoughts are all one has. The mind is a creative angel or monster, depending on the tilt of one's life. Francis's mind, being angled so steeply toward the bad, has turned ugly. What is left for him in the wake of his last burst of optimism is a fatigue that makes every joint ache and muscle sear with pain, weighing upon his eyes until even the middle and near distances grow blurry and his eyelids become almost chronically heavy. He begins to lie down on his bed of salty blankets more often than he rows, losing sight of the difference between the life he dreams and the one he wakes to inside this endless, unsheltered blue, where he spills finally the last drop of water, sweet with the tinge of champagne, across his cracked and swollen tongue.

Blue

SPLAYED OUT IN the heat of the sun pounding through his shower curtain shade cover, his body stiffened and sweltering with dehydration, Francis hears the voice of an angel singing in his ear. Joni Mitchell. *Blue... Songs are like tattoos. You know I've been to sea before. Crown and anchor me, or let me sail away...* He hears her as though she were right there in the boat with him, her piano fingerings floating down from the cloudless heavens in accompaniment. When he occasionally comes to, he prays for the less angelic tone of Annie Lennox instead to fill his ears, but neither her song nor rain falls upon him. Just the relentless rays of the sun. When something finally, suddenly, shrouds him in shadow, he's too far gone for it to cohere across the distance his mind has receded to. He hears a great rumbling in the shadow and thinks it must be the thunder of death, his brain in his boiling skull imploding, the end of the world, and sees a vision of the black-footed albatross, god-sized, its dark wings wrapped around the flame-forked, furious sun.

IT HAS TAKEN us less than a week to make it to Hawaii. Now what? Vericombe and his first mate—a bald, very small, very serious man named Smith—rarely descend from the captain's deck. The one time I ventured up they gave me a polite tour of the instruments and such, then made it quite clear that I was to leave and not come up again unless invited. So I've turned my attention in the opposite direction, down to the engine room instead, befriending Figgs over the past week. I ran out of smokes two days into our passage and I've been bumming them from him ever since.

He's down in the engine room or out on deck doing repairs and maintenance most daylight hours. But at night he's always in his quarters, the forward fo'c'sle. Between him and the towering aft cabin where the rest of us sleep is the open steel deck, and below it the hold, probably sixty feet long by twenty feet wide by fifteen feet deep, which Vericombe has, as Figgs tells me, "stuffed with enough diesel to keep us running till the end of the world." Funny he should state it as such given all that he's told me over the past five days. I now know where the name of the skiff *Sohqui* comes from, and with that knowledge I've picked up a basic understanding of all that Ferris's finding of the fish float has us caught up in.

I come down here to smoke with Figgs every night once I've put

Willow to bed. I'm too full of anxiety and upheaval to sleep much. It's getting more and more difficult to keep Willow calm too. My ill-ease is infectious I'm sure, especially to my own son. But Willow is a good, level-headed eleven year old. He's self-sufficient really, for a kid, and as I watch him sleep in the bunk beside me at night by the passage light leaking in under our stateroom door, I can only guess at what he thinks and feels of all that has gone on this past month. The quake. His father's leaving. And now this. Us on this boat with these bizarre strangers. He doesn't say much, which isn't uncom-mon, though he's been even quieter than usual the past couple of days, which tells me he's starting to feel the strain of it all. Tumultu-ous or not, what with Ferris and I fighting, our home has been a stable one for Willow for as long as he can remember. Aside from trips to my hometown to visit his grandparents, we don't travel, on principle, and we're fairly reclusive and routine-oriented people. So I know this is a lot for Willow to absorb, and I keep waiting for his nightmares to return. It's been a couple years now since they de-sisted last, but being the mother of a child who is haunted the way Willow is, the worry is never far from my thoughts.

So I don't usually stay long visiting with Figgs, dreading the thought of Willow waking without me. We share a smoke, a story or two, then I return to my bunk. But tonight we've been talk-ing for hours. We're on our fifth, maybe sixth smoke each. Figgs has been telling me more about Mu and the Sohqui, and I have to admit I'm a sucker for the magical beauty. The mystery. I read fantasy throughout my entire childhood, Tolkien and Lewis and later Marion Zimmer Bradley. It might be safe to say that I secretly enjoyed reading the Harry Potter books with Willow more than he did. Figgs usually seems indifferent as he tells me of the Naacal, but tonight he's engaged and it's got me wondering if he actually believes in it all. So I ask.

"Do you know why I became a marine engineer?" he asks me in response. Figgs has a voice both rough and smooth at once, like the sound of broken sea waves raking back on a pebble beach. It's a voice easy to get lost in listening to. "Those engines back there. The reduction gear and the pitch of the wheel. Those are all things I know you know very little about. My father was the son of a poor farmer. I grew up in Odessa in a two-room house with five sisters. A marine engineer is someone who has knowledge that very few people have. And so we're always useful. There is always work because not very many people know how to keep boats running, but many depend on them doing so. Maybe it's the same with these kinds of things. Arnault Vericombe is not a stupid man, I can tell you that. He's spent much of his life learning about the Naacal, and he's seen and read the tablets that tell the stories I've been telling you. I won't be the one to question his knowledge now. Not while the ship's going down."

He takes a long drag from his cigarette and butts it out in the ashtray beside his bunk. He's been lying on it with his feet up, in shadow, while I sit at his small table and chair beneath a dim light fixed to the ceiling. "It's a big ship Anna. And it's one I don't have the first clue how to keep running." This is the first time Figgs has pointedly mentioned the state of the world. Of course I'm dying to get into it with him. It's so much of what I've made my life about, I'm a bit of a junkie at this point, one who hasn't had a good fix since Ferris left.

"Do you think anyone really does?" I ask, looking for more.

"That's the question, isn't it? The big question." He pulls his burly body up and sits facing me as he says this, his bare feet now out of the shadows.

"It is the big question, you're right," I reply. "It's the only question now, I think. So, do you think someone's got an answer?"

"I think a whole lot of people have an answer, Anna. Everyone's got an answer. Which is why none of them are enough. Look at the accords. They're all full of you-give-me-this-and-I'll-take-from-you-that. It's not about keeping the whole ship afloat. No. People don't give a shit about the ship, they just want to know that the little section they're floating on isn't going to go down with the rest. And they'll do whatever it takes to keep thinking so, because life otherwise is overwhelming and intolerable."

"And don't you think that's exactly what Vericombe and his cronies are up to here? They've got this fantastical idea in their heads, and it sure helps stave off the reality of what's really going on doesn't it? Just imagine if all we really had to do was break a glass ball and poof, the fish stocks replenished and the corals unbleached. Wouldn't that be something."

"It would. But then where would it leave you? You say you work with a woman who is fighting the aquaculture companies. But what if this thing that Vericombe is doing works and all your efforts amount to nothing while his fantasy changes the world? Of course you don't want to believe it could be so. It's not the corner of the ship you're sailing on. Not right now, at least."

Figgs stands up and clears his bedside table—a wooden produce crate turned on its side, strapped with two bungee cords to the wall—of his ashtray and books. He unhooks the bungees and carries the crate over to the table I'm seated at, places it on the floor and sits across from me. Then he rolls the sleeves of his flannel work shirt up to his elbows.

"This one," he says, pointing to a faded tattoo of a pirate flag on his left forearm. "It was given to me by the third mate on a Swedish carrier after we passed through the Malacca Straits. I was twenty-one, having just entered the merchant marine. Back then I was the great explorer. The sailor. The drinker. Me and my mates brawled in the streets of Bombay and Cape Town. This one," he continues, pointing to the tattoo on his right forearm, one of a white whale with a harpoon pierced in its side. "I got that done at a parlour in Tierra del Fuego. I was a bit younger than you are now, in my late twenties, working on a Norwegian whaling ship. A mate of mine in the merchant marine gave me an old copy of *Moby Dick*. He told me I had the mind of a scholar but the sensibility of a snake, and that I better get out of the sailor's gutter before it was too late. *Before you end up like me*, he'd say, then he'd drink himself sick on Jim Beam. So I became the whaling adventurer, fisherman and poet. You'll like this one," he says, lifting his shirt off his back.

There's a tattoo across his entire chest of a wave with the heads of a flock of big-horn sheep rising from the cresting foam. "I got this one at a parlour in San Francisco. This was me in my mid-thirties. Eventually the lustre wore off on the whaling and all the blood got to me. I had what I guess you'd call a mid-life crisis, so I did an about-face and signed on with Sea Shepherd. I engineered on the *Farley Mowat* for five years, fighting the fleet I'd just been working with. Then I was the storied sailor who'd seen the world and wrought destruction with his own hands, and I was doing penance. I drank more than ever then." He turns his right shoulder to me. *Live and let Live*, is written in black across it, arched over a black and gold crucifix. "Here's where I had AA and God. I did two years in a rehab centre up the Fraser Valley. A working farm for drunks and addicts. At first I loved being off the sea and I blamed her for all my troubles with the bottle. But after a couple of years I couldn't take it any longer so I got a job on the tugs out of Vancouver."

He turns his left shoulder to me and there's a tattoo of a black, red and white tug with the name *Husky King* scrawled beneath it in black ink. "This one was done by an artist on Commercial Drive, Quincy, a Native guy I met on the farm. He also did this one for me."

He turns around and shows me the tattoo on his back. It reaches from his waist to his shoulder blades, a circle of red and black Coast Salish art. "It's a whale swallowing a serpent swallowing a grizzly swallowing the whale," Figgs explains. The three figures are wrapped around a ball of black with a reddened centre. "And that thing in the centre of the circle?" I ask. "That's the earth. It's Quincy's depiction of my life upon the earth. I'm the bear." Figgs sits back down and puts his shirt on.

"And the serpent's the bottle?" I ask.

"The bottle, and everything that leads to it, and everything that threatens to take its place. For me, really, I think it's anger Anna. Maybe it is for everyone, I don't know. I'm not sure of much anymore. Which is why I've taken this job working for Arnault. It's a quiet life this one. And I think for now I've heard and seen enough."

"So what about that whale on your back. Is it not worth fighting for anymore?"

"It's not that it's not worth fighting for. I just don't have the fight in me. And I think maybe there has to be another way. Those five years I spent with Paul Watson and Sea Shepherd, what did we accomplish? We saved a few whales from the harpoon. So what? At one point we were all out on deck: Paul, the crew and a group of young volunteers, university kids who had come with us to the whaling grounds to help stop the Japanese fleet. We'd just been through a major confrontation with one of the whalers who had sent his crew out on deck with semi-automatic rifles and threatened to open fire on the *Mowat* if we didn't get out of the way of his fishing. So Paul had us all, the twelve kids included, surround the deck to make a human shield. He'd just put all those young people in the line of fire. And there we were, victorious, but all I could see in the eyes of those around me was anger. Those young kids with the same anger and defiance I had when I was their age. And I couldn't blame them, but I couldn't feel it any longer. I realized then it was a life source for them as it had been for me, but I'd grown to want something different. Which isn't to say that's what I've found. But in leaving it behind at least I've left myself open to possibility."

"Did it work?" I ask.

"I don't know if I can say it worked. But I think it's working," he replies, misunderstanding my question.

"No. I mean putting those kids out on that deck. Did it keep the whalers from killing whales?"

"Oh. Yes, for a time. But it didn't stop the rest of the fleet from filling the quota. Which means the whales got killed and would have even if the Japs had fired on those kids."

"But what if there were more *Farley Mowat*s out there? What if there was a fleet large enough to actually rival the whalers?"

"Then armies would be sent in to clear them out. That's the thing. If the defiance gets large enough they snuff it out. You can't fight their fire. You have to unfuel it. And anger is the fuel, I think."

"I think it's ignorance."

"Ignorance has nothing to do with it Anna. Ignorance is benign. We all live with it because we have to. You know a lot about fish farms and salmon, but what do you know about engineering, or physics, or plumbing? What about the struggles of women in Sierra Leone? Or Afghanistan? What about the life beneath us now at the bottom of the sea? There are people who've made it their life's work to know about these things and would call you ignorant. But that's just their place on the ship. We can't know it all Anna. So we all do what we can with what we have. There's a guy right now driving cab in London trying to figure out how he's going to get his wife and children out of Bombay. That he's there at all means his life has been, for him, lucky. It's all he can handle. Does it make him ignorant that he doesn't protest the war or the WTO? He knows more about survival, I mean in the emotional sense, about living life stripped of certainty and dignity, than you or I could possibly imagine. So who's ignorant Anna?"

Figgs lights himself another smoke while his question lingers in the air between us. There's this knee-jerk reaction in me that wants to thrash against the wall of his logic. "It's an endgame then," I say, taking another smoke, too.

"Possibly. Or maybe there's much more going on here than we can account for. Maybe Arnault's little tale is the truth and we're caught inside a curse long cast and not for us to undo." He takes a hard drag, then places the butt still burning in the ashtray. "Give me a moment," he says, and walks to the sink at the far end of his room. There he flicks on a fluorescent light over a wall-mounted mirror and again takes his shirt off. From the under-sink cabinet he takes a cordless hair clipper and begins shaving off his scraggly grey hair. He keeps his back to me as I watch the strands drift slowly down his tattooed back to the floor, then he turns the fluorescent light out and comes back to the table. He sits and bows the crown of his head toward me.

There's a bright blue and white tattoo of a coiled, scaly, snake-like creature on the top of his head. It has a tale with three fins fanned out at its tip. "Sohqui," he says, his head still bowed down. "At this point Anna, they're both as real and fictitious as any hope we have." He sits up and pulls his shirt once more over his broad shoulders. Quite hairy, I realize now, in light of the shaven contrast he's just created. And I can't help but laugh at the thought, and he laughs too, though I don't share with him the source of my humour, as he doesn't share his with me. We just laugh like that together for a good long time while our cigarettes burn down side by side in their tray.

⌒

WHEN I FINALLY climb back to the stern quarters, well into the early hours, I find Willow in the galley with Fairwin' playing cards and drinking warm cups of Krakus, milk and honey. I couldn't feel more like a rotten mother, though Willow seems happy enough to be up with the old kook, and Fairwin' seems happy too for his company. "He's teaching me a game called hearts," Willow says as I sit down beside him. He's putting up his cute-boy shield to deflect the shit he expects me to give him for being out of bed so late, but under these circumstances I'm just happy he's happy and I can't blame him for not sleeping.

There's a lot of anticipation in the air since we arrived in Hawaii. This morning we pulled in close to shore—I'm not sure where, some large, sandy bay with a long man-made spit stretching across it—and Arnault's man Smith launched the skiff and left the boat on a "reconnaissance mission." These guys think they're in some kind of 007 flick or something. And as ridiculous as it all seems, the three of us at this table tonight want nothing more than to find Ferris and the woman, and so it's contagious, Arnault and Smith's sense of seriousness and urgency. I suppose it's testament to how much Willow has grown up into a little man over the past year, how much like his father he's becoming, that he's woken up without me and sat down calmly to a game of cards with Fairwin' instead of turning hysterical.

"Couldn't sleep, hey Bub?" I ask him, taking a sip of his Krakus. I give Fairwin' my very best, adult-to-adult, *Thank you, and is this okay?* look, to which he responds with kinder eyes than I would have expected he were capable of, and I realize again that I've been judging Fairwin' on an erroneous assumption of who he is. Were I to pursue the kind of life that Fairwin' has cultivated, the choice to do so would be based in misanthropy, that disposition in me which is tempered only by my love for my son, Ferris and my parents, and by my stubborn though dwindling belief that people are, despite it all, inherently good. So I've assumed Fairwin', being a man who, as far as I know, has no children or close family, must logically be himself a deeply misanthropic person, and so consequently hardened to others. That he is again challenging my assumptions with his warmness toward my son and myself irks me, as it is just one more hand on the rope pulling down the little walls I've been living behind.

"I'm tired," I say, and stand from the table, wanting to make my exit before my disharmony disrupts the friendly countenance between them. "I'm going to bed, Bub. Why don't you finish up here and come to bed, too." Willow looks up at me with his pleading-child eyes. He's clearly not tired, wired on the restless energy that seems to crackle in the air on this boat like the static charge preceding the electrical storms that gather in the mountains where I was born. "When you're ready," I say, and tousle his hair. I thank Fairwin' and head to our stateroom knowing I should get some sleep, but not feeling the least bit tired.

I lie awake in the dark for a while thinking about what Figgs and I talked about, about Ferris and his role in all this, and about his role in our son's life, in my life, in our life together. I have a mind to write him another letter, but there's too much and too little to say. I can't seem to sort it all out, flooded as I am with the awareness of so many different things I've kept myself from, with my fighter's will, and flooded too with the awareness of all the ways in which I've done so. How I've narrowed everything and everyone down to positions and players in a war, and in so doing made my life, my family's life, one of conflict. War eliminates possibility, compassion and diversity. That's not a sentence I'd have applied to myself, not readily, not without the qualifier that such sacrifice is the nuts and bolts of necessity and this war, this one in which I've enlisted myself, and so too my family, demands it. And the war *is*, whether one admits it or not, which is the point that always hangs up my free-fall into self-doubt.

What choice do I have? That others, Ferris included, find within themselves the ability to ignore the war only makes it all the more impossible for me to do so. But perhaps there's a way of acknowledging that some people prefer to remain civilians; to find a different way of assessing those who continue on with life-as-usual, despite the deaths and the deep, deep damage. Ferris has surrendered to join the ranks of the disillusioned and the conscientious objectors, those who concede the war is on, but opt out of the fight. Does this have to mean I can no longer love him? Can no longer share my life with him? Perhaps turning my sights on him and on my parents and on others who have been close to me in the past is a product of the enemy's elusiveness, of its ability to obscure itself, avoid definition or direct engagement, to hide behind its walls of wealth, litigious language and institutions. And so in my very human limitations I've fought against those I love and who love me, and have risked losing the very ground that needs more than any other to remain protected, undefeated. It's what Ferris has been saying all along. If they destroy our ability to love, to laugh and feel joy with one another, they've won.

My son comes into the dark quietly and slips into bed. I cradle him close the way I used to when he was younger and he dissolves into me without resistance. It's been a long time since I've held him like this. "Mom?" he asks in that timid voice he gets when he's troubled and uncertain. "Is Dad going to be okay?" I'm surprised that it hasn't come to this sooner. I have to listen deep down inside myself now to know what to say.

"He's going to be okay," I finally answer, and I have the sense I'm speaking the truth, I do, though right as the words pass from my lips I feel the strangle-hold of my helplessness in this situation. Ferris is a needle in a haystack, somewhere out here, and I haven't the slightest clue how we're going to find him. I wonder if Vericombe does, if he has some sort of method or plan, and I decide I'm going to find out. Fuck him. This is the father of my child—this warm and fragile little boy in my arms—we're looking for, and from now on I'm going to be up there in the wheelhouse helping, because who's to say it won't be the very intuition I'm feeling now that will lead us to Ferris? Who's to say that's not worth a million times more than all his radars and radios and satellite phones and faxes?

I stroke the hair on my son's head and he quickly falls asleep, his skinny body relaxing beside me while I lie awake and smell the scent of his father on him, just faintly, and listen to the wash of the ocean along the hull over the steady hum of Figgs's well-tuned diesels. I'm thankful at least for *his* capability and kindness, quietly

keeping us going along, just as Ferris would. Which is all I'm rely-
ing upon now, more than ever, on Ferris's ability to keep it together
no matter what the weather, to keep himself from sinking no matter how bad the storm.

⤻

I LEAVE WILLOW out on deck with Figgs. It's a sunny, calm day
offshore of Hawaii, and Figgs lets my son sit in the cockpit of the
helicopter while he does routine maintenance, "readying her for
flight," as he puts it. Vericombe accepts me invitingly up into the
wheelhouse. He must have known it was only a matter of time before I would defy his order because he's ready with answers and
a task for me as soon as I come up. "This is where we're at with
things," he explains. "We're going to return to shore in two hours
to pick up Smith. He's been up to my house above Hilo, the Sunimoto house, and found nothing. It's all blown apart and shot up
with bullets, but other than that the fellows who did the shooting
did a good job of cleaning up after themselves. We know Ferris and
Miriam escaped, and we know their boat is not docked or moored
anywhere within reasonable range of Hilo. Smith has checked into
all that. So now all we can do is follow the most likely scenario,
which is as follows. They got back to the boat, they refuelled somewhere, then they headed north for the return trip to Canada."

"Doesn't really give us much to work with, does it?"

"No it doesn't, but this does," he says, and hands me a stack of papers three inches thick. "That's a list of all the EPIRB signals picked
up by Cospas-Sarsat in the past two weeks within a thousand-mile
radius of Hilo." I haven't the slightest clue what an EPIRB is, so I
ask. "Emergency Position Indicating Radio Beacon," Vericombe replies. I look at him quizzically still, so he asks me to follow him and

leads me out on to the small upper deck off the back of the wheel-house. "This," he says, pointing to what looks like a plastic torch mounted to the wheelhouse wall. "In the event of an emergency, this device sends a signal out that can be detected by a network of dedicated satellites orbiting the earth."

"Meaning what, Arnault? What sets it off?" I ask, trying not to let the implications of this thing he's talking about cause me to panic at the thought of Ferris being in the trouble I've feared all this time.

"It can be done manually, like this," he answers, and takes the torch from its harness. He flips the clear plastic cover off the top and points to a switch. "It also has a sea-switch. It's designed to deploy from its harness and float to the surface if the boat sinks. There's a little filament inside the switch that erodes from the salt water and sets the signal off." This he tells me in a very matter-of-fact way, but I don't take it so easily.

"Okay. So you're telling me that what we have to feel hopeful about is a stack of papers which may or may not tell us where Ferris sank? Fuck, Arnault, what the fuck are we doing out here?"

"It's not that simple, Anna. What we're looking for is an indica-tion. For all we know they could be broken down right now out there waiting for their rescue." Without scoffing at this, as I'm in-clined to, I point out to him the obvious, that they're on a sailboat and don't need power. "But if they left Hawaii a couple of weeks ago now, like we suspect, they could be stranded a thousand miles north of here in the middle of the subtropical high, and there's no wind there. Say they panicked when leaving Hawaii and didn't re-fuel before setting out. It's not out of the question. Miriam and your husband might be sitting out on deck in the sun drinking gin and tonics for all we know. The boat they're on is as seaworthy as they come, and they've got provisions for months of sailing, so there's an awful good chance they're still out there. We're just covering our bases before we start flying around over the open ocean checking every vessel that comes within radar range."

"Ferris doesn't drink," I say to this, stupidly, then ask the obvious. "What about the people who shot up your house, what if they sank the boat?"

"They wouldn't have. They'd have no reason to."

"How do you know?"

"Because they got the float, Anna, which is all they wanted."

"Did they? How can you be so certain?"

"Because a major earthquake just occurred in New Delhi, which is where the man who stole it lives, that's how."

"And you're absolutely certain of that are you?"

"We wouldn't be here on this boat if I wasn't. I'm so certain that I've paid a group of men a very large sum of money to go and retrieve it for me, with great risk, but all that is beside the point and none of your business."

"None of my business? Vericombe, I wouldn't be out here on this boat if it weren't my business, and neither would my son. You've got my husband and my son caught in the middle of some war you're having, and whether I like it or not, right now protecting them from you and whatever other lunatics are involved is my only business." I'm yelling at him now and he reacts to my hostility by quite calmly walking away, back into the cabin. Shit. I don't want him to shut me out again, so I take a deep breath, collect myself, and follow after him.

"Wouldn't they already have been rescued then, if their EPIRB had gone off in the past couple of weeks? Isn't that the idea?"

"At least ninety-five percent of EPIRB signals are false alarms," he answers, not turning from the window he's looking out of, keeping his back rigidly to me. "The US Coast Guard spends over five million dollars a year sending search and rescue crews out to idiots who have accidentally set off their EPIRB, or even worse, pranksters who think it's good party fun to have the boys in red show up to the yacht. So no, *if* their EPIRB has been set off, it may not yet have come to the point where a rescue has been launched to find them. It depends on the timing. They'll first go through the registered contact numbers, and they'll try to get any boats in the area to respond with whatever information they might have. That can take hours, even longer, and for all we know you might find a transmission in there that's more recent than that. I imagine too with the eruptions here and tsunamis in the southeast, the Coast Guard are stretched fairly thin. From what our contact at the Rescue Coordination Center in Honolulu tells us, there are an excessive amount of distress signals listed on that stack of paper. They're swamped. It was all she could do to fax us that information. It could be they don't have the manpower to attempt a rescue that far north of here. So it's up to us to sort through those papers and do what we can."

He still doesn't turn his back, but his tone is growing more and more aggravated. "What am I looking for then?" I ask, as I sit down at the table behind him, the stack of paper before me. "*Princess Belle*. Belle with two Es. That's the name of the boat they're on. Find that somewhere in there and we may be one step closer to getting your son's father back and getting you all away from this little war," he says, not turning from the window, and I realize that he must be watching Willow with Figgs out on the deck below. Maybe he's been watching out for Willow more than I know. I look him up and down and for the first time notice the extreme tension in his shoulders and posture not as some rigid uptightness, but as a bearing of stress. Such is my nature, I'm coming to see, that I have not given him the credit that may be his due. So I say nothing more and put my head down to the work he's given me, resolved to do what I can to help this man find my husband.

〜

HALFWAY THROUGH SCANNING the pages I find it. Distress Signal Received: 11:38:53. 06/14/10. Coordinates: 32°58'30.83"N. 158°3'49.21"W. Hex #90356D83659DE381XX47 9553225712. Registered Vessel: *Princess Belle*. Status: Distress Signal Discontinued: 20:14:52. 06/14/10. Brimming as I am with both excitement and fear I carry the page forward to Vericombe and hand it to him.

"Okay," he says. "Now we've got something to go on." His eyes are instantly alight with what I can only think of as the wilds of adventure, and it makes me uneasy. He's like a little kid who has just found out where the candy is hidden. "Couldn't be better timing," he continues. "We'll pick up Smith and be off." He puts the boat in gear and throttles up, at the same time setting a track to the EPIRB coordinates on his GPS computer. "Nine hundred and thirty-eight miles. We should be there within three days."

I want to contain my dissent, but I can't believe what I'm seeing and hearing from him, and it gets the better of me. "Three days! Vericombe, how out of it are you? This signal was detected a fucking week ago. What good does that do? They could be another thousand miles from there by now." Or long since drowned at the bottom of the ocean, I'm thinking, though I can't bring myself to say it, not right off, and when I do try it stifles my voice, cracking it in two, and I have to choke back the sobs as the tears start.

I don't cry much, so when I do it always comes in a torrent, and I'm bawling right now in front of Vericombe. Veritably bawling. I surrender to this tall, skinny Frenchman's arms, sobbing into his linen collar, and though it's beyond awkward when I finally release myself from him, it's a necessary awkwardness, an acknowledgement between us, each of the other, of our mutual human vulnerability out here. Whether out of compassion or hope or despair I'm not sure, Vericombe has the streak of one tear down his cheek, too. I understand for the first time how similar he and I actually are, and I think he does, too. The two of us fighters in our little private wars. We tell ourselves we're fighting for the survival of all, and mostly we believe it, mostly it's true. But then there are these moments, clusters of days even, when that reasoning comes into question, and we're left as though suddenly stranded in a no man's land, wondering what it's all worth, what it's all really been for. We question the casualties and the damage, all the energy given over, before we come back to ourselves—where else is there to go?—and continue on with our waging, despite everything and everyone's doubts and admonishments, because if we don't who then will in our place?

"Okay," I say, looking up into his glass-obscured eyes. "Okay, Captain. Let's go find them." I straighten his crinkled collar for him and smile as kindly as I can, and I hope he sees in it that I understand and appreciate what he's doing, and hope too that I can remember to do so in the coming days when things are bound to push the boundaries of what I can bear.

⤸

FIGGS IS UNBOLTING and unstrapping the helicopter. Lack of sleep finally got the better of me and I've been in bed most of the past two days, drifting in and out of dream and anxiety, trusting Willow mostly to the care of Fairwin' and Figgs. I suppose it's taken me all this time to feel comfortable enough to sleep; to let my guard down on this boat with these men I don't know. It's amazing what a couple days of solid rest will do, though. I've had a shower, washed and brushed my hair, and right now I'm feeling a million years from the vulnerability that overwhelmed me with Vericombe. "You going for a little whirl?" I ask Figgs, sauntering up to him with my hands in my jean pockets.

"Not me. I hate these things. She's Arnault's, and only he flies her." Figgs slides a steel bar into a slotted handle and leans over on it, torquing the last of the tie-downs free. "Why has he waited until now to use that?" I ask, considering for the first time the usefulness of this machine given the vastness of the ocean we must search to find Ferris.

"We've got a lot of fuel on this boat Anna, but most of it is diesel. Jet A fuel is expensive, not that that should be any reason for Arnault not to have as much as he wants. You want to know the truth, I think he hates the thing, too." Figgs winks at me when he says this, then climbs up into the cockpit of the helicopter. "You ever flown in one?" he asks, grinning from above me. I shrug my shoulders in response, meaning no. "Get in," he says, a flare of mischief in his eyes.

"No fucking way," I say, but I don't mean it. It's like the me of a couple of days past, exhausted and caution-prone, is doing the talking, while the me of the present is walking around the front of the bird, opening the door and climbing in beside him.

I've never even sat in one of these things before and the thought of lifting off this deck into the sky sends a shiver straight through me. "We're not flying," Figgs says as I start to put my arms into the seat belt straps. "I meant it, I hate these things. If you want to go for a ride you'll have to convince Arnault to take you. But I need to tell you something." With this Figgs turns serious, almost grave. He closes the door beside him. "Anna, this thing that we're doing out here, looking for your husband. I know it's all the hope you've got, but I don't want to see you crash and burn, so I have to say this. The chances are slim. They're next to nothing."

I start fidgeting with the buckle on the strap hanging down beside me. "I know Figgs. It's a big ocean."

"It's not just that. If anyone could find your husband without the aid of the Coast Guard it's Arnault." He pauses for a second, as though trying to decide what to say next, or if even to say it. "I'm going to tell you something, but you need to promise not to talk about this with Arnault." He's got an aged, weary look on his face.

It's much more lined, his skin rougher, as though calloused by all the wind it's weathered, than I'd noticed before, and it occurs to me this is the first time I've spoken at length with Figgs in full, open daylight.

"Why not?" I ask, though I have a feeling whatever answer he gives will be only a portion of what it is that motivates him. Figgs, the lifelong seaman. It's a storied life he's lived, no doubt, and I'm starting to wonder if getting even as close to him as I've gotten, which isn't saying much, was such a good idea. Then he smiles, and my upswelling paranoia subsides. "Because Arnault's a dreamer and it's part of how things work for him and me that I don't burst his many little bubbles. But that's the thing I need to talk to you about, though first I need your promise. This job is important to me, and I want it to stay just as it is. It's all I've got now and if its current harmony is disrupted it will only be a matter of time before I lose it. So if we're to have this conversation I need you to swear it stays here between us."

I'd noticed right away that Figgs takes his job seriously, but this is a whole other level. Whatever. "I promise," I say, those simple two words that can mean so much and at the same time so little. Now Figgs is the one fidgeting with the buckle of his shoulder strap.

"Jeremy Gibbon is his name," he says. "The man who's looking for your husband. He's from Quebec, sort of. Now he lives in India. He's a young man, and very wealthy like Arnault, and he's equally intelligent. The thing is this, Anna. It's almost certain he's already found your husband. Arnault informed me of the coordinates you found, and I'd bet my life on the fact that EPIRB got set off when Jeremy found Miriam and your husband." I keep calm as he tells me this, remarkably so, not sure why he's telling me or whether even to take him seriously.

"And?" I ask, as in, *What's your point?*

"And I don't want you to get your hopes up when Arnault starts flying this thing around, because your husband's not out here."

Not out here. Got it. "What you're telling me is we've just travelled for a thousand miles, in the wrong direction, when you know where my husband already is. Is he even alive, Figgs?" I'm starting to lose it again. "Is he? Are you telling me my husband's been murdered?"

Figgs takes both my hands, which are beginning to flail before me like the blades of this machine, and holds them steady. "No, Anna," he says. "He's not been, but he's not out here, either. Listen. It would be foolish for Gibbon to kill your husband, because then, according to the myth, his presence would no longer be required in order for your son to break the float. But if he has him, he won't readily give him over. And that, I think, is why Arnault is continuing on this search, because he knows as difficult as this search is, getting your husband back from Gibbon is going to be infinitely more challenging. He and Gibbon have known each other for a long time and as I understand it there is nothing but bitterness between them now. Arnault is not a man who wants blood on his hands. He'll do whatever it takes to get your husband back, Anna, but it may end up costing him more than you or I could imagine."

"Okay. So we just go along with this then. Wasting time while my husband's been kidnapped to where, India?"

"I would suspect so. That's a very big, very crowded country though. Gibbon could be keeping him anywhere. It'll be impossible to find him, just as Arnault knows it will be impossible to find the float without Gibbon handing it over. Though I'm sure he has people trying as we speak. I'd say Gibbon's gone after your husband so he's got something to bargain with to keep Arnault and his people at bay."

"Why?" I ask. "Why does this Gibbon guy want the float so badly? Why wouldn't he want Arnault to help Ferris and Willow break it?" I can't believe I'm asking that question, as stupid and fairy-taleish as this all is, but I've decided to give over to the whole scenario for the time being, because right now these men on this boat are all I've got to work with and it seems more and more that my husband is in great danger. This is no longer the time to argue the premise of the thing, though part of me even now wants to yell at Figgs to give it up, to stop trying to place responsibility for all the problems we've created on this earth on some ancient myth of questionable legitimacy.

"I don't know, Anna. I haven't a clue why he wants the float. I've just overheard enough over the years to know about the rift between Arnault and him, and I thought you should know what we're really in for here."

"And now I'm just supposed to sit back and watch the show?"

"You promised Anna."

"Right. I promised. Well fuck your precious job, Figgs. This is the father of my son we're talking about." I unlatch the door and jump from the helicopter. I'm going to go have it out with Vericombe, the old moron. I'll commandeer this goddamn ship if I have to.

Figgs grabs my arm from behind and pulls me around and to him, hard. "I've already said it all to him, Anna. It won't make any difference. Please. Just give it a few days. Think about it. If Gibbon wants to harm your husband he'll have already done so. So just let the old man go through his motions. We'll get to the next stage of things eventually." I tear myself away from him and start walking again toward the cabin. "I'd leave it if I were you, Anna. You don't know what you're dealing with. There's a good chance your husband is safer now than he will be if and when we go after Gibbon." I don't turn back to answer. I'm going to see Vericombe. I'm going to give that old fucker's head a shake.

When I storm into the wheelhouse I find him there with Smith and my son. Willow is seated at the helm, his hands on the wheel, a great big smile ear to ear on his face. I glare at Vericombe, who seems to accept it without hostility. Smith, too, looks at me with a kind of sympathy, and I realize that they've just watched from their window my and Figgs's little spat out on deck. I'm about to launch into them both, into the absolute fallacy of what I suspect they assume they were just witness to, but then Willow interjects. "Guess what, Anna?" he says. "Arnault says I can go up in the helicopter with him." He's so thrilled I can hardly believe the position I've been put in.

"Only if your mother will allow it," Vericombe corrects Willow. "Anna," he says to me, "this is of course your decision." I tighten my glare on him. It smells of musty old man in here and I find it hard to breathe.

"We need to talk," I say, and walk as calmly as I can out to the back deck. For my son's sake, I'm trying to contain myself.

Vericombe steps from the wheelhouse, his impeccable white linen shirt almost impossible to look at in the sunlight. "First of all, don't get my son excited about something and then leave it to me to spoil the party ever again. It's hard enough keeping things on the straight and narrow without you giving him some reason to freak out. Secondly, what the hell are we doing wasting our time out here?"

Vericombe considers for a moment before responding. "I apologize Anna, for offering Willow a ride before asking your permission to do so first. I have very limited experience with children. I had none of my own. It didn't cross my mind that this might create a problem for you and I'm sorry if it has. As for your question, I thought we already discussed this the other day. We're doing everything we can to find your husband. I suspect the little row I just witnessed between you and Figgs might have something to do with your asking me about this again, and in answer to that I can tell you that Figgs has his own notions of what is going on here, which I have already discussed with him, and which are based on a very limited, peripheral knowledge of the situation. There are things Figgs can not and does not know. Just as I respect that you know what is best for your son, you'll have to respect that I know what is best for this boat and this crew and this situation. I understand it must be hard for you right now, but you're going to have to trust me. There's no other way this is going to work."

Vericombe has this candour that's completely disarming, the problem with it being that I'm so thrown off-kilter by all this that my guard falling means my tears do the same, and before I know it I'm choking on my sobs again. This time I step away from him, avoiding any embrace he might offer me. I grab the steel rail with both hands and steady myself before turning back to him. "What if you're wrong Arnault? What if Gibbon has my husband already, and the woman that's with him, too?"

"Miriam."

"Right. What if he's got them both? Figgs says he won't harm them, but anyone who sends a bunch of men to shoot up a house the way he did can't be all that safe."

"He doesn't have them, Anna."

"How do you know? How could you possibly know?"

"I have more eyes than the two looking at you right now. That's all you need to know, and that's between you and me. Okay? I know for a fact that Jeremy Gibbon does not have your husband or Miriam. And I'm telling you only because I know you're not a player in all this. I can't be entirely certain of anyone else on this vessel, Fairwin' included. I've gotten to people in Jeremy's inner circle and it's clear by what happened in Hilo that he's done the same in return. So if you want to see your husband again, you do two things. First of all you keep this conversation between us. I mean that with the gravest of gravity. The only person I can trust on this boat entirely is you, because I know the only reason you're here is to find your son's father. The others I'm less certain of. Secondly, you start trusting me, too. I want your husband safe and sound on this boat as much as you do, albeit for different reasons, and if we're going to find him we have to be orderly and efficient in our efforts. Now clean yourself up." He takes a handkerchief from his back pocket and hands it to me.

"Please decide whether or not you would like your son to go for a helicopter ride, and let's go back in there with composure." He puts his hand on my shoulder. "Keep it," he says, smiling, as I offer him the hanky back. "We'll find your husband, Anna. Come hell or high water, we'll find him. And we'll finish this as it is supposed to be finished no matter what it takes. Then we can all get back to our lives as they should be. You'll see."

I follow him back into the cabin, my eyes still stinging, and give my son a big hug and a kiss on the top of his shiny blond head. "Lucky boy," I say to him. "It's going to be fun to fly, hey Bub?" This lights his eyes up instantly and he wraps his arms around me while I reach behind him and knock on the strip of wood trim lining the instrument console, hoping Vericombe knows, in so many different ways, exactly what he's doing.

⤟

I'M NOT A dreamy person. Ferris is, and Willow inherited the disposition from him, but my dreams are very seldom vivid. It's like they're low-lit movies, filmed in sepia tones, and I'm always in the audience, at least one step removed from all that's occurring. As a consequence I'm normally unaffected, unlike Willow and Ferris, who both seem to wander around some days as though still half-asleep, caught as they are in that other world. These past few days have been different, though.

Since the day Vericombe and Fairwin' started taking to the sky to search for Ferris I've been overwhelmed by a wild, boundless dreamscape that spills so far over into my waking I almost can't decipher what is real and what is not. I see Ferris in all different shapes and sizes and species. Ferris as a howler monkey, a grey whale, a mirage-like visage in a rolling desert. I've seen him old and infantile, crippled and more alive and powerful than I've ever known him. I've been sleeping at random intervals whenever the need takes me, like a wave breaking: morning, noon, the middle of the night. Willow has asked me several times if I'm okay, and I answer him yes, yes I am, and because the answer is genuine he believes me, and is reassured. And so I've been allowed to drift in and out of my dream—I think of it as this, as one long sequential dream—for almost a week now, happy to be with Ferris when I'm asleep, in whatever form he takes, and assured when awake of his still being alive and well, and of us coming nearer and nearer to him with each moment that passes, despite Vericombe's many disheartening returns, having found nothing out there in the endlessness that surrounds us.

Which is why when I wake to the sound of the helicopter coming down in the middle of a bright afternoon, and lie for a time with the dream of Ferris, young and strong, making love to me in our bedroom back home by the bay, keeping it with me even as I rise and walk to the galley, even as I pour myself a cup of coffee with cream and honey, becoming more and more aware of the commotion on deck as I do, so that I walk with my mug to the window and look out, and see the skin-and-bones likeness of Ferris laid out on the deck, naked, his body both sunburnt red and gauntly pale—it is why at that moment I don't believe it, don't believe I'm actually awake and that it is actually him. I walk to the galley table, set my mug down and smile at the dream's turn, its dark offering, before rising again to head out on deck to face it.

Which is when I realize this is actually happening, the sun's heat too real, the scene before me too tangible. Willow is on his knees beside his emaciated father, Vericombe, Smith, Fairwin' and Figgs all gathered around them. Vericombe is discussing something with Smith while Fairwin' is trying to lift Willow, dragging his feet in defiance, from his father's side. Figgs is nodding up at Smith and grabbing hold of Ferris under his arms. Smith takes his legs and they start to carry him toward me, toward the cabin. "He's alive," Fairwin' is saying to my son. "He's going to be all right Willow."

Just like that I'm jolted from my dreaminess and a severe clarity, an extremity of the state I normally function in, sets upon my mind. This is my husband passing by me, hanging limp as a hammock in the arms of Figgs and Smith, unconscious, with the appearance of one who has only the slightest veil between himself and death. I watch him pass, wanting to lunge down and take him in my arms, but my limbs are heavy as though frozen still with the inertia of sleep. I look up to see Willow coming toward me, tears gushing, so I take him instead in my arms, looking to Fairwin' and Vericombe for something, anything.

"He's going to be fine," Vericombe replies to my unspoken question. "He's severely dehydrated, but we're prepared for that. Smith is a doctor. My own personal doctor, the best I've ever known, and we've got everything we need to treat this." Okay, I think. Okay. This man has been right so far, hasn't he, despite Figgs's doubts, despite my own? Ferris is here now, and whatever his state it's better than him being out there still, unprotected, uncared for, alone.

"It's going to be okay," I tell my son, soothing him as best I can. "He's going to be okay. He's here now. We found him."

Part III

SOME WOMEN HAVE the sea in them. They have its fierceness and its tranquility. Such a woman has its depth in her body and a wind always blows around her. It rises from her. Heat transfer. They're rare. I've been to every major port on this earth, where I've bedded more whores than I care to remember. It's on my soul, that sex, those nights black as base oil, the whiskey. But that's not what's brought me to this dilemma. It's two of the few women I've known with the sea in them, Miriam and Anna—how knowing the one has led to knowing the other, and now has led me to this choice I have to make.

I first met Miriam nearly a decade ago. I'd just come off the farm, out of rehab, and after a year or so on the tugs in the Fraser and the strait I ended up in French Creek on Vancouver Island, living in a small seaside Pan-Abode at the French Creek Cottages. A friend I'd made on the farm—the son of a fisherman, and a fisherman himself whenever he wasn't too far gone on the needle—got me a job helping his old man drop a new engine into his seiner. It turned out he was doing a major refit on the whole boat, and he kept me on most of the winter, through which I picked up work on other boats in the French Creek fleet whenever we were stalled up waiting for parts, or fabrications, or decisions to be made. By the time the seiner was finished I'd built up a reputation, and so my work was in enough demand that it seemed only sensible to stay on at the cottages, as I did for a number of years, until I got this job with Arnault. But that's getting ahead of myself a bit. First, Miriam.

I met her through her husband at the time, Horace Maynard. He'd bought a hand-built wooden ketch off a bush pilot from Port Hardy, a guy who'd spent the better part of his life building her only to sell her upon completion. His retirement plan I guess, building that boat, labouring passionately—you can see it in the detailing, the precision joinery—for years just to sell her off to the first rich man willing to pay the price. Such is our lot in life, brother... So Horace was that rich man, and Miriam his wife, a woman more suited to that bush pilot for certain, just as the boat was, but it was Horace who had the bucks, and so he had it all, including me to care for his boat and desire his wife like I had not desired a woman before in my life, and haven't since, until I met Anna.

Horace bought the boat, then named the *Tsulquate River*, for a song. He had no idea the calibre of boat he had acquired, and neither did the bush pilot, obviously. At any rate, he hired me to care for her, which seemed a fine side-job to me, a bit of wood polishing and light duty maintenance instead of the usual heavy wrenching I was being hired to do by the fishermen. First thing I did was have the boat moved from French Creek to Schooner Cove, a more suitable home for her. First thing Horace did, unfortunately, was rename her.

Every seaman knows if you want to keep a boat under good stars you don't do that. Of course Horace was no seaman, and he was insistent that the word *Tsulquate* was too awkward and meant nothing to him. So he renamed her *Princess Belle*, after Miriam's second daughter, Mirabelle, and it was at the re-christening that I first met his wife. Miriam, with the long legs and hair like a head full of sunlight. She wore a white sleeveless dress with little purple flowers stitched across it. Let me be clear, I rarely if ever remember such details. I've been a man mostly driven by my own darkness and the sea-wind inside me, and I've not often taken notice of a woman in my life.

Alone is how I've preferred to be, with the sea. I've known men who've tried to have both and I've seen nothing but divisiveness and sorrow come of it. I don't claim to be a man of wisdom, but if the sea has taught me one thing it's this: of all that a man desires he can have and hold only a precious small amount, and even that is ephemeral and always under threat of being lost in the ever-coming storm. It may be different for those who live their lives on land, relatively safe and stable as it is, but out here the limits are well set, and no one survives well who doesn't live within them. So I'd forgone the comfort and love of women for the sea, and it was for the first time at that christening that I felt what it might be like to be in love, or want to be in love, with a woman.

Perhaps it was because I'd been off the deep sea for years by that point, two on the farm, one on the tugs and one in French Creek, or perhaps it was that I was ageing and it's only natural to find someone who might care for you, be there for you, in those years when caring for yourself becomes a difficulty. Maybe I had a sense the days I would still be capable of going to sea were numbered, that eventually the sea inside a woman like Miriam would be the closest I would be able to come. At any rate, I lost myself to her as I watched her break the bottle over the bowsprit, and I've not been the same man since.

It's been one thing for me to feel as I have. It's another to do something about those feelings. What I did with Miriam those first few years was to remain in French Creek, connected to her through her husband's boat, which I cared for as if it were my own. Knowing the curse brought upon it with its re-christening, and that this woman whom I loved might someday sail out onto the open ocean with her clueless husband at the helm, meant the *Princess Belle* needed to be as seaworthy as she could be to see them through.

It was quite some time after Horace's death that I finally made my feelings known to her. Another thing I've learned at sea is that timing really is everything. It means the difference between taking the right wave broadside when turning in the midst of a storm, or taking the wrong one on the stern-quarter. It's the split seconds in life that often make the difference. In this case I was months if not years off, and I can only say again it must have been my years on land that handicapped me. For me there's no clarity when the day-to-day is spent in too close a proximity to too many other people.

And so when Miriam asked me to take her up to Chatterbox Falls on the boat, I misread her. To make a long story short, she was paying her final respects to her husband while I was anticipating romance. It's hard to believe when one feels so strongly for another that they can't or don't feel the same way. And perhaps she would have come to it, given time, but while she was carrying an urn of her husband's ashes on that trip, intent on spreading them below the falls, I was carrying the expectation, as I've said, of a romantic voyage. The disparity of the two eventually led to my being replaced as caretaker of the *Princess Belle*, though in the gracious way Miriam operates it came in the way of a job offer from her husband's old friend Arnault Vericombe, and I've worked happily for him the four years since. In that time, living here aboard the *Naacal Warrior*, I've come to accept the sea as my rightful bride, and I've thought less and less of Miriam and of women in general, forgoing even my usual excursions to brothels, learning instead to be at peace with my sobriety and my solitude. Living that first truth of the sea, keeping only what I need—my clothes, my glasses, my books and my tools—here with me.

Setting out on this crossing in search of Miriam has been enough to blow me wide open, though. And then a day into it, Anna. Anna with her all-salt-and-tears body. Her angry eyes and mother's wrists, elegant and strong. I'd give anything for a taste of her, while all the while she thinks of nothing but her husband. I've had half a mind to sabotage the main just to strand us out here, but I'm too proud of my work to do that. If there's one thing I'm not, it's a lousy engineer. No ship I've ever worked on has not made its crossing soundly on account of mechanical failure and I can't, despite myself, bring myself to tarnish that record. At any rate, he's here now, contrary to what I'd planned for or expected, and I now have a much bigger decision to make.

This cellphone I'm holding in my hand was given to me a year ago by Jeremy Gibbon. I first met him also through Horace. Shortly after the re-christening of the boat he invited me to the Glass Globe to share Christmas with his family. It's true Horace and I took an instant liking to each other. Of the books I keep, the works of Herman Melville are prominent, not only for their sheer volume, but for their importance to me. Once a whaler, always a whaler, I suppose. Herman said that friendship at first sight, like love at first sight, is the only truth. That's how it was with Horace and I, despite the fact that he was a piss-poor excuse for a seaman and I was jealous of both his boat and his woman. Still, I would have turned down the invitation if it weren't for my even stronger feelings for Miriam and my inability to deny myself the opportunity to be around her. So I went for three days and nights and that's where I met Jeremy.

He was a scrawny little schoolboy then. He must have been no more than twenty-one. Miriam's daughter, Mirabelle, had met him at school in Montreal and they'd been dating for a number of years by then, I think. Long enough that he was spending the holidays there with her family instead of with his own, though I've since learned that his own isn't much of a family at all as far as holiday get-togethers go. He's the only child of two American foreign aid diplomats and he spent his childhood moving from one poor, war-torn region of the world to the next. By the time he began his secondary studies at McGill—Montreal being the closest thing he has to a home city as his parents keep a rural farmhouse in the

Gatineau Hills—he'd studied at ten different international schools, having been moved almost once a year throughout his whole childhood, quite often from father to mother and back to father, pinballing between his parents' different postings, living in hotels or guarded rentals, even at times in refugee camps. As he tells it, his longest stint in one place before he moved as a young man to Montreal was inside an armoured compound in Kigali, Rwanda, where his parents were given a rare posting together for two years following the genocide.

After he completed his studies at McGill, Jeremy joined the Peace Corps and spent a number of years living in East Africa. As I understand it, the distance eventually put an end to his relationship with Mirabelle, so you can imagine my surprise when Arnault came down to the boat a couple of years ago, Jeremy Gibbon in tow. Freshly shaven, in clean blue khakis and a button-up shirt, I almost didn't recognize him, though I've yet to forget a face. He'd put on plenty of pounds since I'd last seen him that Christmas many years past, and he'd acquired a businessman-like air he'd not had back then either. As it turns out, after his time in Africa Jeremy did an MBA at Stanford, and his visit with Arnault was precipitated by his need for venture capital investors.

While Jeremy was living in Benin, building schoolhouses and irrigation systems and mud cook-ovens in the poorest of poor people's homes, he'd lost his closest friend at the time—a young African man who was his neighbour and as Jeremy tells it now, his "dark doppelganger"—to a kerosene house fire. When he was at Stanford he and his new best friend, now his partner and president of B Light Social Enterprises, brainstormed on Jeremy's desire to rid the poor, rural world of kerosene lighting, and they eventually came up with the B Light (as in, "Let there be light") Suntorch, a little plastic lantern filled with LED lights, topped with a small solar panel and equipped with another auxiliary panel to be mounted outside the owner's home or on their roof. For ten bucks, or six months' kerosene costs, they offered the peasants of the world a safe, clean, environmentally friendly way to light their lives. It was ingenious, and the timing couldn't have been better. Over the years it has made Jeremy a reasonably wealthy man, which is why this cellphone he's given me presents such a dilemma now.

Miriam was one of the first people Jeremy went to for money with his idea, and just as she had with me, she tactfully pawned him off on Arnault. Which, at first, was a match made in heaven. Arnault invested, and took a keen interest in Jeremy and his endeavour. This was reciprocated by Jeremy's interest in Arnault's Churchwardian ideas, his obsession with all things Mu. Jeremy became as curious about and involved in Arnault's Children of Mu as Arnault did in the momentous fortunes of B Light and in the triple-bottom-line world of social enterprise and First World altruism which was the legacy given to Jeremy by his parents. At a certain point it seemed Arnault was always headed overseas to see Jeremy, or else off to some conference on the Naacal that Jeremy would also be attending.

Arnault, I think, was so tickled pink by Jeremy's success, and by the validation his interest in the Children of Mu offered, that he failed to see him for what he was: an ambitious, self-congratulatory, self-driven young man with an angel's tongue and a head full of devil's ideas. It has been to his own detriment that he's done so, and thus far to my gain, though I'm not sure where my best interests now lie. There's that old saying, it takes a rat to sniff out a rat, and Jeremy and I are in many ways of the same ilk. We both see the angles and play them all to our own best advantage.

He came to me shortly after he and Arnault had their falling-out. They'd both been first-hand audience to the Sohqui myth tablets found in the Marquesas and had contributed together to the efforts to decipher the symbols that were their text. It was in the aftermath of that deciphering that their friendship fell apart. They became polarized in their ideas of how to respond to this new, potentially world-altering prophecy. Arnault felt, as is plain to see, that in discovering the tablets they'd been entrusted by the same power that cast the curse to see now to its proper undoing. He felt it was clear that humans had done their penance, that enough of us had come to see our wrongs clearly, and that we were now being offered a miraculous means of redemption. I didn't know, nor could I guess, what other view Jeremy could possibly have on the subject until he showed up at the boat a few months after Arnault informed me of his withdrawal from the group of investors supporting B Light and of Jeremy's expulsion from the Children of Mu.

He came at night, alone, and from the moment he stepped into the cabin I knew his visit was of the secretive kind. I almost immediately asked him to leave, not wanting to get caught up in anything which might lead to the kind of situation I'm in now, standing at the bow of this boat as it cuts quickly through black water beneath a bright full moon, trying to decide which is the lesser of two evils, to give up the chance for money or for love, though it may be, if I play things properly, that I can still find a way to come out of this with both.

Jeremy cut to the chase at that meeting before I had much of a chance to decide whether I wanted to hear him out or not. He offered me this phone and said there could very well come a time when I might have information he required, and that if I were to use the phone to share that information with him I would be greatly rewarded. He slid the phone across the galley table toward me as he said this, then picked up my pack of cigarettes beside it, took one out, and lit up. A clear gesture of dominance. I had a mind to snap the little rich prick in half right then and there. But any man of my class will understand when I say that, hate the money men as we may, they're the hand that feeds us, and breaking that hand only ever leads to one's own hunger. Better to polish the rings on each finger, take what crumbs are offered, and learn to turn the anger elsewhere, inward if it must be, because a little of that eating at the insides is a lot better than the body eating itself for lack of nourishment. I took the phone, but first I had to ask.

"So what's the deal?" I'd said to him, lighting myself a smoke as well, so that we were both sitting together in the cloud of our making, reluctant confidants, co-conspirators now against the man who'd given me the best living I'd ever managed, and Jeremy the chance to build the company of his dreams and grow rich in doing so. "What could you possibly have against Arnault's preparations? Why wouldn't you want to help the prophesy be fulfilled if the float is found?"

"*When* the float is found," he'd said in reply. "Not if. It will be found. The tablets are very clear. It will be found soon." I was less sure of his and Arnault's convictions then than I am now, after all that has happened since Anna's husband found the float, but I wasn't interested in that argument then, I wanted an answer to my question, so I just flicked my ash into the tray between us and sat back, conceding the point, and he continued.

"I've seen all kinds of horrors in my life. Piles of bodies five feet high lining the streets. I had a friend in Kigali who watched his uncle disembowel his entire family, his pregnant sister—my friend's mother—included, because they were Tutsi sympathizers and he was Interahamwe. In Calcutta I knew a girl who was forced to suck off the landlord as part of her family's rent every Friday. She was fifteen when I knew her and had been living like that since she could remember."

"I know," I said. "I've seen my share of such things."

"I know what you've seen, Figgs. You've seen bars and brothels in rough port towns full of fifteen-year-old whores and men with nothing but hate in their eyes. You've seen some violence and some poverty. You've lived and worked with mates who couldn't kick the smack and were walking wraiths. But have you ever seen a father cut his son's arm off at the elbow while soldiers half his age rape his wife and his daughter? There is no limit to the vileness of humanity when it's driven in desperation beyond sanity. If we see these kinds of things in our wealthy world it's only rarely, if ever. They're freak episodes, not the endemic symptoms of poverty. We've had the assistance of our technologies so long, we don't even realize the half of what's in our nature, what we'd be like, were like, without it. Those people doing those things, that's what we are, given the impetus, given lesser conditions than you or I are accustomed to. We take for granted the superiority of our reason in the West, and that doesn't come without some legitimacy, but I'll tell you this much. Take the buffer our technologies have given us from our own selves and from nature away, and we're back to the baseness of every other species. It's all about survival, and the people I've known in my life, and I've known both the richest and the poorest, they're all the same. It's their circumstances that differ. And what makes those circumstances different is access to wealth and technology."

"What does that have to do with not wanting to see the prophesy fulfilled?"

"The tablets say that there will be brought upon the earth a great shift, a sea change, as a result of the Sohqui extinction. It is Arnault's belief that fulfillment of the cursed fisherman's quest, the shattering of the float, is the only rightful outcome. But nowhere in the tablets does it say that this must occur, or even that it should. As our technologies have become more advanced and ubiquitous, so has the abundance of the natural, non-human world been diminished. There is no question of this. But there's also been a great diminishment in human suffering. We've built a society here in the West where a majority of people can live long, reasonably healthy and happy lives if they so choose, relatively free of tyranny, scarcity, discomfort and disease. It is thousands of years of our ancestors' toil and struggle and suffering upon which we stand with that choice. Arnault subscribes to a Garden-of-Eden environmentalism, and in so doing he makes much of all that's been lost and little of what we've gained, all the while living with all those comforts and conveniences as a wealthy man in the safety and plenty of the First World, as if it's all just a matter of course. What do you think will happen if the float is broken and cast into the Mauna Kea? Do you think the Sohqui will reappear and with all their magic bring about a fundamental change in who we are? There is ample evidence of war and vulgarity and oppression amongst the Naacal. It was them who fished the Sohqui to extinction. They were no different than us Figgs. They were us."

"But they weren't, because they didn't have our technologies. You misunderstand Arnault. He believes in our advancements as much as anyone. And he believes that if we're given another chance, if the abundance of the world is restored, this time we'll have the foresight and the tools, the technologies, to use it and care for it properly."

"Right. And we'll all do it together, in cooperation. One big family of brotherly love. And what do you think, Figgs? Do you think we'll all just calmly share that renewed abundance?"

"I don't know, Jeremy. This isn't about what I think."

"Yes it is. It's about what every one of us thinks, or perhaps doesn't think. It's about when and how we don't think, or that point at which our thinking changes from the kind we are engaged in here to the kind that's hard-wired to survival. We're a complicated animal, but that's all. If Arnault's renewal were to come to fruition its only real outcome would be to postpone the inevitable, and in so doing proliferate and prolong the kinds of human suffering I've seen. We are right now coming to the fullness of our waxing as the animal world is waning. It's only natural. And as we're able to rely less and less on the non-human world for our survival, we've been forced to develop and proliferate our technologies to take its place, and we've had to cooperate in doing so. It is our common connection, our reliance upon the tools of our making, and therefore upon each other, that will bring us closer and closer to the end of suffering."

"What about the Nazis? Their barbarism was only enhanced by technology. What about nukes and chemical warfare? So we've acquired the means to spill off our aggression elsewhere. Folks send their sons and daughters overseas to do the dirty work nowadays so they can stay home and quietly hate their neighbours. What's the difference?"

"I think you know what the difference is. Of course there will always be war. But it will be contained and restrained because we eventually won't have the resources for it. As the natural world dies, we'll be forced more and more to focus on our own collective survival. And this will in turn force us away from our tribalisms and nationalisms, toward a new ethos of cooperation because our self-interest will dictate it as such. The Nazis were like a bunch of five-year-old boys playing with loaded rifles. They'd come from the farm into the throes of modernity. They were out of sync, of two worlds. The further we move away from our agrarian past, the more comfortable we become with technology, the more control we attain. It's evolution, Figgs. We'll never be free of its growing pains. We're not going to arrive suddenly or eventually at some state of enlightenment. But we're learning with each generation's advancements, and to wind the clock back, to take away the impetus of scarcity that is right now accelerating our mutual development, that will only lead to the prolonging of war and poverty as we know it."

"And you're certain of this, are you?" I stared into him as I said this, searching for any sign of doubt or falsity; of any ulterior motive at play, but I couldn't detect any. I've seen all kinds of crooks and deceivers, and Jeremy Gibbon's not one of them. As calculated and cold as his ideas are, there is a genuineness about him, even an earnestness. He placed his burnt-out cigarette in the tray and slid the cellphone to my far edge of the table, standing as he did so. "I'll give you $500,000 if the information you supply leads the float to me or me to the float. It's that simple. I haven't the time or the inclination to seek out the float the way that Arnault does, and it is futile for me to try to duplicate the coverage the Children of Mu has. So I'll let them locate it for me. And if you want the money, you'll help me do this."

"And if I don't?"

"Then you don't. And that's your choice. You know I'm good for the money. And you should also rest assured that any violence which may arise as a result of all this will only be dictated by that which Arnault and his men may escalate it to in resistance. I have no intention of bringing harm to anyone. That being so, the men I have contracted to take care of this for me have their way of handling such things, and I will not be with them when the situation arises, so it will be out of my hands. If Arnault were a wiser man he would see the wisdom in what we have discussed. I'm of the mind that humanity should not be made victim to his stupidity, and if that stupidity brings about some casualties in the course of all this it will be greatly sad, but the casualties and the sadness that will result if he is allowed to do what he proposes to is a million times greater. I'll do whatever it takes to keep that from happening. Do you understand, Figgs?"

I only nodded in response, as there was nothing more to say. It was clear these two men had declared war on each other and I was now caught in the crossfire, and my only choice was to walk away—to where though, and for what?—or choose which of them I'd stand beside.

That was a long time ago now, and it was the last I'd seen of or spoken with Jeremy Gibbon until I called him from Halfmoon Bay with the news of Fairwin' Verge's call to Arnault, and of Anna's husband's and Miriam's imminent arrival in Hawaii. That phone call earned me my five hundred grand, and just as Gibbon promised, the money has been deposited in my account. That should have been the end of it, and if I were wise, or of greater means, it would have been. But I'm neither. And I have my ever-approaching old age to consider.

So when Jeremy Gibbon offered me another fifty thousand to keep the phone on standby, I took it. And when he offered me another hundred thousand for the whereabouts of Anna's husband if and when I received that information, I took him up on it also, and I called him as soon as I was able to learn the EPIRB coordinates Anna found. I supplied this information with the understanding of course that he and Miriam would not be harmed, but now Anna's husband has been picked up in the middle of the ocean floating half-dead in a dinghy. Miriam is nowhere to be found. I don't know even if she's still alive, and Anna's husband has yet to speak. All I know is that if my actions have led Miriam to harm in any way I'll never forgive myself. And I'll hunt down Gibbon if it takes me to the end of my days. I've tried calling him and he doesn't answer, which makes me all the more suspicious. If I were of a weaker stomach I'd be sick with what I'm feeling. There's one thing I can't stand and that's being helpless. It's against every fibre of my being.

Gibbon embedded a tiny magnetic tracking device in this phone. He didn't tell me, of course, but I had the electronics guy in Parksville who works on all the boats, one of these ultra-geeks, check it over and he found it right away. You should have seen the look in his eyes, pure pleasure, at viewing such a high-tech little piece of tin and plastic. And you should have seen the look in mine. Because if there's one other thing I can't stand it's being lied to, and Jeremy's not telling me about that little thing amounts to as much. I should have tossed the phone right then and there, and I thought at least to remove the device, though I feared it might nullify our deal, and by then I'd already grown pretty warm to the idea of an extra half a million dollars padding my pocket.

But now Miriam's gone and for the first time Jeremy is not answering my calls, and I don't like what it adds up to. Since he brought Anna's husband aboard Arnault has been steaming southward full throttle back toward Hawaii and I can only imagine he's got some plan to recapture the float from Jeremy now that he has what he otherwise needs to fulfill the prophesy. And in thinking through all this it isn't hard to imagine also that the phone I'm holding now in my hand puts myself and everyone on this boat suddenly in the realm of danger, which leads to the inevitable conclusion that I have to get rid of it, even if it might, in Gibbon's eyes, negate my right to the funds I've already received. Even if it leads to his trying to recuperate them in the future. Five hundred and fifty grand, maybe more if he paid me for the EPIRB coordinates, which obviously didn't lead him to Anna's husband as I'd thought it would. I was in fact so sure it would that I baited Anna with the idea that the EPIRB had most likely been set off when Gibbon had found her husband and Miriam.

Fiery as Anna is, I knew she'd break the oath I made her swear to and go to Arnault with the idea, just as I had earlier in the day. It seemed a good way to deflect the suspicion I'd started to feel coming from him. I reasoned that if it appeared to him that I believed wholeheartedly in their abduction having already taken place a week previous, it's unlikely I would be implicated either now or in the future as having anything to do with the abduction I assumed was taking place as a result of my phone call. And of course her husband's being found only lends more credibility to my story, though Arnault still seems to look at me darkly, and the whole thing has grown much larger and more convoluted than I signed on for.

So it seems the best thing to do is to hurl this phone into the chuck, but that leaves me without my line of contact to Jeremy, and so it leaves me with far less possibility of manipulating things as they arise. If he'd answer my calls I might decide. I might be able to learn something in what he has to say, or in how he says it, which could give me a sense of what's gone on with Miriam and what might be happening in the future. But he's not answering, and so I can't bring myself to toss the phone overboard, not yet, uncomfortable as I am in knowing that by not doing so I'm allowing Jeremy

Gibbon to follow this boat's every course of direction. As the tech-geek informed me, the sensor is hardwired into the phone in such a way that it would be complicated to remove it without considerable expertise. He may have been trying to milk me, but I'm not willing to risk it.

So I'll keep the thing, for now, the sensor intact. It's against the better judgment of any good marine engineer to discard a potentially useful tool. And it would be untrue of me to say that the removal of Anna's husband from this boat, and even of her son, would be unwelcome. It might even be, after all, the overriding reason I keep this phone with me. With Miriam having already rejected me, and perhaps now no longer even alive, Anna may be the last woman I meet in this god-forsaken life who carries the sea as she does inside her, in whom I could so easily swim and sink and drown.

⌒

THIS IS THE first night since our voyage began that Anna hasn't come to see me. I've been waiting in the dim light of my room for hours. The smoke suspended over me makes the light even dimmer, and though I'm tired in my body my mind won't rest. Her husband must have finally awoken. That's the only reason she wouldn't have come. The thought of it lights a flame in my chest.

She's spoken often of her husband over the past couple of weeks. She said the other night she didn't know what she'd do if we didn't find him, and all I could think was that I did, that I knew exactly what she should do. But I've had so little experience in speaking of matters of the heart that all I could do was listen and offer her another smoke like I was offering her my life, though I know she didn't sense it as such. I was sure her husband would never be on this boat, especially then, days after I'd called Jeremy with the EPI-RB coordinates. So I thought it best to just be there for her, to go through it all with her, be her confidant. I thought there would be time after this was all over to make my feelings known, to find out first who she is and what she desires, so my advances wouldn't be met with the same rejection they received from Miriam.

But now she's in the medic room with her husband and I'm here with this jealousy burning in me like some fire that's waited my whole life for the right wind to work as its bellows and is suddenly, unfamiliarly, scorching through me. The sea and the bottle are all-consuming lovers, the kind that take and take and give only the little necessary to keep you coming back for more; this jealousy is not something I've known before and the first and only thing I can think to do as it flares through me is eliminate its fuel source, Anna's husband.

Anyone who says that killing a man is easy is both speaking a great lie and the greatest of truths. The body dies easily if you know how to make it do so. The first time I killed a man was in a back-alley brawl in Djibouti. It was gruesome how I bludgeoned him with my fists and my boots, and when I left him he was still convulsing in his blood and the red dirt of that alley. I only learned many days later that he'd died, but I realized as my mate told me that I'd already known, had already felt him enter the depths of me. It was like his soul had flown out of the body I'd beaten the life from and straight into my own. I'd been carrying the weight of it inside me for days. I still do to this day. Just as I carry the weight of the other men I've killed, and all the whales and other animals, too. They're all heavy inside me. Which is as it should be, I'm certain, but it's the part that's hard about the killing, and anyone who says otherwise is lying, or has never taken a life, or is one of those whose soul has passed far into some dark place where nothing, not grief or remorse or love, can reach to.

As for me I've felt the full heft of every life I've taken, and so don't think on it lightly when I consider how I might relieve Anna of her husband. But I can tell, can sense, that the love she thinks she has for him is merely the vestige of something which was once with her but is now gone. And I can see how she has built it back up so that it appears as though it has returned, and is with her now, and that she has done so as a means to protect herself from the prospect of losing him to the sea instead of ridding him from her life on her own terms. Control is everything to us humans and Anna is no exception. We'll go to great lengths against our better judgment and interests to retain it, and that's what Anna has done in his absence, in the face of his possible disappearance at sea. Somehow, for her, clinging to the notion of her love for him has kept her in control. So now she has to play it all out, and she is doing so right now while I lie here, waiting for her though I know she won't come, trying to make sense of everything I've felt and am feeling. Trying to decide the right thing to do. Which is, in this world, not a simple thing to come to.

I'm not sure of our coordinates, but I know we're getting close to the Hawaiis now. Arnault asked me tonight to ready the chopper again first thing tomorrow morning. It could be he's gotten his hands again on the float. It could be Jeremy Gibbon is dead, which would account for his not returning my phone calls. Or it could be Arnault is taking us right into the centre of a shitstorm. Underestimating one's adversary is the greatest mistake in any fight. It's why Sea Shepherd lost that two-million-dollar speedboat to the Japanese whalers last winter. Paul didn't think they had it in them to tear it in two, just as Arnault might not appreciate what Jeremy Gibbon may do now. If he were smart he'd have purged this boat of its crew the minute the float was stolen from Sunimoto. As it is, he's only mentioned it in passing, as though it were to be expected, a matter of course, while every moment he's handicapped by my presence still on this boat, by the cellphone in my drawer sending its little signal up to the sky.

I take it from the drawer and put my boots and coat on. As I climb the fo'c'sle ladder up to the deck I'm calculating it all, the money, Anna, the risks of losing both, though neither is actually with me here, in my hands. I take the phone to the edge of the deck and toss it overboard. Now I've got nothing but the old sea, my desire for Anna and the ghosts I carry, with a little room maybe for one more now, way down in the darkest part of me, a place I've not entered into since I last drank the whiskey, and it occurs to me that if I'm going to do this there's one thing I'll have to do first.

⇝

ARNAULT KEEPS HIS single malt in the galley, in the high pantry cupboards beside the diesel stove. He's the only one who drinks on-board, aside from the odd nip Smith shares with him some evenings, so it's as good a place as any for it. I've been sober now for a decade, but the first ounce goes down easy. I'd have taken this as a fall, and taken it hard, even a couple of years ago, but something changed for me when I turned fifty. It's not that I stopped caring, but I stopped being concerned. I'm in the firing range now, and time spent dwelling on what's past isn't a luxury I can afford any longer. Back in the days when I fought for the whales I fought always for the future. But the only future I've got to look forward to is my own old age, my own being put out to pasture, and I've paid my dues to the future beyond that, the one I won't live to see. So what I work with now is just that, the here and now. One day at a time, as the adage goes.

The Scotch plies me open as it slides down my throat. I light a smoke to temper the rush. It's like a flood tearing a widening trough in me just as a river does when it swallows its banks, then its entire valley. The fifth ounce is always the sweet spot, where everything comes clear before it disappears into the fog that follows. It's here I can take the true measure of myself and it strikes me how essential this has been throughout my life. I've been hiding under Arnault's wing for years now because without access to this point of clarity I'm lost, and impotent, and it's made a coward of me in the world.

An old friend of mine in the program once told me there are cycles to sobriety, just as there is to everything in life, and to deny this, to keep from the drink beyond what is necessary, is to live in stasis, caught in a net of one's own fear. He'd been in and out of the program for twenty years and he had this unorthodox reverence for the twelve steps and the bottle both. The life worth living, he said, was the one lived skipping from edge to edge. I always thought of this as his own complex denial. But now I'm seeing it in a different light, feeling the liquor opening me in ways and in places I thought lost to the past, and I can see there's room in me, more capacity maybe than there's ever been before, and it makes my decision easy knowing this, so as I pour myself another drink, I take it.

⤸

I WOKE UP this morning with my resolve unwavering. I'm not one of those men who is of one mind in the night and another in the morning, the liquor worn off. Those are the weakest of men, the kind who have nothing at their core. I quit drinking not because it made me into some sort of monster I'm otherwise not, but because it seemed to be suppressing something in me I wanted to come to the fore. Which I've found now, and it makes this kill I'll make easy. It's lack of clarity that confounds things in life. Anna doesn't see me, not entirely, because the father of her son is perpetually cast like a veil before her eyes. I'll lift it and be standing there before her when her eyes adjust their focus.

I enter the medic room and see him for the first time since Smith and I hauled him in off the deck two days ago. It's dark in here, a towel tacked over the small porthole and all the lights out. By the hallway light casting in over my shoulder I can see he's as gaunt still as he was when he first came aboard, his damaged body sunken in on itself. He's on the edge, and will go easily over, having next to nothing in him to fight for the air I'll keep from his lungs. I close the door behind me and its little click wakes him. He turns toward the sound and there's fright in his eyes as he struggles to set them upon me. I walk to the opposite end of the room and take the towel from the window, letting the last of the day's light into the antiseptic whiteness. I'll ease him into this and I'll find out what's become of Miriam while I do so.

I pull a chair up close to his bedside so he can bring me into focus through his weakness. I've been close to death before, much as he is now, stranded in the aftermath of a wicked storm for nearly two weeks alone inside an inflatable life raft on the Indian Ocean. There was no relief in being finally rescued. It gets like that, or at least it did for me. The closer I got to death the more I wanted to finish the journey. I can see that same disappointment in this man's eyes, the pain of being forced to find desire for life again when death has already been resigned to, and I'm almost inclined to think he might hold the pillow over his own face for me.

"I'm Figgs," I say to him. "I'm the engineer." He only nods, and only slightly, in reply. "I was a good friend of Miriam's at one time, when her husband was still alive." He nods again. "You want some water?" I ask, and again he nods.

I draw him a glass of water at the sink, then set it down beside him and help him sit, arranging his pillows so he's propped up on a forty-five-degree angle. I drop one down at my feet as I do this, for later, then I hold the glass to his lips and help him drink. Smith has him hooked up to a couple of different bags so it's awkward accomplishing all this, but I do it to put him at ease. I think a man ought to die as he ought to live, with as much dignity and grace as this world will offer, and if it will be my hand that brings death upon him then it will be a hand of light turning him to the darkness. He manages a meek "Thanks," as I take the glass from his lips, his voice passing through them like wind through a dry, hollow reed.

I can hear the thrumming of Arnault's chopper approaching outside the room's walls. He radioed in ten minutes ago to let Smith know he'd be arriving, to be ready for his landing, as we'll be steaming full speed from here as soon as he touches down. We're ten miles or so off the coast of Maui and Arnault's been gone the better part of the day. If he told Smith what he's doing on the island, or even which island he's on, Smith hasn't let on. When he came down to inform me of Arnault's approach, I knew now was the time to take care of this. They'll all be rushing out to the deck to meet Arnault as he lands. If you can count on one thing about people at sea it's that their boredom eventually gets the better of them and they'll go running like clockwork to the slightest stimulus.

"What happened to her? Where's Miriam?"

He closes his eyes when I ask this, and when he reopens them they're glazed over with the look of tears, though none form, his ducts likely too dry. But the look is unmistakable, and I can see in it instantly that he loved her, and that he watched her die helplessly, against his best efforts and every bit of his will. I'm not sure what kind of response I'd been expecting, but it wasn't this. I suppose I assumed she'd drowned, or been taken or killed in violence, but I can already tell by the grief in his eyes that hers was a death of a different nature. She told me once after Horace passed away that she figured he was the luckiest man in the world to go out so quick and easy the way he did. No drawn-out fuss. An acute pain perhaps, but then an end almost instantly following. The only way to go. "How?" I ask. "How did she go?"

"Blood," he manages, though I have to lean in close to his lips to hear him, and he has to repeat it so I do. "Blood."

"Did you do it?" I ask him. I know the answer. Still something, perhaps what I'm about to do, makes me ask it. He moves his face once side to side in reply.

"Inside her," he says now, and I'm starting to get the picture.

"Did it go on for long?" I ask, the thought of Miriam suffering as she must have starting to burn inside me. He nods in reply. I want to ask him why he didn't help her, but I can see in his eyes he would have done anything, would have given his own life to save hers, and I'm starting to see that he might want this death I'm here to give him more than I know. Or as much as I've known during those times in my life when I've felt I couldn't live with the things I'd done or seen.

"Did you love her?" I ask, and there's the flame of jealousy stoking inside me again. Both these extraordinary women. He's had both of them. He's had the love in his life I've never been granted, and I can't comprehend why it's been like this, how he's been so fulfilled as I've been left so devoid, so vacant, except to say that for whatever reason, all that I've had in this life I've taken by guts and sweat and force. Nothing has been easily given, and it's been my own folly that I've waited for love to be as though it should be the one exception, the one thing I shouldn't have to snatch from the jaws of a life that won't relinquish to me the slightest sustenance without a struggle. So be it. This man's had his share of what will be mine for the taking. He can be with Miriam in heaven or hell, it's of little concern to me now where she is and where he's going. I hear the faintest "Yes," slither off his tongue as I reach down to grab the pillow from the floor. I lift it before his face, his eyes wild with fright as he realizes what I mean to do.

There's a deceleration of time that occurs in such moments, a honing of the world down to a singular tunnel of space. In this his mind and my mind are conjoined, and as I press the pillow down over his mouth and his nose and his eyes, it's like I'm doing so over my own. We both give only the slightest struggle, his in his body's weak resistance and mine in the slight stirring of emotion, the one that makes murder a counterintuitive act, that makes most people so certain that what I'm doing here is the gravest of wrongs, though they're all only the perfect storm of circumstances away from doing the same themselves. I lean in on him as his feeble hands try one last resistant grasp on my forearms before they slacken, and it's then that I come back to the world and hear the commotion approaching from beyond the door. Quickly I pull off him, drop the pillow to the floor, and kick it beneath his bed as I sit.

Anna comes into the room in a rush of excitement. "He got it!" she blurts out as she approaches the bed. Willow, Arnault, Smith and Fairwin' all enter the room behind her, Arnault holding the float in his arms. He turns the bright overhead fluorescent on. Oscillating as I am in that state of heightened, piercing perception I just went into with Anna's husband, the float comes into enhanced view in my eyes, and I could swear there is a swirl of colour whirling inside it, like it has its own centrifugal energy, its own orbited centre. An entire world in that orb of glass.

"Wake up Ferris," Anna is saying to her husband from the opposite side of the bed. "Wake up." She shakes him at the shoulders as Smith leans across me. "Oh my God, he's not breathing!" she yells out, hysterical, as Smith palpates his neck for a pulse. I slip out from beneath him and step back behind them all.

Smith looks up at Arnault quickly. "The resuscitator," he says, and he immediately pries open the unbreathing mouth and seals his lips over it. Arnault begins rifling through the cabinets beside the sink. "Other side, under the anaesthetics," Smith instructs him, then breathes again, trying to give back to the body the breath I've just taken from it. Anna's husband is still here, I can still feel him, not inside me but locked like a shackle around a link of chain, so that now it is me who feels suffocated, feels the need to struggle for release. I'm about to leave the room when Arnault tears the ventilator from its bag, attaches the mask to the tube, and hands it to Smith, who sets it down over the face I've just leaned the full weight of my life upon and starts to pump.

As soon as the breath comes back to the body Arnault leads the kid, who's now holding the float in his hands, to his father's side. Then he turns toward me, looking me square in the eyes. I have the sense he knows, which doesn't occupy me as much as it maybe should, lost as my concern is in the sight of Anna falling over her husband, tears gushing from her eyes. "Get a tray from the galley and a hammer," Arnault commands me. I slip out of the room, freeing myself from the spellbind between Anna's husband and myself.

In the galley I retrieve what Arnault requested, pausing for a second at his drawer of well-sharpened knives, considering... but that's just the intensity of the past few minutes getting the better of me. There will be other times, and better ways, and so I come back to the room with the tray and hammer. Arnault takes them both from me and sets the tray down on the bed beside Anna's husband.

"Hold your father's hand," he says to the kid, taking the glass float from his hands and putting the hammer in its place. The float he sets down in the tray. "Lightly, son, just as we talked about. Start by cracking it a bit, so we don't lose the pieces." Anna's husband is still unconscious, but everyone else is riveted to the child. He taps at the glass with the hammer, to no consequence. "A bit harder," Arnault says.

Standing as I am in the doorway I can hear a distant thunder pulsating the air. I step from the room out to the galley and look out the window. I can see the silhouettes of two choppers coming straight at the boat against the last light in the southwest sky. Gibbon. I run back into the room as Arnault nearly screams at the kid. "Smash the fucking thing then!" Willow brings the hammer down on the float with all his force, but it just ricochets off.

"Arnault," I say, but he doesn't even turn in response. He tears the hammer from the kid's hand and puts it in the unconscious hand of Anna's husband. "Here," he says tersely, putting the kid's hand over his father's. "Now. Strike it like this. Hard." The kid does, but still nothing happens.

"Arnault!" I holler at him now, and he turns to me finally as something explodes out on deck. Then there's another explosion that shakes the boat violently. I run down the hallway, through the galley and out onto deck.

Arnault's chopper is in flames and there's black smoke billowing up from below the cap rail of the bow. I watch as a fire blaze issues from one of the circling choppers and slams into the hull, again shuddering the boat across its length. The alarms start wailing under the compressive thunder of the choppers and Arnault comes out on deck as another shot issues from one of them and again the hull is torn open and set ablaze.

We each have our duties in such a scenario, and mine is to get the pumps drawing from the bilge. I jump back into the cabin and start to the back of the hallway. Smith is before me in the middle of the passageway, fumbling frantically with a phone in his hands. As I arrive at his side I see it's a red Motorola, the duplicate of the one Jeremy Gibbon had given me, and as he looks up at me the panic in his eyes is laced with the kind of terror that comes over someone when they suddenly recognize that it is only by their own mishandling of circumstance that things have turned terribly wrong. But there's no time for that, not now, so I push past him and through to the engine room access, where I look below and see water swirling in. I drop down the ladder and land in it up to my shins. The washdown hoses on this boat both draw from different thru-hull ports, and on each one there is a ball valve that can be switched over so the intake is rerouted to two screened wide-diameter pipes in the bilge: one under the main engine, and one on the other side of the bulkhead separating the engine room from the hold.

I slosh over to the main and plunge my arm into the water, feeling for the first of these valves. As I get my fingers on it another artillery slams the boat, throwing me face down into the water. I emerge just as another tears open the sidewall of the engine room and the sea rushes in, a gushing white torrent, and I go under again and feel my body slam against the steel stairs I've just descended. Then I'm blind and inside it, the dark sea, I'm inside it and there's no escaping this time. It's inside me, and in this there's a completion, a perfection, just as I've always wanted and dreamt there would be.

IF HE SPEAKS of it at all it's in the middle of the night. He'll wake beside me, feverish with sweat, in a terrified panic. That's also when he'll allow me to make love to him. It's always one or the other. He'll climb on top of me and put himself quickly, fully inside me, or else he'll start talking. When he does it's more like he's telling himself the story than he is telling it to me, staring up at the shadow of the bars on our bedroom window cast across the ceiling. We lie beneath it together like two captives, staring up at it as he speaks. A couple of nights ago, after he'd finished telling me again about the man he sees in his dreams—the man with the roughest of hands, the smell of bearing grease on his skin, the look of death in his coal-black eyes—he said to me how odd it was to him that the shadow never shifted.

At first I didn't get what it was he meant by that, and then I understood. If it were cast by the moon it would be ever-changing, tilting and stretching out and in through the nights. But here in our little house on the corner of Fraser and Fourteenth there's only the street light's glare falling through our window, and the sound of the traffic sweeping past at all hours is a far cry from the wash of the waves on the beach beyond the bedroom he once shared with Anna. I know he longs for her. For his son, for their home and for that time. The time before he found the float. He came back to me changed, without the love I know I once had for me. I know he has it for Emily still, and I see him some days choosing to feel it for me, too.

Some days even, I think maybe that choice he's making, that effort, might lead him back to me, back to how it used to be between us, but then we go to sleep and he wakes in the middle of the night from one of his dreams and he puts himself inside me and it feels nothing like what it used to. Like it's not me he's loving at all but his own grief and anger, his memories of what he's lost, of what he'll no longer have in this life. In the morning I know he is ashamed, but there's nothing that I can do for him. He has to find his own way back to me, and though I can see him trying, for now he is still somewhere out there on that sailboat with that woman, or on the boat that sank and took Willow down with it. Or maybe he's still drifting alone, unconscious, yet to be washed ashore, his arms wrapped tightly around the glass float that lives now under this bed that we share, beneath this shadow-cage cast in perpetual stasis across our ceiling.

But I'm kidding myself with such thoughts. The fact is Francis washed up on a black-sand beach on the north coast of Maui some time after Arnault Vericombe's boat sank. His arms were locked around the float. He'd been holding onto it for dear life, literally, though he remembers nothing of this. What he does recall of the time following his rescue from the rowboat are only hazy snippets. Soaring in a roaring chamber. Anna singing to him in a white room. The man with the black eyes smothering him. He remembers Willow cupping his hand, something cold and hard in his palm. If it weren't for the fact that the Coast Guard also found Fairwin' Verge and Anna floating off the coast of Maui, that's all he would know of what went on. Which would be for the better, in one respect. But as it is, Francis has been to visit Fairwin' several times out on Lasqueti Island, and after each visit he seems to return with a greater sense of things.

When he first began these visits I had hoped it would bring some kind of clarity for him, some kind of closure, but every time he comes back with greater sadness and with more questions, and quite often upon his return I have to call in sick to my uncle for him so he can stay home in bed. He sleeps these days away, and then he's up in the middle of the night, going over again how he doesn't understand why the float wouldn't break, why it still won't break, and doesn't know why that man, the engineer, would have wanted to kill him—though he's not even sure that he tried to, only that he feels like he did, he dreams it. Fairwin' says the engineer was the only one in the room when Francis stopped breathing and that he was the kind of man that was capable of doing such a thing, though why he would have wanted to kill Francis Fairwin' can't say either.

Francis goes around and around these things in his head, obsessively, and I sometimes fear he'll never stop, that he's doing it to keep from facing what is for him still unfaceable, that Willow is dead, and that it is his fault, a result of the whole thing he got his son wrapped up in with the float. Sometimes I feel like the only thing that will ever release him from all this is its breaking, and in those times I take it from beneath our bed and I try to smash it myself. I've beaten it with a hammer as hard as I can. I've tossed it with all my might down onto the sidewalk in front of our house. I'd throw it in the trash, or back to the sea, if I didn't think it would lead only to Francis forever searching for it, forever lost to Emily and me.

After his first visit to Lasqueti, he came back with some of the old fire in his eyes. At first I thought it was because he'd been out on the water for the first time since his return. He swore he'd never fish again the very first day he arrived home. Within a month he'd sold the boat, settled up with Anna, and we'd bought this house with the money he had left and a letter to the bank from my uncle that said he would keep Francis employed. For the first few months living here, he refused to go see Fairwin' because that meant going by boat. This house was considerably cheaper than it would have been before the quake, but it's still all we can afford to make the mortgage and feed ourselves on what Francis earns, so chartering a plane is out of the question, and regardless Francis says he won't fly either. I think he feels like death is stalking him, like somehow he's living on borrowed time. Some days this makes him uncontrollably anxious and he skips work to take long walks all day alone. He says he just wanders around the city looking at all the restoration and new construction work. He says it helps him think, the aimlessness, but I think there's more to it than that. I think on those days he feels death is somehow at his heels and his walking and walking is an attempt to shake it. It was after one of these walks that he declared he had to go to Lasqueti, and the next morning he woke up before dawn and left.

He came back, as I said, with the old look in his eyes, focused intensity. And for a while it seemed that his spirit was finally returning to him from wherever he'd lost it out on the sea. He was still distant, distracted, but every day he grew more lively, animated, more like the Francis I'd known before he found the float. So I was hopeful, for a time.

Then he went to visit Fairwin' again. This time he returned with a near-manic look and energy about him. Over his shoulder he carried a duffle bag I hadn't seen before. He set it down in the living room, not bothering even to take his shoes or coat off first, unzipped it, and lifted out the float. Then he took my pestle from its mortar and placed them both on the coffee table in the living room. I was nursing Emily while I watched him do this. "Give her to me," he said, holding his arms out toward her and me. It was with the same certainty of desire that he did this as he used to have when he'd reach for us, and seeing it there in him almost made me weep. But I held back my tears as I unlatched Emily and handed her to him. He set her on his lap and put her little fingers around the pestle, wrapping his hand around hers and the pestle as well. Then he struck the float, but nothing happened. He struck it again and again like this, but it stayed round and perfect as ever each time.

Eventually he batted it from the table, set Emily down at his feet, and left the house cursing. He didn't come back until well past dark, well past the time I'd put Emily down. I'd been sitting up waiting for him, worrying, for many hours when he finally came through the door. He was soaked right through, dripping a puddle on the old wood floor in the entranceway where he stood, shivering. I went to him and stood in front of him, saying nothing, looking for the look that had been there earlier. But he looked again as though he were staring out from inside a dream. All he said was, "It's so cold this year, Jin Su. Why is it always so cold?"

It's true, it's been colder this fall than I have ever seen or thought was possible, but I knew then as I know now there is more in what he was asking than that. I have no answer for him. The truth is I don't know Francis well enough to know what it is he needs from me or anyone else, so I keep most of my thoughts to myself and go through these days with him, caring for our daughter, trying to care for him, hoping something will change inside him so he will eventually come back to me, to us, fully himself and alive, instead of as this ghost that wanders through our home, sleeps beside me in this bed, and wakes from one dream into another, trying to take from me something I can't give him, something no one can give him, because what has happened has happened and nothing can change that. Nothing can bring back what's died from the world. Not any amount of wishing or hoping. Not the breaking of any magic antique fishing float. I have no way of explaining why it won't break. But to take it as evidence of some mystical prophecy is a leap of faith, and it's that faith that Francis is clinging to now; and it's that faith that is keeping him locked away in the past, like he's caught inside a globe of glass himself, and I fear sometimes that, as with the float, we'll never find a way to break it.

⌐

THIS MORNING I decided to take the float from beneath the bed and let it loose. I thought while I lay awake after Francis fell back asleep last night that keeping the float hidden from view isn't going to help. Treating the thing like some sacred object has only given it more power than it already has over Francis, and if I can't break the thing the least I can do is try to break the spell it has him under. He has never explained to me why it was he was striking the float with Emily that day. He won't discuss much of whatever it is he and Fairwin' do, or what it is Fairwin' has told him, during their visits. Aside from his middle-of-the-night recallings of what he remembers, Francis won't discuss any of it with me. He won't let it out into the light of day and I've realized this must end. Until now I haven't challenged him on anything, but this way of being is killing him, slowly, and it has to stop. So I took the float from its box beneath the bed and gave it to Emily to play with. She's been batting it around the house most of the day, crawling after it as it rolls across the kitchen floor, down the hallway, across the living room. I wish I could do the same with all of Francis's grief. Just wrap it up into a ball and give it to our daughter for her to bash around the house.

With that in mind I've decided to tell Francis I want him to go back to being a fisherman. I'm sure this will upset him at first. But I also know that his decision to sell the boat was one made in grief and out of fear, and I know he'll never emerge from either until he faces them. Until he faces the sea. He says he won't go back out because he won't give the sea a chance to take more than it already has from him. But what about all that it's given? My family have been fishermen on both my mother's and my father's side for as long back as anyone can remember, and if I know one thing it's that once a fisherman, always a fisherman. For those who come to love working on the sea, no job, no life, can ever compare. Even my uncle, as wealthy as he's become since immigrating to this country and working in the city as a fish buyer, bought himself a salmon troller a few years ago so he could get back out onto the sea. He earns nothing fishing compared to what his business makes him, and some trips out he really does make nothing, but that's not the point.

And it's not the point for Francis either. This life we're living isn't his. He's a fisherman, and the look I no longer see in his eyes is the look every lover of the sea gets from being out upon it. I want him to go and find that again, because I've come to realize this shroud of fear we're living under is killing me, too, and I didn't come to this country to live like this. People here don't realize the opportunity for freedom they have. They seem to use whatever they can to make it so their lives are ones of suffering and loss. Francis, I've come to see, is no exception, and without the infusion of freedom he used to get from fishing he's turned into another one of the hungry ghosts in this city, oppressed by his own fear and inertia.

I hear his footsteps coming up the front porch. I've thought all day of how I'll get this through to him. How I'll tell him without turning him further away from me, without presenting my thoughts as ultimatums. But as I hear him approaching the front door I act without thinking. I go to the entrance hallway so that I'm standing before him as he comes in, shivering again from the cold. "You should wear more layers," I say, as he closes the door behind him. He hadn't noticed I was here, and this is unlike the habit I have of giving him time to enter the house unaccosted. So my words startle him, which is what I want. I want him shaken.

"Jesus Jin Su," he says as he takes off his jacket. "What's going on?" he asks, a faint, forced smile on his face. I reach up and kiss that smile, and take him by the hand, pulling him into the house. "I've got to get out of these clothes. I'm freezing," he protests, but I don't care, I want this out of me right now. It's been almost five months of this and enough is enough.

I lead him into the living room and sit him down on the sofa. It's a long, narrow room that looks to the east, to the wall of our neighbour's house, so close you can almost touch it. Emily is on the far end of the room opposite us and as I sit down beside her father I watch her look up with the joy she gets when she hears his voice for the first time at the end of the day. "Yiiiieeeee!" she shrieks, and rolls the float toward us, crawling after it. It rolls quick and smooth across the floor and stops at my feet. I pick it up and hold it before Francis.

"This," I say. "This thing may never break Francis. But I won't live my life with it hidden like some sickness beneath our bed." An anger rises to his eyes as I say this, which is what I want. Anger, hatred, joy, it doesn't matter. I just want a reaction from him, some emotion, and as he reaches for the float I see the contempt in his eyes and I hold it away from him so more might come. I stand and walk across the room, pick up Emily, and hand her the float. "What's the problem Francis?" I ask as he rises, too. "What the hell's going to happen? It's not like she's going to wreck the thing. What the hell does keeping it hidden accomplish?"

Afraid to go himself, Francis sent Fairwin' to Hawaii to retrieve the float. Ever since his return Francis has wished it was still there buried in the sand. He fears whoever it was that sunk the boat will come looking for it. But that hasn't happened. "You're not hiding it from anyone but yourself now, Francis," I say.

"Give it to me," he says. I turn to put myself between the float and him, holding Emily tight in my arms.

"I won't do it anymore. I won't live like this," I say. I've not wanted to do this, to force him, to be the way he always told me Anna was. But I can see now it may be the only way he knows how to be,

307

and it occurs to me that perhaps it's as much my lack of engagement as anything else that has allowed him to sink further into his grief instead of emerging out of it. He spins me around violently so Emily is facing him again. It's the first time I've felt him, really him, touching me since he came back, and I want more. I take the float from Emily's hands and she starts to cry. She's lived in a world of pain with us, but this is the first fight she's seen. The mother in me flares for a moment and I consider letting it go, giving him the float and letting enough be enough for now.

But then Francis speaks. "You don't have the first fucking clue of what you're talking about, Jin Su. At least you're alive." This raises me back to it instead and I respond with an anger to equal his.

"And so are you Francis. But you walk around this house like the living dead. Look at your daughter. Look at me. Do you even see us here? Do you?"

"What kind of question is that?" he asks, and this sets me even further into it.

"You're with Anna and Willow, Francis. You can't let them go and you've got us around you like stray dogs waiting for scraps."

"That's not fair, Jin Su," he yells at me over Emily's wailing. "I'm not with Anna am I? No. I'm right here. Every day. In this stupid fucking house we live in, in this fucking hell-hole city. For Christ's sake Jin Su, my son's dead. My fucking son. Dead." He's crying too now. The first tears I've seen from him, ever. "I'm trying. Every day I'm trying. What the fuck more do you want from me?"

"You Francis. Like this. I want you here with us."

"What the fuck does that mean? I am here. See." He tugs at his shirt, then twists his hands together in front of my face as I back away.

"No you're not. That's the thing. You're here. But you're not here. You're a ghost Francis, and you're starting to scare me." I'm crying now, with my daughter. We're both bawling. I hold the float up in front of him. "This," I say. "You're lost inside this ball of glass

Francis. And I suppose if that's what you want, if that's all you want is to be trapped with this thing, you might as well take it." I want him to say something. Something we're on the brink of now. Something of recognition. But it's not in me to fight like this. If this is what he needs, for me to call him out of himself the way Anna did, screaming and yelling like this, he should go back to her. I can't do it.

He reaches out to take the float from me. As he does Emily lunges at it with a burst of that fire she has in her and swats it out of my hand. It hits the floor and explodes between us, sending shards across the room, scattering flecks even into the hand-woven silk rug my father sent from China after my mother died. An heirloom passed down for generations in my family from mother to daughter, mother to daughter. The one Emily will leave to her daughter one day, long after I'm gone.

WHEN I AWOKE on the beach in Hawaii I had no idea where I was or what had happened. I don't remember the boat going down, the helicopters, any of it. The last thing I recall before waking on the shore is the black eyes of the man whom I think tried to kill me. Everything I know now of what occurred on that boat I've learned since from Fairwin' Verge. But when I woke up that day on the dark sand, the breaking waves rushing up and down my body, I knew nothing but fear and confusion. There I was, naked but for my underwear, wrapped foetal around the glass float, the one I'd lost, with no idea of how it had come back into my possession. I could recall only traces of Anna and Willow at my side, Anna singing, her warm hand on my heart. Willow with fear in his eyes.

I dragged myself up to the top of the beach, a small cove with high volcanic cliffs all around, and there, well above high water mark in the centre of the cove's arc, I dug a deep hole in the sand, placed the float in, and buried it. I took dead reckoning off two points: a towering tree to my left that loomed its broad, splayed leaves over the beach, and a cave-like impression in the cliff to my right. Two hundred and thirty-one paces to the one, 418 paces to the other. I blazed those numbers into memory. Then I laboured across the clean beach and into the otherwise non-descript foliage, up a forested slope, till the land plateaued. For a distance I made my way over open fields of grass till I finally found a road. The first car that came by stopped.

"Where am I?" I asked the man at the wheel. I'd used what little energy I had burying the float, and by then it was all I could do to push the words from my mouth. "Can you tell me exactly where this is?" He looked at me as though I were some kind of freak show—I must have looked frightening, bearded and emaciated as I was—and very nearly drove off till I explained to him that I'd been at sea, had just now woken up on the shore, and that I had no idea what had happened to me, but thought it important to at least remember where it was I had washed up. We recorded the reading on his odometer, and when we got to the hospital in Kahului, we recorded it again. Then I had him draw a map for me of the route we'd taken to get to the hospital and I walked into the ER without him.

Eventually I was taken to the local police station, where I told them who I was and the story of Miriam and I, leaving out the float, the meeting with Sunimoto, and Miriam's death. I told them I had no idea what had happened to her or the boat, which was in a sense true, or how I'd come to be back in Hawaii, which was also true. Then I was taken back to the hospital and kept there for what must have been over a week before they finally released me with a fresh change of clothes, a temporary passport and a ticket home.

I had a severe anxiety attack on the plane ride over the Pacific, and I was met at YVR by Jin Su, Emily and Jin Su's uncle (who had covered the hospital bill as well as my airfare and other expenses), and by paramedics. I spent another night in hospital trying to catch my breath, basically, before finally going home to Jin Su and Emily at her uncle's house. I still didn't know what had happened to Anna or to Willow. And it wasn't till I returned to Halfmoon Bay a few days later and found them gone that I started to understand my hazy memories and the hollow I felt at the centre of myself. The one I still feel now, and always will, now that Willow is dead and Anna is gone.

⌇

ANNA SURVIVED THE sinking by clinging to an insulated plastic tote for two days before the Coast Guard found her. By the time I arrived home she had already returned, taken some clothes, and left with her parents up to Sicamous. I've seen her only once since, at the lawyer's office when the boat sold. She wouldn't look me in the eye. Wouldn't speak with me or open to me when I tried to take her in my arms. I'm not sure what's worse, Willow's death, or her scorn. I had Svend clean out our rental house for me once Anna's father called to say they'd been back again to retrieve the few things she wanted. I couldn't do it, so I told Svend to just empty it out and take it all to the thrift store or the landfill. I didn't care. If I couldn't have my old life back as it was, I wanted none of it.

Since then, Jin Su, Emily and I have settled into something comfortable, especially now that Fairwin' Verge has come and taken the shards back to Hawaii. I keep waiting to hear word from him that it's been done, that the pieces have been thrown into the Mauna Kea. I'm hopeful for some kind of release in that moment, but I know it's a false hope. Maybe all hope is. I'm not sure. Any sense of certainty I had about such things drowned with my son. Now it's enough to just get through the day, and when I say that I mean it not in the *one day at a time* kind of way. I mean it absolutely.

Each day is enough for me. It has to be. I don't have any idea whether the shards of glass being cast into the Mauna Kea will bring about some sudden re-seeding of the sea, and I'm not sure that I even care. It was another lifetime, in another world, wherein such things seemed so important. Now I go to work, I do the job I'm given to do, and I come home grateful for the woman and the child I still have with me. And although the love we share is different than the love Anna and I had, and even the love I felt with Miriam, I'm a different man now without Miriam in the world or Anna in my life, and that different man that I am wants nothing more than what we have. The hollow at the centre of me is something I'm learning to live with, and I've come to understand it's not just the loss of Anna and Willow that has left it in me, but it is also the shrinking of the mammoth desire I used to carry inside. The one that wanted more than what Anna and I had, that ultimately led to everything happening as it has. Now I carry it like a small chest of dark treasure locked and buried, and I allow myself to dig it up and admire its glittering fool's gold only on the long walks I take through this city, alone inside this year's cold that won't seem to relent.

Jin Su says she wants me to go back to the sea, to being a fisherman, and I know it's the desire in me she wants brought back. The thing is, she doesn't see how dangerous it can be. Or she can and she doesn't care perhaps, because she hasn't lost to it what I've lost. To the contrary. Changed or not, she has gained me through all this. I'm now unquestionably hers, though she argues otherwise. That I still have my memories and my grief and my love for Anna is beside the point, ultimately, because I live with them tucked away inside me here, in this city, with her and our daughter, and those other things will diminish, as all things do, with time.

When Fairwin' Verge told me everything he'd learned from Arnault Vericombe about the true meaning of the myth and about my role within it, we were both ecstatic at the possibility that Emily might be the one to break the float. He said he'd realized this potential long before the moment when Willow wasn't able to break it, but he'd been caught between this awareness and the vow of secrecy he'd made to me. So he did what he felt was right and kept Emily's existence to himself. Arnault had said so many times, *Passed down through the generations, father to son.* He'd given no indication that the curse might also include daughters, let alone that it might be strictly matrilineal, as it turns out is likely the case. When he saw that the float wouldn't break, Arnault panicking, hollering at Willow, Fairwin' realized the error in his secrecy, but by then it was too late, and the next thing he knew he was clinging to a piece of the destroyed boat, floating through the dark, watching the last of it burn and sink.

When my attempts to break the float with Emily failed, it brought upon me finally a darkness so complete I know now I could see nothing other than that failure, all my failures, and it's what has brought rise now to Jin Su's insisting that I return to fishing, to the sea. She thinks that is what's gone from me, its energy, its vitality. How do you tell the woman who needs more than anything for you to be strong and sure in a world full of threats and vulnerabilities that what you've lost is your very centre of gravity, even your buoyancy? That you're a hull full of holes and she's the float you're moored to, the only thing keeping you from sinking?

I've come out of that now that the float has been broken and Fairwin' has taken the shards to Hawaii. But there are all these lingering things I live with. Today I saw a man on the SkyTrain who I could swear had the eyes I see in my nightmares, the ones that plunge into mine like an auger and sluice, sucking the life from my skull. At first all I felt was fright standing there defenceless in that sealed-up tube, but when he looked away from me I thought I must be mistaken—though how there could be another pair of eyes like those in this world or any other I couldn't fathom. So I moved toward him, squeezing myself through the jam-packed people, but then the next stop came and he got off. And I wouldn't have given it much more thought if it weren't for the scent of him that cut through the perfumes and body odours of the other passengers, bearing grease and sea salt, too unmistakable to deny.

Now I'm here, on the eve of my daughter's first birthday, the eve of the new year, not knowing what to do with all these memories and this fear. I went to great pains to make my emergence in Hawaii as normal and public as possible, though I lied about which direction I'd come into town from, reasoning that whoever had stolen the float at Sunimoto's and had somehow lost it to me would be watching to see if I re-emerged with it. So I left it there in Hawaii, too afraid I might be followed if I tried to retrieve it from the beach where I'd buried it.

When I finally reunited with Fairwin' on Lasqueti he told me he'd been flabbergasted to learn that I'd survived, and he couldn't see how I could have, except that it must have been the float's potency that saved me. Which is how he knew I'd kept hold of it before I even told him. When I spoke with him about the man, the eyes, he told me it made sense, that it must be the engineer Figgs I was remembering, as he'd been there at my bedside when I began to die. What exactly he might have done to me, Fairwin' wasn't sure, and he couldn't see any reason why Figgs would have wanted me dead.

Still, I can't excise the fear no matter what I do, no matter that Fairwin' saw no evidence on that beach to suggest that anyone had ever been there searching for the float. No matter that the float is now broken and will any day now, knock on wood, be thrown into the Mauna Kea's newly formed caldera. There is this feeling in me that I'm being hunted, stalked, by something, perhaps this Figgs character I see in my dreams, or perhaps the man who, for some reason I can't begin to imagine, wanted to stop the float from being broken so badly that he was willing to kill for it. Sometimes I think what follows me is something other, some being or energy, and it is so strong that I can't trust my own sense of things; I don't know if the scent of the grease and sea I smelled on my ride home was an illusion I created in my own paranoia, or if it was reality. And I'm not sure what frightens me more now, these things that haunt me, or the frailty of mind that haunting has brought me to.

The phone rings and I realize I've been sitting here on the living room couch staring out at the neighbour's pink shingles for a long time. I hear Jin Su answer the call, then I hear her say Fairwin's name. I walk into the kitchen where she's holding Emily in one hand, stirring the dinner she's making with the other, and talking to Fairwin', the phone pinched between her shoulder and chin. I take it from her and put it to my ear.

"Fairwin," I say, "Is it done?" There's a long silence at the other end of the line, the faint hoots and hollers of New Year's Eve revellers in the background. "I'm going out on a fishing charter tomorrow Ferris," he finally says, his voice as boisterous as those behind his. "And I wouldn't be entirely surprised if I hauled up a long scaly fish with three fins for a tail."

~

I WAKE IN the morning at first light to what sounds like a knock at the front door. I open my eyes and listen for the dog's bark from the neighbour's yard, then I remember that I'm no longer in Halfmoon Bay, that my neighbours here on Fourteenth Street have no dog, and so I rise from bed, pull on a t-shirt, and head to the front of the house. I open the door to nothing but the street, quiet in the grey light of another dark winter morning. I step out onto the porch and look east and west over the rows of parked cars as the streetlights flicker out. Nothing. Turning back to the house I nudge something with my bare feet, a black leather satchel, small, the size of a manila envelope. I look again behind me, but still there's no one and nothing to be seen.

I carry the satchel into the living room and turn the light on beside the couch where I often sit. Inside I find a key, small, silver, and a note written on plain white paper in black ink.

Ferris,

Go to 505 W. Broadway with this key. You will find what is right-
fully yours there. I am sorry about what happened to your son. From
what I knew of him, he loved you very much. As for what occurred
between us, I can only say you have nothing to fear from me now, as
you have nothing to fear from Jeremy Gibbon either.
Figgs

I go up into the office above our bedroom and turn on the computer. When I google Jeremy Gibbon I learn that a rich young man
by that name has gone missing somewhere in India and that it's
been almost a month since he was last seen or heard of. I recall the
earthquakes that took place there shortly after the float was stolen
from Sunimoto's, and it makes sense. Then I search the Broadway
address in Figgs's note. It's the Royal Bank of Canada on the corner
of Broadway and Cambie. It must be a safety deposit box key I hold
here in my hand. I can only imagine what's in it. Perhaps the cash
I was to be paid for the float? Or something of Anna's or Willow's
this man managed to hold onto as the boat went down?

I'm not sure what to think of this. Whether to take this as the
end of things, or the beginning. Aside from the very little Fairwin'
has told me, that he was a rough man, and that Anna seemed to
like him, I have no idea who Figgs is or why he tried to kill me, as I
now can confirm from his letter that he did. But who are Figgs and
Gibbon, and how do they fit into all this? I can only assume Gibbon to be the man responsible for Willow's death, though I have
no idea what Figgs would have done to him. I suppose I can well
imagine. But how much am I missing, and how will I ever find out?

A telephone wire runs from a pole in the back lane to the roof
of this house just above the window beside me. There's a little bird
that's just landed upon it and I can hear its chirping and trilling
through the closed single-pane glass. Leonard Cohen. "Bird on a

Wire." I was never much of a fan, but the song's ubiquitous. And I suppose it has its place. I suppose Leonard has his point. Today is my daughter's first birthday. Later some of Jin Su's family and friends will come to our home to celebrate with us. There will be gifts and laughter, candles and cake. Simple things. Maybe more than enough. Maybe these questions can go unanswered. Maybe I can take this letter on my desk at face value and put the rest behind me. It's a new year, not something I've ever made much of. But maybe this one is of greater significance than most. For me. For Anna. For Jin Su and Emily. For everyone. Maybe the past is the past, and what's done is done. It's hard, I think, for anyone to say.

But regardless, I know where I belong today, and whom I belong to, and I'm going to walk downstairs to the kitchen to put the coffee on now, quiet so as not to wake them. And when they do, when Emily finally finishes her morning nursing and Jin Su carries her out into the living room, I'm going to kiss them both, and I'm going to take my feisty daughter from her mother's arms and put this shiny little key in her hands.

Ferris,

I've had a letter I wrote to you sealed in a stamped envelope beside my bed for months now. Almost every day I think to send it, but don't. It's a letter I wrote the night before Willow and I left with Arnault and Fairwin' to find you. That was the last night our son slept in his own bed, in our home. I found it where I left it, tucked under your pillow, when I came back with my parents to clear out my things. I found a few strands of Willow's hair under his pillow then, too, and I've kept both things together since, sealed in that envelope with your new address written on it. Tonight I put it in an old coffee tin and set it out to sea on a piece of driftwood. I lit the envelope on fire as I did so. I'll send this letter instead.

Today is the first anniversary of our son's death, Ferris. The last time I saw him he was running from me back into the ship's cabin to save you. How it is you survived and he didn't, given the shape you were in, I'll never know or understand. It's taken all this year for me to forgive you for surviving. It doesn't make much sense to me. None of it does.

I met your daughter and her mother once, as I'm sure you know, in front of the general store. They came to our home for dinner the night before we left to find you. They are both lovely. Still, I'm not sure what it is you found in them that you couldn't find in Willow and I, but whatever it is I hope it's enough for you now.

I've been so angry with you, Ferris. Tonight, at least, I've set that aside. The letter I put to flames spoke of my love for you, of how much a part of me you are. It spoke too of how we'd both made such a mess of things. And we have, haven't we?

I'm living up here in Echo Bay now, doing good work. I don't think we're winning, but I can't say what the future will bring. I would have never thought what happened to us, to our son, could have. Often it feels I'm still waiting to wake from a dream. To our little house with its crooked floor and its crappy plumbing. To our dear son getting himself ready for another day down by the sea.

Love Always,
A.

THIS FIRST LETTER arrived late this spring, nearly a year after it was written. I suppose it spent a bit of time by Anna's bedside too before she finally sent it off. This one I'm glad she didn't burn.

Before I opened it I thought it might be a very belated thank you for the portion of Figgs's money I sent her. That she made no mention of it is just like her, and I'm happy for that too. More than any of the words in her letters it tells me that, despite it all, her spirit's intact. Anna the independent fighter. It's what I've always loved about her.

I spent the night she wrote that letter, June 28th, the date Fairwin' told me would be the anniversary of my son's death, with Svend and a bottle of Scotch just a block from our old home. I suppose I wanted to be with her that night, and with Willow. I suppose Svend and the bottle was the closest I could come.

In the middle of the night I went down to the water, to the beach Willow always used to play at. It was warm, mid-summer, and the sea was calm. Just little waves stroking against the shore. Nothing more. No visions of my son building castles in the sand or digging clams from the intertidal muck. I realized then that even my memories of him were beginning to wear thin. It's not what I'd expected to find there that night. But what ever is? Not much seems certain in this life beyond the waves that keep on breaking against the shore. The forgiveness Anna wrote of eludes me, too.

That night I fell asleep in the sand above high water mark. When I awoke there was a blue heron standing in the shallows, perfectly still. I lay there watching him for a long time, admiring the innate patience, the gift of the species. Then finally, suddenly, his head plunged into the water, and he came up with a small silvery fish flashing in his beak.

Fishing. Patience. The given catch. The grace of survival. For a moment it seemed that simple. Then the heron flew off with the fish still struggling in its beak, and I stood, brushed the sand from my clothes, and climbed through the tall grasses, between the houses, and up to the road.

At the gate that leads into our old yard I stopped and stood, leaning against its waist-high, weathered pickets. Anna's garden had been left untended, the beds overgrown with weeds. Around them there were various plastic toys strewn. A wagon, a slide, a car, a collection of dump trucks and diggers, and as I looked them over I noticed that the ground was soaked, a continuous stream of water flooding beneath them. With my eyes I followed the path of water to its source, the shallow pool I'd found for Willow at the landfill when he was a toddler. A plastic, green, turtle-shaped pool, Anna had kept it around as a bird bath long after our son outgrew it. And there it was, still in its same spot, being used again by this new family that had moved in after us. Someone had left the hose on overnight, Anna's old garden hose, and the pool was overflowing with water.

I opened the gate as quietly as I could, its rusty hinges creaking in the dark blue light before dawn, and walked into the yard. I stepped over the toys, between Anna's garden beds, approaching the sleeping house. The tap hissed and groaned lightly as I shut it off. Then I unthreaded the hose, drained what water I could from its end, and coiled it over my shoulder.

I use that hose to water the small garden of peas, nasturtiums, kohlrabi and kale Jin Su and I keep in the backyard now. It's the only thing I have of my life with Willow and Anna. Occasionally I receive a letter from her and I write back. With each one there is a widening of the distance between us, a diminishing intimacy. She's still so angry. I write to her of the thirty-seven million sockeye that returned to the Fraser last fall, the greatest run in over a century; and of Joni Mitchell's rumoured plans to donate her land and new home to the local community as an ecological reserve and interpretive centre. But when she writes back, she ignores my overtures toward a more hopeful dialogue. She rails, just as she always has. The last letter I received was the first in which she failed to mention Willow. I've yet to respond. I'm not ready to let him die in that way, too.

With the money Figgs left, Jin Su and I bought a more expensive house in Deep Cove on the outskirts of the city. It feels more like home here, at the end of the road, tucked into the mountains up Indian Arm. When we sleep, we sleep in darkness. There is a trail across the street from our house that leads down through a small forest to a beach of pebbles and stones.

Often I go in the morning. I wake in the dark, slide from bed and leave the house quietly without disturbing Emily and Jin Su. The forest is thick and silent before dawn, an entirely other world from the one I spend my days working in downtown, the fish plant's fluorescent-lit concrete and steel.

When I reach the beach I go to the water, dip my cupped hands in and splash it cold and salty on my face. Then I skip a few smooth, flat stones across its surface. When the sun begins to rise I walk a little further along the beach toward it, my back to the city, to a little spot I found where the rocks are just right for sitting. There I look up the channel, like I used to look upon the mountains above Sechelt Inlet from the deck of the *Prevailer*, and watch night give way to day. Sometimes this occurs, when the mountains are holding thick clouds across their slopes, as only a lightening and lightening of grey. But when the sky is clear the sun casts an array of colours—oranges and pinks and golds—over the peaks. Some mornings there is a gentle wind sweeping up the channel, churning its surface to a rippling chop. It's these mornings I think Willow, as a man, would have loved: the moment the colours fade to blue in the sky, and the sun comes beaming over the dark mountains, speckling down across the water like the sea is made of countless flecks of glass, each one holding the light.

NOTES

The Albert Camus passages are from Stuart Gilbert's translation of *The Plague.*

The John Berger passages are from his novel *From A to X: A Story in Letters.*

GRATITUDE

To Sue Wheeler for the Velella velella; to Stu Farnsworth for 1949; and to Doug Beguin, for everything you've taught me through the years about fishing and boats and the sea.

For reading the manuscript early on, and for your thoughts and support: Alison, Katherine, and Nancy Denham; River Rohlicek; David Drury. To Theresa Kishkan, for the same, and all the careful red ink along with it. And to Liz Marshall, for the late read, and for all your invaluable insights and encouragement.

To Bob Doleman, for helping me see the centre clearly.

To Silas White for everything: early and late edits, interest, advice, and all the work bringing the book into print.

To everyone at Harbour/Nightwood for all your diligence and enthusiasm.

To Carleton Wilson for the cover, and to Adam Lewis Schroeder and Angie Abdou for the kind words which grace its back.

To Vicki Ziegler and Peter Taylor, for your time and effort.

To Alexandra, Joni, and David, for being fuel and fodder for Anna's passion and fury, and for all your good work in the world.

To John Pass and Theresa Kishkan, for the encouragement and advice over the years.

To John and Nancy, for all your faith and support.

And finally to Amy. For all the invaluable, essential reading and editing from the first draft to the last. For the life we share which makes this writing possible. For the ballast and the buoyancy, the strong and steady mooring.

About the Author

Joe Denham is the author of two poetry collections, *Flux* (2003) and *Windstorm* (2009). His work has appeared in numerous magazines and anthologies including *Open Field: 30 Contemporary Canadian Poets, The New Canon: An Anthology of Canadian Poetry* and *Breathing Fire 2: Canada's New Poets*. He lives with his wife and two children in Halfmoon Bay, BC, and works as a commercial fisherman throughout coastal British Columbia.

joedenham.ca